STARLING

isabel strychacz

SIMON & SCHUSTER BFYR

New York London Toronto Sydney New Delhi

SIMON & SCHUSTER BFYR

An imprint of Simon & Schuster Children's Publishing Division
1230 Avenue of the Americas, New York, New York 10020

SIMON & SCHUSTER BOOKS FOR YOUNG READERS
and related marks are trademarks of Simon & Schuster, Inc.
For information about special discounts for bulk purchases, please contact Simon &
Schuster Special Sales at 1-866-506-1949 or business@simonandschuster.com.
The Simon & Schuster Speakers Bureau can bring authors to your live event. For
more information or to book an event, contact the Simon & Schuster Speakers Bureau
at 1-866-248-3049 or visit our website at www.simonspeakers.com.
Interior design by Laura Eckes | The text for this book was set in Bell MT Std.
Manufactured in the United States of America
First Edition | 2 4 6 8 10 9 7 5 3 1
Library of Congress Cataloging-in-Publication Data
Names: Strychacz, Isabel, author. | Title: Starling / Isabel Strychacz.
Description: First edition. | New York : Simon & Schuster Books for Young Readers,
2021. | Audience: Ages 12 up. | Audience: Grades 7–9. | Summary: Darling is a small
isolated town, made up of small-town people who have small-town kids who rarely
leave; it is the last place anyone would expect to find a visitor from another world, but
that is what Starling Rust claims to be, and the town-folk, led by their corrupt mayor,
are terrified—the Wilding sisters, Delta and Bee, are determined to protect Starling
from the town's escalating xenophobia but the growing feelings between Starling and
Delta may prove to be the greatest threat of all.
Identifiers: LCCN 2021009647 (print) | LCCN 2021009648 (ebook) |
ISBN 9781534481107 (hardcover) | ISBN 9781534481121 (ebook)
Subjects: LCSH: Human-alien encounters—Juvenile fiction. | Strangers—Juvenile
fiction. | Xenophobia—Juvenile fiction. | Sisters—Juvenile fiction. | Romance fiction.
| Science fiction. | Young adult fiction. | CYAC: Extraterrestrial beings—Fiction |
Strangers—Fiction. | Sisters—Fiction. | Love—Fiction. | Science fiction. | LCGFT:
Science fiction. | Romance fiction. | Classification: LCC PZ7.1.S7974 St 2021 (print) |
LCC PZ7.1.S7974 (ebook) | DDC 813.6 [Fic]—dc23
LC record available at https://lccn.loc.gov/2021009647
LC ebook record available at https://lccn.loc.gov/2021009648

For my dad, who read me stories of magic and adventure,
and for my mom, who showed me how to write my own.

And for Henry—how sweet it is to be loved by you.

We . . . are all in the same boat, upon a stormy sea.
We owe to each other a terrible and tragic loyalty.

—G. K. CHESTERTON

✧

Whatever our souls are made of,
his and mine are the same.

—EMILY BRONTË, *Wuthering Heights*

✧

You were made to soar,
to crash to earth,
then to rise and soar again.

—ALFRED WAINWRIGHT

1

THERE WERE TOWNS, and then there were small towns, and then there was Darling.

It was a place utterly cut off from the world, nestled down in the flat valley between craggy California-brown mountains that peaked around its sides. The town rose up like a wellspring around the one single road that bisected the entire valley. Over the years a few barely paved streets branched off Main Street, collecting houses in cul-de-sacs lined with quaking aspens. Their leaves always trembled in the breeze and gave the whole town a permanent earthquake-like effect, in a melancholy, arborous type of way.

Darling was a town made up of small-town kids, who'd grown up and never left and had small-town kids of their own. Darling was dry and golden and lonely, sprinkled with sections of rustling woods that seemed to emerge from nowhere; it was sagging porches and sunburn summers and sputtering trucks with flaking paint. Despite the fact that there was nowhere to take wrong turns, confused tourists en route to somewhere else often found themselves stranded, somehow, at the town's diner. The weight of eyes, heavy upon you, was ever present, although no one could really tell where it came from. Darling itself existed in a vacuum, and all passers-through looked back on their hazy recollections of the town and wondered if it had even really happened, or if Darling, with its gabled Victorians and dead-brown fields and fluorescent-lighted diner was simply some bizarre hallucination.

It was a curious place, sitting alone with miles of nothingness stretching out on all sides, and it kept its 333 citizens and their millions of secrets close.

Delta Wilding had lived in Darling her whole life, and she knew its oddness better than anybody. Sometimes she thought her town did things simply to amuse itself. Sometimes she thought her town was playing its own great game, and they were all just pieces on its chessboard.

Darling was not just a town, and the Wildings were not a typical family.

Strange things happened to them. Strange things just found them.

Even in times of utter mundanity—like right now, as Delta curled up on her window seat, waiting for Tag to text her back— Darling always seemed like it was holding its breath, quietly *waiting* for something unusual to happen. The air through the open window was shimmering with heat, and the call of the common starling bird repeatedly shattered the still air. It was the type of day that doesn't let you know it will end in something completely unexpected, until the unexpected arrives.

Delta sighed, drawing her knees into her chest as she watched the starlings swooping outside. From her vantage point, she could see the strip of asphalt that led past her house into Darling proper. But if she were to open the wavy-glass window and lean out, she would see Victorian houses springing up a mile or so down the road, leaping into existence like a pop-up book. The Wildings' home was settled on the very outskirts of the town. Along the flat stretch of highway, there was a dirt road that veered suddenly left. It bordered the town line, fields of Darling on one side and fields not in Darling on the other, and wound its way in and out of bone-dry, California-golden grass. The dirt road was bumpy and rocky, pocked with holes and wear, and it ended at a farmhouse.

The Wild West was white clapboard, once grand, and it had a wraparound porch, thin columns holding up the wooden awnings, and a gabled roof. Its best days were far in Darling's past; nevertheless, it sat proudly amongst the abandoned fields while Queen Anne's lace crept up toward the front steps. The house was all wooden floors that creaked and dusty windows with the original glass, warped and distorted. When the weather was sunny and hot, Delta rushed around throwing open the still-unbarred windows so that light streamed in, illuminating the dust that shimmered in the air. When it rained, she hurried on top of creaking floorboards, slamming down pails to catch the leaks, until the entire house sounded like a rainwater symphony.

Despite it all, the house was beautiful and full of memories and a quiet sort of magic, and Delta loved it. Every memory of her childhood was centered within the creaking walls. The Wild West had a *feeling* about it, a feeling like something fantastical was just around the corner. And in Darling, something usually was.

But in the minds of the citizens of Darling, anyone who

preferred to live anywhere other than the central Darling cul-de-sacs was not to be trusted. At least, this is what they whispered amongst themselves, usually during the seventh inning of Darling Devils baseball games or after Book Club, three glasses of Merlot in. Delta knew it; she heard the whispers, she saw the stares.

She knew that she, her sister, and her dad were considered oddities in their town. *There's something* off *about them*, came the whispers. *There's something not* ordinary *about those girls. There's something* strange *about that house.*

And they were right.

Because a dusty dirt road, a window seat, and waiting for a text back: these were the ordinary things about Delta.

The fact that the music playing from the dock next to her bed changed itself according to her mood: that was not.

The fact that her house, the Wild West, moved around her with a strange sort of sentience: that, too, was not.

The fact that her father had walked into their hallway closet and never come back out: that was perhaps the strangest thing of all.

And the worst.

Delta closed her eyes as if the sudden darkness could ward away the thought. *Don't think about it.* Delta had to remind herself this multiple times a day. *Don't think about it, it didn't happen, he'll be back soon.* He'd been gone for seventy-seven days—she'd been counting—and each day that passed without him returning made the knot in her stomach grow. It had risen to her throat now, clogging it—he was *gone,* and she was here, alone, in charge of everything, in charge of *too much* . . .

Don't think about it. Sometimes she was worried if she allowed herself to really realize what her father being gone meant—for Bee, for their house, for the rest of their lives—she might start crying and never stop. *Don't think about it* seemed easier.

Delta swallowed hard and set her jaw, glancing again out the window at the swooping birds. One flew down to perch on the windowsill, cocking its pure black eye toward her, fluttering its feathers. The wing shimmered like an oil slick in the sun.

Delta stared at it, the loud silence of the empty rooms echoing around her. She couldn't hear Bee—and Bee, her flighty, freckly, flouncy sister, usually made her presence known. It was just Delta and the bird. Did it have a knowing look in its eye, or was she imagining that? Delta shook her head. *Come on, Delta.* It was a *bird*, for God's sake, and birds didn't care about humans. Birds didn't watch humans—why should they? They had better things to do, like fly toward the stars.

Delta met its round eye. "Lucky you," she murmured, and her heart clenched painfully tight as the bird took flight. She was just about to get fully into bed and pull the covers over her head and hope tomorrow would somehow bring her dad back, when her phone pinged with a text at the same time as the front door banged open and Bee's voice carried up the stairs: "Del-*taaa*?" She heard the door slam again, then the sound of their fluffy Australian shepherd Abby's feet click-clacking on the hardwood floor of the living room and the louder clatter of Abby's leash landing on the floor from wherever Bee threw it.

Delta sighed again, sitting up and grabbing her phone. Tag

had answered her Hey, miss you! text—the one that had been composed from melancholy and empty rooms, the one she'd sort of regretted sending the second her finger pressed send— with Miss u too! Everyone's at the diner, u should come.

Maybe, she texted back, fingers flying across the screen. I'll check with Bee. It was a ridiculous excuse, because of course Bee would want to come. Bee, after all, was the fancy-free whirlwind Wilding sister, completely the opposite of quiet Delta, who watched her world go by with careful green eyes, silently filing away strangers' secrets.

Delta read Tag's text again, eyes skimming over and over across the Miss u too! The words made the knot in her stomach both loosen and tighten all at once.

"Delta!" Bee's voice called again, closer now, and her footsteps sounded heavy on the stairs.

"Yeah, I'm here," Delta called back.

"Where's here?"

"Bedroom," she answered, the word hanging in the air as Bee burst into her room, blond and fierce, a tornado in the body of a girl, a hurricane of glitter and throwaway smiles and highlighted hair.

"Oh, hey," Bee said, one of her signature smiles coming out in full brilliance. Bee had a way of always smiling, but often Delta thought her sister's smiles held more anger and sadness than anything that looked happy. But Bee smiled through it all. Delta sometimes wished she could be more like her younger sister; *God*, did she wish she could hide her emotions away in a smile. She wished she could pretend everything was okay. Most days it was hard to even summon up a stoic expression, much less anything beyond that.

"Where've you been?"

"Walking Abby," Bee replied, her voice lilting, and she threw herself down on the bed next to her sister, closing her eyes and throwing an arm up over her forehead like a swooning starlet. "I am *so* hungry."

Everyone's at the diner, u should come.

Did she want to see Tag? Her emotions were petals: she did, she did not, she did, she did not. *She did.* If only to remind herself that she didn't.

"We can go to the Diner," Delta offered, and Bee sat straight up, her face the very picture of incredulity.

"We *can*?"

"I mean . . ." Delta trailed off; she could feel herself becoming unconvinced already. She could quickly cook up some pasta instead. . . . That would be the responsible thing to do.

"No, no," Bee replied hastily. "That sounds so *fun.*"

"Well, I don't know now," Delta said, unable to keep a bit of fretfulness from creeping into her voice. She hadn't checked the emergency money box, currently their sole supply of money, for a while—again, it was something that stressed her out to her core so badly, it was easier to pretend it didn't exist—but she was fairly certain they weren't flush with cash. Not anymore.

Not after seventy-seven days.

"Delta," Bee replied, fixing her sister with a stare. "Don't be so boring."

Which is how Delta found herself behind Bee, following

as her sister skipped down the stairs. While Bee grabbed the car keys from the peg by the kitchen door, Delta hurried into the living room. The room was tired. The furniture was old and sagging, the throw pillows almost threadbare, the fireplace boarded up. The two human-sized indents in the couch cushions were the only signs that this room was used. The wooden floor creaked ominously as Delta crossed it, and she shivered, moving over the floorboards quickly. Sometimes her house unnerved even her, with its constant sighs and creaks, as though it knew something they didn't. As though the very walls were trying to tell her something. She knew the Wild West was strange, but she certainly couldn't fathom the extent of its oddities, and Delta considered, not for the first time, that one day the floor might give way and she would fall into whatever was under their house. Maybe simply dirt, maybe a cellar, maybe another world.

There was just no way to tell.

Delta crossed to the mantel above the boarded-up fireplace. There were three objects on the wooden mantel: a photo of Delta and Bee as little girls, their long hair in identical braids; a faded photo of a young woman with a face like Delta and sparkling eyes like Bee; and a carved wooden box. Delta lingered for a moment near the photo of her mother—her eyes were always drawn to it, but she didn't pause long enough for her mind to unravel into thoughts of *What would my mother do?*; not long enough to unravel into an empty feeling of loss. It was the box that Delta was here for: opening it, she glimpsed cash—too little, always too little—before she grabbed a twenty and stuffed it into the pocket of her jeans. She hesitated, then walked to the hallway closet and pulled open the door.

It was just a closet, full of boots caked in mud and winter coats and umbrellas and an ancient, barely used vacuum cleaner.

It had been just a closet the other times she'd checked, the other seventy-seven times she'd checked: once a day for seventy-seven days. But it didn't matter about those times—what mattered was the time when it had *not* been just a closet.

That time, seventy-seven days ago, on a chilly March afternoon, the Wilding sisters' father, Roark Wilding, had walked into the closet and had never come out. She imagined him standing there amongst the boots and coats and disappearing into nothingness. She shut the door, counted to ten, and then flung it wide open.

Boots and coats and Abby's leash and stray umbrellas and the vacuum cleaner.

Nothing more.

While their dilapidated farmhouse was most definitely settled in Darling, it wasn't settled quite as *firmly* as all the other houses. Things went missing—pepper grinders, half-read books, rarely worn earrings—and none of it had seemed to matter much until the thing that went missing was not an old sweater but their dad.

Don't think about it. Delta's hand trembled in her pocket, fingers still clenched around the twenty-dollar bill. The emergency cash fund was running low, and there was still no sign of anything but dusty winter wear in the place her father had disappeared. *Don't think about it.* Who was she kidding? All she did day in and day out was think about it. She couldn't stop. The twenty in her pocket felt like a twenty-ton weight. The electricity and water hadn't been shut off yet—Delta guessed she should feel lucky that their father seemed to have prepaid his bills. Lucky, yes. Lucky that the sisters had water and electric for at least another couple months. *Lucky.*

Delta didn't feel lucky, not at all.

"Hey," said Bee, and Delta quickly snapped shut the closet door, trying to keep her face calm and composed. She even managed a small smile toward her sister, although it came out more like a pained grimace.

"Hey. I'm ready." She pointed to the sofa, and Abby obediently climbed up and nestled down into the cushions.

"Still a closet?"

Delta forced her mouth to keep smiling. Her sister was smiling back at her, and her smile was more like a grimace as well. "Yeah."

"Oh."

"Yeah." There was silence. For a moment Delta stared at the scuffed floorboards, stared at her shoes, and then she shook her head. She had to get out of this house. "Come on, let's go."

Bee looked like she might say something, but Delta couldn't imagine anything she'd like less than to *talk* about what already pressed on her heart and lungs every second of every day. She knew Bee didn't want to talk about it either; both sisters wanted to pretend nothing was wrong. Talking about it made it real, so Delta pushed past Bee and stalked out of the hallway and into the kitchen, grabbing a faded red-and-black checked flannel from the hook by the door.

Outside, above the woods pressing in against the back of their house, the flock of shimmering starlings wheeled about, forming murmurations of shining feathers and letting out deafening screeches. The sky was darkening from a soft pink to a murderous sort of orange, casting a fiery glow over everything. Bee swung out behind her and beelined for the old Ford truck that sat, weathered and solid and rusty, in the damp grass.

"I'm driving," Delta said, heading immediately for the driver's side door.

"I'm driving," Bee replied, smacking Delta's hand away.

"*I'm* driving."

"No, *I'm* dri—"

They struggled momentarily over the handle of the door before Delta gave up with a frustrated grumble and muttered obscenities and crossed to the passenger side. The truck roared to a start and they rumbled around the farmhouse, passing the sign heralding their house, and picked up speed as Bee maneuvered onto the unpaved, dusty lane. She wound the truck through the fields filled with deadened grass and Queen Anne's lace and not much else, finally pulling onto the road that led into Darling.

Bee drove with confidence. She was sixteen and *barely* had her driving permit, so she wasn't technically allowed to drive in a car with anyone under the age of twenty-five, but both sisters disregarded this fact completely. They were alone, after all.

Delta sat in the passenger seat, watching the waving grass pass by in a blur as they roared toward town. She was composed of elbows and harsh edges and freckles, and the gauntness of her cheeks and dull brown hair reflected her position as a teenager who held her universe together by a snapping thread. She hadn't *always* looked like she wore despair as a shroud; disappearing fathers had that sort of effect on eighteen-year-olds. Delta, as unexpectedly as a sudden shot, was now in charge of Bee and the Wild West and shouldered the responsibility of keeping their lives moving forward.

Don't think about it.

Who was she supposed to go to? There was no one at all. No one to tell, no one to help; their mother had died of cancer when Bee was still a baby. Delta had only vague memories of soft hands and the feeling of comfort that she wasn't quite sure were even real. There were no other family members, no cousins, no aunts. She had Tag and she had Anders, but could she trust on-again-off-again boyfriends and friends from school with something like this?

No, there was no one to tell, no one who could step in and take over. There was no one at all. There was only her and the emergency money box on the mantel.

The neon sign of the Diner appeared through the evening haze. *Don't think about it.* Delta attempted to pull some semblance of normality into her expression and tried to forget the rest.

2

DARLING PROPER WAS
getting closer and closer; Delta could now see the white spire of
the church and the pointy roofs peeking through the quivering
green leaves of the aspens. Delta's hands were clenched in her
lap. Maybe coming here had been a bad decision, brought on by
loneliness and the thrill that comes from the *ping* of a text.

"Maybe we should get pizza or something?"

"No," said Bee.

"We have some pasta at home . . ."

"No," replied Bee decidedly. "I want to go to the Diner."

"But—"

"You're the one who suggested it," Bee said, her voice verging
on a snap.

Delta couldn't really think of anything to say in response
to the truth, so she just swooped her hair up into a ponytail,
fastening it with the black hair tie at her wrist. The Diner was
where she, Bee, and their father used to go every Sunday night.
Pulling into the parking lot still made her stomach clench at the
remembrance that he wouldn't be there when they got home. It
was also the hangout spot for all of Darling's under-twenties,
who apparently all forwent studying and doing anything useful

to sit in the leather upholstered booths and gossip. But now the thought of sitting in a booth with Tag and all the people she'd just graduated with, smiling and giggling and gossiping, was exhausting. She'd barely tolerated it at the best of times, and now . . .

Delta frowned out the window. Now she was father and mother and sister, tied up in one. She was the protector, guardian, heroine . . . She was an eighteen-year-old Atlas, holding both her and Bee's dreams above the dusty hard ground of reality. Now glowering was often all she could manage.

The Diner was a squat building right off the road, painted a pale, sickly green, and its parking lot was gravelly and overgrown with weeds. It was open twenty-four hours, and an electric sign was mounted on the roof, proclaiming DINER in neon bloodred. A huge Joshua tree grew, spiky and distorted, near the entrance. The Diner's large windows showed the inside goings-on: a family having dinner; a couple of tourists with backpacks and hiking shoes and particularly shell-shocked looks on their faces; a couple of grumpy, silent men in their usual booth; and a bunch of glittering, loud, authoritative Darling Academy students in theirs.

Darling Academy was not an academy at all—it was just a normal rabbit-warren of a school inside an old converted Victorian house where all Darling kids supposedly became educated. It was a perfect representation of everything in Darling: it was a little bit magical, a little bit melancholy, a little bit decrepit. It had the distinct air of being left to its own devices.

It was filled with downtrodden students with the highest of hopes.

But it was summer now, sticky with heat and stretching with time: school was now a distant memory for Delta, who had just graduated, and a hazy future for Bee, who'd be starting her junior year in a couple of months.

Bee was halfway to the door before she realized Delta wasn't following. "Come on!" she yelled toward the truck, then turned and waved madly through the window to the kids in the booth. A few of the girls from Bee's year furiously waved back.

"Hey, Tag's here!" Bee called to Delta, who could see perfectly well that Tag was there, then turned and flounced into the Diner, the bell tinkling above her head as she entered.

Delta stayed in the truck, watching as Bee easily entered the fold of the group, meshing herself right in the middle of the arms and hot breath and giggles. Bee flourished when she was surrounded with people. Delta wilted. She just couldn't help it: the more people gathered around her, the more she felt her energy being sucked away, little by little.

Finally, she edged her way out of the truck, slamming the door behind her and locking it—not that there was anything to steal. She continued toward the entrance, discomfort growing in her stomach as each step brought her closer to the spectacle of the Darling Academy booth. There were only seven kids there, but to Delta it seemed like half the school had turned out to the Diner. Unease nettled her.

The bell above the door tinkled. Delta braced herself.

As one, all the faces in the Diner glanced up. The old men with the grizzled beards eyed her, suspicious, and then returned to their whiskies. The family eyed her, suspicious, and pulled their kids in a little closer. Delta could see what they were all thinking: *A Wilding. The Wildings are strange. The Wildings are not to be trusted.*

Her unease quickly hardened into something more like resentment, and she frowned at them, folding her arms across her chest.

"Delta!"

Her attention was diverted from glowering at the diners as her name was called in a loud, commanding voice. She knew that voice—there wasn't anyone in Darling who didn't.

One of the boys in the booth stood up and made his way over to her. He was a vision of unintentional arrogance, with his blond gelled coif and perfectly starched blue jeans, his dazed blue eyes and checked button-down. His breath heavy with the cinnamon aroma of Fireball whisky. He was the promise of puppy love and biting rose-hued lips of honey. Despite the fact that he'd been in Delta's school year and therefore had just graduated, he was still wearing his Darling Devils letterman jacket proudly over the blue-and-white checked shirt. His eyes were *very* blue.

Delta breathed in, the scent of cinnamon and distrust and expensive cologne filling her nose. "Tag."

"Delta. You're—you're here."

He sounded more than a little surprised, and she supposed it made sense. Their relationship was a mountain full of switchbacks and perilous cliffs. It was a single heartbeat: up and down, up and down, a series of never-ending uncertainty. They had been in a valley for a while now, despite Tag's insistent texts and four a.m. phone calls.

"You invited me," she replied a little frostily. She peered over his shoulder at the table, where Bee was chatting and smiling, her face a sunbeam.

"Oh—I know I did. I'm happy you're here. I just didn't think you would actually come."

He sounded hurt. Delta tried really hard to make herself care the way she knew she was supposed to. She knew she was supposed to want Tag in the way Tag wanted her, because who wouldn't want Tag Rockford III's attentions? Sometimes she did, but she couldn't seem to keep those feelings within her grasp for long. She knew there must be something wrong with her, because Tag wanted her, and most of the time she wanted nothing but to get out of Darling and run and run and run until nothing was familiar.

"I know. Things have been really busy." That was only part of the reason. The smallest part. Because how could she explain to Tag—*Tag Rockford* of all people—the plights of her disappearing father and all the trouble it brought upon the Wildings? She wanted nothing more than a low profile, and discussing her life with her sort-of-ex, the mayor's son, was the exact opposite of that.

Tag visibly sagged. His blue eyes looked at her with so much sadness, she could've taken the sadness and written with it. She was surprised he hadn't yet collapsed on the floor, a puddle of misery and pride and *God, I miss you.*

"God, I miss you," said Tag.

Delta hesitated. Finally: "I miss you too." And . . . she did, in a way. It would hit her at strange moments, when the sky was dark and her sheets were very cold and the silence of her empty house overwhelmed her. *I miss him, I miss him not.*

His face lit up. "You do?"

She sighed. "Maybe we can talk about this later."

The Rockfords were all about normalcy. The town of Darling had an odd relationship with the Rockfords—they'd been there since the town's founding, and had always been in positions of power, despite the fact that everyone disliked them. Darling's citizens liked nothing more than to sit back and reelect the Rockfords and then mutter complaints behind their backs. Tag's father, Tag Rockford II, was the current mayor of Darling and he ran the town with an iron fist. *Darling needs order, Darling needs tradition.* Delta knew the only reason Tag Senior had put up with the eccentricities of Delta and Bee's father and the eccentricity that was, by proxy, theirs, was because of Tag III. Tag Rockford III was, for reasons Delta didn't really understand, completely head over heels in love with her. Sometimes she felt like Tag secretly had some subconscious need to rebel against his order-obsessed father and authoritative family.

She didn't know. She'd never asked.

"We haven't seen your dad around recently," Tag said, and his use of the royal *we* made Delta try very hard not to roll her eyes. She wasn't even sure if Tag *knew* that the town didn't particularly like the Rockfords. He certainly acted as if his family were beloved. "Has he gone out of town?" His eyes were very beseeching, and very blue. His question—because it *was* a question, no matter how casually he said it—was posed so lightly, it almost sounded unimportant, just an observation, friend to friend, but she saw how his blue eyes got brighter, got harder.

Delta had seen his eyes get that way only a few times, and it always made her shiver, because it broke the illusion that Tag was not the shallow rich kid most of the town believed he was. At least not *only* that kid. There was something under his skin that was whip-smart and saw right through her, and it smiled at her. It was obvious in that moment that when he said *we*, he meant, *My dad hasn't seen your dad around and wants to Big Brother the hell out of you. Where is he? Why has he gone?*

Delta tried to keep any emotion out of her voice. She would not be scared of the Rockfords. It wasn't her fault her dad was gone—the Rockfords couldn't do anything even if they found out, right? She had nothing to hide. *Delta, you have everything to hide.* The little voice was loud, insistent. She made herself meet his eyes, wondering if whatever steeliness that lurked inside Tag's father would be gleaming out of Tag's own baby blues. But—no, it was just Tag who looked at her, golden-haired golden boy Tag, his face clear, innocent, his lips kicked up in a smile.

"Oh?" Delta said noncommittally, remembering he hadn't posed his question as a question, and she wasn't required to give an answer. This was just Tag. The blue eyes flashed. *Just Tag.* She accompanied her vague answer with a wonderfully evasive, mysterious shrug, and Tag visibly wilted at her obvious attempt to not talk to him. Maybe she'd misinterpreted his not-question? She immediately felt bad—*sort of* bad—for being so closed off, and tried to quickly remedy the situation. The Diner was growing increasingly hot, the voices growing louder and more animated until they rang in her ears. She clenched her jaw. "Well, he's around. Doesn't get into town much. He's been on a business trip."

"That's a long business trip."

"It's been a lot of different business trips."

Tag gave a hesitant laugh. "Of course." He gave her a tilted, awkward smile that, coming from him, didn't look tilted or awkward at all. It made him look like he was ready to run for mayor next year, or now. She returned the tilted, awkward half smile, and hers looked both those things, completely.

"And is he still obsessed with the paranormal?" Tag said with another easy laugh, like they were in on some kind of conspiratorial joke together. Delta let her smile drop, mimicking her stomach. Her ribs felt too tight, her teeth clenched so firmly, she thought some of them might just give way and come tumbling out.

"He was never *obsessed*," Delta ground out, heart tight, heart hurting. That was the thing: her father *had* been obsessed with everything strange, everything mysterious. It was just one more reason the town thought them odd. Delta and Bee had been raised on it, raised on jumping in the truck and racing off with their dad to stand in the middle of a deserted field while he arranged rocks in circles on the ground. Raised on *Never go into the woods alone, especially at night*, and *A* is for *Astrology*, *B* is for *Bilocation*, *C* is for *Close Encounter*. She'd called her dad *obsessed* many times before: they had laughed about it together as he sat on the floor of his tornado-like study and pored over maps of the world for hours on end, searching for hotspots, where lines of energy converged into one place.

But when Tag said it, it didn't have the same ring to it. It didn't have her dad, looking up and laughing along with her and saying, *I know, I know, I'll be done soon.* Tag said it like a bad word. When Tag said it, it sounded less like *obsessed* and more like *insane.*

"I . . . I just meant . . ." Tag tried to backtrack, and once again Delta felt pangs of guilt. What was wrong with her? Obviously Tag wasn't *trying* to be rude. People like Tag never *tried* to be rude. She lifted the corners of her mouth, trying to force the smile back onto it. His eyes were so blue, and so innocent. He met her smile, encouraged.

Keep smiling, Delta, she thought. It was hard with Tag's next words.

"Anyways, I'm glad you're here, because, as you know, the mayoral election is coming up."

"Ye-es," Delta got out, hesitant. Oh God, he was going to ask her to the Mayor's Ball, *again.* She thought after last year his dad would have disallowed Tag bringing someone so ordinary. She'd had quite enough stares at the last ball to last her a lifetime or five, but . . .

"And the Mayor's Ball is the day before election night," Tag continued. Delta sucked in a breath. He smiled, his perfect, straight teeth strangely glinty in the reflective fluorescent light. "And I would love if you allowed me to escort you." He zipped the zipper of his crimson letterman jacket up and down and up and down until the metallic sound made Delta's skin crawl. *Zip, zip, ziiiiip.*

Last year's Mayor's Ball had been an opulent affair, back

when her dad was still around and she wasn't holding the whole world together. Back when she and Tag had been up on the mountaintop, together, and the cliff's edge didn't seem so close. Back when she thought maybe kissing under the streetlights might be enough for her. Her dad had allowed her to drive the truck to downtown Sonora, where she'd bought a long black dress covered in black sparkles, so formfitting, it was almost a second skin. She'd looked lovely, at the time, almost ethereal in a strange, funereal type of way, and had piled all her hair in an intricate updo. She'd danced and laughed at Tag's jokes as he'd continuously, stealthily, supplied them both with flutes of champagne. There'd been too many awkward conversations with the Rockfords' rich, well-connected, well-to-do friends, the ones who lived in the nicest Victorian houses on the nicest cul-de-sacs. There was no one who didn't know Delta Wilding, and whispers had followed her the whole night. And the two of them had made out on the hood of his car, parked around the side of the house where no one could see, the lights of the party twinkling out around them.

But while Tag had looked at her, Delta had just wanted to lie back against the windshield and stare up at the stars.

Until, of course, Mayor Rockford had found them, shirt half-unbuttoned, shoes in the gravel, dress around her waist. She could still remember it now: the mayor's cold blue eyes glinting in the light from the windows. Each word a hiss, his fingers so tight around Tag's upper arm, his knuckles went white.

What the hell are you doing?

You're a disgrace to the Rockford family, Taggart.

To Tag: *Worthless.*

To her: *Whore.*

Get away from that girl and get back inside. You're a Rockford—act like one.

And Tag . . . had. He'd slid off the car, tugged on his shoes and hurriedly rebuttoned his crumpled white shirt, and left. Left with his father, back into the party, without looking back.

And of course, everything had fallen apart after that. *Again.*

She knew it still lingered in the forefront of both of their minds. She could see the fight in his eyes now. *Worthless. Whore.* She was sure he could see it in hers.

And even after she'd taken off the dress completely back at the Wild West, stoic and grim, anger coursing through her, the black sparkles remained. They seemed almost embedded in her skin, reminding her each day of Tag. *Worthless.* Of the Rockfords. *Whore.* She'd find them under the bed, on the floor, under her fingernails, in her hairline, in the crooks of her freckly arms. She just couldn't get rid of the black sparkles, just like she couldn't seem to get rid of Tag.

But he had gotten rid of her much more easily.

"Am I *allowed* to come?" she said, her voice cold.

Tag stilled, his smile frozen, then shook it off and settled back into his easy charm. "Of course you are—why wouldn't you be?"

"You know."

"Del," Tag murmured. He was very close to her now, and half of her wanted to crumble into his arms, kiss his

Fireball-flavored mouth. "We talked about this. I said sorry."

"It was a half-assed apology."

"But I meant it."

Delta sighed. He probably had; with Tag, who knew? She couldn't read his drowsy eyes, not anymore. And she didn't know what he'd do if she forced the issue, made them talk. If she made a scene. But Delta only made scenes in her mind, after everything was said and done.

So she edged a strained smile on her face and managed a "Then I guess I'll see you there." There was no use denying Tag what he wanted, because he always found a way to get it anyways. Tag smiled in a horribly presidential way, too perfect, too stiff, and exclaimed a long stream of "Great!" and "I really did miss you, you know" and "I think I'll be wearing blue," as he hooked his broad hand into the crook of her elbow before letting it drift down to capture her fingers.

He looked at her, met her gaze. She squeezed his hand, and he led her toward the table of Darling Academy pupils.

Delta could feel their eyes tracking. There were a few mumbled hellos, and Delta couldn't miss the raised eyebrows as they took in Tag's hand in hers. *Back together again?* She could already hear the gossip that would make its way around Darling, quicker than the speed of light. She mumbled hello back, saving her only smile for Anders Houston, Tag's best friend, and the only one who didn't glance at their entwined hands.

The burgers and fries, Delta thought morosely as everyone talked around her and over her, were taking excruciatingly long to arrive. For a moment she wondered if Tag had asked the chefs to purposefully slow it down, just so he could continue to press his leg against hers and inch his arm, millimeter by millimeter, over her shoulder. Delta honestly didn't care. She just wanted food. If she was going to spend her precious twenty-dollar bill on a feast for her and Bee, she wanted it quickly and in peace.

The others were talking about the upcoming start of school, despite it still being months away. They discussed outfits and homework and parties, all while leaning on elbows and hands as laughter burbled perpetually around them. It was like being trapped in the eye of a hurricane.

High school had not been Delta's glory days. Before her dad's disappearance, her mantra had been *One more year. One more year, and then I can be out forever.* She wasn't sure why she was so desperate to leave Darling. The feeling had always been twisting in her stomach, the feeling to get out, to explore. Maybe it was their father's influence, of growing up always believing that something *more* was out there, just beyond their grasp. Maybe she was just irrevocably weird. She didn't care which. She just wanted out.

She was glad to be done with Darling Academy, but there was no way she'd be able to leave Darling. Not now, with her dad gone and Bee completely dependent upon her. Delta sighed. She just wanted to leave, to sleep, to dream of something besides both herself and her father falling, falling, falling into a gaping black void that never ended until she woke up screaming.

But she lived in this bubble of a town. She had to pretend that she, too, felt the same nostalgia about high school, and not a vague memory of impending doom. As finally their burgers were placed before them by a vacant-eyed waiter, the owner's son, who smelled strongly of weed and cigarettes, she had to pretend that she, too, enjoyed sitting amongst her peers.

She didn't.

After some time, Delta cleared her throat, and her voice came out unused and hoarse, the words scratchy and clinging to her vocal cords. She shook them loose. "Bee? Abby is waiting."

Blank eyes turned to her.

"Our dog, Abby," she said softly. "She hasn't been fed yet. Or walked."

She had been both fed *and* walked, something Bee knew, as she'd been the one to dump kibble in her bowl and had just returned from a walk minutes before they'd left for the Diner, but she nodded calmly at her sister, her face revealing none of the lie.

"Yeah. Okay. Let's go."

Delta had never been so grateful for her sister as Bee inched out of the booth, thighs squeaking against the red leather seat, and grabbed for her. Delta allowed herself to be grabbed, allowed Bee to continue to build the excuses, allowed goodbyes to be made for her. It was nice to have someone else in control, even just for a few seconds. It hardly happened anymore.

"Hey," Tag said, reaching out to catch her hand before she could edge out the door. He ran his thumb back and forth over her knuckles. "I'm really glad you came tonight."

Delta gave a close-lipped smile as her stomach twisted. She shouldn't have come, because now Tag would think they were back together. She could feel Anders's eyes heavy upon her from the corner of the booth, and when she glanced at him, he just said, "It was nice seeing you, Delta." The rest of the kids in the booth raised their eyes at one another, but Anders ignored them.

"You too," she murmured back.

Tag squeezed her hand. "Call me later?"

This was a mistake. "Mm-hmm," Delta replied, tempering the noncommittal answer with what she hoped was a comforting, winning sort of smile. It must have worked, because Tag sat back in his booth, back in his element, and Delta hurried for the door.

When they were out in the parking lot, alone, Bee said, "Delta—"

Delta held up a hand. "Seriously, don't."

Bee snorted. "*Abby*. Of all the excuses."

Delta, who'd thought Abby was a pretty damn wonderful excuse, put her hands on her thin hips, miffed. "I wanted to leave."

"You always want to leave."

"We'd been there forever."

"We'd been there *thirty minutes*."

They pursed their lips at each other, not identical, but close.

Bee crossed her arms and pouted. Although to outsiders Delta was the cold one and Bee the sparkly one, things were much more complicated than that, as things usually are. Delta *was* colder, harder—because she had to be. She was the guardian. She was the shield. Bee didn't have to be any of those things. She was carefree, effervescent merging with flighty, but almost always thoughtless with romance and sisters and feelings.

She didn't have to be anything but. And Delta couldn't be anything but strong and cold.

They walked together toward their truck, settled in between another old truck, belonging to one of the bearded locals, and a shiny vintage purple Porsche, which belonged, quite obviously, to Tag.

The license plate read ROCKFORD.

"I'm driving," said Bee.

"No, I'm—"

"I'm driving."

Bee swung the truck out of the parking lot and swerved along the road as she pushed a CD into the CD player: the low rasp of Bruce Springsteen morphed slowly into the strummed chords of David Bowie's "Starman" within seconds.

"You know what would be nice?" Bee began, crashing her fist down upon the dashboard. "If we could listen to a CD—any CD, I don't care—without that happening."

"Yeah," Delta replied. "But that's just how things are."

She settled her head back against the headrest, watching Tag and Anders talk animatedly together through the dusty window of the Diner. They looked different through the glass, as if all the small things that made them *them* had been wiped away. As if they were just golden boys under bright strip light-ing. She liked them like that, held steady behind the glass. Was that how she had looked from the outside, sitting there, wedged in next to Tag? Happy and light?

Bee accelerated. Delta watched the figures behind the window, as separate as if they were from another world.

They are, she told herself, and the truth of it weighed heavily upon her. They went home to families that didn't disappear. They went home to houses that weren't somewhat sentient.

But the Wildings didn't. And that would always set them apart.

There was nothing Delta could do about it.

It was, clearly, as Bowie continued to sing instead of Bruce, just how things were.

3

THE EDGES OF THE

sky had been slowly gathering darkness while the sisters drove home, wrapping the twilight around itself like a skirt as they parked the rumbling Ford behind the Wild West, shutting off Bowie's ceaseless singing. Abby was whuffling at the back kitchen door, excited to see the girls returning—and, with sudden conviction, Delta decided she *would* take her on another walk after all. Delta didn't like lying, even when the lie got her out of excruciating social situations. She had an extremely— perhaps *overly*—well-developed conscience. Which, when you are a teenage girl lying about your father disappearing via mysterious circumstances, is not always the best thing to have. Lying made her stomach uneasy, like someone knew she was being untruthful. Like someone was watching.

"Do you want to come with?" she asked Bee.

Bee shrugged. "I guess."

They headed out, grass swishing around their ankles as Abby sniffed along in their wake.

The fields around the house couldn't really be called a yard—it was just dry grassland with a fence around the distant border. Delta had searched every inch of it for clues about her father's whereabouts; anything to show that he was still on Earth somewhere, that he hadn't simply disappeared into the ether. But there was nothing. Just golden-brown grasses waving in the wind.

Delta and Bee stood shoulder to shoulder as Abby picked her way around patches of thistles so dry, they'd turned prickly, before stopping to sniff at a mangy-looking bush.

"You and Tag seemed a little awkward." Bee's voice broke through the quiet.

Delta stiffened. "I don't want to talk about it."

"I like Tag."

"I know."

"I don't know why you don't just—"

"I don't know." Delta cut off her sister, her face flushing. She didn't know how to put into words the strange pull away from Tag, away from the town she'd grown up in, away from everything she knew. But she did know that however she said it, Bee would smile in that horrible way that was actually a frown.

"I just don't understand," Bee began, and Delta got the sense that she was choosing her words with pointed precision. "Why you won't talk to me anymore."

"We're talking right now."

"*Delta*," said Bee.

Delta sighed and turned to face her sister. In the gathering gloom, Bee's face was shadowy, her eyes dark. She wasn't smiling now, but Delta could still pick out the exact thoughts whirling through her sister's head. The sisters had always been close. They'd always been able to read each other.

That's why Delta wanted to go. Because Bee wanted to stay in Darling, and Delta wanted to leave, and each of them knew it. And each pretended they didn't.

"I don't know what you want me to say," Delta said in a low voice. "I don't want to talk about Tag. I don't want to talk about"—the word choked in her throat—"Dad. I just want to try to figure out what to do next."

Bee had just opened her mouth to speak when a bark cut through the night. Both girls jumped in fright at the sudden noise, then turned as Abby came sprinting back toward them, sliding to a panting halt near their feet. She tilted her head toward the sky and began to yowl. This was such unexpected behavior from old, gentle Abby that for a moment the Wilding sisters just stared at her, and then at each other, identical expressions of confusion blooming on their faces.

Delta had just crouched down to pet Abby, to calm her, when the earth began to shudder and roll beneath her feet.

The shaking was hard but not so hard to use words like *violent* and *severe*; in any case, this was California, and the sisters were used to duck-and-cover and standing in doorways and diving under desks. In fact, earthquakes around their town were even more commonplace than most of California. No one knew why—it was just how it was. They were in Darling, after all.

Darling did what it wanted.

But tonight, something was different.

Delta could feel it in her heart, in the way her chest tightened, even as the ground stuttered under them. Abby continued to yowl, the sound shrill and horrible, and then trailed off into a low whine, accompanied by loud, jarring barks. There was something in the air. Something in the way the wind whipped around them, no longer sultry and sticky but bitingly sharp. Delta pulled her flannel tighter around her slim frame with one arm and hugged Abby with the other. She glanced up at Bee, who was looking around in alarm, her air whipping about in the chilly breeze.

"Something's wrong," Delta said. That was all she *could* say, because she knew with every atom in her body that something was happening, something was changing. She just didn't know what. She'd never felt this way before: the hair on her arms stood up, her fingers trembled. The air had begun to buzz, a reverberating fizzle that tingled around the yard. The single porch light, hanging at an angle above their front door, flickered and then went out. Everything was plunged into darkness.

"Yes," said Bee, because it was obvious.

"We need to get inside the house," Delta said, dread rising in her throat. It came out of nowhere, the dread—she was worried and then, suddenly, she was terrified. The feeling of unease, of total wrongness, mounted, swirling, eddying in her stomach. Without knowing why, still kneeling in the crackling dry grass holding tightly to Abby's collar, she ignored the convulsing earth and instead turned her face to the black sky.

Bee fell to her knees too, grasping Delta's arm so firmly, Delta gasped with the sudden pain of it. "We're in the middle of a field, we're safest here!" she said, almost shouting.

Bee was right, of course, and Delta managed to squash down enough of the adrenaline coursing through her to realize that.

She gasped in—her lungs felt like they couldn't get enough air; it was a horrible feeling—and turned her face back to the sky just as the *thing* appeared.

She first thought it was light. It looked like light, if you glanced at it quickly and then away, not focusing—just glittering light arcing its way through the dusty, hazy air. It was backlit brilliantly against the darkening sky, a crescent moon curving its way to Earth.

A star, falling gracefully from its place in the sky.

It was beautiful. It was, certainly, unusual.

And it looked to be headed straight toward the ground.

"It's going to hit the house!" Bee said in a half-strangled yell, her body twitching upward like she wanted to run back and stop the collision herself. Delta didn't move, *couldn't* move. It was light, but it was more than light. . . . She blinked, and suddenly the light banked and it became very clear it was *not* light.

Not just. A dark object came to the forefront, the light now waving behind it like a luminous tail. Wrapping itself around the shape of—of—

She opened her eyes wider, as if that might make what she was seeing—*no, this can't be true, this can't be what I'm seeing*—anything less than impossible.

"A meteor!" screamed Bee.

How was Bee able to speak? Delta felt as though her vocal cords had been sliced to ribbons; she just gaped above as the light—the *thing*—soared overhead. She knew it wasn't a meteor, but couldn't bring herself to say so. If she said it wasn't a meteor, then Bee would ask what it was. And then she'd be forced to say—to say . . .

"It's not a meteor." Delta forced the words out, excitement and fear gripping her simultaneously. "*Look*. Look at the outline of it. It's . . ." She trailed off, her breath leaving her as the thing dropped closer, the light arcing down into the woods.

There may have been an earthshaking crash.

The Wildings wouldn't know, because the earth was already shaking.

But it didn't shake for long. As soon as the *thing* dropped down, disappearing from view, the rolling earth fell still, almost as if it hadn't happened at all. The sound of chirping crickets and rustling grass flooded back into the night; Abby stopped barking with a final low whine and lay down on the ground; the breeze that had whipped around the sisters during the earthquake coiled away and the syrupy heat descended again, draping itself around their shoulders. The porch light flickered dimly once, twice, and then turned on again.

Everything returned to normal. It was, once more, a completely normal night in Darling.

All her breath leaving her, Delta let out a *whoosh* and sat down on the ground beside Abby, who, although she wasn't growling or barking anymore, sat squarely beside the girls and looked around into the night mistrustfully.

Delta didn't know what to think; her thoughts were pounding in her head, a drumbeat thrumming out impossible knowledge under the guise of a headache. Unseen things rustled in the grass and Abby sniffed uneasily. Delta didn't know what had just happened, but she knew it wasn't a meteor. And she knew that however innocent and normal Darling now tried to behave, something had broken. The *thing* that had fallen from the night sky with its tail of streaming light had shattered something.

Darling had never been normal. Now it was extraordinary.

"So," said Bee in a measured voice, as though she was about to start commenting on the weather. *So, some rain we've been having, huh?* She didn't follow up her *so* with anything, though. She gave Abby a pat with a trembling hand, and that was it.

"So," Delta echoed back to her, also unsure of what to say next. *So* was a word to start some fantastic and bizarre adventure story; *so* was for the battles between Beowulf and Grendel. *So* wasn't for a small town with lights flashing overhead in a meteor shower of one single, normalcy-breaking *something.*

"Delta," Bee whispered. "Do you think anyone else saw it?"

"Yes . . . I'm sure they did."

Her first thought was Tag, his drowsy blue eyes watching the light streak through the sky from behind the glass of the Diner. And then Tag morphed into another Tag . . . a harder Tag, older, with no warmth in his eyes. She felt her lungs tighten, the air suspended in her throat. Her heart was suddenly too loud, the beat of a drum signaling their location.

The thought of Tag Senior coming to find out what had fallen from the sky made her skin go cold. Because she'd seen the outline in the falling light. The outline of—

"*Delta!*" Bee hissed again, and Delta glanced at her sister, then did a double take as she saw Bee's green eyes had a gleam in them, and a strange smile unsteady on her lips. The smile wavered, like Bee wasn't sure it was a smiling sort of time. "Let's go and find it."

Just like that, the daze was broken. *Let's go and find it.* It was real, it had been there, and that *thing* was now somewhere in the woods behind the Wild West. The falling light was on their property. Beckoning to her. *Calling* her. She suspected that sooner or later the mayor would make his way to the Wild West, and she wanted to find—whatever it was—before anyone else came looking.

You can't have seen what you thought you saw. But Delta was so sure, *so sure*, she had . . .

The girls moved even quicker now, practically running toward the farmhouse. It loomed suddenly out of the darkness, mist curling around its dormer windows and the metal weathervane. The grimy windows peered at them, interested, as though wanting to see the events unfolding before their blank and staring eyes. As though the house itself knew that something singularly remarkable had happened, that Darling had shifted, changed. Abby ran beside them, seeming only too happy to get away from the gloom of the yard, and flung her old body into the kitchen as soon as they opened the door. A small part of Delta felt like doing the same—burying herself under her covers and pretending that she hadn't seen a thing.

The other, larger part of her was buzzing with anticipation, with adrenaline. That internal drumbeat had returned, hammering away at her skull. *It wasn't a meteor. It wasn't a shooting star. You know what it is. You know what it is.*

Was she imagining it, or was the Wild West holding its breath? It was still empty, still somber and filled with memories that sat in corners like shadows . . . but now there was something else. Something more. And the Wild West knew it.

Darling knew it.

She forced herself to be calm as she stood in the kitchen, but her eyes were fixed on the trees behind their house. All she could see was the blazing trail of light in the sky, heading for the woods. And they were about to go find it now—they would enter the woods and search for the streak of light that had descended, intruder-like, into their midst.

Her dad would be so excited. The thought hit her so hard, she reached out a hand to steady herself against the doorframe. She could hear Bee behind her, checking the batteries of their old, heavy flashlights.

Delta thought back to the last time she'd seen her dad: they'd been side by side in his study, comfortable silence reigning, while he pored over his books and she poked colored pushpins into a map, using coordinates from his handwritten list. She'd been anxious to leave; she'd had a date with Tag. He'd waved her away, he'd smiled and said, *Be back before ten.* She was. But he hadn't been there to know; there had only been a hysterical Bee and an empty hallway closet.

Grief, razor-sharp and hot, washed over her, her sudden longing for her dad so strong, it felt like needles in her chest. *Something* was happening; the something was what her dad had always hoped for, prepared for, wished for.

Now *something* had arrived, but her dad was gone.

4

DARLING AFTER HOURS
was like a town of the dead: lighted house after lighted house
went suddenly dark, leaving only the buzzing neon of the DINER
sign and the lonely, flickering streetlights standing sentinel on
abandoned streets. Delta and Bee leaving seemed to have been
the catalyst; one by one, everyone else in the diner made their
excuses and said their goodbyes. The bewildered couple with
the backpacks—*"I don't know* how *we arrived here, we never even
saw an exit"*—picked up their to-go cups and left with directions.
The family finished their burgers, and even the two muttering
old men checked their battered watches and filed out.

Tag slumped down on an elbow, staring out the window
into the dark parking lot out front, full of cracks in the asphalt
and sprouting dandelions. The jingling of the door faded away
and he sighed. There were only four people still in their booth:
Tag, Anders, and two soon-to-be-senior girls who kept leaning close to whisper things to each other. He knew their names
were Allison and Marnie—everyone in Darling knew everyone
else—but he'd never had any classes with them. They weren't
who he wanted to spend this night with, but he didn't have any
other options.

Tag sighed. It was time again for the Rockford Act. For the presidential smile and the vacant eyes as the rest of them rambled about nothing and everything.

He didn't necessarily *like* the people he hung out with—except for Anders—but he was quite obviously their leader, and that was enough for Tag. He didn't need to like people, as long as they liked him. And in a town like Darling, where his family was both revered and hated in equal amounts, he couldn't be choosy about who wanted to be his friend.

He liked Delta, though. He had absolutely no idea what went on in her head, or in her life. Half the time he couldn't even tell if she really liked him. If he went off how often Delta answered the phone when he called, his chances were very low indeed. And he called Delta a lot.

He knew he seemed desperate.

He was.

Things typically came easily for Tag, but getting Delta Wilding to pick up the phone was not one of them. Tag, the once-great ruler of Darling Academy, the lord of the Diner, driving around in his Porsche with the windows down and music blaring, the king of the castle . . . he couldn't even get his sometimes-girlfriend to answer his call.

He supposed he could go to her house to try to talk it out. They lived just a few miles apart, for God's sake, but the distance between them might've been the distance to the moon.

And at least when Delta ignored his calls, the rejection, while very clear, was from a distance. Going to her house would make it all very real. In any case, Rockfords didn't do things like that—Rockfords didn't wait around, or beg, or stand out-side houses with boomboxes. They also didn't mope around a deathly quiet mansion and leave multiple voice mails a day to girls who wanted nothing to do with them, either, so Tag wasn't quite sure what that made him.

Not really a Rockford?

Being Tag Rockford III was all he knew. He wore the title like a crown.

"All right," he said abruptly, loudly, sitting up straight. *I don't want to think about this. I can't think about this.* He was vaguely aware he'd interrupted another conversation, but both the seniors trailed off. "I'm done with this." He said the only thing that he could think of in the moment, the first thing he knew would let him forget Darling, his dad, and Delta. "Let's get drunk."

The girls giggled to each other. "Okay."

"Anders?"

"You know I'm there," Anders said lightly, although Tag noticed the way his friend's dark eyes followed him as he stood up, his eyebrows furrowed in something that might've been concern. "Your house?"

"No, my dad is home."

The bolder of the seniors, Allison, piped in, "Wishing Well?"

Tag sighed. He should've known the girls would want to go there; *everyone* always chose the Darling Wishing Well—an old abandoned well deep in the pocket of woods near the Wilding house, its water littered with years upon years of pennies from the hopeful—but it was so close to Delta. Back before they'd imploded, he and Delta spent countless hours tossing pennies into the pool, casting stupid wishes that always turned serious an hour and a drink or two in. It was *their place*. It was where he'd first kissed her.

If he tossed a penny in those deep waters tonight, would the wish be heard by whatever mysterious force cradled Darling in its hands? Maybe Delta would be there too by some twist of fate. Maybe this would be the night they'd stop fighting, and Delta would realize he hadn't intended for anything to happen how it did. As the penny dropped out of sight, maybe Delta would fall for him all over again.

"Wishing Well, yeah, okay," Tag agreed.

"I'll drive us," said Anders, and Tag nodded, tossing him the keys to the Porsche. The Fireball whisky still coated his tongue, syrupy cinnamon rising to his head. The small group shuffled out of the booth and left the air-conditioned Diner, stepping out into the lingering warmth of night. Beyond the light shining from the Diner windows was pure, undulating dark. It might have been another world, some underground land where there was no one left but the four of them.

Their feet crunched in the broken gravel of the asphalt as they crossed to Tag's shiny car and all loaded in. No one spoke until the car purred to life and Anders flicked on the headlights, the twin beams of light cutting a pathway through the pressing blackness.

Yes, Darling at night was a town of the dead, and they were its ghostly inhabitants.

The drive was mere minutes, and Anders chattered animat-

edly the whole way as only Anders could, saving Tag from having to say a word. Tag couldn't tell if this was on purpose or not,
but either way, he appreciated being able to sit back and let the
conversation float over him in a hum. It was only when Anders
turned the car down a winding dirt road midway between the
Diner and the Wilding house that Tag sat up. He couldn't help
but notice lights on in the large farmhouse, and once again the
distance between him and Delta loomed. He was so close, half a
mile, maybe less, but the trees blocked the way, and the walls of
the Wild West crossed their arms against him.

They parked in the makeshift lot—the Wishing Well had
become a favorite with the passing tourists—and followed the
narrow path into the woods.

Tag was aware of everyone talking again; they laughed and
joked, their lilting voices echoing loudly throughout the woods.
He heard them as if from far away, as if he'd fallen into the
Wishing Well and was separated by a thin film of glassy water.

He didn't want to be here—he didn't *care*.

But it was better than his house. It was better than sitting
alone at the Diner with his whirling thoughts. That's what Tag
told himself, because he had to believe it. The clearing with the
Wishing Well was enclosed by dark trees, and it had felt like
a magical place those nights he'd sat here with Delta, but now
the seniors gabbled over each other, their voices intertwining in
one loud roar, and they brought out clinking bottles and took
sharply scented shots that spilled onto the mossy forest floor.

"Come on, crack a bottle," Anders said, smiling wide. Tag
smiled back as he grabbed one; it felt like an act. It *was* an act,

and he was so good at it by now that even Anders didn't see through it. He tilted the bottle and threw back a shot. It burned its way down his throat, and Anders reached to take the bottle, but Tag held up a finger to wait. "Another," he coughed.

If he were drunk, he wouldn't wish he were alone.

He wouldn't wish he were sitting in silence, staring up at the mass of stars above.

He took his second drink, then passed the bottle on, an unexpected lump growing in his throat. He kept smiling; everyone was laughing, and no one noticed his glassy eyes, the wetness there.

Tag lay back on the mossy earth, throwing an arm under the back of his head. If he tilted his head, he could see the pitch-dark sky above through the canopy of leaves. He could feel the drink in him, dizzying his sight, smoothing down his thoughts, pulling at his eyelids. He didn't remember giving in and falling asleep, but when he next opened his eyes, the warm summer air was pressing down upon the sleeping bodies of Anders and the senior girls. Mini bottles littered the ground, and Allison was cradling a half-empty tequila bottle like it was a teddy bear.

The warmth in Tag's stomach had curdled, turned sharp and acidic in the time he'd been unconscious, and he lay back again to try to ward off the sick feeling that was sweeping its way through his body. He couldn't decide if he was still half-drunk or if he'd passed the verge to hungover, but his mouth was already dry and he swallowed hard against his cottony tongue.

He wasn't sure why he'd suddenly awoken, and he was just thinking about whether he could manage walking home when the ground began to shake around him. The others awoke too,

Anders blinking heavily, small twigs in his dark hair; Marnie opened her eyes and ran off into the underbrush to throw up while Allison kept mumbling, *"Whaz going on?"*

Anders closed his eyes with a groan. Tag turned his gaze up to the sky once more, even as the stars seemed to wheel around him. There was a light there, a light in the sky, and it was coming closer—it was *moving*—

"Anders!" Tag said hoarsely.

Anders gave another moan but didn't open his eyes.

Tag stared blearily up, trying to discern what was happening from under the canopy of leaves. A light was falling from the sky—a shooting star? It was heading right for them, and Tag was just about to yell, or try to get up and run, or *something*, when the earthquake stopped abruptly, the earth quieting around them. And the light was gone.

"Anders, did you see that?"

Anders moaned.

Marnie came back into the clearing, her face leached of color, her blond hair lank around her face. "I'm gonna walk back home," she murmured. "Anyone coming?"

"Did you see that light?" Tag asked.

She stared at him blankly.

"The light," Tag pressed. Had he imagined it? It had been hard to order his thoughts with the shaking earth, but he knew something had fallen from the sky.

Marnie shook her head. "I didn't see anything. I just wanna go home."

Tag's throat clenched: how he wished he could say the same.

But he nodded, pushing himself up with a groan. "We should all go." Anders was still lying on the ground by the well, his white shirt now streaked with dirt, and Tag nudged him with the toe of his shoe. "Come on, bro, we're leaving."

"Hmm?"

"We're going home."

"I have to text Colson," Anders slurred. "My phone—where—"

"It's here," Tag said, picking Anders's phone off the ground, brushing off the dirt, and slipping it into his back pocket as his friend leaned heavily against him. "You can text him once you're home. Okay? Let's get you home." He shifted Anders, unsure of when he'd become the responsible friend.

"The car—"

"I'll get it tomorrow, it doesn't matter," Tag mumbled. "Let's just go."

One by one, they filed out of the clearing, walking heavily, heads drooping. *Why the hell did I ever agree to this?* Tag thought as he held tightly to Anders's arm to keep him upright.

What the hell am I doing?

They stumbled out of the woods, back past the Porsche, down the dirt road, and onto the expanse of flat road stretching off into nothingness. Soon houses would start springing up out of the darkness. Soft beds and splitting headaches awaited them. A roar of a car sounded in the night, and the group stumbled to the side of the road. The car that squealed by them had no headlights on; it was just a dark shape shooting by. It was driving fast, too fast, but even so, for a second Tag thought he recognized the shape of it. But then it was gone, and Tag shook his head. He was drunk and hungover at the same time; everything was blurry and vague.

And there was no reason his father would be driving with no headlights toward the Wilding house.

Tag turned once, glancing back at the dark mass of trees and, beyond, the dark outline of the Wild West. Everything was quiet; all lights were out. Nothing arced its way out of the sky. No signal came that anything out of the ordinary had happened.

Maybe nothing had.

Maybe you imagined it.

Tag's stomach twisted again, and he didn't know if it was the alcohol or the knowledge that *something* had happened, and Darling was acting innocent. He turned back to the disheveled, glassy-eyed group and trudged on through the night.

5

DELTA SHIVERED AS
Bee handed her the flashlight. The creeping dark had sucked
away the day's lingering heat, but Delta's hairline still felt
damp with perspiration. Even so, she pulled her checked flannel
tighter around her waist, unable to stop the hair on her arms
from standing up as a shiver tremored through her. She flicked
on the flashlight, Bee following suit, and the thin beam of light
trembled in the night air as Delta's hand shook.

"You ready?" she said to Bee, talking louder than necessary.
She was trying to convince herself, too. Now that it was time,
now that they stood fifty paces from the woods, she felt almost
sick with restlessness and apprehension.

Bee stood stock-still, looked nervously out over the trees.
There was no sign of the gleam that had been in her eyes when
she'd set things in motion with her *Let's go and find it*. She
clicked on her flashlight too, and the dim shaft of light hovered
next to Delta's, illuminating the trunks of the first trees.

The woods had always been there behind the farmhouse,
looking like a thicket had exploded outward and then suddenly
and abruptly stopped. The trees formed an almost perfectly
straight line at the backyard's edge, and swelled away from the

house, petering out only when they hit the start of the cliff face
a good three miles or so in the distance. The cliff face was actually the south side of a small mountain, and no one in Darling
knew what it was really named, or if it even had a name, so they
called it Mount Darling.

They couldn't see the cliff face now; it was too dark and their
flashlights shone on nothing but the straight line of trees before
them, leaves whispering in the girls' uneasy silence. A starling
squawked angrily as Delta's beam of light hit it, and it launched
itself into the sky in a flapping of glossy wings.

"Should we take Dad's service road?" Bee whispered.

Along their property line was an unpaved road that ran
parallel to the edge of the woods and, just like the trees, only
tapered off when it hit the base of Mount Darling. Their dad
had cleared the grasses in order to create the dirt road; it was
flat enough that technically he could take the truck along it for
easier access to the depths of the woods, and bumpy enough that
Delta could remember him ever driving along it only a handful
of times in her whole life.

"No," Delta whispered after a moment of thought. "It looked
like it would've landed somewhere in the center. We might as
well just . . ." She jerked her head toward the trees.

Bee took a couple of steps forward and nodded. Her mouth
was set in a straight little line and she looked unusually stern—
she looked, in that moment, very much like Delta. Scared and
unsure and grave. This more than anything got Delta's feet
moving and pushed her ahead of her sister, taking the lead
as they hurried past the first few trees. She didn't want Bee

looking like that—glittery, happy Bee, of all people.

A blanket of quiet settled over their shoulders as they picked their way through the trees. They stayed within a step or two of each other, not wanting to get separated. They could find their way out, sure, but it was night and it was dark and *something* was here that shouldn't be. That was enough to make them jittery.

It got progressively darker the deeper they descended into the woods. The night had been filled with stars only half-covered by clouds, but the leafy canopy above blotted out whatever twinkling lights could be seen. Dead leaves crunched under the two sets of sneakers; two sets of flashlight beams swung in all directions, illuminating gnarled trunks and dark green leaves and, once, the too-bright eyes of a raccoon. The flashlights were rarely used and the beams were dim, but they still lit the forest in a welcome, if perhaps a bit eerie, way. The stifling heat that had surrounded them near the house couldn't seem to follow them this far into the trees, and swirls of fog curled around their ankles. They had never had a reason to come this far into the woods; in fact, their father had expressly forbidden it.

"Shouldn't we have found it by now?" Bee whispered, her breath hot on Delta's neck. Delta felt as if they should have: the woods went deep behind the house, but not *that* deep. Another mile and they'd have walked through to the other side, to the base of Mount Darling. It had to be here somewhere.

She stepped on a twig; the resounding crack was too loud in her ear, more like a gunshot in the dark than a small piece of wood breaking in two. She stopped still, causing Bee to step on her heels and whisper apologies. Neither girl wanted to raise her voice above a whisper; there was something about the pressing darkness that spoke of things unseen and trees that listened. The trees were slumbering. Delta, for one, did not want them to wake.

"Maybe we imagined it?" Delta replied, her voice rising uncertainly, leaving the question open. She knew she hadn't imagined it. She knew what she'd seen. But it was also true that she felt they should've stumbled upon it by now. Whatever *it* was.

You know what you saw.

"I didn't imagine anything." Bee's voice was sure.

Delta paused, wondering if Bee could hear how her heart was hammering in her chest. "I know."

They kept moving, slower now, almost as one body. Their flashlight beams jumped frantically between tree, rock, and bird, roving in agitation over anything that moved, anything that made the slightest sound. Delta swallowed hard, peering through the trees as they moved. It was so dark, and any second she expected something to jump out at her. Anything was possible in woods as dark as these. Delta reached down, fingers grasping for her sister's. She wanted to feel another's heartbeat, hear another's breath. Bee pressed closer as they stumbled along: a three-legged race through the dormant woods.

From somewhere in the woods came a shout.

Both girls stilled. Delta could see the whites of Bee's eyes in the light of the flashlight, wide and terrified.

"Did you hear that?"

"I think," Delta said, her voice shaking as she tried to whisper, "that someone else might be in here too." She tried to stay calm—*after all, it's probably just someone else who saw the falling light.* Why did that make her stomach drop and her hands shake?

Bee didn't reply, but Delta could hear her breath coming faster. They continued on, quicker now, until Bee stopped suddenly, throwing an arm out to bring Delta to a halt. "Do you see that?" Bee whispered. She directed her own beam of light about twenty yards away, through the trees.

"What?" Delta whispered back, lowering her voice to the softest of whispers, so that she could hardly be heard. The trees rustled around them in a chilly wind, listening in. Her eyes darted toward Bee's light, wandering over moss-covered trunks hung with ivy and hard-packed ground. There was nothing she could see that was out of the ordinary. "No. What?"

"There," Bee said, and with a click turned off her flashlight, disappearing into the blackness besides Delta. "Turn yours off too."

Delta complied, a prickle of fear sliding down her back as the world around them plunged into inky darkness.

"Look," came Bee's voice from beside her, and Bee squeezed her fingers hard.

Delta peered around, hearing nothing but her own sharp intakes of breath. She couldn't hear any more shouts from behind them, couldn't hear any other footsteps through the undergrowth. But that didn't mean they weren't there.

For a few moments, her eyes couldn't seem to adjust to the dark. But then, slowly, a shimmer of dim light came from the place Bee had pointed out with her flashlight. The light was faint, a dull golden glow that somehow still lit up the trees surrounding it.

"That must be it," Delta whispered. The trees rustled back at her, agreeing.

For a moment, she stood stationary and simply *shook*; her hands trembled, her breath came low and fast. *This was it.* She wanted to turn back, to run, to—no. No, she didn't. This was the start of—something. The start of something unbelievable, unknowable . . . and the end of normalcy. She took a deep breath and then flicked back on her flashlight. *This was it.*

Growing up with her father, she'd always been taught there was something else out there. Something besides the Wild West, besides Darling, besides California. The world was ever expanding, filled to the brim with *others*, things they couldn't understand. There was magic in the air, if only one would reach out and grab it. That, their dad had explained, was what the Wildings were put on Earth to do.

It was in Delta's bones. She ached for something . . . more. Anything more. It was out there, and she wanted it. Whatever was out there, she wanted it. But her feelings warred: she both craved and feared the unknown.

"Let's go," Bee whispered, squeezing Delta's hand once more and then letting it slip out of her grasp. She switched her flashlight on again, and the twin beams cast a thin glow on the forest around them. They tripped forward as one, trying to stay as quiet as possible as they tromped through the moss and climbed unsteadily over fallen logs. The glow grew brighter and brighter. They skirted around a huge tree, and

Delta dragged her fingertips across the rough bark as though reminding herself that *this is real, this is real*.

They were close. As they crouched behind a particularly large fern, they could now see that the strange glow coated the trees and grass before them. Delta heard her sister's breath hitch slightly before a long breath out, and she reached for Bee's hand in the darkness. This time, neither girl let go.

They emerged at the edge of a clearing. Stars winked dully above them; finally, the thick tree cover that had enveloped them the whole way through the woods had vanished with the grove. And in the center of the grove was—

"That . . . that's impossible." Bee whispered the words so softly that Delta barely heard her, except for the fact that she'd been thinking the same thing herself. There was no other way to put it. It wasn't a meteor at all—of course, she'd known it wasn't from the moment she'd seen it descending through the sky. She'd known from the moment the tail of light illuminated the shape of the falling *thing*.

"I know it's impossible. But . . . but . . ."

Bee made a noise from the tree line, a mix of sudden hysteria and the noise that comes before a scream. When she spoke, it came out strangled and loud, although the words were casual. "It fell from the sky. *It fell from the sky, Delta.*"

Delta met her sister's wild eyes, followed her stare, Delta's heart *thump-thump-thumping* with every second.

On the ground in the clearing, nestled atop crushed stalks of grass and shining with a dull glow, was a boy.

6

THE SISTERS DIDN'T
speak a word to each other, just tried to keep breathing.

This isn't possible. This isn't possible. Delta felt a spark of unbridled hysteria rush to her head. *It's not possible, but . . . he's there.* Someone *is there.* Delta took a hesitant step farther into the clearing. "I . . . I'm going closer."

"Delta, no!" Bee's fingers tightened painfully around Delta's, holding her back against the trees.

"We *have* to look, Bee. He might be . . . hurt."

"I mean," Bee began, her voice shrinking to a mere echo of a voice. "He did *fall* from the *sky.*"

Delta breathed out. The words rattled around in her brain, bouncing through her thoughts. *Fell from the sky.* She couldn't stop staring at the boy: his torso was bare, but he was wearing what looked like loose, dark trousers. He was so still in the night, Delta wondered if he was asleep. Or . . . Delta's eyes widened. *Or he might be something worse. . . .*

Delta shook off Bee's hand and stepped toward him, peering into the glow, trying to get a better look.

"Delta!" Bee said sharply. "Seriously."

"We *have* to," Delta repeated, mostly to herself. Her heart was in her head, her stomach was on the ground. . . . She felt light-headed and crazed, and also slightly foggy, as though she was wandering through a highly stressful dream. In that moment Bee could've said anything and it wouldn't have changed Delta's mind. "We have to see." She waved her hand toward the boy. "We have to. There's nothing else we can do. This is . . ." She didn't know what it was. *Everything*. "This is bigger than us. Everyone will be coming to find it. *Him*." She took a deep breath, then repeated, "There's nothing else we can do."

There were actually, probably, quite a lot of things they could do, but with a boy from the stars there—right there—before them, all those other ideas seemed very small and very far away.

Delta walked slowly toward the prone body. She thought she heard Bee whisper *Be careful* from behind her, but her mind was whirling too fast to pay much attention. The sheer wonder of what was before her had burned away her fear.

She stopped a mere foot from the body in the clearing and stared down at the boy in front of her. His whole body was suffused in that strange glow, pale yellow light wrapping itself around his arms and legs like vines of sunlight. But besides that, he looked more or less *normal*.

He was tall and thin, and his eyes and mouth were closed, the expression in his unconscious state almost peaceful. While the boy's lips were pink, beneath the golden glow his skin was pale with a bluish tinge, as though he was sleeping in the snow rather than a grassy clearing. The tinge was so faint, Delta kept thinking she'd imagined it, until his cheek or shoulder would once again reflect the slight color. The boy had dark brows, furrowed even in the comatose state, and his hair was colored the same dark brown, almost black, and was wavy and knotted. The snarls were plastered to his forehead and neck in a sweaty tangle.

Wrapping around his body, on every bit of bare skin Delta could see, were strange black tattoos, all identical. The repeating tattoo looked like an elongated roman numeral *III*, and the long lines wrapped around both of his arms and his entire chest and back. Delta couldn't fathom what they meant, but that didn't stop her from trying.

"Is he dead?" Bee whispered from the edge of the grove.

Delta stared down at the boy, focusing on his chest. Was that movement there, or was it her own hammering heartbeat? *It's a boy . . . a boy who fell from the sky.*

Which is impossible.

And yet . . . and yet.

Delta crouched down, shuffling a little closer. She couldn't keep her eyes from darting back to the boy's face, at his upturned lips and long lashes. *Please don't be dead.* She knelt over the body, her hand hovering above his tattooed chest. This would change everything. She shook the thought away, placing her hand gently on his chest. His skin was warm beneath her fingers, and she felt a flush rise on her cheeks. She turned her head away from Bee, ducking her face toward the boy and willing her own heart to calm down its frantic beating. All at once, she felt his heart— or *something* moving beneath his skin. She quickly rocked back onto her heels. "Well, *something* is moving in there."

"A heartbeat?" Bee whispered back.

"It didn't . . . I don't know," Delta replied.

"What do you mean? What did it feel like?"

"I . . . I don't know." Delta reached out again, placed a cautious hand once more on the boy's chest. There wasn't a single heartbeat so much as a cacophony of them, a fluttering, a pounding, a strange rhythmic beating. . . . It was like a song. It was beautiful.

The words rushed out of her before she could stop them, before she could think about what they meant. Each word tumbled into the next, jumbling together in one scattered, impossible sentence: "Bee, I think he has more than one heart." She stared at her sister with wide, turbulent eyes. Nothing about this was expected, or possible, and yet the boy lay between them with his multiple hearts pounding wildly inside his chest.

And then they heard the voices. They were still far away enough that the words were indistinct, but they were deep, male voices and they were coming closer. Delta and Bee gestured wildly to each other for a moment, frozen in place in the clearing, but it only took a split second for Delta to decide to take charge.

They had to take him home. They had to get him out. She didn't know who was in the woods with them, but it was dark, and late, and she didn't want to leave him there, alone and unconscious, for someone else to stumble upon. She *couldn't* let that happen to him.

To this strange, tattooed, unconscious boy.

To this boy from the stars.

"We're bringing him home," Delta said, and her voice broke

the spell. Was that a flashlight beam she saw through the trees? Were those footsteps coming closer and closer? She didn't let herself consider what was happening. She could feel it pressing against the bones of her skull, tapping persistently against her forehead, putting pressure on the jelly of her eyeballs. But just as it had been easier to search when she'd told herself it was a falling meteor, it was easier to carry this comatose boy through the rustling woods when she told herself he was just a boy, just a boy. Nothing more. "Get him, now. Get his ankles. We have to go." When Bee just stared at her, shaking her head, Delta snapped, "*Now*, Bee!"

Bee took his ankles hesitantly, and Delta grasped the boy's wrists. His unconscious body was heavy, deadweight, but between them they managed a carrying, dragging movement away from the clearing. Away from the footsteps and cracking twigs.

As they moved through the crunching leaves and slick moss, the forest awoke around them. The trees leaned in, stirring and murmuring, branches waving and leaves swishing knowingly. The trees listened. The trees watched.

How had the girls ever thought the woods were quiet? Each step sounded like a gunshot, each breath the rattling of a horror-movie zombie. The birds screamed in the branches above them, announcing their presence to the world. Delta could feel the boy's many heartbeats through the pulse going at his wrist— was she imagining it or were they progressively slowing down? She didn't want to look down at him to check; every time she glanced down at the body hoisted between them, her breath didn't seem to flow correctly and she staggered over the flat ground. His angular face with its furrowed brows was so . . . peaceful. He was almost . . . *handsome.*

She kept her eyes trained on Bee.

Just a boy. Just a boy.

But he wasn't.

While the journey into the woods to find the meteor had taken just under an hour and seemed like much longer, the way back flew by in what felt like mere seconds, a mad rush of stumbling feet, tripping over twigs, of branches caught in hair, of gasping breaths and wild eyes and the beating of five hearts in three bodies.

Before they knew it, the trees were spaced farther apart and their hastily trod trail through the underbrush met with the well-trimmed path their father had created years before. The oppressive watchfulness of the trees gave way to the stars shining from their places in the sky.

Delta tightened her grip on the boy's wrists. The stars didn't seem as far away as they had when she'd entered the woods just two hours ago.

The Wild West met them, breaking the sisters out of their wavering course. They careened toward the house, half running, half falling, suddenly desperate to get into the safety of the enclosed walls and lockable doors. On the issue of locked doors, they discovered—as the back door swung readily open with a hasty turning of the knob—that they hadn't even locked the door on the way out to the woods, a fact that seemed horribly innocent and naive now that they had a boy from the sky, glowing with otherworldly light, slung between them.

A boy.

An . . . alien?

The world once again tilted dangerously, threatening to slough off its facade of normalcy, but Delta pushed back. She had no illusions that Darling was normal, and she had always believed there were other things in the universe besides humans. She just hadn't ever truly believed those other things would be held in her grasp. That she'd carry them into her house by the wrists.

"Where should we put him?" Bee asked as they tripped through the doorway, accidentally bumping the boy's head on the doorframe. He didn't stir; his head lolled back, the curls hanging down in a dark tangle.

"Guest bedroom," Delta replied. The guest bedroom had only been used when their mother had died, years before, and relatives came to stay for the funeral. It was across the hall from Delta's bedroom, so at least she'd be able to keep an eye on him. At least he'd be farther away from Bee, just in case.

"Okay, yeah, good idea," Bee replied, sounding relieved that Delta hadn't suggested their dad's bedroom, which was across from Bee's, or the living room couch, with its open archways and no doors.

They headed for the stairs and hurried up them toward the guest bedroom. There were four stories to the Wild West: the first floor, with the kitchen and drafty living room and mostly unused dining room; the second floor, containing Delta's room, the guest bedroom, and the bathroom; the third floor, with Bee's bedroom, the closed door to their dad's room that Delta couldn't bear to open, and their dad's study; and at the end of the hallway was a pull-down set of stairs, more like a hastily constructed ladder than anything, that led to the attic.

The guest bedroom was neat and orderly, as most rooms are when no one lives in them. It was pretty in a sad sort of way, as though it had taken on all the sadness of the last people who'd stayed in it and kept the sadness hidden under the floorboards. There was an air of undisturbed quiet, like the room had a sleeping, but invisible, inhabitant.

The still air quickly roiled and fled as the panting of the sisters took its place. They heaved the prone body onto the mattress, which let out the tiniest of groans at the pressure, accompanied with a small puff of unsettled dust. The boy's eyelids didn't even flutter with the movement, although his naked chest continued to slowly rise and fall.

Delta unfolded the top of the sheets and pulled the blankets up over his chest. His skin, besides the blue-tinged pallor and the strange golden glow and the fact that it was currently damp with perspiration, felt fairly similar to a human's skin— maybe just a bit smoother. Although this should've comforted her, instead it made her quickly step back from the bed. Boys who fall from the sky, who are seemingly *aliens*, she decided, should *look* like aliens. They shouldn't be human-shaped with dark curls and slightly parted lips and long, thick lashes and high cheekbones. They shouldn't look like handsome, ethereal boys.

She walked to the doorway, where Bee stood, shifting back and forth on her feet. Bee stared at the bed, and Delta chanced a glance back too. The boy lay still and unmoving, eyes closed, jaw slack.

When Bee spoke, Delta could hear the layered fear in her voice, despite the attempt at nonchalance. "We don't have to *stay* in here with him, do we?"

"Of course not," Delta replied.

"But how will we know if he wakes up?"

For a second Delta imagined waking up to find the boy—an *alien*—standing over her, very much awake. She imagined seeing eyes peering through those dark curls, the smile that might bloom on his lips. The thought shot a tiny thrill through her, and she shook her head to dispel the sudden flush that crept up her cheeks. Somehow she didn't think Bee was imagining the same thing.

"What if he dies in his sleep? What if he needs something?" Bee continued. "What if—"

"I get it," Delta interrupted. She backed out of the doorway into the hall, floorboards creaking with each step, and beckoned for Bee to join her. She snapped the door shut with a click. "I'll . . ." She thought. What *did* they do now? They'd found the alien, rescued him from the woods, brought him into their home. But the fact remained that he was not a human—*couldn't* be a human—no matter how much he might resemble one, and they didn't know if he was peaceful or not.

She nodded confidently before she actually had anything to say, because that's what big sisters are supposed to do: look confident and make it up as they go along. "I'll get those walkie-talkies from Dad's study. You go to the kitchen and get a glass of water to put by his bed. If you don't want to go in there alone," she continued, waving a hand and heading off the apprehensive look she knew Bee was about to give her, "just leave it by his door and I'll do it later."

"Okay," Bee said agreeably, and Delta saw relief in her eyes before she hurried down the stairs to the kitchen. Delta stood for a moment, alone in the hallway, the ache in her arms from carrying the boy becoming sorer by the second.

They had an alien in their house. A falling star. A celestial boy.

A wild, hysterical burble of laughter threatened to rise, but she bit it down and hurried to the door of her dad's study. She paused before going in, leaning against the solid wood of the door, breathing deeply. She knew exactly where the walkie-talkies were, which meant she didn't have to look at the disarray of the office, dusty and forlorn in its abandonment. *One, two, three. Come on, Delta.* She pushed open the door and grabbed the walkie-talkies off the top of an old suitcase. Despite the effort not to look around, the smell of old books and her dad's soft sweaters made her heart clench.

She hurried back down the stairs, desperate to get out of the study, so full of reminders of what was gone. Lost. *Missing.* Bee stood outside the closed door of the guest bedroom, holding a glass of water in both hands. When she saw Delta, she visibly brightened. "Did you find them?"

Delta showed her. "Replace the batteries in these monitors and we'll be able to know if—I mean," she amended, "*when* the boy wakes up." She paused, then said, "The alien."

The words sounded strange in her mouth. *The alien.* She said it again, aloud: "The alien." Bee looked alarmed, her green eyes widening, as if she'd just realized what they'd found. Delta said it again. It had hit her, too, all at once, and she felt as winded as if she'd run a marathon.

As Bee headed back downstairs to rummage for batteries, Delta took the glass of water and braved the room. She tried to turn the doorknob as quietly as possible, bracing herself for the fact that maybe the alien had already awoken and was lying in wait behind the door, or under the bed, or on the ceiling, or . . .

The boy was where she'd left him, tucked in and unconscious. She crept over and placed the tumbler on the bedside table, the water sloshing inside the glass. Then she stood and looked down at their comatose ward, a strange feeling coming over her. It was a mix of disbelief, of fading adrenaline, of . . . interest. Curiosity. *Attraction.*

What are you doing, *Delta?*

A noise sounded behind her as Bee stepped into the room, her eyes narrowing as she took in Delta standing by the bed. She stayed close to the door as she held out both of the walkie-talkies, now working, refreshed by the batteries. Delta placed one on the bedside table, carefully locking in the talk button so it was permanently on, always listening. She slipped the other into her pocket.

Then she backed out of the room, making sure Bee didn't see her eyes stray to the light-infused boy, and shut the door behind them.

7

THE ROCKFORDS' HOUSE

was a dream of a house, all glittering gold and sparkling chandeliers swaying from the ceiling and gilt brocade upholstery on the couches. The rooms were expansive and airy, with fifteen-foot ceilings and huge windows peeking out from expensive velvet curtains. It was a house that was obviously extravagant in its false simplicity; bookcases carved out of mahogany and end tables that were just props to exhibit glass-blown paperweights and stacks of hundred-year-old books no one was allowed to touch.

There was a place for everything, and everything was in its place. Including the people: Tag Rockford III, still in his dirt-streaked, blue-and-white checked button-down, lying prone and rumpled and hungover on his canopied bed, ibuprofen tablets littered on the bedside table. His parents in their different rooms: the mayor in his study, blue suit unrumpled, pocket square perfectly pointed, eyes narrowed as he turned the carved bone handle of an ornamental dagger around and around in his fingers; Annabelle Rockford in the darkened kitchen, sitting prettily in a slim-cut shift dress, fingers trembling around a crystal tumbler filled with honeyed scotch.

Everyone in the Rockford house was well-dressed, and everyone was a mess.

Because that was the thing about the Rockford estate: It was a dream of a house in that it was gorgeous, and glistening, and very, very much an illusion. It was not the house containing the upstanding mayor and his perfect wife and son. It was not the house, not really, where lavish parties were held and smiles were passed. It had no broken windows, no broken floorboards, no broken appliances. Just gold and daggers and money and very broken people.

"Tag, darling?"

Tag groaned from the bed, a tiny noise that meant *Go away*. There came the clicking of high heels, and a soft touch landed on the side of his head. The smell of his father's favorite scotch washed over him as his mother sat primly, if slightly drunkenly, on the edge of his bed.

"Darling, your father wishes to see you in his study." Annabelle Rockford said this sentence with one too many pauses as she tried very hard not to slur any words. She gave her son a pat on his head again, slightly harder now.

Tag cracked an eyelid open. God, his head.

"What time's it?"

"Just past eleven," his mom replied, already drifting back to the door.

A sliver of light came through the half-pulled curtains. Tag sat up slowly, but even so, as soon as he swung his legs off the bed, the room began to spin around him. The movement sparked a memory from the night before—spinning.

Shaking. *Earthquake.* And the light—he was the only one who saw the light, streaking through the clouds. He was the only one who saw as a dark shape came to the forefront of the light. It looked like a . . .

Tag shook his head. He'd been drunk.

But it had been *strange.* And now his father wanted to see him, something that rarely happened.

Tag stumbled to the doorway. His head pounded and his stomach heaved. He felt like death. He breathed through his mouth, shallowly, pushing away the waves of nausea that hit him. The door to his father's study was closed, and before he entered, he tucked his shirt into the band of his jeans and smoothed down his mussy hair. There was nothing he could do about his bloodshot eyes, but he knocked on the door anyways. If there was one thing Mayor Rockford hated, it was to be kept waiting.

"Come in," came a low voice from inside the room, and Tag swung open the door and stepped inside. His father was seated at his ornate desk of dark, polished wood. His whole study, in fact, was dark and gleaming. Wood-paneled walls and built-in bookcases with glass doors, showcasing book spines like a neat line of maniacally grinning teeth. His desk was clear except for some loose papers and a chess set, the pieces carved from wood so shiny, Tag could see the lights from the candelabra above reflected in the board.

"Take a seat," his father said. Tag sat. The two Tags sat across from each other, one young and pale and glowering with the pressure that came with trying not to seem drunk, one

powerful and steely and carefully studying the other over the
peaks of his steepled fingers.

Finally Tag shifted in the chair and coughed.

"What did you need?" he said cautiously. He always had to
speak cautiously around his father. He never knew if he'd be
talking to his dad or the mayor of Darling, and honestly, they
were no different. They were family, weren't they? Tag wasn't
really sure how much that actually counted for. The position of
mayor had been in the Rockfords' family for decades. Tag Senior
treated his role as both his God-given right, and as though it
might be taken from him any day, a strange conglomeration of
predestined arrogance and unscrupulous desperation.

Tag couldn't really remember when he realized that his
father was not the hero most little boys thought their dads were.
He couldn't remember when he realized his dad was not really
a good person at all. Maybe he'd always known it. Maybe being
bad was in the Rockford blood.

"You're a mess," his father said, his voice low and slow.

"I—" Tag glanced down. He hadn't showered or changed
when he'd finally walked the mile and a half back to his house;
he'd just crept inside and thrown himself facedown onto the
covers, letting sleep pull him under.

"Where were you last night?"

"Out."

"Taggart."

"I was out with my friends," Tag mumbled.

"I do not want you hanging around the Wilding girl."

"Who, Delta?"

"Yes," his father replied, his mouth verging on a sneer. "*Delta.* I thought I made myself more than clear last year at my reelection ball. You're not to see her. At all. Understood?"

Tag's heart sank. He knew his dad didn't like the Wildings, and his dad *had* said he didn't think Tag should continue seeing Delta, but he'd never given an outright *ban* on it before. And Tag had never gone outright against something his father didn't want.

"Why not?" he said.

"Because," Tag Senior said, "I said so."

"But *why not?*" Tag repeated, very aware that he was balancing on a knife's edge.

"Because Rockfords don't associate with people like the Wildings."

Tag sat up in his chair, his anger flaring and for a moment burning away the sick, hungover feeling in his stomach. His father regarded him from the other side of the desk: calm and amused.

"Maybe," Tag said coldly, "I don't want to be a Rockford."

There was a heavy, long silence. And then his father smiled, and it was a wolf's smile that was much, much worse than if his dad had begun to yell. The smile spoke of secrets and grudges. It was a smile of someone playing the long game. A game they knew they'd win.

Worthless.

Tag swallowed, then murmured, "I wasn't even with Delta."

"Hmm." Tag's father looked down at his desk and shuffled some papers around idly. He liked to do things on his own time.

He liked to make people wait. Finally he glanced up and said, "Did you find out where Roark Wilding is?"

Tag's I-Am-Not-Drunk expression grew more pronounced. Okay, he knew the answer to this question. He could answer normally. He tried to not let his eyes wander as he replied. *I'm sober. I'm not hungover. I feel fine.*

"No," he said. Damn it. He glanced toward the bookcases. Why did his father never open them? Why—no, now was not the time. Sober. He was sober. "Delta said he's on a business trip."

"Yes," Tag Senior said, then tilted his head back in his chair, eyes still fixed on his son. His blue eyes were too light and too glossy. Tag didn't like looking his father in the eye; his eyes were uncomfortable. Tag didn't know, or knew and chose to ignore, that he had his father's eyes. He vigorously pretended he didn't.

Silence reigned. Tag Senior picked up a shining wooden pawn from the chessboard and examined it thoughtfully.

"Can I go?" Tag ventured. He tilted his own head to rest against the back of the chair, hoping the move came across calm and powerful like his father, and not like he was so hungover, he wanted to vomit all over the study's red Persian rug. He thought wistfully of his dark room and soft bed and the ibuprofens that awaited his return.

"Did you happen to feel the earthquake last night?" his father asked.

"Yeah," Tag replied, wondering if it would look calm and powerful to close his eyes.

"And did you happen to see a certain *light* fall from the sky?"

Tag sat up a little straighter. So he hadn't imagined it. Tag Senior glanced from the pawn to Tag, noticing the change in Tag's expression. "Is that a yes?"

Tag pulled at the collar of his blue shirt. "The meteor, or something? Yes."

Tag Senior nodded. "The meteor." He continued nodding. "Or something."

Tag didn't like the look in his father's eyes, but then again, he never liked the look in his father's eyes.

"It looked like it was heading toward the Wilding dump," his father said musingly. "I do hope it hasn't *damaged* their property in any way. In any case, I should go over there today. Make sure they're all . . . safe and sound."

Tag nodded, nod, nod, nod. There was nothing else to do.

His father waved a careless hand to dismiss Tag from the room. Tag edged away, snapping the study door behind him. His stomach roiled with queasiness, and something else—a feeling that, growing up in the Rockford estate, he was used to. He'd never really had a name for it, the feeling that hung over him and brushed against him every time he talked with his father or met those searching, flinty eyes. But now that feeling wasn't simply hanging over him, ever present—it was pressing, heavy and painful, against his lungs.

It felt a lot like unease.

It felt a lot like fear.

He tried to stay calm, as a Rockford should, but he only made it to the end of the hallway before he broke into a run.

8

IT WAS LATE MORNING

and the Wilding sisters sat on the sagging couch, the walkie-talkie alone on the coffee table before them. They stared at it. It made no noise. They stared some more.

Delta had slept in Bee's room, the farthest bedroom from where the alien lay unconcious. But neither girl had gotten much sleep at all; every time Delta's eyes drifted closed, she'd suddenly jerk awake, sure she'd heard the walkie-talkie crackle with noise. She'd come downstairs when it was still dark to sit in the living room and wait for something to happen.

They'd been staring silently for so long that when Delta's phone vibrated next to her on the couch, they both jumped. Bee let out a strangled scream.

"Who is it?" Bee asked, her voice coming out scratchy.

Delta checked the screen, then glanced up at Bee. "It's a text."

"From?"

"I don't know the number."

Bee nestled in next to her sister, her limbs relaxing around Delta's waist, her head coming down to rest on Delta's bony shoulder. "Darling area code," she noted.

Delta nodded slowly, staring at the line of numbers. She'd

noticed that too—the Darling area code preceding the phone number. The only person she texted regularly was Bee—other than that, she sporadically texted Anders Houston, or sometimes Tag if she was in one of her *I miss him* moods.

So which unknown Darling resident was texting her now, mere hours after they'd dragged an alien into their home?

She read the message. There were only two words, all lowercase, as if the message wasn't even important enough to bother with proper capitalization or punctuation. Two words, but Delta felt her throat clogging with fear. Her stomach curdled with each word.

we know

Bee peered at the message, then turned wide eyes on her sister.

"They know? Who knows? Knows what?"

"I'm not sure," Delta said in a low voice, trying to keep it from wavering. She was the strong one. *You have to be the strong one.* "I assume . . . they know about . . . him. The—you know."

Bee looked thunderstruck. "Do you think it was whoever was in the woods with us?"

It was a thought that had hit Delta as well, and it wasn't comforting. She'd thought that she and Bee had left the clearing before the footsteps and voices had reached them, but it had been so dark. . . . Anyone could have been there, scattered like ghosts amongst the trees, watching as the sisters carried the alien back to the house. Had Delta and Bee's panting breaths been joined by others? Had their flight through the forest been watched by careful, calculating eyes?

The Wildings were already regarded as too strange for those who lived in Darling. Delta didn't like to think what the townspeople might do to a boy who had drifted down to Earth.

The unease making its way through Delta's body sharpened. He was in their house now—he was *their* responsibility. "Let's check all the doors," she said, abruptly standing. "Make sure everything is locked." The floor groaned as she crossed it, the boards creaking ominously beneath her feet as if the planks themselves could sense the anxiety that ran like a current through the house, through Delta. Her fingers tingled with anticipation, but she pushed the feeling down, stolidly checking the front door, then crossing into the kitchen to check the back door too. All locked, and she was sure the townspeople—or whoever it was that sent the text—couldn't get into second-story windows. . . .

Well, no. She wasn't sure at all.

She was no longer sure about anything.

The kitchen was warm, the June air seeping in under the back door. The fridge hummed in the quiet. Water from the tap dripped into the sink.

The quiet pressed in.

With a loud, jangling ringtone, Delta's phone, still held clenched in her fist, went off. She shrieked at the sudden vibration and hurried back into the living room, Bee's scared face poking out around the doorframe. Abby's white-and-brown head nosed around her knees; then she turned tail and retreated back into the room to once more take up safe haven on the couch.

"You scared me!" Bee said accusingly.

Delta took a deep breath, shrugging her way into an apology. She didn't want to admit the fear that had hit her as well. Instead, she held up the phone, still ringing.

"From them?" Bee whispered.

Delta shook her head. "Tag." He'd just seen her last night.

Last night? It seemed like a lifetime ago.

She accepted the call, sidling out from under Bee's watchful eyes.

"Hello?"

"Oh—hey," Tag said, slow and drawling. But Delta still thought she could detect a tense undercurrent running through his voice. "I didn't think you'd pick up."

"Why wouldn't I?"

"You rarely do."

"That's—" Delta pressed her lips together. *Accurate.* "Well. I have to do something to keep you interested, don't I." That wasn't it at all, and it wasn't true, but she didn't know what to say. She didn't know how she *felt.*

"God, Delta, you couldn't stop me from being interested."

His voice did things to her heart, even now, when they weren't together. Now, when she wasn't even sure how she felt about him at all. "Stop it." Her voice was suddenly breathless.

"It's true."

"Are you drunk?"

"No," Tag said immediately, in a way that made Delta think he was lying. He gave a low chuckle, then added, "A little hungover."

Of course. There wasn't a whole lot for the kids of Darling to do, what with their odd little town in the middle of a valley, surrounded by mountains, with nothing but dry fields for miles and miles on end.

Tag had once told her that he drank to forget he was a Rockford, and although he'd been drunk at the time, and although he'd laughed, Delta still remembered the way his eyes had looked when he'd said it.

"From last night?"

"Yeah."

"Were you drinking alone?" Delta said lightly.

A pause, and when Tag answered, his voice was even lower than before, almost a purr. "If you want to know if I'm seeing anyone else, you can just ask."

"That's *not* what I want to know," Delta replied, but her heart kicked up its pace.

Tag just laughed. "Sure. If you must know, I wasn't alone." He paused, and Delta's heart constricted before he added, "A few of us kept the party going after you left. Anders, those two senior girls. Allison and Marnie?"

"Sounds . . . fun," Delta said, biting her lip. "Was it?"

"Honestly, not really."

"No?"

"It would have been a lot better if you were there."

Delta closed her eyes, taking a long moment before she replied, as if in the space of a breath she would be able to unwind all her feelings and figure out exactly what she wanted. It was so easy to talk to Tag like this, to fall into their familiar back and forth. They'd grown up with each other, went to school together from day care through senior year. Their lives were so interwoven, so complicated, and every time she tried to extricate herself, she ended up pulling a hundred other strings. Starting a hundred other fights, ending a hundred more, making up with a hundred kisses.

"I wish you had invited me," she blurted out.

For a second, all she could hear was breathing on the other end, and then when Tag spoke again, his voice was nothing but a sigh. "But Del, would you have come?"

"I . . . I'm not sure." She chewed on the inside of her lip now. It gave her something to do, something else to focus on besides her quickly beating heart. If she'd been with Tag, she never would have found the alien in the clearing.

"I wish you would've." There was that low chuckle again. He still sounded a little drunk, but he'd had so much practice that half the time she couldn't really tell. She could just picture him, lying on the bed in his darkened room, drowsy-eyed, his blond hair disheveled and messy, the only light coming from his phone screen.

She blinked, and the languid, familiar Tag was replaced with another boy on another bed: long limbs and tattoos and dark hair. The only light coming from his very skin.

Delta bit her lip, hard enough to force her mind back to the conversation. *Pull yourself together, Delta.* "Did you need something?"

"Do I need a reason to call my—" He stopped, the unsaid word heavy in the air.

"Your what?" she whispered. She didn't even know what she

wanted him to say, or if she wanted him to say anything at all.

"Delta . . ." He said her name as a half word, half groan, and Delta's heart fluttered traitorously.

"What?" she whispered again.

Tag sighed into the phone. A long pause. Then: "D'you remember when this used to be simple?"

"Us?"

"Us. Life. Everything."

Delta nodded into the phone, squeezing her eyes shut: stumbling through the woods with an unearthly creature. Her dad, disappearing into thin air. Mysterious threatening text messages. An alien upstairs. Her relationship with Tag that kept crashing down around her no matter how hard they tried. She let out her breath. "Yes. I wish it still was."

Tag was quiet for a moment, then, in a different tone, muttered, "Hold on a second." She heard his voice, far away: *"No one. Where are you going? Just—yeah. Why? Okay. I told you, it's no one. It's Anders. Yeah. Bye."*

Tag came back on the phone with a loud, "Sure, that sounds good, Anders."

"Your dad?"

"Yeah," Tag said, but his voice was different, all sleepiness and that soft, heart-to-heart tone gone. He added, "He's coming to your house."

Her mind still turning with the simplicity of her life one year ago, it took Delta a second to process what he'd said. When the words sank in, her veins went cold, her fingers tightening around the edges of her phone. "He's coming *here*? Why?"

"I dunno," Tag said, then hesitated. "But . . . he was talking about that meteor thing. Did you see it?"

"I saw it," Delta replied, tendrils of dread creeping around her stomach.

Tag started to say something else, but Delta cut him off. "I'm sorry, Tag, but I have to go." She hung up halfway through his startled goodbye and hurried into the living room, where Bee looked up in alarm.

"The mayor is coming here," Delta said, the words heavy on her tongue as she processed them. Then: "The *mayor* is coming."

She knew it wasn't a coincidence. She'd known the towns-people would come calling—it was more *when*. It was more *what would they do when they arrived.*

A noise, like someone sighing, issued with a preceding crackle from the walkie-talkie. Delta and Bee glanced at each other, alarm mounting, and then rushed up the stairs, stopping anxiously outside the guest room. Delta took a deep breath and opened the door, just a tiny crack. She poked half of her head inside, craning it around to look at the bed. The boy still looked asleep, although his head was now at an angle, as if he'd shifted in his sleep.

"Still asleep," Delta whispered, and pushed the door open some more, creeping toward the bed. She reached out a hand, breath held, and touched it gently to the boy's forehead. She abruptly pulled it back, cradling it to her chest. His skin was hotter than it had been; it felt like he was burning up from the inside out.

"I think . . . he has a fever," she said to Bee. *No, no, no.* She had not thought this through at all. She'd acted on instinct, bringing him into their home. But what if he was sick? What if he was injured? She had no idea what to do. She was clueless. Helpless.

She didn't want to be the one in charge. Tears pricked at the corners of her eyes, and she angrily brushed them away.

"What are we supposed to do about it?" Bee replied. She kept glancing back down the stairs at the front door, as if any second the mayor would pound on it so hard, it would be ripped off its hinges.

What to do about it? She had to be rational. She could do this. Okay.

"Get the thermometer from the bathroom," she instructed Bee, and Bee scurried away for just a moment before returning holding the mouth thermometer. It was old, a spindly glass tube filled with silvery mercury. Delta took it from her, trying to seem like this was normal, like she wasn't afraid of going near the boy's mouth.

"Careful," was all Bee said, but she inched after Delta anyways, as if her mere presence in the room provided protection. She left the door open a tiny crack, just enough so they could hear when the mayor knocked on the door.

Delta nodded, eyes trained on the boy, ears strained toward downstairs. She sidled up to the edge of the bed and bent over the body. Hesitantly, feeling more and more like this was probably the worst idea in the world, she brought her fingers to the boy's lips and opened his mouth, pulling his lower lip downward so his jaw fell open. She jumped back in automatic recoil.

She wasn't sure what she'd been expecting—if she was honest with herself, she'd been hoping for a straight row of pearly whites. It would have been much easier to take, a sigh of relief, if at least that had been normal.

But that wasn't what she got.

The boy had teeth, and most of them were square in shape, a bit crooked, but more or less human-sized. His canines, however, were sharp and elongated, a wolf's teeth in a boy's body.

"What is it?" Bee asked, peering over Delta's shoulder.

"It's . . ." Delta tried to control her heartbeat. She couldn't freak out now. He needed their help. She focused instead on his closed eyes, on his curls, on the hollow of his tattooed collarbone. "It's nothing. Just . . . sharper teeth than I was expecting."

"What, like a vampire?"

"He's not a vampire, Bee," Delta said, although now that she thought about it—she didn't really know this for sure.

"Well, good thing he's unconscious," Bee whispered.

"Yeah," Delta replied uncomfortably, suddenly very aware that any second this boy could open his eyelids and wake up. It made her want to throw the thermometer on the floor and run from the room. What if he woke up while her fingers were holding his lips open? This time, the thought of his eyes opening and finding her there did not send a flush through her body. *No. Everything is fine.* The alien *was* unconscious, after all, and didn't pose much of a threat in this state.

She hoped.

Delta took a deep breath and edged the delicate glass tube under the alien's forked tongue, nestling it in the valley between his bottom two teeth. Then she quickly closed his jaw, so the thermometer stuck out from between his lips. And they waited, with bated breath.

After three full minutes of staring anxiously at the alien's unmoving face, Delta eased the thermometer out from the alien's mouth. She held it up and examined the mercury inside, and a laugh broke through from her mouth unbridled before she could stop it. The laugh was half-hysterical, half-panicked: the mercury had shot straight to the top of the glass tube. The numbers printed on the thermometer only went up to 110 degrees Fahrenheit, and the mercury had passed that. His fever must have been upward of 150 degrees.

There was no way this boy could be alive.

Except . . . she stared at the golden light that streaked along his skin. It seemed like it was fading now; it certainly wasn't as bright as it had been in the dark clearing. She touched a finger gently to his arm. It was like . . . sunlight. Starlight.

She set the thermometer carefully on the bedside table, then knelt by the side of the bed. His mouth was closed now, and he looked once more like a sleeping boy. Before she could convince herself out of it, she leaned forward very slowly and put her ear against his chest. She knew it was intimate, and from Bee's expression, she might've been throwing herself on top of him, but the pounding that spoke to his otherworldly life drew her in. His skin was warm where it brushed against her earlobe; she could hear his hearts beating solidly: one, two, three, all pulsing at different times and in different rhythms.

He couldn't be alive, but he most definitely was.

She stayed still, kneeling beside him, listening to his heartbeats: *thump-thump, thumpthumpthump, thump—thump—thump.*

It was beautiful, and haunting, a celestial drumbeat. The cadence of heartbeats melded together into a symphony; they beat in time with her own solitary heart.

She'd just closed her eyes when three loud thuds broke her from her reverie. *The mayor.* He'd arrived. Delta snapped her head up, the moment broken. Bee was standing by the door, her eyes wide.

"I'll handle it," she said to Bee. "Make sure he's okay. Make sure he doesn't come out." Bee nodded, slipping out onto the landing and hiding at the top of the stairs. Delta darted from the room, shutting the door completely behind her, then made herself walk calmly down the staircase.

She opened the door leisurely, peering out curiously as if she had no idea who stood on her porch. The mayor stood squarely in front of the door, in a blue suit with his hands clasped behind his back. His white-blond hair was combed neatly and gleamed in the morning sun. Parked behind him was a shining sports car, elegantly out of place on the tangled weeds that made up the Wildings' front yard.

"Oh! Mayor Rockford!" she exclaimed, and the word sounded too fake, too bright, to her ears. His too-blue eyes suddenly went glinty in a way that made Delta think her exclamation had sounded false to him as well.

"Delta Wilding," replied the mayor, in a way that made Delta's skin go cold. He was smiling a smile that showed too many teeth. It felt like dislike had hardened into something more.

Worthless.

Whore.

"What brings you all the way out here?" Delta asked casually. She made sure the front door was only opened just enough for the mayor to see her, and nothing else.

"Of course, I do apologize for stopping by unannounced," the mayor replied. "But I couldn't sleep last night after the earthquake."

He paused, and Delta studied him, her jaw clenched. It seemed strange to think of the mayor sleeping. He didn't seem like the type to do something as trivial as *sleep*. She'd assumed he was always awake behind the monstrous gates of the Rockford estate, planning and plotting and scheming at all hours.

Finally, he spoke. "When I saw the *meteor* hurl its way to Earth, I was, ah, *quite* concerned about the welfare of you and your sister." He paused just a little too long. "All alone out here in this big old house."

A cold stone, hard and expanding, dropped into Delta's stomach. She tried to school her expression into neutral, to betray nothing. She couldn't keep her knuckles from going white on the doorframe, and hoped he hadn't noticed.

"Well, the meteor didn't land anywhere near the house that I could see," she said lightly, looking around from the doorway as if the meteor would pop up behind the mayor with a friendly wave. "And we're not alone, Mayor."

"Oh," the mayor replied. "I was under the impression that—"

"I know what your impression was," Delta said. *Worthless. Whore.* The coldness in her stomach was creeping into her lungs. She carefully dropped her arm from the doorframe and tucked it behind her body so the mayor wouldn't see it trembling with anxiety. She had to stay calm. *Stay calm. Be polite, Delta. Get him out of here.* She was all too aware that if Mayor Rockford tried to force himself inside, she wouldn't be able to stop him. "Thank you very much for your concern, Mayor. But I can assure you that my sister and I are perfectly fine, and we are not alone in this house."

She thought of the sleeping boy upstairs. That part, at least, wasn't a lie. But all the next words that dropped from her mouth were. For once, there was no accompanying guilt, and she lied as easily as if she were the Great Deceiver himself.

"We're well looked after."

"Oh, really?" said the mayor. "Because my son informed me that your father is away. That you're alone."

Goddamnit, Tag. She could just imagine him, snitching his way into his dad's good graces and then calling to say he missed her. "My dad is on a business trip at the moment," Delta said, her voice so tight, she could barely recognize it, "but should be back very soon."

"A business trip, hmm?" the mayor replied.

"Yes."

"He has been on a business trip for quite some time now," he said.

"He's been on lots of little trips."

"Ah," said the mayor quietly. The light flickered around him. "Of course." He stared at her, and she met his cold blue eyes defiantly. He opened his mouth, and his eyes flashed, and for a moment Delta wondered if he *was* about to push her out of the way and march straight into the house. Then thudding steps sounded behind her, and she felt Bee slide her freckled arms around Delta's waist and tilt her head against Delta's.

"Oh hello, Mayor Rockford!" she said brightly, loudly. "Wow, this is unexpected! Is everything okay?"

"Yes," the mayor ground out. "I was just checking up on you girls in your father's absence."

"Oh, that's so nice!" Bee said, widening her eyes and smiling beguilingly. "Our dad will be so happy when he gets home and hears that we've been so well looked after by our town."

"Yes, yes," the mayor said again, then shot a stony look in Delta's direction, who met it with a firm stare. The mayor stepped back slightly, glancing away as if he couldn't bear to look at the two of them anymore. As if the wildness that ran through them—the wildness the townspeople couldn't stand—was something to be feared. *Worthless. Whore.*

Being feared by all those who passed her on the street didn't make Delta feel strong or bold. It just made her sad.

Bee continued to smile at him. "Get home safe," she said, then added a sharp, *"sir."*

It was such an obvious dismissal that for a moment Delta thought the mayor would yell at them, or force his way into the house to look for the mysterious meteor, but he just smiled at them. Delta found this even worse; staring at his hard smile made her skin crawl.

He continued to smile as he leaned in toward them and said softly, "Be careful, girls. All the way out here in the wilderness . . ."

The girls stayed silent, and Delta gripped Bee's arm. It sounded like a threat, but she didn't know what to do about it.

She was all too aware of the secret they were keeping; all too aware of the alien just upstairs.

"All sorts of things in these woods," the mayor continued, still with the horrible smile. "You'll want to be very careful. Do you understand me? I don't want any trouble in my town."

"Neither do we," Delta finally said.

"Good," the mayor breathed, and then with a nod in their direction, turned on his heel and sauntered down the steps toward his expensive car. Before he'd even reached it, Delta closed and locked the door. For the first time in a while, she latched the three security chains her dad had attached some years before, when he was paranoid that his paranormal research would attract the wrong sorts of people.

It looked like he'd been right.

He'd been so, so right. About everything. Delta leaned back against the locked front door, breathing shallowly. She felt physically drained after talking to the mayor, and the cold feeling still hadn't left. She wanted a long, hot shower to wash away the cold. The fright. Did he somehow know what they'd found, what was sleeping in the guest bedroom? No, he couldn't know. He hated Delta; he hated her family. He was just taking shots in the dark, trying to assert his power and authority. She dropped the back of her head to the door, resting it there, eyes closed.

"You okay, Delta?" Bee's voice came, accompanied by a soft touch on her arm.

Delta didn't answer, couldn't answer. Her throat seemed to have closed up, so she just nodded and hoped Bee understood the nod was actually a *thank-you*.

"I'll go check on him," Bee said, even though there had been no noises from the walkie-talkie.

Delta nodded, then cracked an eye open and rasped, "I'll go check Dad's study. See if there's anything helpful." She walked mechanically over to the coffee table and picked up the walkie-talkie, taking it with her.

She wanted to get away, to be alone. No, no—she didn't want to be alone: she wanted her dad. The dull ache that sometimes hit her when thinking about the mother she couldn't really remember suddenly hit her with full force, but this time she was missing her *dad*. And she remembered every bit of him: his wild hair, his glasses, his favorite striped sweater. She wanted her dad to tell her what to do, to be in charge, to lift all the weight off her shoulders. She wanted her dad to see that he'd been right all along, that there were really aliens out there.

He'd have been so excited. . . .

She hardly noticed she'd started walking until her hand turned the knob of his study door, and the familiar smell of her dad greeted her. The room was small and square, and felt even smaller and squarer because of the labyrinthine piles of books stacked waist-high in piles on the floor and desk. They half covered the windows, and the sun shone down onto the stacks of books, illuminating the dust that now settled there. There was no free wall space: every inch was covered with photos and lists and maps—strange maps. There were large maps of the universe, maps of assumed close encounters, maps of faerie sightings and ghost sightings. The maps were covered in multi-colored pushpins, with strings strung up between and around them, triangulating and zoning off certain sections. There were lists of government employees, psychics, and mediums; lists of galaxies and star charts. The photos showed the barren desert of Roswell, stills from alien movies with handwritten notes in Sharpie (*wrong—similar but not quite—this seems accurate*) scrawled over them. There were lists in her dad's familiar scribble, detailing planet names and cold spots and unexplained phenomena and science terms and words Delta was fairly sure might've taken a turn into gibberish.

It was the room of a madman, the type of room where a dedicated detective would track down a killer. It was the room of someone obsessed, someone consumed.

But it was her dad's study. And Delta had always felt safe in here, surrounded by the thoughts of her father.

She took a couple of steps into the room. Where to even start? What was she even looking for? Her hands shook as she began to sift through piles of loose-leaf papers; piles upon piles of unfinished lists and half-formed ideas.

"There has to be something here," Delta whispered to herself. Her words didn't echo—there were too many things in the room, soaking up the sounds. But the words felt empty just the same, as though her dad's study had swallowed them. "There has to be something that can help."

She wasn't expecting a reply, obviously, but the lack of one made her stomach clench and her arms tremble harder. She grabbed a half-open box from atop the nearest piles of books and lugged it to the desk. The books swayed precariously, but she ignored them and began to rummage desperately through the box, upturning moth-eaten, forgotten sweaters, a Magic 8-Ball, and hundreds more illegible shorthand and drawings and mathematical equations on tiny scraps of paper. The pressure in Delta's throat returned. What was she supposed to *do*? She had a star-flung boy in the other room, and she was completely out of her depth. Did she feed him? Did he drink water? Could he speak English? Could he speak at all? What if he was dangerous, murderous?

She pushed the box off the desk; it tumbled to the floor, knocking over a stack of thick books. A plume of dust followed the thud of the falling tomes. Why hadn't their father given them anything useful?! Why had he just left them alone with nothing but the emergency cash box? She made a noise of despair, a noise she didn't even know came from her until she made it again. She threw another box onto the desk and ripped off the lid. More junk.

Junk, junk, junk! He'd left them with junk. He'd left them with nothing but junk, all because of a madman's dream of finding other life.

What was wrong with this *life, Dad?* Delta thought, furiously knocking the next box off the desk too, where it joined its broken companion on the floor. *She* was the one who was allowed to want to leave; *she* was the one who dreamed of other worlds and other places. Her dad was supposed to be there, steady and solid and present, for when she returned.

Where are you? And then the words weren't being thought— they were ripping from her throat in a scream. "Where are you? Why did you leave us?"

There was no answer, just the sound of the apple tree scratching its branches against the windowpane. No answer except the breaths that wretched themselves from her chest. The lump was back, her throat was closing, and her eyes prickled painfully.

"Why did you leave us?" she asked again to the empty room, then slumped to the floor as her exhausted legs gave way beneath her. Her back hit the desk, and she leaned her head against the wooden leg, staring up at the stacks of books that surrounded her on all sides, rising over her like walls against reality. She curled her legs up to her chest, clutching them close. And Delta, for the first time in two months, for the first time since her dad disappeared, began to cry.

The weight of the world dripped off her shoulders with the tears, forming puddles around her feet. She cried until she physically couldn't cry anymore, until her throat was dry and her head splitting, until her nose was running and raw and her eyes puffy and glazed with dried tears. She cried for her dad and for Bee and for herself.

She was still crying when the walkie-talkie beside her crackled: first with soft sounds, and then, suddenly, with a voice.

9

DELTA NEVER RAN

so fast in her life. She jumped up from the floor and flew out of the study, taking the steps down to the second floor three at a time, hardly able to see through eyes still itchy with dried tears and the encrusted salt that accompanied them.

Bee was standing outside the door to the guest room, holding it closed with both hands, although it didn't look like anyone was trying to come out. The walkie-talkie in Delta's hand continued to give off crackles and sighs: the sounds of someone waking up.

The sisters stared at each other wide-eyed as Delta came to a halt, breathless, before the door. Bee didn't comment on Delta's wan, tear-streaked face and red eyes, and Delta knew it was just because crying people made Bee uncomfortable, but she appreciated the silence just the same.

"He's awake?"

"He's awake," Bee confirmed. "I was sitting on the chair, and then he made a sound, and he sort of turned his head, and . . . I ran."

More sounds, faint, like someone talking to themselves, issued from the walkie-talkie, and Bee gave it a look of alarm.

Delta held the walkie-talkie out for her to take, then put a hand on the doorknob.

"Wait—" Bee said.

Delta glanced at her.

"He could be dangerous," Bee breathed. "He's not *human*, Delta."

"If he's dangerous, keeping him locked in a room won't make things any better for us," Delta replied. "We brought him here. We have to deal with the consequences."

Bee gave her a look that clearly said she would rather keep the boy locked in the room regardless of the consequences, but took a tiny step back.

Delta turned the doorknob and stepped inside, snapping the door shut behind her.

The boy was most certainly awake. He was sitting up, the blanket draped over his legs, his whole body coiled as though ready to spring at her, or maybe flee out the window. His head was tucked down, his hair sticking to his forehead; his jaw dropped slightly and she saw the dart of that forked tongue leave the interior of his mouth. And then, slowly, he lifted his head, the movement graceful, almost sinuous, and stared at her.

Delta took a deep breath, counted *one, two, three*. She could do this. She *had* to do this; there was no one else. She made sure to stay rigid and still by the door, then raised her eyes to meet his.

His eyes were slightly bigger than a human's, as well as completely black. He had no irises, no surrounding white. Just shining and empty and dark as a void. Dark as a night sky. But the black orbs *swirled*, as if he had trapped galaxies instead of pupils.

She could tell he was watching her.

"Oh my God," she murmured, unable to stop herself. Her breath rose in her lungs, and she pressed her lips together to stop from whimpering; clasped her hands together to keep from running out the door.

"Is he awake?!" Bee's voice came through the closed door, the words muffled.

"Yes," Delta breathed. He was sitting up in the bed, his orb-eyes reflecting the tiny image of her own body back at her, the darkness shimmering almost liquidly beneath the surface. He hadn't moved a muscle; maybe he could tell she was frightened and was now trying to remedy that, the way one might still themselves in the presence of a frightened, jumpy deer.

Or maybe not. Delta had no way of knowing if this boy even understood human reactions, human feelings. Maybe he was deciding if she was going to try to hurt him. Or maybe he was just very confused.

At least he wasn't attacking, Delta thought. *Yet*. That was something.

"Hello," Delta said, raising a hand and waving it awkwardly in his direction. The black eyes were so large, they didn't even need to flick back and forth to follow the movements; they took it all in with that same depthless stare. What was she supposed to say? She cleared her throat and began, "I . . . um, I come in peace."

He just stared and didn't reply. She heard the door being opened slowly behind her, and then Bee's voice whispered breathlessly, "Delta? Are you okay?"

"Fine," she breathed, not taking her eyes from the boy. She

hadn't blinked yet, and neither had he, and Delta felt like she was in a staring contest with . . . with a what? Not a boy, not with those depthless eyes. Not a monster, not with the remnants of golden light still seeping from his veins. But still, she didn't want to risk being the first one to break, because she wasn't sure what would happen if she blinked—would the alien take it as a sign of disrespect? Oh God, her eyes were watering. She tried to hold them open, but she was only human, after all. She blinked rapidly a few times, feeling the relief, and then returned her gaze to the boy. He hadn't moved a muscle; he didn't make any moves toward her.

"Can you speak?" she whispered, feeling slightly more confident with Bee standing close to her. "I speak . . . English? Can you understand me?" The boy said nothing, but he did slump back against the pillows and close his eyes momentarily, then let out a strange string of what might have been words of some faraway, otherworldly language. It sounded like a mix between sounds rasped from the back of someone's throat and a lispy, serpentine hiss.

"Okay, not English," Delta murmured. How to communicate? She racked her brain quickly and tried the most basic standard of communication. It worked for Earthlings, so maybe it could be adapted for aliens? She pointed at her own chest with her finger and said loudly and clearly, "Delta. I am Delta. Delta Wilding." She wasn't sure if the alien was looking at her, but those starry-black eyes were definitely focused somewhere in her direction, and she was sure she could feel the weight of his gaze. She took this as a sign to keep going. She pointed at Bee, who looked alarmed at suddenly being the center of the boy's attention, and stood as still as a statue. "This is Bee." She pointed at herself—"Delta"—and at Bee—"Bee." Finally, she pointed her finger toward him, trying to school her features into a casual, curious expression like this was all normal. Just a standard day in the Wilding house.

The alien said nothing for a moment, then murmured something in that hissing, lisping language. He paused and looked at them.

"S-sorry," Delta said. "What was that?" The words certainly weren't English, but they were beautiful, a jumble of sounds and lisps and strange syllables that fell from his forked tongue. The language fit him: fit his otherworldly presence, his dark eyes and furrowed brow. She wanted to hear it again.

Bee nudged Delta in the side with a sharp elbow. "I think he said *Star King*."

It *had* sort of sounded like the boy had said the words *Star King*, albeit a very hissed, serpentine version of them.

"Well, we're not calling him that."

"But if that's his name . . ."

"Bee, we can't go around calling him *Star King*. Come on."

"*Star Boy?*"

"No."

"Well, what do you think he's saying?"

Delta glanced at the boy. As if he knew what their predicament was, as though he was trying to help, he opened his mouth—Delta caught a glimpse of the glint of his vampirish canines—and then repeated the words, slowing it down. *Shtaaarlkeeeng Rwuuuusssst.*

She tried to repeat it back at him, lisping the letters and pursing her lips to try to roll the *R*'s and hiss the *S*'s. One of his furrowed eyebrows became less furrowed, kicking upward in what, Delta thought, looked like amusement. He said it again; Delta repeated it back.

"I think you're frustrating him," Bee whispered.

Delta said his name again, her best approximation of it, dropping the sounds she couldn't make and the hissing that wouldn't come from her non-forked tongue. "Staaaarlinnnng."

"Starling?" Bee echoed.

The starling on the windowsill shrieked and jumped from the ledge, swooping off toward the forest in a rustle of shining black feathers. Both sisters looked from it to each other. Delta mouthed the name to herself, flicking her glance to the boy.

She thought he looked resigned to the name, so she took a stab at the second set of sounds he'd made. Maybe his last name, maybe part of his first name—there was really no way to tell. She once again dropped the lisps and hisses and said "Rust."

He definitely looked resigned.

"Delta, Bee, and"—she pointed at him—"Starling Rust?"

He inclined his head, just the smallest tilt.

"That's a yes!" Bee said.

Delta ignored Bee and nodded slowly. "Starling," she said, turning the syllables over in her mouth. The name was fitting, she supposed, for a man who had been flung from the sky, the free bird felled from above. "Nice . . . nice to meet you." She took a hesitant step forward and held out her hand.

Starling stared at her fingers, then glanced up at her.

"You shake it," she said, awkwardly shifting from one foot to the next. "It's a way to say hello."

Starling reached out and brushed one finger along the curve of her outstretched hand, as light as a breath. Delta's fingers shook, and then she couldn't help but let out a little gasp as Starling enveloped her hand with his own, his thumb pressing into the skin at her palm. His skin was warm, as if the faint glow was not just light but heat as well. Then he opened his mouth and said, in a low, rasping voice, "Hello." The word sounded strange coming from him, as if his unearthly mouth wasn't meant to utter earthly words.

Delta's eyes widened. He *could* speak English! He *could* understand. She was speaking with a boy from the stars. She didn't let go of his hand, and neither did he. She felt the pressure of his thumb once again, and then he brushed it along the inside of her hand as if he was reminding himself that she was real. The touch sent a thrill up her entire arm, and she glanced up. He was watching her too, and the depthless eyes didn't seem as intimidating now with his hand in hers.

"You," he began, each word carefully picked and hesitant, "brought me here."

"Yes," Delta whispered. She could feel Bee's barbed gaze on her, lasering in on the place their hands met. "Yes, we did. We found you in the woods."

"The woods," the boy repeated. Then, almost to himself, he murmured, "Yes, the woods."

"Do you remember how you came to be there?" Delta continued.

Starling frowned, then dropped his head back onto his pillow. His gaze went to the window, where only the tips of the trees outside could be seen. He didn't reply.

Delta tried again: "Is there anything you need? Are you feeling okay?"

Starling's dark eyes darted between the two sisters, and then he said in a low voice, "Thirsty."

Bee edged up beside Delta and whispered, "What if he wants blood?"

"Blood?" repeated the boy, his voice low and scratchy, and Bee widened her eyes and stepped away, throwing open the bedroom door.

"Here, look," said Delta, pointing toward the bedside table. She pulled her hand from his and picked up the glass of water, holding it out to him. He took it from her, his fingers brushing against hers.

He gave another slight incline of his head, then took a long gulp and promptly spat it back out onto the covers.

"Oh my *God*, he's a vampire," she heard Bee squeal, and then the sharp thudding of her panicked feet as she ran into the hallway. Delta stood frozen, remembering the sharp canines, but Starling didn't leap out of bed to attack her and drink her blood. She heard a shuffle of feet from behind her and knew that Bee had hesitantly come back into the room.

Starling thrust the glass back toward Delta and gasped out, "No."

"No? It's water . . ." She tried to think of what else this falling star of a boy might need. "I don't know what else . . . I'm sorry . . ."

The boy took a deep breath and closed his eyes, then said, "F-f-ferment?"

She stared at him blankly. "Ferment? You need . . . ?"

"Ferment," he insisted again.

Delta turned to Bee, who was leaning against the doorjamb. "Does he mean . . . alcohol? That's fermented, right?"

"*Alcohol?* I wouldn't know; I have never, ever tried alcohol in my life," Bee said automatically, then shot Delta a wicked grin as she hurried out of the room. Delta heard her running down the stairs to the kitchen, where their dad kept a couple of wine bottles neatly stacked on the counter.

Delta turned back to Starling. "We're getting some now," she said, but there was nothing but silence in return. Something kept nagging at Delta, and she couldn't hold it back any longer: biting her lip, she said, hesitatingly, "And you . . . you *do* come in peace, right?"

"Peace," echoed Starling. His eyes narrowed, as though he was considering.

Bee came back into the room then with a bottle of twist-cap wine, which she passed first to Delta, keeping at least a couple of steps from Starling. Delta, the middleman, gave the bottle to Starling, who untwisted the cap, raised the bottle to his lips, and chugged the entire thing.

"Better," he rasped, slouching back onto the pillows almost wearily. His voice, while still scratchy and hissing, sounded slightly clearer.

Delta felt her mouth drop open. *I wasn't expecting that.* And yet she couldn't stop watching him, the way his eyelids closed over those swirling black eyes, the slight flush that had come into his cheeks with the wine. She wanted to perch on the end of his bed and just listen to his gravelly voice. She wanted his celestial hand back in hers.

But then Bee pulled on her arm, insistently, and she let herself be pulled away.

Delta stopped by the door. "You should get some rest," she said. "It was a long fall." And then she backed out of the room, leaving the boy who fell from the sky alone with his thoughts.

10

EVERYTHING HURT.

His whole body raged with fiery hot agony, and every bone was as achy and tender as if they'd been snapped and remade.

The humans—the *girls*—had left the room, taking their bright eyes and shared glances with them. And he lay still, staring at the empty bottle of fermented drink they'd provided him, trying to think, trying to remain calm. He took long, slow blinks, each blink reminding him of the pain that registered throughout his entire body.

From beyond the closed door he heard muffled voices, but the murmurs quickly grew fainter, and two pairs of footsteps diverged.

Then there was silence.

When he'd first awoken, he'd been nothing but a bundle of frayed nerves and adrenaline, coming to in an unfamiliar house in an unfamiliar place after being rendered unconscious by the impact of his appearance on Earth. His eyes had been blurry and scratchy, but when his vision finally cleared, he took in the metal bedframe and a strange chair made of what looked like woven wood. He hadn't been able to look around much more before his body spasmed with pain: he knew by the burning agony currently razing his skin that his body had invoked a fever to heal itself. He'd had to ignore the agony through gritted teeth when the door had opened and two young humans had entered, with questions and human words and faces that showed each and every emotion. He was in a strange body, and—he touched the skin at his neck—the chain was gone, and he could already feel the energy draining from him. He looked blearily at his hands, noticing how the celestial glow was already fading. *He had to find the chain; he had to get back to the place he'd been found. . . .*

But now there was quiet. He settled back into the cushions and tried to breathe, tried to order his thoughts.

He couldn't *remember.* That was the problem. He could feel the energy writhing in the ground beneath this house—did that have something to do with how he had ended up here? Was he pulled to this place? Did he trip through a thin spot between worlds? There was just a swash of blackness where his memory once was.

He glanced around the room, noting the position of each chair, each window. Somehow he'd been taken to these Earthlings' house. Had they carried him? Dragged him? His eyelids fluttered shut and he squeezed them tight, trying to remember. *How did he get into this room?* But there was nothing. It was no use.

Suddenly, from behind the closed door came footsteps once more, and the door cracked open. He shifted immediately, tensing up, getting ready to—what? Flee? He didn't even know where to go. But he had to be prepared for anything. He was a stranger here, after all. And humans were small, erratic beings.

A small hand, pale and shaky, crept around the edge of the

door. There was the echo of an inhalation, and then green eyes met his as the taller, brown-haired human stepped into the room. It was the human who had touched his hand, the one who had asked if he came in peace.

"Hello," she whispered, and held out another bottle of the humans' fermented drink. "Sorry, I thought you might be sleeping. I brought you another bottle of wine, if you need it."

The human's eyes flicked down to his tensed shoulders, his hands clenched tight from pain, and she stumbled backward. Trepidation fluttered across her face, but it was obvious she was trying to seem calm.

This single tiny human posed no danger to him that he could see. He slowly settled back against the frame of the bed and tried to look unthreatening.

"Coming here has—hurt me."

"Oh." Understanding flitted across her face, coupled with shock. At least, that's what he thought she was thinking. Her face changed so often with emotion, but he didn't truly know what any of it meant. "Of course. The crash—the meteor. When we brought you here, did we hurt you? We just . . . we just wanted to help you." She edged forward, coming to stand by the end of the bed. "My room is across the hall. If you need anything . . . just come and get me." She gulped, as though she had suddenly imagined him standing above her in the night and was quickly rethinking her offer. Or was she thinking something else? He was so terrible at reading her.

The girl chewed her bottom lip, then took another step closer and held out the dust-lined bottle. "Here."

He inclined his head, then said, "I . . . thank you." The words were strange in his mouth, and for a moment he couldn't help but feel a traitorous thump to his hearts. Thanking a *human*. He curled his fingers around the bottle and set it on the small table beside the bed.

The human girl—*Delta Wilding*, that was the name she had used—gave him a hesitant smile. It looked so natural on her face, and he struggled against not allowing his own lips upward to match. Not to a human. Not to her.

And yet . . .

And yet currently the fermented liquid she brought him was keeping him alive, here on this strange planet. He couldn't afford to not have her trust, not until he knew where he was.

"You . . . stay?" He swept a hand over the edge of the blanket and tried to make sense of the human tongue. His brain didn't formulate the words, everything sounded jarring and ugly. "Would you—like—want—to stay?" He looked at her closely, watching her reaction.

It was as if her face had lit up; as if she, too, was suffused with the same light that coated his body.

"Yes," she breathed. "Yes, I would." There was hesitancy in the way she moved, but it was graceful, refined, and she perched on the end of the bed. "I—I'm glad you're here," Delta said, then paused before continuing, "Why *are* you here? How did you get here?"

"I do not remember," Starling replied hoarsely.

"We saw you fall. You fell . . . from the sky."

"Yes," murmured Starling. The tiniest hint of a memory

twinged at the back of his mind, and he glanced down at his hands, at his chest, noticing the glow of his skin. He knew it was important—knew this town was important. He could feel it. And he *knew* something about it, about how to get back to the stars . . . but the memory wouldn't come. "I do not remember," he repeated, then winced as another lightning-sharp bolt of pain arced through his bones. He shifted on the bed, delicately moving his shoulders, stretching his arms above his head, trying to get into a more comfortable position.

He glanced back at Delta Wilding to find her staring at him, her eyes roving over his bare chest, caught on his rib cage, on his collarbone, on the tattoos there. He saw the moment she noticed him noticing her, and she quickly focused on an innocuous spot on his neck, where the stark black edge of line faded into his chin. A red flush stained its way up over her cheeks.

Would there be heat if he placed his hand against the blush?

Would she let him?

Delta gestured her hands vaguely in the direction of his body and said, "What do your tattoos mean?"

Starling's breath hitched. The blackness in his memory seemed so dense, it blocked out everything else, but little bits of himself came through. Celestial markings etched on his skin. A reminder of how different he was from these humans. He was not a human. He was so much more.

Finally he said, "A reminder."

"Of what?" Her eyes tracked over the lines.

"Of where I'm from." He stretched his arms again, turning

them back and forth. His skin was nothing but black etched marks. *A reminder.*

"And where is that?" Her voice shook.

In reply, he simply pointed up. Up past the ceiling, past the roof. Up to the sky above. His memory was a mostly blank slate, but some things were stark and clear. He was not from any-where near here.

Delta moved her foot off the bed, put her weight on it. The floorboard creaked. And then she stayed still, frozen. Starling dropped his arms back to rest on the covers, dropped his eyes to stare at his tattooed fingers. Maybe she'd finally realized the enormity of what lay in the bed before her; maybe he'd fright-ened her. He'd just tried to be truthful, but perhaps the truth wasn't really what was needed.

"Are you going to hurt me?" she blurted out.

He stared at her. Her mouth was a thin line; her eyes were glinting. She was scared—that was obvious from her trembling hands—and yet she still stayed defiantly on the mattress, arms folded, the keeper of a crumbling castle.

He could hurt them *all* without a second thought. They were so fragile.

"No." His voice was soft and low, although he was very aware of each hiss that came from his tongue swishing over his teeth.

He saw the swell of emotion in her: relief? What must it be like to be so saturated with feeling?

"That's good."

"Are you going to hurt *me*?"

"I rescued you."

"What I mean is," Starling said, "am I safe here?" He knew

the answer: he knew he wasn't. It was why he had to leave as soon as possible. A being like him did not belong on a planet with *humans*.

She shut her eyes for a moment, then loosed a long, drawn-out breath. Her answer was short. "Honestly, I don't think so."

It was more or less what he'd expected as a stranger in a strange land, but still, he didn't like the answer. All it would cause was problems. And any problems would cause his time here to stretch out.

"I'll make sure I keep you safe while you recover," she added. "I'll do anything I can."

Starling lay back against the cushions, so overwhelmed with the sights and sounds and smells of this place—another *world*—that he didn't question any further. He didn't want to talk, anyways—he wanted to listen to *her* talk. While the Wildings' language sounded harsh and strange on his lips, it fell easily from Delta's, melodic and . . . beautiful.

He pushed the thought forcefully from his mind. *No.* It would not do to be interested in these tiny creatures. He had to find his chain and leave. Gritting his teeth against the pain, Starling threw off the covers and made to swing his legs out of the bed.

"Hey—hey, what are you doing?" Delta moved quickly, her hand on his shoulder, her fingers firmly pushing him back. "You can't get up yet!"

Starling glowered at her and brushed off the point of contact, his long fingers sweeping hers away. "I lost something when I fell. I must retrieve it."

"What did you lose?"

Starling narrowed his eyes. These questions unnerved him—and so did the music in her voice. "Nothing."

Delta bit her bottom lip and shifted from one foot to the other. "I can help. I *want* to help."

"I do not need your help," Starling said, the words coming out almost a growl. He didn't want to talk anymore; he didn't want to think. He was enjoying lying in this soft bed while the human's words washed over him, but he *couldn't* enjoy it.

"You'll get lost—you were unconscious when we brought you here. You don't know these woods, and I do."

"I will find the way."

"You can barely walk!"

"I am *fine.*"

She crossed her arms, insistent. "You just fell who knows how far, and you're hurt. I bet you still have a fever." She edged forward and quickly put her hand on his forehead. Her skin was cool against the fire burning through his veins, but he swatted her hand away anyways.

"See? You're burning up."

Starling refused to look her way. He'd never fully realized how irritating humans could be.

Delta continued speaking through his silence, her quick human words filling up the space. "You don't know where you are, but I know those woods like the back of my hand. Let me help you—I *want* to help. And people are already suspicious. We're not the only ones who saw you fall, you know. The mayor was here. Who knows who will come next? What if they find you? What if—"

Starling sighed, finally flicking his eyes to watch her as she babbled. He supposed the human was right in some ways—he could certainly find the place he'd landed eventually, but he *didn't* know these woods, or this planet. Humans baffled and aggravated him in equal measure; these tiny talkative things with their whims and impulsive moods.

"Fine," he snapped, cutting her off. *"Fine."*

"You know you have to tell us what we're looking for."

"No."

"Starling, we can't help if—"

"Something important. A way for me to leave."

"Oh." Delta took a deep breath. "Okay. Well—of course we'll help you."

Silence fell once more, and this time, Delta didn't fill it. She sat on the edge of his bed, twisting her fingers together, then cleared her throat, her eyes darting toward him. "You look like a human," she said eventually. "A little bit."

The words were silvery and sweet, tripping over her tongue. But it was this, and the fire racing through his bones, that made him flare up with sudden indignation. Who did this human think she was, comparing himself—his celestial self—to the erratic beings that populated this planet? He turned his dark eyes upon her and snapped, "But I am *not* like you." It was said as much for himself as it was for her.

"No," Delta whispered, and for a moment Starling felt a tiny prick of feeling that could have been relief or disappointment. Hopefully she understood now: they were so different. Humans were nothing; he was so much more.

But then she smiled at him. "No, you're not. But hopefully we can be—um, friends—anyways." She offered up another tentative smile, then slid off the bed and headed for the door. "I'll go get Bee. We can all go out to the woods." She backed out of the room. The space where she'd sat by his feet went cold as her heat leached away.

Friends.

Friends. It was impossible, it was ridiculous. *Friends, with a human?* Never. He was just passing through, he couldn't stay. . . . But he couldn't help the disparate flutter of his three hearts as he remembered the earnest, open look on Delta's face as she'd spoken. *Friends.* Spoken with such hope, like she'd believed it possible. As if she'd wanted more than anything for it to be true.

11

DELTA SNAPPED THE door to Starling's room shut, then turned and called up the stairs, "Bee?" Her sister had disappeared into her room after Mayor Rockford left, and Delta wasn't sure why—it was almost as if Bee wasn't curious in the least by Starling's arrival. As far as Delta knew, her sister hadn't said one word to the man from the stars. Delta wasn't even sure how it was possible to be so uncaring to the sudden and miraculous mystery that had landed in their backyard. "Bee!" she called again, louder now.

There was the long creak of Bee's bedroom door opening, and then Bee stood at the top of the stairs. "What?" She was wearing sweatpants and an oversized striped sweater, and her eyes were very red. Had Bee been *crying*? Why?

"You okay?" Delta asked.

"Yeah," Bee replied, and Delta couldn't help but think she sounded sulky. Her sister crossed her arms over her chest and stared down at her socks before her eyes flicked between Delta and the closed door. "Were you in there with him?"

"Yes. We're taking Starling back to the clearing."

Bee's face lifted, her mouth creeping into a tiny half smile. "He's leaving?"

"Not yet," Delta said. "He lost something, and we're going to help."

"What is it?"

"I . . . I'm not sure. He wouldn't say, but it's important and—"

"So," Bee interrupted, "he's keeping secrets and you're okay with that? Delta—" She dropped her voice, as if any second Starling might appear, yelling *Gotcha!* "I don't think we should trust him. We don't *know* him, or anything about him, and . . ." She swallowed hard. "How do we even know he's safe?"

"If he wanted to hurt us, don't you think he would have done it by now?"

"Delta . . ."

"He's an alien, Bee," Delta said, lowering her voice to a whisper to hide the tremble in her words. "An *alien*. I just . . . I need to know. I need to talk to him. We might be the only people in the world who can honestly say they've made contact." She could hear her voice edge into a pleading tone, but she didn't know how else to make her sister understand. She barely understood it herself, but she did know there was a man from the stars inside their home, and she wouldn't—couldn't—waste this chance to learn what more was out there.

Bee stood there sullenly, arms crossed tightly across her chest.

"Whatever it is he's lost will allow him to return to wherever he's from."

Bee glanced up. "It lets him leave?"

"That's what he said." Delta shrugged. "But fine, you don't have to come. Stay here."

"Oh no, I'm coming with you," Bee shot back immediately.

"I'm not letting you go waltzing off into the woods with an
alien."

"Bee," Delta sighed, then looked beseechingly at her sister.
"We just found out we're not alone in the universe. Isn't that
incredible? Doesn't it make you excited?"

Bee walked down the stairs heavily, glaring at Delta as she
passed, and stood with one hand on the handle to the guest
room door. "No," she whispered, half to herself, so softly, Delta
almost missed it. "It makes me scared." She took a deep breath
and held it. Her hands were shaking as she quickly pushed open
the door, then jumped to stand a good three feet away from the
doorway. She peered in with narrowed eyes and a frown. "Okay,
alien. Let's go."

"Bee!" hissed Delta, pushing Bee out of the way and taking
her place in the doorway. She took one single deep breath, then
smiled and entered the room.

Starling pushed the covers off and slowly stood up, his body
unfolding off the mattress. It was the first time Delta had seen
him standing, and the sight of him seemed to steal her breath
from her lungs. He was an *alien*, and he was here, standing
before her. He was no longer an unconscious body, no longer
safely tucked away in bed. She couldn't seem to look away. He
was a full head taller than her, and although she couldn't see his
skin's glow as well in the light-filled room, it was obvious he
was an unearthly creature. He stood in a stilted way, as though
his body was a thing he didn't understand. One long-fingered
hand rested on the bedpost, and the ink markings tracked up
and around his skin. His swirling black eyes bored into hers,

then flicked over her head to where Bee hovered nervously out on the landing.

"Lead the way, human," he ground out, his voice a mere rasp.

Bee gave a squeak and ran downstairs. Delta, whose eyes were still locked on the being before her, swore she saw Starling's lips flick for just a second into a wry-looking smirk. But when she looked again, he was walking toward her, brushing past her to follow Bee, and his face was stoic, his mouth set.

She watched as he took the steps carefully, one at a time, holding tightly to the banister. Once or twice she thought she saw him wince in apparent pain, but before she could say anything, the emotionless mask tightened once more over his features.

Bee was waiting in the kitchen, pouring kibble into a bowl for Abby.

Starling edged into the room, then stopped as though struck. Abby ignored her bowl of food and came toward him, sniffing at his bare feet and the cuffs of his dark pants.

"What is that?" he murmured.

Delta passed him, looking quickly around the room. "What's what?" She tried to imagine seeing this space through an alien's eyes. Pots and pans hung from the metal rack above, light slanted through the red-and-yellow checked curtains, and used mugs sat in the sink, waiting to be washed.

"That," Starling repeated, then lifted a finger and pointed at Abby.

"Oh," said Delta, biting back the strongest urge to laugh. "That's Abby, our dog. Don't worry," she added as Abby licked his ankle and Starling locked into a statuelike position, frozen in place. Abby was a protective dog, always had been—the mail carrier didn't come within a hundred feet of the Wild West anymore—but Delta would never guess this by the way Abby sniffed around the alien.

"A dog?"

"Our pet," Delta continued. Abby licked his ankle again. "She likes you. You can pet her, if you want."

Starling reached out a hand and brushed his fingers through her fur. A fleeting emotion crossed his face, but before Delta could tell what it was, Starling raised one hand to his bare chest and abruptly stepped away. "Come," he said imperiously, sweeping a hand toward the kitchen door.

Behind his back, Bee rolled her eyes and shot Delta a *look*, which Delta studiously ignored. She spent a solid three minutes peering out all the windows before finally cracking open the door, letting the warm breeze carry in the smell of dry grass and dark trees. "Okay," she whispered, once again eyeing the empty backyard.

The three of them had just stepped outside when a sharp, loud knock echoed through the house. There was a pause, and then another knock sounded.

"Delta?" Bee squeaked.

Delta froze, her hand clenched on the back door. Was it the mayor, coming back for another round? Or someone else from town? Delta's heart dropped low into her stomach. She knew what the people in Darling thought of them, holed up there in their old crumbling farmhouse. She wouldn't put it past the townspeople to do something—anything—if they suspected the falling star had landed here.

"Run," Delta whispered. She jerked her gaze toward the tree line. "I'll distract whoever it is, and follow you."

"Delta, *no!*" Bee said, her voice rising, and Delta couldn't tell if it was because she was scared for her sister or simply didn't want to be alone with an alien. Perhaps it was both.

Another knock came. If Delta didn't open the front door soon, whoever it was could simply slip around the side of the house and find them all congregating at the back door. Caught.

"Go!" she said frantically, then pulled her arm out of Bee's grasp and shut the back door, the wood and glass separating herself and her sister. She waited until Bee turned and ran, Starling following in her wake.

Delta ran down the hallway, the floorboards singing and creaking beneath each step. She peered through the mullioned glass that sided the front door, cold fright dousing her when she saw a woman standing on the sagging porch. She'd never seen this person before, but a gleaming golden badge proclaiming SHERIFF was pinned to the woman's chest.

This cannot be happening.

A black Escalade was parked where Mayor Rockford's car had been parked earlier that morning. The woman was maybe Delta's height, with long black hair braided down her back and warm brown skin. She had inquisitive eyes that took account of the porch, the surroundings, Delta, the small sliver of house interior she could see through the side window. Delta could *tell* she was surveying, and surveying wasn't something Delta usually approved of unless she herself was the one doing it. But the woman's eyes were curious. They were kind. She held herself with surety, the type of woman who knows what she believes and won't let anyone tell her differently.

The woman knocked again, and Delta waited a couple of seconds before opening the door.

"Hello, I'm Ramona Schuyler," said the woman, sticking out her hand. It was small and had a callused look about it, like it had done great things, or at least attempted them. Delta met the handshake reluctantly, and the woman pumped her limp fingers up and down energetically.

She dropped the woman's hand, nodding to her, and didn't give her own name. Her mind was racing, and she didn't want to accidentally give away more information than she should. Her perception of people usually consisted of a battle between clear, cool-headed judgment, overactive imagination, and a heightened worry of strangers. It was this worry of strangers that made her say tightly, "I'm sorry, but why are you here?"

She realized a little too late this could make her sound guilty. But the woman's eyes just lit up.

"We-ell," she began, and tapped the shiny badge. "I'm the new sheriff in town. Just started last week."

"Does the mayor know?" As soon as she said it, Delta realized how silly it sounded, but still—the Rockfords did not give up their power lightly. The old sheriff was in his eighties; it was mostly an honorary title now. Mayor Rockford was judge, jury, and executioner in the town of Darling.

But the sheriff just put her hands on her hips and smiled. "Funnily enough, the mayor of Darling *does* know there's a new sheriff in town. I've always wanted to say that. It sounded just as good as I imagined."

"Oh. Well, welcome to Darling. Most people who live here have been here forever."

"Yeah, judging by the stares I got driving down Main Street— oh sorry, the only street—doesn't seem like you get many newbies."

Delta chuckled, but then the smile slid off her face as the new sheriff segued into what was obviously the real reason she'd come by. "There was an earthquake last night—I'm sure you felt it—*but* I'm not sure if you noticed, a . . ." The sheriff paused, seemingly choosing her choice of words, then continued, "*Something* seems to have descended into the woods behind your house. A meteor, perhaps."

"What?!" Delta gasped, because she didn't know what else to do. There was a silence as Sheriff Schuyler surveyed her with her knowing eyes and Delta said *"What?!"* again, for effect.

"Something crashed last night, and my calculations place it somewhere in your woods."

"Your calculations?"

"Yeah, that and my eyes."

"I didn't see anything," Delta said nervously. Okay, that sounded fake. She backtracked, to firmer ground. "And it's private property. I mean, we felt the earthquake. But we didn't see anything." Oh God, she was making it worse. *Stop talking!* she yelled to herself, giving the sheriff what she hoped was an honest sort of smile. She really was the worst liar. She would need to work on that.

"We?"

"My sister and I," Delta said. At least she could say that with complete confidence, complete honesty.

"May I speak with your parents?"

She gave a tight smile and said, "My dad is on a business trip."

"Your mother?"

"Dead."

"I'm sorry," said the sheriff, and she actually sounded it.

Delta met Sheriff Schuyler's eyes. "I'm sorry I can't be more of a help. I didn't see anything like what you described, though."

Sheriff Schuyler just nodded, sucking her bottom lip. Then she smiled, and while the smile didn't say *I believe you*, it didn't look menacing, either. Delta would take that over Mayor Rockford's threats any day.

"Thank you for your time," she said.

"You're welcome," said Delta, already starting to inch the door shut.

Sheriff Schuyler thrust her hand through the gap. She held a card with her name and profession and work phone number. On the back of the card she'd scribbled another number. "My cell," she said seriously. "Call me if you *do* see anything. Or," she added thoughtfully, "if anyone else comes asking after the—uh, meteor."

"Will do," said Delta nervously. "Bye." She snapped the door shut and took a deep breath through her mouth, trying to refill all the air that had slowly compressed out of her lungs. Then she locked the door behind her and slipped the card into her pocket. She couldn't imagine ever calling the sheriff, for any reason at all. It just wasn't worth the questions it would bring. The questions she already *had*.

She leaned against the hallway wall, nerves fluttering in her stomach. First the mayor, now the sheriff. Who would come knocking on their door next? She remembered when Starling had asked if he was safe here.

Honestly, I don't think so.

And she *had* been honest. She couldn't trust the mayor, she didn't know this new inquisitive sheriff, and she certainly couldn't trust the townspeople, not when they so hated her strange, odd family and everything they represented. To those in Darling, the Wildings were as good as town witches; whenever Delta felt the weight of eyes on her as she walked down Main Street, she just knew they were wishing it was the olden days when they could take matters of witches and strange things into their own hands.

But if officials were already coming to her house to see what had fallen from the sky . . . Delta had a bad feeling it was only a matter of time before those in Darling did as well.

The text on her phone swirled into her mind: *we know.*

She peeked out the thin window by the front door, waiting until she saw the sheriff's shiny car do a wide turn in the grass and pull back onto the main road, heading for town. Then she turned and ran for the woods.

Bee and Starling appeared from behind two trees at least twenty feet away from each other when Delta finally slid around the first few mossy trunks and entered the woods. Starling was running his fingers lightly up and down the moss that coated the tree closest to him, and Bee shot Starling a distrustful look that only Delta saw.

"You were supposed to keep an eye on him," Delta whispered

as Bee inched closer. Her sister just wrapped her fingers tightly around Delta's and didn't reply.

"Who was that?" Starling asked, his voice still gravelly, although the words came smoother every time he spoke.

Delta swallowed. "The sheriff."

"What, Mr. Stanley?" Bee piped in.

"No," Delta replied grimly. "There's a new sheriff. Ramona Schuyler."

"And was she . . ."

"Suspicious? Yeah. She asked about the meteor. Gave me her card. I have a feeling she'll be back, though," Delta said, her stomach squirming uncomfortably with the thought. She turned to Starling. "Don't worry, Starling. We'll find what you lost and help you get home." She tried to smile reassuringly, but it didn't quite reach her eyes. Already Starling was ready to leave. There was so much she hadn't asked him yet. So much she still needed to know about the universe.

She was keenly aware of his presence, of his every movement. She'd always considered herself fairly tall at five foot eight, but Starling was at least six foot two or three, and his mere proximity to her made her nerves on edge. She couldn't explain it; she was slightly frightened by the sheer reality of him, but the fright seemed to coalesce with awe and excitement until she couldn't tell if she was scared or just completely and acutely *conscious* of him, of every step he took. The alien walked slowly and carefully beside her, choosing each step with silent precision. While Delta and Bee tripped over twigs and slipped on patches of damp, slick moss, Starling simply walked between them, his steps faltering but silent, his orb-eyes taking in the whispering of the forest as it tracked their journey. His steps were halting, but his eyes were alive with a steady and confident gaze.

The woods blocked out the daylight, until within the trees it seemed almost night; Delta, too late, realized they should have brought the flashlights. But the darkness was wanted: the thick cover of the trees guarded them from any prying eyes. She felt safer here than at the house, especially as the Wild West seemed to be overrun with sudden visitors.

They continued to follow the path they'd made before, and Delta had lost track of all time when Starling suddenly came to a halt next to her. The sudden stop took Delta aback, with Bee falling into place beside Delta; they stumbled and looked around the woods warily. Had the alien seen something, some hidden danger? Starling sniffed the air, and his eyelids blinked languorously once, twice, as though he was mulling over whatever it was he smelled. He touched the bark of the tree nearest him, running his finger down its textured crust. In its wake he left a thin line of light.

Finally, he moved his head, his black eyes glancing at Bee for only a second before his unearthly gaze rested on Delta. She tried not to blink or move: as an eighteen-year-old human girl, she'd never given much thought to squirrels and their respective feelings. But in that moment, as Starling's heavy, starry gaze settled over her shoulders, she fully understood what it felt like to be a squirrel caught in the gaze of a wolf. There were secrets in his eyes; there were untold years.

"Are we close?" he asked Delta, but he spoke as if he already knew they were. Could he sense that his secret missing possession was close by?

Delta peered around the woods, trying to ignore the shiver that felt like watching eyes. "Yes, I think so." She pointed to a sinuous trail of crushed moss and grass. "That way, I think. That's from when we dragged you out of here." She took a step forward, ready to lead the way, but Bee immediately pulled hard on her hand, wedging herself between Delta and Starling, jerking her sister back.

"If we're close, then you can go first," she said, her words harsh. She glared at Starling; in the dark, all Delta could see of her was the glint of her eyes.

"Bee," Delta whispered, but Starling just gave a short nod and pushed past Bee, and despite his faltering steps, he still looked like he was weaving in and out of the trees like liquid. A flash of light. He stopped by a collection of thick ferns covered with dew and sniffed the air again. Delta and Bee followed more slowly.

"I don't like how he looks at you," Bee finally muttered. She kept her fingers clasped around the bottom of Delta's flannel.

"He doesn't look at me like anything."

"He does," Bee maintained. "Like this." She turned to Delta and widened her eyes, staring deeply and intensely into her sister's.

"He does *not*," Delta repeated in return. She spoke in a low voice. She wasn't sure how good Starling's hearing was. Possibly he was listening to every word they said, no matter how softly they spoke.

"I don't trust him," said Bee.

"Neither do I," Delta said, nettled, stepping over the ferns. Starling was walking faster now; perhaps it was the nearness of the clearing that gave him sudden energy. He pushed aside branches and stepped lithely, gracefully, over any obstacles the woods put in his path.

"You do," Bee said. "I can see it. You *do*."

"I *don't*," Delta insisted.

Bee sighed, then said in a quiet, resigned tone, "Yeah, maybe. But you will."

Delta didn't know what to say, so she said nothing. Bee was always dramatic about everything; it was just how she was. Delta felt faintly annoyed that Bee was being so oddly unlike her usual carefree self; there was a time and place, Delta thought, to develop a protective streak.

"I don't trust him, Bee," Delta whispered finally. "This all just . . . feels like a dream. It's unreal."

"He's too good to be true," Bee shot back. "You'll see."

They could see the clearing now, and Delta's heart clenched in both worry and wonder as she took in the disconcerting sight before her: light everywhere. The grass was completely coated in the strange viscous light, as though the impact had splattered it around when Starling hit the ground. The trees and shrubs were streaked with it, and there in the middle of the clearing where Starling had lain, unconscious, was a starry pool.

Starling stared around, his expression inscrutable, then sighed and edged forward into the clearing, his eyes on the grass.

"So what is it we're looking for?" Delta asked, keeping her voice low. She didn't want to disturb the scene before her.

Starling didn't reply, but he glanced at her mistrustfully

from across the clearing before dropping his gaze and restarting his search.

"Glad we came," Bee whispered derisively, staying a few feet behind Delta. "We're obviously wanted here."

Delta kept her eyes on Starling, but kept her distance. He stalked around the clearing, his movements smooth but searching, almost predatory. "I can help you if you let me."

"No."

"We're not your enemies, Starling," she bit out. "All we've done is protect you and help you."

Whereas Delta could see the glint in Bee's eyes even in the cool shade of the woods, Starling's swirling eyes seemed to draw light away. Pools of black watched her, darker and more viscous than the murky gloom around them.

"How am I to know that?" His voice was sharp. "All humans do is lie."

"That's not true," Delta replied, stung.

"It is true. And I do not trust you humans to help me, because what I am looking for can do *so many* things. It's pure power, pure energy. With it I can leave, I can stay, I can—" Starling stopped and swallowed, his throat bobbing, his eyes going wide as if he couldn't believe what he was admitting to. He shook his head, then muttered, "Small humans cannot be trusted with such power."

His words swirled around her as she pinpointed one single phrase: *I can stay.* A glance at Bee showed her sister had zeroed in on that admission as well; her eyes were narrowed, her posture tense.

"When you find this thing," Bee said, her voice loud in the gloom, "you'll use it to leave, right?"

"Stop *questioning* me," Starling ground out, turning away from them and stalking around the light-filled clearing. "I will do what I *want* with it, as it is *mine.*"

She heard Bee's light footsteps behind her. "Del, let's just go. He obviously doesn't want us here. He can find whatever he's lost, and go away, and we can go home and just forget this ever happened."

"I can't *forget it ever happened,*" Delta said. Each word was sharp-edged. She waited for Starling to say something, say anything, but he was quiet, kneeling in the grass, his hands gently searching. "Starling?"

"I do not care what you do," he said, and Delta reeled back. She had made contact and had a chance to discover the mysteries of the universe, and the alien before her didn't trust them, didn't like them, didn't want anything to do with them.

Bee caught Delta's hand in her own. "Come on, Del." She pulled on her sister's fingers, then called out to Starling, "*Sorry* we tried to help you. *Sorry* that we don't fit with how you think humans are. *Sorry* that Delta *cares.*" She paused, then muttered, "I wish we hadn't been the ones to see you fall."

Delta wished she could feel the same. If her dad was here, he would know exactly the right words to make Starling trust them. Her tongue felt coated in sawdust; she'd had the universe in the bedroom across the hall for barely a day, and already it was all slipping through her fingers.

She and Bee turned and walked away, leaving footsteps of light as they left. They'd only walked fifty feet when a branch cracked somewhere in the distance. And then . . . another light.

Faint, far away through the trees. Another branch cracked, and the light swung.

A flashlight.

"Delta!" Bee's voice shattered the stillness. "Someone's coming."

"Run back home," she said, the words tumbling over each other. "Lock the doors."

"But—you—"

Delta gave her sister a shove. "Go, go!" Bee only hesitated another second before she turned and ran, crashing through the woods. Delta turned and ran in the opposite direction, trying to be quiet, trying to be quick. She burst back into the light-soaked clearing and Starling looked up, startled.

"Someone's—coming—" she gasped.

Starling reacted immediately, turning and darting nimbly away from the clearing. She hurried after him. The trees were close, and she ran flat out, a whirlwind of panting breath and pounding feet. Starling moved silently, just in front of her.

He abruptly stopped, and right before she slammed into his suddenly still body, he whirled around and grabbed her by the waist, swinging her body in a circle and preemptively stopping the collision. Delta tried to scream—she opened her mouth to shout for help, to shout to Bee that *you were right, I shouldn't have trusted this alien!* But before she could even draw in a breath, Starling clapped a hand over her mouth. Her scream became nothing but a breathy squeak, inching past his fingers. She struggled violently against him as he hauled her behind a wide tree, his feet not making a single sound.

"Stop fighting me," he breathed.

Delta's heart crashed furiously in her chest and she writhed against him, panicked, trying to pull free.

"I am not going to hurt you," he hissed into her ear. "Stop, stop. I will put you down—here."

True to his word, his arm loosened and his hand dropped from over her mouth. Delta slapped his hand away, whirling to face him, to yell at him.

"Do not speak," he murmured again. "Whoever is coming is almost in the clearing now."

"Maybe I don't care," Delta whispered back, glaring up at him. Once again, she had gone back to help him, and once again, he obviously didn't care in the least. "I don't even know why I came back to warn you, honestly."

"Do not speak," Starling muttered again.

Delta began to retort when a soft voice sounded from the clearing, carrying over the still air, over the chirping of the birds. "Oh my God."

Delta recognized the voice: it was the new sheriff, Ramona Schuyler. She could imagine her there facing the light-splattered clearing, gaping. Delta heard the woman whisper to herself: "This . . . is impossible."

Delta almost smiled; she'd thought the exact same thing when she'd seen the boy falling from the sky, and now here she was, hiding behind a tree next to him.

The sheriff continued, "I *knew* I'd seen someone falling." A pause, then: "What *is* this stuff?" Footsteps sounded as the sheriff walked around, examining.

Delta felt her heart speed up—what if the new sheriff decided to search farther into the woods? It was dark, but even so, it would be difficult to get away unseen or unheard. If the sheriff decided to look where Delta and Starling were standing behind the tree, sentinel and silent, they would be found one way or another: either by staying put, or by the noise they made by running away.

Delta's breath hitched with sudden panic, a quick, loud inhale that she couldn't help. Starling raised his hand and edged it over her mouth, slowly, gently, different from before. He left a tiny gap through his fingers for her to breathe. The heel of his palm rested lightly on the right side of her jaw, and the tips of his fingers reached all the way over her mouth. Delta could feel each and every callus, each and every ridged bone of his fingers as they pressed against her cheeks. Would she have a light-streaked face now? She'd have to wash it off before she saw Bee—her sister would *freak out*.

But still, now that the panic had drained away, she found she didn't feel as frightened. She couldn't see him, but she could feel the closeness of his body behind her. She couldn't see the starry eyes or the light-streaked skin; if she closed her eyes and imagined, she could be in anyone's arms.

She tuned everything out: she couldn't hear the sheriff, or the rustling of the leaves above her, or the screeching of the birds that swooped low overhead. She could only feel Starling Rust's warm skin and the wildly thunderous thumping of her own heartbeat mingling with the disparate rhythms of Starling's three. She reached up, edging Starling's hand off her

mouth, then twisted in his arms to stand face-to-face. Her boldness surprised even her; but perhaps Starling wouldn't take it
as boldness—he wasn't human, he might not know. His face
was shadowed, but she could see the slight tightening of his lips
as his hands dropped back to his sides. She felt the hitch of his
breath against her chest.

Was it because of her?

She stared up into his face; instead of the usual galaxy-filled
eyes, his eyes were as dark and fathomless as black holes.

They stood behind the tree for what felt to Delta like ages,
and finally they heard Sheriff Schuyler's footsteps getting
fainter as she moved back through the woods. Delta nervously
wiggled her fingers by her side.

She tilted her face back and up and mouthed, *We need to leave*,
the words barely forming, the sounds hardly dancing on the
air before disappearing under the chittering of the birds. Her
mouth was very close to his. She hadn't realized just how close
until now. Starling licked his lips, his tongue running along his
bottom lip. Delta couldn't find the air in her lungs; it had been
sucked away into nothingness.

He spared one more look toward the clearing, his hand reaching up to touch the empty hollow at the base of his neck with
something like longing. But he was *stardust*, he wasn't human;
he didn't understand longing and desire.

Starling Rust placed a hand at the small of her back, and
quickly led her back toward the Wild West.

12

BEE LAY CURLED IN

bed, the patchwork quilt passed down through generations of Wildings pulled up over her head, even though the warmth of the afternoon made the room heavy with heat. Her phone was plugged into the docking station on her bedside table; she'd turned the music up loud enough to drown out the sounds of creaking floorboards echoing up through the Wild West's old walls. Bee had originally put on her summer playlist full of pop songs, but as usual the Wild West took musical matters into its own hands. Apparently, her house thought in her current mood she needed some melancholy music, and Oasis was now wafting out of the speakers.

In her hands she held a thin, delicate, glowing chain.

She played with it, ran the chain back and forth between her fingers. Despite lying outside in the woods, the chain was warm. Her fingers tingled with energy, and with each pass a tiny coating of light seemed to stick to her fingertips.

She'd found it as she'd been running back through the dark woods alone, as Delta had been rushing back to warn the alien. It had been nestled in the moss, half-buried under twigs, and as soon as Bee had paused to pick it up, her hand had grown hot.

Could this have been what Starling was searching for?

Bee had dropped it into her pocket and hurried on. She hadn't dared take it out again until she was safely inside her room.

She thought of Starling's words in the woods; this chain was surely the mysterious item that would let him leave—or stay. She ran a fingertip over the dainty links.

The events of the past couple days beat a pattern furiously inside Bee's head. She felt like it had been a dream: she'd been swept up in carrying him—a real live otherworldly body— through the woods; she'd been so excited when she'd first seen the unconscious boy lying there in the grass. She had held Delta's hand tightly in the clearing, before they'd seen the prone figure, and they'd stood so close, she'd felt as if they were one person: *DeltaandBee*, the way they used to be growing up.

Growing up. Maybe this separation she'd been feeling with Delta was just part of growing up. But before the meteor, before Starling, before yesterday, the distance was slight enough to ignore. Now she felt like they were living in two different worlds, in two different realities.

Delta's reality: fiery high hopes, an almost-delirious excitement over the arrival of Starling Rust.

Bee's reality: a sudden, terrifying, unexplainable loneliness and a sudden, terrifying chasm between her and her sister, too far to jump. Too far to even call over to the other side.

If this was growing up, she didn't want to do it.

She felt like she was turning into her sister, bit by bit. Delta was the one who was supposed to be practical and always on the lookout. And now everything was wrong. All Bee knew was that Delta's eyes changed whenever she looked at the alien, as much as she insisted they didn't.

Bee rolled over onto her side, drawing her knees into her chest, eyes burning with unshed tears. She could feel the tears welling over in her heart and stomach, but when they reached her tear ducts, they just pooled there, taunting her, reminding her of her sadness. She pushed the heels of her hands into her eyes, giving a little groan of frustration, trying to dispel the sadness she couldn't quite place.

Liam Gallagher's voice warbling through the speakers abruptly stopped mid-"Wonderwall," and after a few seconds Paul McCartney began crooning "Golden Slumbers," a song that, for Bee's entire life, had made her cry.

Bee's stomach clenched as the lyrics came through the patchwork quilt, talking about getting back home. Bee *was* home, but she didn't feel like it. The loneliness began to fill up inside her again.

"Can you not?" she muttered, and in response, the Wild West upped the speaker volume a couple of notches, just in time for "Carry That Weight" to come bursting through. She pushed the quilt off her head and turned off the music. "I get it," she snapped, then flopped back against the headboard morosely.

The silence rushed in, and everything was quiet in the absence of music until suddenly the speakers burst back to life with Simon and Garfunkel, coinciding with Bee's door bursting open. Bee stuffed the chain under the covers, into the pocket of her sweatpants.

Delta rushed in, so full of energy it was like a pulse running through her. She crossed the room and turned off "Bridge Over Troubled Water"—the music stayed off this time—and turned to face Bee. Bee didn't like the look in Delta's eyes: they were excited, sure, but there was something else just below the surface, a sort of brightness. It was like Delta had been awakened and all stirred up with passion and magic and fire.

Bee didn't want her sister to be wistful and morose, and she *knew* that Delta was both of those things, and had been for a very long time. Even before their dad had disappeared, Delta had preferred to be by herself, or alone with a book, or carefully zigzagging in and out of the tree line, staring up into the sky as though she was seeing things nobody else could. The sadness had amplified tenfold when their father never came out of the hallway closet; Bee could feel it flowing from Delta in waves. Bee didn't want that for Delta. She *didn't*.

But Bee also didn't want a Delta with wild tumult gleaming through her green eyes as she thought about her alien.

"Where were you?" Bee said. *I was so worried* shivered on the tip of her tongue, but she swallowed it down. Instead: "You took your sweet time coming back."

"Sorry," said Delta in a decidedly un-sorry tone that made Bee frown. "Bee, it was the *sheriff* in the woods. We only just got away in time. She's seen the clearing, the light, but thankfully, she didn't see Starling."

"Because you went back for him," Bee said, the words so soft, she could hardly hear them leave her own lips.

"Yes," her sister said. "I did."

"And did you . . . did you find whatever *he* was looking for?" she asked, sure Delta could see the lie on her cheeks. "The thing that will let him leave?" The light-infused chain was hot in her pocket.

"No," Delta sighed, then raised her eyes to meet Bee's. "The thing that will let him leave or *stay*. You heard him."

The two girls stared at each other. Bee's heart pounded hard and painful in her chest, and she was the first to break, changing the subject and dragging the conversation back into safer waters.

"If the sheriff had seen you, you would've been in so much trouble, Delta. You have to think of yourself. If you get arrested, or questioned, or—or *anything*, where am I going to go?"

"Nothing like that will happen. Everything is fine."

Everything did not feel fine to Bee. How could her sister be so sure? She pressed again: "The boy might be dangerous . . ."

"His name is Starling."

"Whatever," Bee muttered. She didn't care what his name was, not anymore.

The mattress sank as Delta sat on the edge of the bed and pulled her knees to her chest. "What is wrong with you?"

"Nothing!" Bee said. "I'm just trying to protect you!"

"From what?"

Bee glowered at her sister. "Yourself."

Delta rolled her eyes. "Oh, please."

"You have to admit that he's not very nice."

"I think," Delta said slowly, "that he's scared." She met Bee's eyes. "Wouldn't you be? Alone in a different world? That's why I'm trying to help him, Bee. He's scared and alone."

So am I! Bee wanted to scream, but instead she stared at her hands in her lap and whispered, "Just be careful."

"I will be," Delta said. "Anyways—why were you listening to your music so loud?"

"It wasn't me," Bee said. A headache was beginning to bloom in her temples, tightening around her neck. "It was the house."

Another citizen of Darling in another, less sentient house might've looked at Bee incredulously in the wake of this statement, but this was Delta Wilding, and this was the Wild West, and so she just nodded in understanding.

Delta got off the bed with a flourish. "I'm going to make dinner, and I'm going to go talk to him. There's so much I want to know."

"Is that . . . a good idea?" Bee asked doubtfully.

"What, dinner?" Delta replied with a throwaway laugh.

"Delta." Bee didn't smile. She didn't like that she was the one who was thinking about things like safety. That was supposed to be Delta's job. That had *always* been Delta's job.

"He's an *alien*," Delta said. Her eyes shined.

"Exactly," Bee replied, uncomfortable.

"You weren't being this weird when he first arrived," Delta said, and Bee could hear the reproach in her sister's voice.

Bee knew she hadn't been. But it had seemed so unreal, so pretend. . . . Now it was very clear it wasn't. And that was the problem.

"I'm not being weird," Bee finally said, although she knew she was. She just didn't want to talk about why. Because for the first time in her life, Delta just wouldn't understand.

"You really *are*."

"Delta, I . . ."

"Think of the things he can tell us, the things he can show us!" Delta said. Her voice sounded almost reverent.

"What is he *doing* here?"

"He fell."

"What do his tattoos mean?"

Delta hesitated. "I—"

"I know you would've asked him."

Delta's eyes flicked to Bee's. "Don't freak out."

Bee raised her eyebrows, even though her heart sank. No good conversation had ever begun with *Don't freak out*.

"Okay?"

Delta cleared her throat and continued, "I think he's a star."

"A *star*?!"

"He fell from the sky, he can't remember anything, and when I asked where he's from, he just pointed *up*."

"A star," Bee repeated. She'd heard Delta perfectly fine the first time, but the word just didn't make sense. Starling was a boy. He had a body. He had hearts that pumped, eyes that blinked. "How does that even work?"

"Well, that's something I'll find out when I talk to him."

"So not only is he not human, he's not even *close* to being human."

"He won't hurt us," said Delta, and she sounded so supremely unconcerned that Bee scoffed aloud.

"Yeah," Bee said. "I bet he said that. And you'd *believe* him?"

"Yes, I would!"

"Well, I don't want to keep him in my house," Bee said, her voice rising. "A star just *becomes* a person, and we're all supposed to be okay with him living with us? Stars don't have *feelings*. They don't have *empathy*, or *thoughts*, or . . ."

Delta pushed herself off the bed, arms crossed. "You're wrong, Bee. Anyways, does it really matter if he's not human?"

"Yes, it matters, because he's an *alien* and he could kill us like *that*." She snapped her fingers, and the ensuing crack made Delta frown at her.

Bee frowned back at her sister. She frowned because it was true, and because Delta was supposed to be the one who said warnings like this to *her*. The discovery of Starling had obviously clicked some switch inside of Delta, and that made Bee feel very testy indeed toward the alien who they'd let invade their house. One discovery, first contact, and the alien—the *star*—was already changing her sister.

Delta went to stand by Bee's window, which overlooked the woods. She was still dressed in jeans and sneakers and a black shirt. She wore her favorite checked flannel over the top of her shirt, unbuttoned and with the sleeves rolled up. Her hair was half-up, the top section twirled into a messy bun. She still looked like Delta—until she turned to face Bee, and Bee could see that her eyes were ablaze.

"He won't," she said. "I know he won't."

Bee frowned. She knew Delta wanted more than anything to explore the universe. It had always been her dream; with a father like theirs, it was possible Delta's desire to quest was innate, set in her DNA. And as Bee watched her sister smile, it was then she knew: this, here, was the change. This was the catalyst. Everything after this moment would be divided as *after*, and everything before—before Starling, before this different

Delta looked out of her sister's body—was nothing but memory. And what if—what if Delta's obvious fascination with this star boy led her away from Darling? In a moment, Bee could see it all; she could see some far-off Delta leaving with this boy. This *alien*. It may not be today, or tomorrow, but one day Delta would leave, and Bee bet anything that Starling and everything he represented would hasten that departure. Fear curled its way around her ribs like vines. There was no way in hell she was going to let her one remaining family member ever leave this earth—or this town—with an alien.

Delta gave her a glittering smile, then hurried from the room. Bee waited until she heard the door to Delta's bedroom close, then swung her feet out of bed just as the speakers once more crackled to life. Neil Young's "Don't Let It Bring You Down" began to warble out, the tune reverberating across the flowery wallpaper and worming itself deep into Bee's heart. She stuck a hand into her pocket; the chain was still warm, curled at the bottom.

With it I can leave, I can stay . . .

Bee padded over to the bedroom door, the chain heavy in her pocket despite being so delicate. It was time to have a conversation with the alien. She had to make him understand that he had to leave. Until she was sure he'd go, she had to keep this chain safe and far, far away from him.

She brought her finger down over the power button, and "Don't Let It Bring You Down" sputtered into silence. "Sorry, House," she said as she stepped onto the landing, and she could feel the heavy, protective gaze of the Wild West shining from the walls, the windows, the floors. "It already has."

13

out the guest room window. The heat of the day had broken just moments after he and Delta had emerged from the woods and hurried to the back door of the humans' house; now, with a crack of thunder and a white snake of lightning splitting the sky, it began to pour. Outside, he could see the trees whispering to the wind in the rain. *Trees.* He liked the trees, liked their hardiness, their longevity. He liked the dark green of their leaves. He liked the smell of the damp moss.

He was a star, a creature from space. He had no emotions, no feelings. He told himself this, over and over. It didn't change the truth of the fact that he craved all these new sights and smells and sounds. The smell of wet, the deep color of green, the ancient feel of the foliage. And in the Wildings' house: the creaking of the floorboards, the softness of their dog's fur, the strange fruity-sweet taste of their fermented drink.

He walked his fingers crablike up the glass, watching the raindrops chase each other. Humanesque bodies were so *strange*; even now, the energy that flowed through his veins wasn't exactly shaped like a normal human. He'd never given any thought to the way his fingers looked, elongated and slender, until now. Until Earth.

Until the Wildings, with their soft hands and small fingers and pink skin and outbursts of feelings. Bee Wilding, with her narrowed eyes and easy walk and spontaneity; Delta Wilding, grave and earnest and analytical, with a storm raging freely behind her green eyes.

Delta Wilding, trying to hide the fact she was roused by his arrival.

Starling closed his eyes briefly, then sat down on the bed. The mattress sank comfortably under him, despite the painful twinge that rocked through his bones. The room was tired and cozy and completely silent, except for the lashing of rain outside. His body was still healing, still hurting, but with each passing moment he was feeling slightly less raw and sore. His mind, though, raced as thousands of new things and words and smells and *feelings* battered his brain. He'd never experienced any of it before.

A star in a man. A boy.

But still a star.

He kept finding himself wanting to talk to Delta Wilding—and then feeling guilty for wanting to talk to Delta Wilding. *She is a human. You are not.* Every time her eyes peered around the door, he got a treasonous flutter of—well, some *emotion* that he had never felt before. Traitorous. It was a traitorous feeling. He could not stay; he should not even *want* to stay.

She was a human.

And he was otherworldly. He was celestial.

A soft knock came from the door, and Delta peered inside. She jumped back for a second when she saw him awake and staring at her, then took a deep breath and returned to the doorway. She gave him a hesitant smile, as though their time in the woods had changed something. And perhaps it had.

He certainly didn't trust her completely, but humans were quick-thinking, impulsive little creatures. Surely if she was going to cause him harm, she would have done so by now. Instead, he'd watched as she'd thrown herself into helping him, again and again.

And he wasn't supposed to care. What was going on? He shouldn't care; he didn't have *emotions*.

Delta Wilding was making it difficult to remain that way.

"Hi," she said. "I was just about to make dinner."

"Dinner?" he replied. He didn't want to answer, but something in the lilt of her voice drew him like a magnet. What she asked, he had to reply. Push and pull.

"What us humans need to survive. Food. Although I bet you wish we would just *starve* and then you wouldn't have to deal with us anymore." She spoke lightly, but her eyebrows were furrowed and she kept glancing at him up from under her eyelashes.

"I . . . may have spoken too harshly, before. In the clearing." He had to force the words out.

Delta gave a half shrug. "I'll be in the kitchen. Feel free to join if you want." She had almost disappeared behind the door when she leaned back in, her eyes dark. "We really aren't so bad, you know. Humans. If you just gave us a chance, I think you'd see that too."

She swept her hair over her shoulder and snapped the door shut behind her. Starling was left staring after her, his three hearts beginning to pound.

Do not follow her.

He wanted to follow her. He couldn't help the tiny spark of curiosity that had been lit within him, or the small twinge of guilt at how he'd treated the humans so far.

He had only taken two steps toward the door when the shadow of a knock sounded, which proceeded to crack open without waiting for a reply from his side. Starling stood still, sure Delta's piercing green eyes were about to appear around the door, but they didn't. It was the human Bee Wilding, the younger sister. Starling almost shook his head as he remembered how young—*sixteen*, and Delta *eighteen*. But Delta's bright eyes . . . they were older. They housed something that went back eons. Something he recognized.

But Bee didn't look young at all as she gave him a cold look and shut the door behind her, standing with her back pressed against the wood, as far from Starling as she could get. When she spoke, it was quiet, but wintry. "I wanted to talk to you."

Starling didn't answer. Bee was looking at him so angrily, raw emotion radiating from her very pores. How could anyone feel so much? He was only just beginning to feel twinges of emotion and he was exhausted.

"Why are you here?"

"I fell," Starling replied. "I believe your sister has informed you of this." Bee narrowed her eyes, but Starling made sure to meet her eyes with his own. He expected her to look fearful, but she didn't; she just frowned at him, fingers shaking slightly.

"Del has told me a lot of things."

He was silent. Human conversations were so full of twists

and turns, hidden pitfalls he didn't recognize until he walked into one. The language was still so strange to him—any language was. It was why he didn't trust them. He could never trust them.

"What do you want with us?"

Starling swallowed. He wanted nothing with them. He *didn't*—and yet suddenly, all he could picture was Delta making human food in the kitchen, Abby at her feet. What was she creating, what would it taste like? Another flicker of curiosity hit him. Would it be so bad to stay, just for a while, and see how these silly creatures lived?

Still, he said, "I want to leave."

Disbelief was written all over her face. "Then leave already."

He watched her carefully and didn't respond. *I want to leave.* It was the truth. Wasn't it?

"What do you want with Delta?" The words shook as she said them.

"Nothing."

"I don't believe you."

He wouldn't either. He wasn't human, after all. To them, he was simply an impossibility.

"You're dangerous, aren't you?" Bee looked up. Bold. She was bold, he could see it in her glance. There was fear—of course there was fear—but she met his eyes.

"Yes." It was true: the energy coursing through his body was pure. The molecules and motes of stardust that made up his flesh and bones and blood were older than anything they could imagine. More than they could fathom.

Bee nodded. It was as if she'd expected the answer.

"I only want to go back," Starling said slowly. "That is all." He did not belong here. He *could not* belong here. Did they not realize it?

Bee sucked in the corner of her bottom lip, eyeing him in what he deemed to be skepticism. Then she took a deep breath and said bluntly, "My sister will want to go with you, when you leave."

Starling didn't think the human would be able to shock him, but this certainly did. For a moment, his three hearts beat as one, a horrible, jolting *thump* of complete surprise, before beginning their separate rhythms once more. It was impossible, of course. There was nowhere to *go* with him. He was simply stardust.

"And," Bee continued, eyeing him. The rain spattered against the window, and a sudden flash of lightning bathed Bee in an eerie glow. Her freckles stood out like pox, and dim light blanched her skin, making her look even younger. It occurred to Starling suddenly that this human was terrified. Bold, maybe, but terrified. "And, I want you to swear to me that you won't take her."

"Bee Wilding," Starling began, searching for the right English words. The entire language sounded bizarre to his ears: disparate and jarring, with sounds that flattened out unharmoniously. "It is impossible, the thing you say."

"You're impossible," Bee said. "Everything about the past couple days is impossible. Just promise me you'll keep away from her." Her hands edged into the pockets of her sweatpants.

"She is my host," Starling said carefully. "She is allowing me to stay here while I recover."

Bee bit her lip again, nervous, and Starling shook his head, amazed with himself that he was even recognizing their strange human mannerisms.

"Just don't take her away," Bee said. Her voice had gotten progressively higher, her eyes progressively brighter.

"I will *never* take her away," Starling replied. The tiny human obviously wanted him to answer her, and what did it really matter? It was the truth. "I *cannot.*"

"Even if she asks?"

Starling sighed. "Even then."

"You promise? You swear?"

"Yes, I swear," Starling said. Did those words *mean* something to the humans? They were sticky on his tongue.

Bee nodded. "Okay, then." She held his gaze, maybe looking for lies. He wasn't sure what she saw in his face. Both her hands were shoved deep in her pockets, her whole body tense. Then she shook her head—such a tiny movement, he wasn't even sure she'd meant to do it—and left the room.

Starling stared at the door, at the window, at the tidy little room bathed in moonlight. The rain was lashing at the windows with passion—even the *weather* was emotive on this strange planet.

Just as emotive as the two girls. The two humans he'd met had *rescued* him, saved his life, were providing him with sustenance and healing. They were full to the brim with feelings and wild eyes. They were brave. He didn't understand them, and that scared him, as much as he tried to pretend otherwise.

But they were still humans. And he was celestial.

He stood at the window and stared out at the raindrops racing each other down the glass panes until his eyes glazed over. Somewhere out there was the clearing where he'd landed, and within it his energy-infused chain, containing all the power he needed to leave this planet.

Or all the power he needed to tether his celestial body to this earth.

And downstairs . . . he could hear Delta moving around the floor below, pots clanging loudly together, her footsteps pacing, the strange *click-click-click-whir* of Delta turning on the stove. His own inhalations and the settling of the old house around him. The sounds mingled into a comfortable quiet.

For the first time, there was no thread of worry running through Starling's mind that the human might be dangerous.

She'd left the invitation open for him to follow her downstairs, but how could he go now, after the younger Wilding had so forcefully warned him away?

And why did he care what they thought of him?

He knew he had to leave. A part of him . . . wanted to stay. *Stop this,* he berated himself silently as he watched the rain spatter against the window. *Humans aren't worth it.* These *humans aren't worth it.*

His doubt was a line of dominos.

Delta and Bee, unknowingly, had neatly flicked the first one down.

14

DELTA AWOKE TO Abby growling.

Her dog stood by her bed, toenails clacking against the floorboards, facing the window. Her lips were pulled back in a very un-Abby-like grimace, and her body rumbled with low growls.

Delta slipped out from under the covers in a second, her bare feet cold on the floor. She'd cracked the window open before she went to sleep, but the rain had continued during the night and now the floor and windowsill were wet. She shivered. Abby continued to growl.

"What is it, girl?"

Abby growled and took a step closer to the window.

Delta crouched low and crawled on hands and knees to the wall, stretching up just enough to peer out the bottom of the glass to the rain-soaked world outside. Her bedroom window looked out over the front yard and beyond; she squinted through the curtain of mist, but the landscape before her seemed quiet. Dreary and cold, but quiet.

"Nothing's there, Ab," Delta whispered, wanting nothing more than to hop back into bed and go back to sleep. She flicked her eyes to the porch, to the fields blowing vigorously in the wind. "Noth—"

She stopped, her breath leaving her. Abby shuffled forward to press her wet nose against her shoulder, and her growling petered off. Delta could see a figure in white creeping across the field toward her house, skirting low through the grasses and avoiding the main driveway. The hazy mist made the figure look insubstantial, a ghostly apparition prowling through fields of dead wheat stalks.

The figure cut through the tall grasses, heading for the house—no, beyond the house. Delta watched, her breath caught in her throat, as the apparition emerged from the fields that bordered the Wild West and glided around the corner of the house. She could no longer see it from the front-facing window. . . .

Her nerves tight, she pulled on socks and a sweatshirt and tiptoed across the hall to the guest room. Without knocking, she cracked open the door. The window was to the right of the bed; maybe she could keep tabs on the apparition without ever waking Starling.

"Delta?" The accented voice cut through the dark room.

Or maybe not.

She quickly stepped inside the doorway, crossing the room in just a couple of steps. She maneuvered the bedside table out of the way—the undrunk water sloshing out of the glass as it wobbled—and peered out the window. Her fingers gripped at the windowpane as she took in the sight before her.

People had gathered in her backyard, half-hidden behind their old Ford—there were at least eight of them. Delta was sure she recognized the tallest of the lot, despite the fact that his back was toward them. The *mayor*? What was he—what were *any* of them—doing here on her property so late at night? Her stomach dropped, and she clasped her shaking hands together. She had a very bad feeling about this.

The squeaking of the mattress heralded Starling's arrival behind her even before the first breath of cold air hit her neck, raising the hairs. For a moment, she saw one of the townspeople, a dark hoodie covering their face, slowly turn to face the upstairs window where they stood. Delta moved so fast, she barely had time to realize her movements before they happened: she turned around and pushed Starling back onto the bed, so hard she toppled on top of him. They became a writhing mass of legs and arms and joints as Starling worked to extricate himself.

"I'm sorry!" Delta breathed as Starling finally picked her up and deposited her on the end of the bed, his eyes wide with apparent incredulity.

"Why?" Starling began, and words seemingly failed him. "Why?" he said again.

"I'm sorry," Delta repeated. "Just . . . don't go to the window. They can't see you. They can't know that you're here."

Starling paused, and Delta took a moment to get her breathing under control. Her hair was in a messy bun atop her head, and she rested her chin on her hand, staring blankly at the floorboards.

Her adrenaline already heightened by the figures below, she gave a loud yelp when the door creaked open. Bee stood there in her pajamas, eyes bleary with sleep but wide with fright. "Delta, are you in the alien's room? There's *people* outside—" Her words broke off when she saw Starling by the pillows, and the fear quickly transformed into hard eyes and a frown.

"I know, Bee," Delta said. "I'll take care of it."

Bee hesitated.

"Bee, I promise. It'll all be okay." *She hoped.* She didn't want to worry Bee, but she didn't want her to come downstairs again either . . . just in case. "Stay up in your room, okay?" Her tone was light. "And lock your door."

Bee stared at her sister. "Are you sure it's okay . . . ?"

"Promise," Delta replied immediately with a bravado she didn't feel. As soon as Bee yielded with a defeated half shrug and headed back upstairs, Delta let her brave smile drop. *This was so bad.*

"Who are they?" Starling asked, his voice low, jerking his head toward the window. In the night, his accent was more pronounced, the hissing more prominent. She lifted her gaze to meet his, and didn't even flinch at the starry orbs that stared back at her. Only two days, and she was already getting used to Starling's otherworldly appearance.

"Starling, meet the citizens of the town of Darling," she said, sarcasm unable to hide the tremble in her voice. "Good thing you didn't fall into *their* backyard."

"Oh?"

"They're not exactly on board with anything out of the ordinary."

"But their town is brimming with energy," Starling said, his voice blank, confused.

"I don't think they even know it," Delta replied. She knew Darling was chock-full of magic, but to hear Starling say it so clearly made her shiver. *Magic surrounds you. Energy is running through your veins.*

"But you know it," Starling whispered. Delta suddenly realized how close she still was; she was mere inches from where he sat on the bed. She couldn't tell if she was imagining the crackle of *something* that fluttered between their two bodies, but she certainly felt something.

"I do," she whispered back.

Starling jerked his head toward the window. "Are we safe here?"

She noticed he said *we*—was he worried for her safety too?

"It'll be fine," she said again, although this time the words sounded hollow. Because what *was* a group of Darling citizens doing outside her house, watching the windows? Did they know something was inside?

Delta remembered the man who looked like the mayor. Was Tag down there, hood up to hide his features?

"You are worried," Starling said, his voice low, raspy. Abby had come over and laid her head on Starling's knee; he was letting his fingers drift through the dog's soft fur with a faraway look in his eyes.

Delta bit her bottom lip, biting into the soft flesh there. "Yes," she admitted finally. "The people in this town aren't too fond of my family. They, um, they think we're witches or something. Which is ridiculous, I know, but the people here love stuff like that. A couple years ago, Mr. Aaronson's cat died while Bee walked by his house. He managed to convince the entire town she had something to do with it—she was only twelve at the time. Bee's basically spent ever since trying to be as normal as possible." Delta peeked out the window; the citizens below hadn't moved. They seemed to be talking to each other, and a few of them were gesturing wildly with their hands. "Maybe that's why she doesn't like you."

"Do they treat you that way too?"

"Usually," she whispered, her eyes locked on the scene outside. Then, without thinking, she added, "Unless I'm with Tag. Then it's just mean looks because they'd never say anything bad in front of—"

"Tag?"

Delta's head shot up. Hearing Tag's name coming from the alien's mouth was so stupefying that for a moment she just gazed at him in a daze. "What?"

"You just said *Tag.* Who or what is a Tag?"

"Oh—" Delta swallowed hard. *You're so stupid, why are you bringing up Tag?* "He's just—he's . . . a boy," she finished lamely.

"Ah," Starling said, his face blank, his voice measured. "A friend of yours?"

"I . . ." Could he see her flush rising in the darkness? "You never really know people," Delta answered finally. She thought of Tag, his charming blue eyes going hard, then guilty, then cast down at the gravelly path as he followed his father away. She sighed, unable to put this into words, especially in front of Starling.

Starling shook his head; his dark hair fell in limp curls over his eyes. "I," he murmured, "do not understand humans."

She shifted on the bed, her eyes sliding to the alien beside her, then rested her head in her hands. "Honestly, Starling? Half the time, neither do I." It was true: she was always scared, always worried, always stressed, always confused. Did everyone crash their way through life like this? Was everyone reeling in their own separate orbit, not knowing everyone else was just as dazed? She had no words, and if she did, she wouldn't say them aloud. So she just shrugged helplessly.

Starling regarded her silently, then rested his chin in the palm of his hand, mimicking her position.

Delta bit back a smile and continued, "I knew it would only be a matter of time before they searched the woods. Found the clearing. We know the sheriff found it, but . . . I didn't see her down there." And she certainly didn't want to go back to the window to check. Because . . . "If they found you . . ." She paused. She had to keep him safe.

He was an alien, but he was *their* alien, whether he trusted them or not.

"And what would they do if they found me?"

"I don't know," Delta admitted. Tendrils of fear wound their way around her ribs. "I don't know what they would do to you. I don't think we want to find out, though."

Starling wet his lips. "No. I don't."

Delta uncurled her legs and carefully moved to the window again. The townspeople were still there, walking in clusters around the truck, their house, the woods. . . . They swung their flashlights to and fro, the lights flickering in the dark night, gleaming through the drizzle.

"They won't try to get in?" Starling's voice sounded from the bed, and Delta broke her eyes away from the phantoms below. Her stomach clenched in fright. She was scared enough of the townspeople *seeing* them in the window. If they tried to get in? Storm the house? But no, that was illegal. Breaking and entering. They wouldn't try that, would they?

But there had never been anything this magical in Darling before.

It seemed to Delta that with Starling's arrival in Darling, suddenly everyone was descending upon the Wild West. The mayor, the townspeople, the sheriff . . .

The sheriff.

Delta remembered Sheriff Schuyler's inquisitive eyes, the way she didn't press Delta for answers. The way she'd whispered to herself, *I* knew *I'd seen someone falling*, when she'd found the light-strewn clearing. Sheriff Schuyler, slipping Delta her business card: *Call me if you* do *see anything. Or if anyone else comes asking after the meteor.*

Delta bit her lip while Starling looked on soberly. She was conflicted: willingly bringing the sheriff into the equation would be madness. But outside, she could hear the footsteps of the townspeople as they crunched their way around the walls of the Wild West. Delta rubbed her face. She doubted that she'd be able to fool Sheriff Schuyler about why the townspeople were snooping around. She would either have to explain everything, or deal with them alone.

Alone. Would she have to continue to do everything in her life alone? The leader, the protector? Suddenly, the prospect of unloading the problem onto someone else, of letting someone else deal with things . . . It was all she could do to not run from the room to call Ramona Schuyler.

"I think maybe calling the sheriff is a good idea," she said to Starling. He looked at her with his unfathomable eyes, and then a small crease appeared on the bridge of his nose, as if he was frustrated.

"I do not understand," he said.

"Oh, well—we have these tiny communication devices, and—" Breaking off, she held up her phone. "It doesn't matter. I can get in touch with the sheriff—that's the woman we saw in the clearing. I think she can help us."

Delta slid off the bed, hurrying to her own room to grab the folded, half-forgotten business card Ramona Schuyler had given to her. She quickly crossed back to Starling's room, standing by the side of the window, peeking out through a gap in the curtains. She pressed in the number, hoping the sheriff would answer; her phone screen displayed the time as just past three in the morning.

Delta couldn't help but be surprised when the phone rang only once before the dial tone disappeared and Schuyler's voice said, "Hello?"

"Um—Sheriff Schuyler?"

"Yes." The voice didn't even sound sleepy.

"I'm sorry to call so late. This is Delta Wilding. You talked to me yesterday. You said to call if anyone else looks for the . . . meteor."

"Yes?" said Sheriff Schuyler again. Delta took a deep breath; the sheriff definitely sounded curious, and not at all disbelieving.

"I told you before that I didn't know anything. That, uh, wasn't true." She peeked out the window; there were only three townspeople still in view. Where were the rest? The knot in her stomach tightened.

"Obviously." The sheriff said it mildly.

"Well, there are others who are looking for it too, and they're here. Here outside my house." She hesitated. How much to reveal? The sheriff had *seemed* kind, the sort of person who believed, but when it came down to it, would she call Delta a liar? Or worse, would she be *so* interested in extraterrestrials that she would want Starling for herself? Would she call in higher powers—the mayor, the FBI? A shadowy government agency so secretive no one knew it was real? But to get someone else involved, someone to help . . . Right then, in the night with hooded figures moving silently around her house, someone to help was all Delta wanted. She didn't want to walk this path alone anymore. She'd just have to be cagey about what she told the sheriff. "I think they might be dangerous."

There was a beat on the other end, and then Sheriff Schuyler's voice said calmly, "Don't you worry about a thing, Delta. I'm on my way. You stay in the house and don't come out for anything. Whoever is outside your house will run, I'm sure of it. If they don't, well . . ." She paused and Delta could almost hear her shrug. "I'm the sheriff. It's their choice."

"Thank you," Delta breathed.

"You go back to sleep. Everything is fine. But tomorrow . . . we need to have a talk."

"Yes, yes," Delta said, almost babbling with relief. The figures outside didn't seem half as terrifying now that she knew someone was on the way to scatter them. "Thank you. I was just . . . so worried. I thought they might try to get into my house if they knew about—"

Delta broke off, silently berating herself.

"Knew about who?"

"Not who," said Delta, keeping her voice even as she winced. "Nothing. There's nothing." She was staring at Starling as she spoke, but the sheriff had no way of knowing that. Delta sounded cool and honest. It didn't matter if her conscience roared; when she truly needed to lie, she could pull it off like a champ.

Sheriff Schuyler made a little skeptical noise, and Delta was just thinking of more things she could say to bolster her lie, when there suddenly came a soft *tap tap* from downstairs. She paused, ignoring the sheriff's next question, and listened. Starling was still and quiet, but he, too, looked as if he was waiting for something.

Tap tap tap.

Delta turned wide eyes on Starling and abruptly hung up the phone, her fingers trembling. Abby's body tightened and she let out a low, long growl, her hackles raised.

Tap tap tap.

Someone was knocking at the door.

Delta and Starling only stared at each other for a moment, and when the knocking stopped, the silence rushed in around them so loudly, she felt she could hear every breath, every clench of sharp teeth. Starling's black eyes bored into hers. They were the center of a storm, held perfectly still, unmoving, gazing unblinkingly . . .

And then from the floor below, a thundering of knocking barraged the front door, no longer quiet, and Abby went wild with barking. Starling jolted off the bed, just managing to catch hold of her collar before she went racing downstairs. Whoever was knocking wanted to be heard. From the landing, Bee reappeared. "Delta?" Her voice wavered. She sounded young. Young and scared.

"Stay upstairs and *lock your door*," Delta shouted. "Take Abby!" Abby would try to protect the girls from these intruders, and while half of her thought that siccing Abby on these townspeople might stop them breaking in, she couldn't bear it if they did something to hurt her dog.

Bee looked like she was about to burst into tears, but she did as Delta asked, and looped her fingers into Abby's collar.

When Bee disappeared up to the third floor, Delta leaned against the wall in the guest bedroom. The banging from downstairs was never-ceasing. Her mind was firing in all directions. She was frantic. Her breath couldn't make its way through her lungs; it curdled there, forcing its way out in a short, sharp panting. She couldn't stop her hands from shaking. She stood there, frozen, trembling. This was finally it. All of the townspeople's skeptical gazes, their murmurings under their breath, the whispers, the gossip. The name-calling.

Weird.

Witches.

Wild ones.

Worthless.

Whore.

The townspeople had finally had enough and had come call-ing. And all it took was an alien falling from the sky to bring them to the Wildings' front door.

A cold touch came on the back of her hand.

"Delta?"

She didn't reply—couldn't reply. She couldn't breathe. She looked at him, met his dark orbs with her own frantic, terrified green eyes.

"Delta."

She trembled.

"*Delta.*" He moved around to clasp both her shaking hands in his own, covering them tightly. He stood very close to her, one foot on either side of hers, hands enclosed around each other as if praying. His dark eyes were depthless, bottomless. She was lost in them. "Are they coming into this house?"

She made her lips move. "Yes." It was less than a whisper.

"You need to hide."

She shook her head, trying to clear the terror that filled her bones with lead. "You—*you* need to hide."

From downstairs, the knocking came again. Loud, batter-ing strikes against the door. Delta couldn't help the sound she made, a half cry, half squeak of fright. The sound jolted her, rocking her out of her hazy fear. This wasn't just townspeople, curious, searching.

They were trying to force their way into the house. This was not a visit; this was a hunting party.

"You need to *hide!*"

"I am not a human. They cannot hurt me."

Delta very much doubted this. She couldn't help thinking that Starling seriously underestimated humans.

"Get under the bed," Starling said.

"*You* get under the bed."

His hands squeezed hers.

"Get under—" They both spoke at the same time, his hissing syllables mixing with her stern emphasis. From down below, there was a resounding crash, a sound that seemed to echo through the house despite the guest room door being closed. Closed, not locked. There was no time. The house was putting up a fight, but its wooden front door wouldn't hold much longer.

Starling let go of Delta's hands and instead grabbed her around her waist. He pulled her down to the floor and rolled under the curling steel frame of the guest bed. Delta scrambled after him, pausing before following him into the darkness under the bed.

Starling was on his side, the slats just above his head. In the darkness she could barely see him. His eyes were black holes. For a moment she hesitated, the outline of his figure an unknown incongruity in the reality of her world. He was an alien—he was an *alien*—and she would be hurt because of him. He was dangerous. He was inhuman. He was—

"Delta." His voice was soft, and the softness had a honeying effect on the grating timbre of his voice.

He was Starling—just Starling. Delta rolled toward him, his body turning into a crash pad as she collided with his chest. He caught his arms around hers and pulled her close, quickly, quickly. When he'd grabbed her in the woods, she'd almost screamed, but now she tucked her head against his bare chest and tried to calm her breath, breathing in and out with the three disparate beats of Starling's heart. She counted the thick black lines etched into his skin.

One, two, three, four, five, six, seven . . .

There was the sound of wood fracturing from downstairs. Around them, the walls of the house groaned with effort as the Wild West tried to hold out the intruders. Delta couldn't help her whimper.

Fifteen, sixteen, seventeen, eighteen . . .

"You do not have to be frightened," Starling whispered.

"I am." Her voice was hardly a whisper, and it still broke.

There were footsteps downstairs. Dozens of footsteps. Delta imagined the townspeople spreading out over the first floor of the Wild West like a swarm of ants.

"I am here."

"That's what I'm scared of."

His arms stiffened slightly, and when he spoke, his voice had a flat tone to it. "I scare you." It wasn't a question.

Footsteps on the stairs. From upstairs, she heard Abby barking from behind closed doors.

Delta's heart clenched painfully, and she clutched at his arms, her nails indenting his black tattoos. She squeezed her eyes shut, not wanting to see the visitors that would appear in her doorway any second now—

The door opened with a slow, sustained creaking.

She held her breath. Two feet stepped into the room. The footsteps were light, measured, not the scary stomping she'd been expecting. Somehow that made it worse. The feet stopped by the side of the unmade bed: they were wearing dress shoes. Polished shoes, shiny and expensive, even as they dripped water onto the floor. She knew those shoes.

Four heartbeats huddled under the bed was all she could hear.

And then suddenly, a cry rose up from the floor below. Delta couldn't distinguish what the person had said, but immediately the feet turned and thundered back down the steps. Delta and Starling stayed where they were; she didn't dare let out her breath, didn't dare make any noise. The closeness of the call shook her, and still she stayed frozen, although a pressure behind her eyes suggested she wouldn't be able to stay that way for long.

The people of Darling had broken in. She never would have thought they'd actually go so far as to break down the door of her house. These were people she'd grown up around, who she saw at the grocery store, who she ate near at the Diner.

And they'd broken into her house.

The knowledge of it began to set in, and the pressure in her head mounted. Her eyes went hot. What did she do next? Buy a new lock, a new door? With what money? Would she and Bee even be safe living here anymore? The sheer responsibility of the decision that she held on her shoulders made her head pound.

She was just about to finally roll over in Starling's arms and ask him if he thought it was safe to get up, when a voice broke through the quiet. "Delta? Delta Wilding? Are you okay?"

Footsteps sounded on the stairs again: harried, frantic footsteps. "Delta? Delta?"

The sheriff. She'd *come.* That must've been what the towns-people had alerted each other about: the new, young sheriff, coming to the Wildings' rescue. Delta scooted out from under the bed, making emphasized *Stay there!* movements at Starling. He watched her, then gave the slightest of nods. Delta ran out of the room, slamming the door shut behind her just as Sheriff Schuyler leapt onto the landing. She'd obviously taken the steps two at a time, and almost collided with Delta as she ran out of the guest room.

Delta and the sheriff stared at each other.

"I got here as soon as I could," Sheriff Schuyler said. She was out of breath.

Delta looked over the sheriff's shoulder, down the stairs. . . . The front door's lock had been splintered, the entire area around it bashed in. The door hung off at an odd angle, broken and sad, and mud was tracked all through the hallway. Delta could *feel* the Wild West's anger; it thrummed through the walls. It seeped from the floorboards into her own bones, filling her with hot fury, with terror. "They . . . they got in," she said. She glanced up at the sheriff, and then, without really knowing how it happened, threw herself into Ramona Schuyler's arms and burst into tears.

15

DELTA SAT AT HER

desk, braiding her hair into two Dutch braids down her back. She'd been awake since dawn, having barely slept the night before—how could she, with a broken door? Sheriff Schuyler had tried to insist on staying, but Delta had insisted just as fiercely that they were *fine*, and she had *overreacted*, and there was absolutely no reason the sheriff should stay in their house overnight. Finally Sheriff Schuyler had reluctantly acquiesced, leaving the property with stern promises that she'd come back the next day to check on them.

Starling had helped Delta and Bee push a large antique curio cabinet from the living room in front of the broken front door, but even so, Delta had lain awake almost all night, every creak or settle of the Wild West making her sit up straight in alarm.

The rain had tired itself out sometime in the night, and now everything was dew-soaked and soggy, but already the heat of another hot summer day in Darling was beginning to creep through her half-open window.

She finished the braid and looped a hair tie around the end, then stared down at her phone, at the name and number displayed there. Before she could talk herself out of it, she pressed call.

Tag picked up on the fifth ring, his voice groggy and full of sleep. "Hmm?"

"Hi," Delta replied. "Did I wake you up?"

There was a pause, and then Tag chuckled and said, "It's summer, Del, I'm allowed to sleep in. Anyways, what's up? You okay?"

"Why would you think I'm not?" Delta said. *Because you were at my house last night? Because you knew your dad was going to break in and didn't warn me?*

"Uh—because the only time you call me now is when something is wrong?"

Oh.

"Sorry," Delta said, heat rising in her cheeks.

"But *is* everything okay?"

Delta hesitated for only a moment before saying, "Not really."

"Need me to come over?"

"No!" The word came out too fierce, too strong. She'd been thinking only about Tag seeing Starling and the secret getting back to his father, but as soon as the *no* was out, it sounded barbed. "I didn't mean it like that," she said immediately, wincing. "I just mean . . . your dad was here last night."

There were rustlings on the other side of the line, as though Tag was sitting up in bed. When he next spoke, his voice was sharp enough to cut glass. "Excuse me? My *dad* was at your house? Why?"

Delta squeezed her eyes shut. She didn't know how to do this; she didn't know how to be friends—or anything more—with such huge secrets on her shoulders. Each conversation was a bramble patch full of thorns, just waiting for her to trip up. "I'm not really sure. There were a lot of people."

"*Why?*" Tag asked again, bemusement coloring his tone.

"I . . ." Delta squeezed her eyes shut even tighter. Tiny star-bursts of light exploded in the blackness on the back of her eyelids. When she opened them, the first thing she saw was the starling on her windowsill. It tapped its beak on the glass and then launched away into the sky with a rustle of feathers. She slid her gaze slowly to the mirror. Starling was reflected behind her, holding a half-drunk bottle of wine. His skin still glowed, although the weak sun shining in from outside made him appear dimmer than he had the night before, in the dark space beneath the bed.

But still otherworldly. Still a star.

It didn't scare her. Not at all, not one bit.

The sight of him there, filling up the doorway to her room with his pale, lit-from-within skin and swirling eyes and strange markings, made her whole body feel tense, like she was holding her breath at the sight of him.

"Tag?"

"Yeah?"

"I actually have to go."

"Oh. I'll ask my dad what he was doing at your house and let you know."

"No, no," Delta said hurriedly. Starling entered the room, coming to stand closer to her. "That's fine, don't ask him. It wasn't a big deal. I just . . . I really have to go. I'm sorry."

"It's fine?" Now Tag just sounded confused. His voice was right at her ear, and Starling moved closer and sat down across from her, perching on the edge of her bed.

"Bye," she murmured, quickly hanging up. She slid her gaze to Starling. "Hi."

Starling dipped his head in reply, eyeing her. She felt nervous under his scrutiny in a way she'd never felt nervous before—but it wasn't unpleasant. With Tag, she was always thinking. Every move he made, she analyzed; everything she did, she rehashed in her head for days afterward. Nothing seemed simple, but at the same time, she understood Tag.

It wasn't simple with Starling, either. But it was *different*. She didn't understand Starling, and this made everything all the more exciting. Was Starling staring at her because he found her interesting? Pretty? Ugly? Baffling? She didn't know; he just *stared*, and she felt bare under his black eyes. She was suddenly all too conscious of her bleary eyes and sharp angles and gaunt cheekbones that looked more and more sallow with each passing week. She couldn't help it; with each week that her dad was still gone, her appetite and sleep decreased while her anxiety and stress mounted. It wasn't the best of combinations. She was too conscious of the night before. Nothing had mattered in the moment then, not with people inside her house, searching. It hadn't mattered that she'd been nestled against him, that his lips had been at her hair as he spoke. But in the light of day, it was suddenly all she could think about.

"Tag," Starling said. "Your friend you mentioned last night."

"Yes," Delta agreed hesitantly.

"Were you telling him that I'm here?"

At this, Delta let out a short laugh. Starling had fallen into this town of secrets and shifting feelings and years of baggage and grudges and breakups. "No. Definitely not."

"And the woman? Will you tell the human about me?" Starling asked.

Delta knew that sometime today Sheriff Schuyler would want to have some kind of *talk* with her, a prospect that usually would have had her shaking. But Sheriff Schuyler hadn't insisted on looking into any rooms. She'd asked what the townspeople had been looking for, and when Delta mumbled an obviously false answer, she hadn't pressed the question again. And then she'd left, with no hovering, no forcefulness. Just a promise to check in later. Delta was feeling very gracious indeed toward Sheriff Schuyler, but she supposed it wasn't only her secret to keep.

"Not if you don't want me to."

Starling said nothing for a moment, then said, in the lowest of voices, "I will trust in your judgment on this."

"Mine?" Delta responded. At first she thought he was being sarcastic, and she followed up with, "Little human me?" But he wasn't laughing. He was just watching her, seriously, his dark eyes tracking every movement she made as if memorizing it. The memory of the night before once again came to the forefront of her mind: the way he'd grabbed her waist, hidden her under the bed, protected her. The way he said *You do not have to be frightened . . . I am here.* A fluttering began in her stomach, and she swallowed hard. Finally she glanced at him and simply said, "Thank you."

Starling looked uncomfortable with the thanks; he gave the tiniest dip of his head in acknowledgment, then cleared his throat and changed the subject. It was really very human of him.

"That is a book," Starling said matter-of-factly, gesturing with his spindly fingers to *Wuthering Heights*. "You can . . . what is the word—read?"

Delta's frown deepened. "Yes, I can read. Of course I can *read*." She paused. "Can you?"

"No," said Starling soberly. "I cannot. I can . . . I can communicate in a different way."

She waited, but he seemed content with that answer, as though he didn't realize how vague it was.

"Which is?" she prompted, curious now.

"I . . . project."

"Sorry, you what?"

"Project."

"I don't know what you mean."

"No," said Starling, and the smallest hint of a smile tugged at the corners of his lips. "I would not expect you to." He sighed and gestured toward her, a little flick of his thin wrist. "Come. I will show you."

"Oh," Delta said, suddenly very nervous, and not wanting at all to find out what *projection* was. "No, that's okay."

"Come," he said again, placing a hand on her bed, and despite herself, Delta crossed to her bed and sat down, clasping her fingers together in her lap.

"What now?" she asked.

"It might not work," he warned her. "I have obviously never tried this with a human."

"Okay," Delta repeated apprehensively, and braced herself for—what? There was nothing but silence at first, and then she felt something, a strange, crawling sensation in her mind. It felt like someone was trailing a finger gently up the back of her neck, and then suddenly the pressure mounted in her head and Starling's lispy, rasping voice spoke right into her mind, almost as if she was thinking the words herself: *Much better than your hieroglyphs, yes?*

"How did you do that?" Delta gasped.

"Astral projection," said Starling. "As I said." He lifted a shoulder in an approximation of a shrug. "You cannot do it. You are just a human."

Just a human. Her jaw tightened, but she forced a smile on her face. Last night she had thought that something might've changed in how Starling looked at her, in how he thought. But obviously it hadn't.

"We could have used that last night," she said. "When *they* were here." Starling's slight smile slid off his face. Had he been as terrified as she had been? It didn't seem possible . . . but he certainly wasn't smiling now. It made her want to look out the window again, to check for the hundredth time that morning that no one was returning for a second try at their home.

"I did not think speaking into your mind without warning would have gone over well."

She laughed weakly. *No, it wouldn't have.* "I guess you're right."

Suddenly Starling's rasp sounded in her head, *I will remember for next time, Delta Wilding.*

"I hope there isn't a *next time* of what happened last night," Delta began, then broke off, still a little shaken from having

Starling's voice wrapped inside her thoughts, as if it had always been there. He was still sitting next to her on the bed, but he felt closer now. It felt almost intimate, the way his words became tendrils of thought in her own head. She shook her head to try to dispel the feeling of having someone else's voice caressing her mind. "Anyways, you're missing out. Books are wonderful. Look." She held up *Wuthering Heights* and showed him the small words printed on the page. Heathcliff was just uttering his famous line: *I cannot live without my life! I cannot live without my soul!* "See the little signs? They tell a story. It's like . . . it's like magic."

Her book didn't seem quite so impressive after Starling had spoken words into her very brain, but he looked at it in apparent fascination anyways. She passed him the book and he flipped through it. The pages fluttered under his deft fingers.

"This is something that humans do?"

"Well, yeah," Delta replied. "We read, we write, we dance, we cook, we listen to music, we sing . . . There's thousands of things that humans do; no one thing to sum everyone up. There's no one way to be human. That's sort of the beauty of it, you know? That's sort of the point."

"The point?"

"Of living. We're all just here, doing our own things, and those things collectively are the *human* thing. I know you say we're all just tiny and stupid, but we're not. We're really not." She thought of the suspicious townspeople, of her flip-flopping feelings for Tag, of Bee pouting and narrowing her eyes, of everyone in the world who lived and made mistakes but not always. No, not always. Starling was, of course, a little bit right—compared to the universe, humans were insignificant. Silly little creatures. But they could also be magnificent.

And that's the point, Delta thought. She just had to find a way to make Starling realize it too.

She waited for the derision, the *stupid humans*, but when she looked at him, Starling met her gaze, his starry eyes fully bright, full of galaxies.

"Will you show me?"

"W-what?"

"Show me something the humans do."

"I thought you don't like humans."

"I . . . I don't," Starling said immediately, but his voice rose as though he wasn't sure.

There was a pause, and then Delta gave a hesitant smile. "Okay, then." She got off the bed and crossed to the bookshelf, crouching down to examine the books there, a collection of classics and favorites, a few nonfiction books on UFO sightings, and a pile of old school textbooks. "This shelf is all my books . . ." She ran her finger over the spines, then glanced back at him to see his reaction. "They're all written by other people. Other humans. They tell all kinds of stories."

He'd come over to kneel beside her. "I can try them?" he asked.

Her heart pounded. The alien wanted to read her books— surely there had never been anyone in the world who had been in the same position. "'Course you can," she said. "You can look at whatever you like."

He mimicked her movement and dragged a long finger over the spines of the books.

Delta pushed herself up and grabbed her phone dock from beside her bed, holding it under her arm. She felt almost giddy at the prospect of showing Starling human things, despite the fact that it wouldn't do much good. He thought he was better than humans, that much was clear. Looking at books or listening to music wouldn't change his mind.

But she could try.

"Come with me," she said, cocking her head toward the door. He followed silently behind her as she walked downstairs; she kept pausing to check he was still there.

She got down to the hallway and then hesitated. There was the closet door, glaring at her, waiting to be opened and checked. She hadn't looked inside since they'd rescued Starling from the woods. It called to her; it dragged her eyes toward it.

"What is in there?" she heard Starling ask quietly from near her shoulder.

She whirled around; he was close to her, and she watched as his eyes flicked up and down the door, then came to rest back on her. There was a strange look on his face as he stared at the door, as if he could see something she could not. Very deliberately, he stepped away.

"Not much now," she said. Should she tell him? Immediately another thought hit her: *Could he help?* After all, he was from the stars. If anyone knew how to find disappearing fathers, wouldn't it be the alien who fell from the sky? "But once . . . once it was a portal."

Starling's gaze sharpened; it was like being caught in a snare. Delta couldn't look away.

"What do you mean?" he asked.

"My father disappeared," she said simply, gesturing to the closed closet. "He walked into this closet and never came out again."

"When did this occur?"

"Two and a half months ago, now."

"Hmm." One of Starling's sharp teeth descended over his lower lip in concentration; Delta stared at it until he smiled a saber-toothed smile at her. She wasn't sure if it was meant to shock her, but she found herself fascinated, not scared, by the teeth inside those lips.

"I still check," she continued. "I still check all the time, but nothing is ever there." She brought her hand to the doorknob and was just about to turn it and open the door when Starling flung out a hand.

His eyes were wider than usual, his mouth in a frown. "No—no, do not."

"Why?" Delta asked, although she dropped her fingers from the cold bronze knob. When Starling didn't reply, she pressed, "Why not? Can you tell me anything about where he may have gone?"

"Your house," he said in a vague non-reply, "is very strange."

"I know," Delta whispered, trying to keep her hopes from rising.

"You are very strange."

She was used to being called strange: she heard it hissed from behind fences and across the grocery store aisle. She'd grown up having notes tossed onto her desk or shoved into her backpack at school: *freak* and *weird wilding* and, yes, *strange*. But somehow it sounded very different coming from Starling. He said the word almost reverently, cradling it and offering it out to her. *Strange*. Like it was something special.

A part of her wanted to ask him what he meant by it, if anything. His gaze had drifted back to the door.

"So?" she whispered.

Starling's brow was furrowed, something like indecision twisting his features. Then his face abruptly cleared and he stepped back. "No. I do not know."

Delta sighed, her hope deflating. "I guess it was a long shot." Swallowing back the rising disappointment inside, she led the way to the living room, where the early-morning light was streaming through the old windowpanes, illuminating the dust motes that swirled through the air. Delta had half expected to see her sister curled on the couch, but the room was empty; Bee must still be in her room. Delta couldn't help but be the tiniest bit relieved—this morning, she had Starling to herself.

Delta perched one of the speakers on the edge of the side table and pushed the battered wooden coffee table out of the way. Abby looked up from her spot on the couch, to survey the situation, then immediately settled her head back down onto the soft cushion.

"This is, uh, music," she said, feeling silly for announcing something so basic, so obvious, but as soon as she put on a playlist and turned the volume up loud enough that the sound vibrated through the wooden floorboards, she saw Starling's face change, and that was everything.

The playlist was full of songs that her dad used to play; he would turn the speakers up loud and blast his favorite classic rock anthems. He'd make them all dance with abandon until they were on the floor, out of breath and wheezing with laughter.

Starling was staring back and forth between the speakers and Delta as if she'd grabbed the moon out of the sky and held it out to him. "Music?" he repeated.

"And if you want, you can dance. It's something humans do." She regretted it as soon as she spoke; Starling's eyes got brighter and he demanded, "Dance? Show me."

"No," she said quickly. Dancing with her dad and Bee was one thing; dancing alone in front of an alien was another.

The alien crossed his arms and waited.

"*No,*" she said.

"Why not?"

"Because I'm embarrassed."

"Why?" he asked again.

Delta considered it. "I . . . don't know. Because people don't just start dancing, usually, especially when others are watching."

"If all music is like this," Starling said seriously, "then they should."

"Fine, fine," Delta said. "You sort of just . . . move." She started dancing, awkwardly stepping side to side and giving her arms a little wave. Her face was flaming, but Starling wasn't laughing. He watched her, entranced, and then mimicked her side-to-side step. The song ended and changed, and Delta turned up the volume knob even higher; she closed her eyes as the music swelled over her, and the familiar giddy feeling rose within her. Song after song burst through the speakers. She was just *moving*, letting her body move to the beat, and Starling was mimicking her every motion, every flick of her wrist or tilt of her head. A bright burst of laughter escaped from her lips—the kind of laugh she hadn't done in months, since her dad left—and then, so suddenly she thought she imagined it, *Starling* laughed too. He stopped immediately, his lips pressed tightly together and his eyes wide, as if he couldn't believe what he'd just done.

"You can laugh, you know," she said breathlessly as she twirled. "You don't have to pretend you're not having fun."

"I am *not* having *fun*," Starling replied automatically, sneering.

She rolled her eyes at him; he rolled his eyes back.

"What is that?" he asked.

"It means I think you're being a little bit stupid," she said.

"*Humans* are stupid," he said.

She just rolled her eyes at him again in response. He opened his mouth—she was sure he was about to snap back something snarky about how he was from the *universe* and so much *better*, when the song changed. Slower, synthy, a little sultry. It might've been that the dreamy music was so loud, it was crawling inside her brain, or maybe she just wasn't thinking straight, but Delta grabbed Starling's hand. His fingers folded around hers; his skin was very warm.

"What are you doing?" he asked immediately, standing still like he was cut from stone.

"Dancing," Delta said shortly.

"You are holding on to my hand."

Delta moved back and forth, dragging his hand around with her, ducking under it in an approximation of a twirl. "I'm aware." She gave him a quick smile. "You said you wanted to see what humans did. Come on, dance with me." When she pulled on his hand again, he stepped forward, taking her other hand in his, following her movements around the room. She could feel his breath on the top of her head, and as the song slowed, so did he, until his movements were sinuous. He slid one of his hands around her waist and she stepped closer, her heart thudding in time to the snapping of the drum.

"Delta?"

The music clicked off; Bee stood by the speakers, her hand hovering above the on/off button.

Delta and Starling broke apart; she realized too late, as Bee's eyes zeroed in on their hands, that their fingers were still intertwined. Delta dropped Starling's hand like it had suddenly burst into flames, and stepped away.

The sisters stared at each other as silence swept through the room.

Delta clenched her fingers nervously; she didn't like the way Bee was looking at her.

"We need to go to the grocery store. We'll need more food soon. And alcohol, although I have no idea how you're going to swing that."

"I'll figure something out," Delta said.

"Let's go," Bee said sternly. "Now."

"All right, fine," Delta agreed, if only to get Bee to stop staring at her like she'd just done some ultimate betrayal. She crossed to the mantel and opened the money box, a heaviness filling in her stomach as she saw how little money was left. A couple hundred dollars. That was it. That was everything. How long would that sustain them? She would have to get a job, but if she got a job in Darling, the truth about her father's disappearance would finally come out. . . .

She just didn't know what to do.

"Everything okay?" Bee asked, eyeing the money box.

Delta grabbed a couple of twenties and stuffed them into her back pocket. She attempted a smile. "Everything's fine." She crossed the room, glancing at Starling as she went. "We won't be too long, hopefully," she told him, then wavered in the doorway. "Feel free to read any of the books or listen to more music." She took a step into the hallway, only to hear Starling make a strange noise that might've been a throat clear. She paused, looked back.

His tall, gangly body looked oddly diminutive standing alone in the living room. "I thank you, Delta Wilding," Starling said, and Delta's heart clenched, her stomach filling with so many fluttering wings, she thought she might rise up and away.

And then, as Delta watched from the doorway, he turned the music back on and closed his eyes, his lashes thick and dark against his pale, gently glowing skin, and started to sway.

16

DELTA AND BEE
drove into town without speaking a word, the leaves of the tree-lined Main Street trembling in the breeze. Delta stared out the passenger-side window, reliving Starling's graceful movements and his hand on her waist. For a moment the memory morphed into another memory, of another's hand on her waist, and whirling around a grand room with another.

Worthless.

Whore.

Tag, walking away, not looking back.

Delta bit down on her lip, forcing away the memory and trying to get her mind to think of the exact weight of Starling's hand in hers. The way his body glimmered with light. The sheer impossibility of it all.

Bee's fingers were tight on the steering wheel, and she pulled into the tiny parking lot of the grocery store with a venomous spin of the wheel. There were three other cars already there, and Delta groaned as she saw the most ostentatious car in Darling parked in the weed-filled lot. Just as everyone in town knew the Wildings' truck—and stayed as far away from it as possible—everyone knew Tag's car as well.

Delta better than anyone.

Was Darling pulling strings? Did simply *thinking* of Tag make him suddenly appear wherever she went?

Not cool, Darling, she thought. The light outside the grocery store flickered, went out, and then flooded back to full brightness.

"Can I wait in the truck?"

"No," said Bee shortly, already halfway out. She clocked the Porsche and narrowed her eyes at Delta. "You're an adult, Del. Come *on.*"

I'm not, Delta thought desperately. *I'm really, really not.*

She'd give anything to not be the older sister right now. She'd give anything to not have to talk to Tag, not when she was so confused.

She frowned at Bee. Her sister frowned back.

"We'll go in there and you will talk to Tag like a nice, normal person. That's your *boyfriend.* Your real boyfriend."

Bee's eyes were still narrow and angry; Delta narrowed hers to match. What did Bee mean, *your* real *boyfriend?* Delta clenched her jaw, a flush creeping up her cheeks.

Bee continued, "You two can talk about what you'll be wearing to the Mayor's Ball."

Delta groaned. She'd completely forgotten about the Mayor's Ball and the fact that she'd agreed to be Tag's date. Although surely nothing could be worse than last year's events. *Okay, you can do this.* She slowly got out of the truck and faced Bee.

"I don't understand why you don't like him," Bee said.

"I do like him," Delta muttered.

"Then why aren't you dating him?"

"Because," Delta replied.

"That's not an answer."

"It's my business."

"I'm your sister."

"That doesn't mean I have to tell you about my relationships in the grocery store parking lot," Delta snapped, but the real reason was that she didn't *know* why she wasn't dating Tag again, and that was the problem. They'd just always been this way: up and down, back and forth. Tag was Darling in a boy's body, just without any of the magic that she knew was there. Tag was Main Street and the Diner; he was fluorescent lights and fancy wine and nights sitting on the hoods of cars in dark fields. He was late nights by the Wishing Well, and he was a song she'd heard from the time she was young. She knew the lyrics by heart. Tag was safe and unadventurous.

Not like Starling.

"He's nice." Bee sounded defensive on Tag's behalf.

"I didn't say he wasn't nice, I just . . ."

"Then *why*?"

"I don't *know*, okay?" Delta cried. Her voice echoed around the empty parking lot, and she bit back her next words, instead letting out a soft and clipped, "I won't talk about this anymore here. Let's just get this shopping over with."

Bee wasn't done. "He's cute," she insisted. "And he's *nice*, and he has a good heart . . ."

"A good heart? Jesus, Bee, maybe *you* should date him, then," huffed Delta, crossing her arms. Bee knew nothing of Tag's heart. *And do you?* The voice was small but insistent. Yes, she did. Of course she did. "Then you could stay in Darling forever and be the mayor's wife."

"I don't want to be the mayor's wife," Bee replied witheringly, but she smirked as she walked toward the smudged doors of the entrance to Darling Grocery. "I'd be the mayor."

Delta allowed a grin, but said, "Why are you suddenly so Team Tag?"

Bee shrugged. "I'm not Team Anyone." She smiled then, suddenly, and for a moment she was back to the normal, chipper Bee. Her smile was bright, but Delta was sure if she looked close enough, she could find the bite within it. "Team Delta, maybe."

"Well, Delta doesn't want to go to the Mayor's Ball with Tag," Delta grumbled, but followed Bee inside all the same.

Darling Grocery had black-and-white checked linoleum floors and harsh white paneled lighting that made blond hair glow with a green tint, and brown hair look grayish and dull. So Bee and Delta walked in looking peculiar, as if they were aliens themselves.

Judging from the sudden collective inhale from the few other shoppers, they were. The woman closest to them gripped the handle of her cart tightly, as though Delta might unexpectedly leap upon her, wild and untethered. From the nearest aisle, somewhere hidden behind stacks of off-brand cereal and loaves of plastic-wrapped bread, came a loud, sharp whisper, "The Wildings are here, Mom." And then there was the sound of a shopping cart trundling away.

Which of you were in my house last night? Delta glared around at the lot of them. They glared back, sharp and suspicious, and then glanced away as if they couldn't bear to look at the strange Wilding girls for long. A lump rose in her throat, and she swallowed it back down. This was how it had always been—her father said even before they'd been born, the town hadn't liked the strange Wilding couple holed up in their mysterious house.

The sisters had only thrown a few things into the basket when the inevitable occurred.

"Delta!"

She heard her name called from somewhere across the store, and Delta flinched, for a moment worrying she'd turn to see some dour-faced Darling citizen accusing her, like some sixteenth-century parody of being a witch. *Burn her at the stake!*

People got irrational in a town this small, and everything was easier when there was someone to push all the blame onto. The proof of it was in the broken locks on her front door.

But it was Tag who was coming down the aisle toward them, pushing a shopping cart with a broken, clattering wheel.

"Tag!" she said, trying to say the word as brightly and Bee-like as she could manage. Bee was looking at Tag brightly and Bee-like as well, and the look suited her much better.

"Hi, Tag! Delta and I were just talking about you," Bee said, her smile still blindingly brilliant. "I'll go grab what we need," she continued, taking hold of the cart and flouncing off into another aisle.

Delta and Tag stood facing each other. Delta was awkward and she couldn't tell what Tag felt—he looked a little blank, a little nervous.

"Talking about me?" Tag said finally. He was wearing jeans

and a flannel button-down that matched the floor of the gro-cery store. He was freshly shaved; Delta could see small cuts where he'd nicked himself with the razor, and his eyes looked sunken and tired. She knew her eyes looked similar—their apparent mutual exhaustion, Delta thought, was the one thing they had in common.

"Not really," Delta replied, and Tag flinched. She imme-diately wished she hadn't spoken; the words hadn't sounded awkward out loud, they had just sounded rude. "I mean," she amended, "we were just talking about the Mayor's Ball. And you . . . ah, you came up."

"Good things, I hope," he said softly. He wasn't looking at her; his shoes held all his interest. But he took a tiny shuffling step closer and reached out to catch at her fingers. His hand was warm and solid, nothing like the long, thin fingers of the alien waiting at home.

Delta's heart was in her throat; being this close to Tag made her want to both run out of the store and run into his arms at the exact same time.

"Tag . . ."

"Del, it's not weird if you don't make it weird," he said with a hesitant chuckle. He tugged on her fingers. "Look, come and give me a hug. You're the one who wanted things to be easy and simple again."

"Did I?" Delta murmured, but she let Tag pull her into a hug and within a few seconds, found herself relaxing in his familiar embrace.

"See? Simple."

"Simple," she repeated, her cheek against the softness of his shirt.

"I miss you, Delta," he said, his voice muffled, and Delta peeked up at him. His hair looked like it had been gelled at some point, but had been slept on wrong and now was a mess of crinkled blond, flickering green from the lights above. She was sure he'd slipped out of the Rockford estate before the mayor had seen him, because Tag certainly wouldn't be allowed to look so tired and faded and crumpled if his father had anything to say about it. Tag let his arms drop and Delta stepped back; as if a spell had been broken, they both laughed awkwardly and glanced away from each other.

"Oh—I meant to ask. What was this morning about? Why does my dad keep going to your house?" he asked.

"Ah," said Delta, her mind suddenly whirring, her smile frozen. What would be a good answer? She couldn't very well say *He needed to threaten me* or *He broke in to find what had fallen from the sky.* "He was just making sure Bee and I were okay. You know, after the earthquake."

"The earthquake." Tag nodded and his eyes went a little blank, as if he was thinking back on something. "Oh, well . . . I'm glad that he wanted to do that."

"That's all he wanted," Delta said, nodding along with Tag. She felt so sure Tag could tell she was lying, but he also seemed like *he* was lying. Did he know something about Starling? Did he know what his dad was doing? There wasn't a way she could really ask.

Another shopper came edging down the aisle, the woman's

face suspicious, her eyes narrowed as she looked between the mayor's son and Delta.

"Hello, Tag," she said stiffly, completely ignoring Delta. "Say hello to your mother, won't you?"

"Sure, Cara," Tag said easily, but as soon as the woman left, he lowered his voice. "These people are the worst."

Delta raised an eyebrow. "Yeah?"

"Well, I know that Cara hates my mom, and my entire family. And . . . how they treat you and Bee . . ." He trailed off awkwardly.

"Don't worry about it," Delta said. "Honestly. I'm used to it. It's okay."

"It's not okay," Tag said immediately, then sighed. "Anyways— I'm glad I ran into you. My parents are out of town for the weekend and I'm having a party. I hope you'll come."

"With people from school?"

"Yeah," said Tag with a wry smile.

"This from the boy who just said *these people are the worst?*" Delta half smiled; it felt good to joke around with Tag. It was like she'd almost forgotten how.

Tag's smile stayed plastered to his face, but his eyes were serious when he replied lightly, "I think you and I deal with being hated very differently."

Delta considered him. She knew Tag threw parties often, especially now that it was the summer and school was just a hazy memory, but she'd never given any thought to *why* he always planned a schedule of never-ending events at the Rockford place. She'd assumed that was just what Rockfords did.

Tag's unexpected admission almost—*almost*—made her want to say she'd go to his party . . . but spending any time at Tag's would just take away from spending time with Starling Rust, and she didn't want to leave Starling on his own any more than necessary.

"So, will you come?" he prompted.

"Come to what?" Bee's voice sounded cheerfully behind her, and Delta whirled around to see her sister with a shopping cart full of food and clothes. As one of the only stores in Darling, the grocery store was more of a one-stop shop, with a little section of used clothes at the back. Delta knew from the size of the flannels and length of the jeans that they weren't meant for her.

"Oh, I'm having a party!" Tag told her sister. Bee brightened visibly as Delta wilted. Of course Bee would reappear just in time to force Delta into going, whether Delta liked it or not.

"But we can't . . . ," Delta began, flashing her eyes at Bee.

Bee smiled innocently back. "Why?"

"We have that—thing."

"I don't remember a thing," Bee said. "What thing?"

"*The thing*," Delta hissed.

"Nope, I don't remember," said Bee. She gave Delta a *look*. "It will be fun to drink *alcohol*, won't it?"

Tag stared at them, his lips half-parted as if to ask what he was missing.

Delta bit her lip. She didn't want to leave Starling alone anymore, especially after last night. And she certainly couldn't bring him to a place crawling with the people of Darling. But they *did* need the alcohol.

Bee nudged Delta out of the way and beamed. "Thanks for the invite—we'll be there! Can't wait. What time?"

"As soon as you want to come over," said Tag happily. Bee just continued to beam. "People are coming as soon as my parents leave."

"Perfect!"

"See you then." Tag's white teeth gleamed in the paneled lights above. He flicked his gaze toward Delta. "See you, Del."

"See you," Bee sang out, and Delta muttered a *See you later* as Tag sauntered to the checkout counter with his shopping cart full of party-sized bags of chips and dip. Bee turned to Delta, slightly guiltily. "A party, woo!"

"Don't even start," snapped Delta, commandeering the shopping cart and pushing it toward the checkout counter. "What about . . ." She glanced around at the other shoppers nearby, who noticed her gaze and squirmed under it, unable to meet her eyes. Delta raised her eyebrows significantly.

"He'll be fine alone," said Bee with a casual shrug.

Delta lowered her voice to a whisper. "We can't leave him at the house for that long. What if *they* come back? Or the mayor? The sheriff said she'd be stopping by to check on us. What if she comes and there's no one there but *him*? What if something happens?"

"We can bring him, then."

"We most certainly *aren't* bringing him." What was Bee thinking? It was like she didn't even care. Delta knew Bee had been upstairs in her room when the townspeople had entered the house and hadn't experienced the terror firsthand, but *still*.

Was she not concerned for Starling's safety at all?

Bee sighed morosely. "You'll have to figure it out, then."

Delta sighed too, clenching her jaw against the tirade that threatened to spill from her lips. *Everything* was her responsibility. Everything came down to her judgment. Yes, she would have to figure it out, as she always did.

I think you and I deal with being hated very differently.

Tag threw his parties, and Delta retreated, step by step, back into the Wild West, away from prying, angry eyes, where she could shoulder the weight of the world alone.

17

ISN'T IT PRETTY TO

think so?

Reading was much better than he'd thought it would be. Starling lowered the novel, brows furrowed; he'd thought reading would be one more human thing that was utterly useless, but as soon as he'd picked up the book and leafed through its pages, the strange letters coalescing into words, he saw that what Delta had said about books was true. They were fascinating, with their shapes that became letters and their letters that became stories. He wasn't sure what Delta would think when she arrived home to find him fluent—no doubt she would pepper him with questions he couldn't remember the answers to. Or perhaps she would just watch him carefully, mouth ticked up in a small smile. Maybe she would tell him, *I knew you would understand.*

And he was beginning to. Because now he'd stroked the humans' pet and read their books. He'd watched the rain fall and sink deep into the earth. His body seemed so different now, too small for all the pounding his hearts were doing, too fragile for the onslaught of feelings he wasn't supposed to be able to feel. His head was full of Delta's dancing in the middle of the living room, joyful and unguarded in a way he'd never seen her before. The way she'd laughed out loud and shaken her shoulders and flung her hands in the air as she spun around and around. The way she'd grabbed his hand and pulled him close, her soft skin under his fingertips. Her eyes had been green and clear, like chips of glass.

And he'd found himself wanting to see all the human things that made her smile in such a way, see what made her eyes shine.

He tossed *The Sun Also Rises* onto the couch beside him; he'd already read through half the books in the top shelf of the bookshelf she'd shown him. He'd enjoyed each and every one, and a sick feeling crept through his body as he thought about wanting to read more, wanting to listen to more human songs, wanting to do more and see more and feel more. Another wave of guilt washed over him when he remembered speaking to Delta through astral projection. Her gaze had been so direct, so intrigued.

She'd been impressed.

And that was the problem: he'd wanted so much to impress her.

When he'd first fallen and first awoken, the only thing on his mind was finding his chain and using the energy it held to leave this world. But now . . . with all the excitement in the past few days, he'd been thoroughly focused on the humans. He hadn't once thought about leaving. All his extra power thrummed through one single chain—still lost—and as he'd told the Wildings, this energy could be used to leave, or stay. Because he could already feel his energy draining away; his glow was fading, and he couldn't stay long in Darling even if he wanted to—unless he found his chain.

He had thought he knew what humans were like.

But he was beginning to realize that humans were like nothing he'd ever believed. The Wildings were so full of feelings and emotions; he was sucked into their passion, their light. That, too, was nothing he'd ever experienced before, and he wanted more of it. He wanted to see Delta smile at him. He wanted her to tell him about her favorite books and songs. He wanted to hear her voice speak about her town, her family, her friends, her thoughts.

He wanted to . . . Starling shook his head. There were a lot of strange, wholly unexpected feelings flooding his body, and he wasn't used to a single one. Most of them revolved around Delta.

What to do? He was celestial, but he found himself at a complete loss.

He didn't want to tell Delta that it could never last. He didn't want to think it to himself. She knew he wasn't human, but she didn't grasp the true fleetingness of him. That he was ephemeral, temporary. He was nothing but motes of stardust, coalescing into matter.

There was something bright inside Delta—he could see it in her searching gaze, in the way the Wilding house responded to her moods. There was something within her that made flickers of energy arc between them when she brushed against him— not, of course, that she realized. She didn't even realize that the hallway closet she'd shown him this morning was brilliant with coiled energy. He could feel it even from behind the closed door—it was the reason he'd barked at her to not open it. Would the power inside react to him in some way? He didn't know, but the possibility was there, and standing so close to her, he'd been suddenly too afraid to try. If her father had found some way to harness the energy inside—well, no wonder he had disappeared into the unknown. Their entire house was a hotspot of thrumming energy and waiting power, and Delta stood at the center of it all, starry-eyed.

Yes, she was unique. Unordinary, certainly.

But she was still a human.

And yet he still didn't want to leave. Could there be some way to stay? Just for a while, just for now. It didn't have to be forever. He couldn't stay forever, not even close, because Delta Wilding couldn't fathom the length of it. Her life would pass in less than a blink of his eyes, a single beat of his treble hearts.

His indecision was eating away at him. Was this a human feeling, this guilt? This uncertainty?

He wanted to stay. He could not stay.

But wouldn't it be pretty to think so?

His hearts beat fast, disparate, *loud*. Too loud, too fast. He trembled. His whole body spasmed. Something was wrong—he wasn't just feeling sick with worry, with guilt, there was something *wrong* . . .

He looked down at his hands. They were gray, mottled. He looked at the bottle of the Earthlings' drink. It was empty. The sun shone through the dark bottle, illuminating the lack of sustenance. Empty. He couldn't remember when he'd finished it; it had been hours, at the very least.

Starling tensed up unwillingly. His throat was fire.

A choke, a spasm, and Starling collapsed, sliding off the edge of the couch until his legs splayed out on the floor. The book fell on top of him, pages fluttering in the sudden breeze of movement and coming to a stop just as Starling's eyes flickered close.

18

"I ALREADY SAID I

would try to figure it out," Delta told Bee as Bee maneuvered
their truck through the grasses bordering their house. Their
shopping trip had turned into a longer outing than Delta had
been wanting, ending with Bee begging desperately for some
Diner fries. Things already felt so weird and strained between
them that Delta hadn't had the heart to say no—and she didn't
want another argument—but as Bee sat and twirled a fry on her
fork, lazy and uncaring as anything, Delta got progressively
more agitated. Starling was at home, and who knew who was
there with him? Anyone could have seen them leave; anyone
could be there now. The sheriff had said she would stop by at
some point; Delta just hoped that Starling would have enough
sense to hide in his room if she did knock.

By the time she managed to get Bee back into the truck,
they'd been gone hours, and worry about Starling kept twining
its way into Delta's stomach, souring the Diner food there. The
sun was high in the sky above the Wild West.

"I just don't know why you're being so *horrible* about it!"

"I'm not being horrible," Delta replied, nettled. A to-go box
of fries for Starling sat on her lap. She couldn't wait to see his

reaction—his first time eating food. Another human experience for an otherworldly boy. "I just don't think it's a good idea, not with Starling."

Bee rolled her eyes. "If you won't come—fine. Can't I just go alone, then?" She threw the truck into park violently, the engine shuddering as she turned the key in the ignition.

"No."

"Why?"

"Because I'm not going to let my little sister go to a party alone."

"I'm sixteen, and everyone from school will be there."

"Well, you know how they are. They don't like us, Bee! I know you wish they did"—the words hovered on the edge of her tongue, *So do I*, but she didn't let them fall—"but they just don't."

"*Well*," Bee mimicked, then sank down under Delta's blazing gaze. "Tag will be there too. And Anders—he's always been cool."

"So?"

"So, I'll just hang out with them, and you'll know I'm safe."

"It's not gonna happen," Delta said.

"You're not my mom," growled Bee, her lips set in a firm, stubborn line.

Delta's stomach twisted. Did Bee think she didn't *know*? Did Bee think she didn't *realize* that she was not a mom, and not a dad, and not in any shape to be Bee's protector?

"This is just not a great time for a party," Delta tried to explain calmly, although she knew that once Bee got it in her head to be upset, she was not so easily swayed. "I can text Tag later and see if he can save a bottle or two for us—for Starling, but I'll make up some excuse. But it's not the time for us to go. You can see that, right? Not with random people *breaking into our house*, remember that?" Delta heard the driver's side door open and close with a metallic slam, and then Bee stormed around the front of the truck, her green eyes afire.

"I am sick of Starling ruining everything," she declared.

"You're being dramatic." Delta shook her head and unlocked the kitchen door. Bee barged inside, pushing past her sister like a battering ram.

"I want to go to a *party*, that's all, and—"

"We need to stay here with Starling! He's more important right now!"

The sisters glared at each other, both their arms crossed, two teams facing off.

"Everything's about Starling around here," muttered Bee.

"He's—an—alien!" Delta cried back, clapping her hands loudly alone with each word to accentuate her point. The claps echoed like gunshots in the still kitchen, the tiles reverberating each sound back to them. "Of course it is!"

"You just don't want to go because *Tag* invited you," sneered Bee, her eyes flashing.

Delta sucked in a breath, then let it out slowly. *Bee loves to talk about things she knows nothing about.* She remembered when she *would* tell Bee things about her and Tag, about their relationship. It hadn't been so long ago, but it seemed like eons. She felt light-years away from Bee now. They might as well have been on different planets as they stood there in the kitchen, arms crossed.

She kept a level gaze on her little sister and said measuredly, "That is not true at all."

"It is."

"It really, really isn't."

"Obviously it is, because otherwise you'd come with me and get alcohol for your precious alien."

"It's not about Tag!"

"Oh, of course," said Bee, and her voice was rising dramatically again. "It's about *Starling*!"

Delta knew exactly what Starling would say if he was watching this argument—something about how volatile and ridiculous it was the way human emotions fluctuated so easily: cold to bitter to angry to accepting, on and on. He would probably say something about—

In fact . . .

Where was Starling?

"Starling?" she called into the hallway as Bee threw her hands up in the air theatrically, as though telling the universe, *See? See how my sister is so focused on this alien?*

There was no answer.

Delta bolted for the living room, where she'd left him, a myriad of worries flooding through her: Had he gone without telling them? Had he been kidnapped? *No, no,* she told herself. *Don't be silly.* But it wasn't silly—it had almost happened. She remembered the glint of the mayor's eyes and the soft footsteps in shiny shoes from the night before. She had the feeling there was not much the mayor wouldn't do if it served his purpose.

No, no. Don't jump to conclusions. He was probably just sleeping. Or reading. Maybe he'd gone for a walk.

She skidded along the hallway, grabbing the doorframe to the living room and barging into the room, breathless.

Starling definitely had not gone for a walk.

He was half on, half off the couch, slumped in a pile of long, bare limbs, as though he'd tried to get off the cushions and failed miserably. Various books were scattered around him; *The Sun Also Rises* was splayed open on top of his body. His dark curls hung down in his face, and his head was lowered so that his chin touched his chest. He was still only wearing his pants, and without a shirt it was all the clearer that something was wrong. His skin, usually pale and golden-veined, was now the harsh gray of a stone quarry, and mottled with flecks of black.

"Starling?!" gasped Delta, rushing in and falling to her knees beside his unmoving body, tossing aside *The Sun Also Rises*. She placed a shaking hand on his chest, and almost collapsed in relief when his hearts moved rhythmically under his skin. "Oh, thank God. Starling? Are you . . ." She trailed off. He obviously wasn't okay, unless becoming rocklike and prone was normal for his species. She somehow doubted it.

He took a shallow breath, then tilted his head up toward her. His black eyes bored into hers. "Drink," he gasped.

"You need—okay, the wine? Where is the bottle you were drinking from?"

"Gone," he got out, his voice quiet and hissing out around her.

"What's happening to you?" Delta asked.

He hissed out something in his own language, then lolled his head back against the bed and managed, "Hydrate. Un—hydrate?"

"You're dehydrated? But you were just drinking this morning—"

"More," rasped Starling. His next breath rattled around in his lungs until Delta was sure she, too, could feel the slow decay of his body from lack of nutrients. How ignorant was she? How had she not thought to ask more questions—*better* questions? There she was, so excited by his very presence all she'd done was dance with him, and show him books and . . .

You're so stupid! she berated herself silently. She'd focused on all the unimportant things. Why hadn't she asked if he—if *stars*—digested things the same way? Why hadn't she asked how long he could go in this body without getting his fermented nutrients?

She had her answer now: not very long at all.

"Okay," she said, and picked up Starling's hand in her own. "Okay. We'll get you something. Don't worry."

Starling's eyes drifted closed. They opened again when Delta screamed, "Bee! Get in here!" but his gaze was unfocused.

She heard Bee's feet thundering down the hallway, and her sister whirled into the room. Delta saw her eyes widen as she took in Delta on the floor, one small hand holding the hand of Starling, stonelike and mottled and looking every inch on his deathbed.

"He's dehydrated," Delta blurted out, trying and failing to keep panic from edging in. "He—needs—right now—"

"The party!" said Bee suddenly.

"Enough about the damn party!" yelled Delta, the panic feeding her emotions. "He's dying!"

"No—Delta—come on! We *have* to go to the party, right now, people will already be there! We can grab him what he needs; I know you don't want to leave him, but—"

Delta took a deep breath, trying to push away the frenzy of dread that was rising in her throat. *Starling was dying.* She squeezed his cold hand in her own.

"I'm *not* leaving him. You go and get the alcohol and come back here and . . ."

Bee was looking past her, at Starling. "I don't think he can wait for that," she said, her voice suddenly very rational and, Delta thought, very Delta-like.

"We can't take him to the party," Delta replied, letting her scoff burn away some of her fear. "That's insane! That's the worst idea ever—"

"Sure we can," said Bee with a shrug. At Delta's glare, she amended, "And leave him in the truck, of course. He's not going anywhere. Look at him. We can just lay him down and cover his body with a blanket and no one will see him. You'll stay with him and I'll run in and grab some bottles. In and out. Starling saved."

Delta stared. When had her sister become more levelheaded in hot water than she was?

"O-okay," she stammered. There was nothing else to say. All her rational thoughts about why this was a bad, horrible idea flew out the window. Starling's hand, usually so warm, was very cold in hers.

Bee crossed the room and grabbed hold of Starling's feet, gesturing for Delta to take his wrists. "Looks like we have a party to get to."

19

BEE DROVE TO THE party, past quaking aspens all aflutter in rows of deep green. The afternoon sun was hanging in the sky, refusing to go down, and it shone into the truck's windows, making Bee's blond hair gleam and illuminating the horrible grayness that had taken hold of Starling's skin.

Delta sat next to her in the middle of the benchlike seat, with Starling slumped against her, his head rolling grotesquely, jolting down onto her shoulder bone with each bump of the wheels.

"It's going to be okay, Starling," Delta whispered to him when his head came down. She should have been tired—they'd had to carry him through the house, out the back door, and push his body into the truck—but adrenaline and fear were coursing through her. She couldn't stop her hands from shaking, even as she held his for some sort of reassurance. She doubted it was helping him at all, but feeling his pulses ticking slowly at his bony wrist made *her* feel better.

Starling made a noise that might've been an agreement.

"We're not going to let you die," she whispered, then repeated it, loudly, forcefully. Bee drove faster.

Starling didn't raise his head, didn't move, but she heard him softly rasp out, "I know."

There was a slight pressure on her fingers, like he was trying to squeeze them back.

Bee accelerated even more, careering through the mostly empty streets of Darling. They passed the Pepperhill B&B, the grocery store, and rows and rows of dilapidated Victorians. Bee's NASCAR-like driving soon put distance behind Darling proper as they shot out onto the empty stretch of road.

"The turnoff is coming up," Delta said.

"I know," Bee replied, taking the gravel exit at fifty miles an hour. Shale flew out from beneath the tires, and for once Delta said nothing about slowing down, or being careful.

Ahead of them, through the open wrought-iron gates, the palatial Rockford mansion rose up like some storybook castle, and although they couldn't see it yet, the sisters knew that just beyond the small hill covered in neat rows of grapevines was the smaller, though still considerably grand, guesthouse. Tag had been holding parties at the guesthouse whenever his parents were out of town since the age of fourteen. If the Rockford mansion was Tag Senior's domain, the guesthouse was the younger Tag's royal throne.

"Remember," said Delta as Bee slowed down slightly at the sight of the horde of cars parked in uneven, careless rows. "Go in, and be normal enough not to draw attention to yourself, but be quick."

There was a great rattling gasp from Starling.

"Very, *very* quick," amended Delta.

"I *know*," said Bee, parking the truck just as haphazardly as all the others and flinging the keys into Delta's lap. "I'll be quick." She met Delta's eyes. "I promise."

Then she was gone, skipping off in her heeled boots, the driver's side door slamming behind her. She glanced back once, and Delta saw the shimmery gold of her eye shadow reflected in the light thrown from the Rockfords' windows; then Bee turned away from the truck and hurried toward the shouts of laughter and drunken singing.

In the sudden quiet, broken only by his shallow breathing and the occasional closing of a car door followed by gravel crunching and loud voices of party newcomers, Delta reached over to Starling and edged the blanket up over his bare shoulders. She scooted over to the driver's side and carefully let Starling's body sink fully down onto the leather. He was so tall that his legs hung off the seat, folded up. She propped his head up on her right leg. If anyone looked toward the truck right now, Delta was certain all they would see was her.

Starling was so *still*. Delta couldn't tear her eyes away from his face. What had she done? Why couldn't she have been smarter? It seemed that despite all her adamant responses to the contrary, humans were just as stupid as Starling believed. Everything she should have done mounted slowly until her breath came in short gasps. *It's not your fault. Not your fault.* But it was. If she had just been *better* at this, they wouldn't be here right now.

And Starling wouldn't be dying.

She knew in a moment that's exactly what was happening. That whatever energy Starling was made of was draining away.

Maybe if they'd been able to find whatever strange *lost item* he kept talking about, that could've helped. But they hadn't, and this boy—this alien—was going to die in her truck.

No, no, no, no . . . She didn't know what to do. She'd never felt so helpless before. Delta glanced wildly through the windshield, but she couldn't see Bee. *Where was Bee?!*

With a shaking hand, Delta carefully brushed the messy curls off Starling's stonelike forehead. His skin was colder than ever now, and the feeling of it was just wrong. *Everything about this is wrong.*

I'm sorry, Starling. She wanted to launch herself out of the truck and get the alcohol herself, but she couldn't leave him.

She heard the running feet before she saw Bee, her sister careening full-tilt back toward their truck, various bottles clinking wildly against each other as she wove around parked cars. Delta had the door open before Bee even reached them, holding out her hands for the bottles.

It's not too late. It can't *be too late.*

Starling didn't move.

"Here, here!" Bee hissed, thrusting a vodka bottle at Delta and dumping the rest of her armful—multiple bottles of cheap gin, Two-Buck Chuck, and even a bottle of Fireball—onto the floor of the truck. There were two small cans of lemonade in the mix too, as if Bee wasn't sure if Starling needed a chaser.

"*Fireball?* Is that even fermented?" Delta's panic made her voice shrill; she felt a wave of hysteria coming over her.

"I don't *know*," Bee whisper-shrieked back. "*Sorry* I don't *know* these things!"

Delta grabbed the vodka bottle and opened it with a crack of breaking sealant. It was cheap stuff, and the sharp scent made her gag, but she just wrinkled her nose and brought a hand to rest on Starling's cheek.

"Starling? I have your—drink."

Starling didn't move. *Was he . . . was he . . . ?* She couldn't bear putting a hand to his chest, just in case.

"S-Starling?"

There was no answer. Hands shaking almost uncontrollably, Delta opened Starling's mouth and poured in a tiny bit of vodka. There was silence.

"Come on," Delta murmured, and her voice broke slightly as her adrenaline surged. She tipped a tiny bit more of the liquid into his mouth.

Silence—and then Starling coughed, and coughed, and coughed, and sat up slightly, grabbed the bottle from her hands, and drained the whole thing.

"More," he rasped, his voice a mere whisper.

She passed him a second bottle; this, too, was completely gone in seconds. Slowly, *too* slowly, the dark stone color of his skin began to fade to a gray-blue, and the black spots disappeared, replaced by the reappearance of crisscrossing, dimly glowing veins. He went through four of the bottles before breathing deeply, looking completely normal—well, completely *strange*, otherworldly—and resting his head back down on her leg.

"Oh my God," Delta said, the words coming out garbled. "*Oh my God.* Thank you, Bee." Bee's eyes were wide as she looked at Starling, but Delta couldn't read her expression. "Thank you," she said again, and she hoped Bee knew how much she meant it.

"It's fine," her sister finally mumbled.

"Did anyone see you come over here?" Delta raised her eyebrows at the stash of empty bottles on the floor.

Bee shook her head. "Don't worry, I didn't bring attention to myself. I told some random kid I would carry these over to the bonfire—and then I booked it up here. No one even saw."

"Good," Delta said faintly. It had been a close call. Too close.

Bee smiled, but this time it was a rigid smile, full of unsaid things. Her eyes kept darting to Starling, breathing slowly and laboriously, his head on Delta's lap. Her smile grew wider, but there were too many teeth and the edges were tight and forced. "It's . . . fine," she said again. "I'm . . . going back to the party now."

"What? No. Get in the truck."

"No."

"Bee—" Delta dropped her voice to a hiss. "Get in the truck! We have to get him home!"

"*No!*" Bee said, and this time the whisper left her voice. It was a shriek, full of bitterness, and the sisters stared at each other. Bee's cheeks were splotchy, her fingers clenching the side of the door. "Delta, just . . ." She took a deep breath. "Just stop, okay?"

Delta stilled, watching her sister closely, noticing how pale she was, how a wet sheen coated her eyes.

Bee's voice was very small and soft when she spoke again. "Right now all I want is to just go and talk with the girls in my class. With Tag, Anders, *anyone*. Talk about anything and everything, and *nothing* will have anything to do with aliens and stars, and pools of light and people breaking into our house, and Dad being gone . . ." Bee stopped and her eyes darted toward the ground, her voice distant.

Delta clenched her teeth together. She felt like maybe she'd done something very wrong—had been so wrapped up in all her decisions that she hadn't seen, or wanted to see, what Bee felt about it all. And she didn't know how to make Bee feel any better, not without making other choices that would hurt *others*. No matter what she did, someone got hurt.

"So stop acting like we're in this together. We're not." Bee's voice broke, and the tears that shimmered in the corners of her eyes broke free, dripping down her cheeks. She turned away.

"Bee—no, stay, let's talk—"

Starling gave a little jerk beside her, and two more kids Delta recognized from Darling Academy got out of their cars nearby. She grabbed the side of the door to pull it closed and shield Starling.

Bee gave a laugh that verged into hysterics. "Yeah, you obviously care about talking to me right now." She slammed the door shut and turned away without another word.

"Bee!" Delta said out the window, trying to stay quiet and call her sister back. "Get *over* here!"

"No!"

"I'm not leaving until you get in the truck!" It sounded so harsh when she said it; as soon as the words fell from her lips, she winced. Just as every choice she made was somehow wrong, everything she said to Bee came out mean and angry, no matter how she meant it. It was like her tone twisted itself in midair into something else.

"Then . . ." Bee spread her hands. She had a smile plastered on her face now, but it was brittle. "Enjoy your night in the parking lot."

"Bee!"

Crunching footsteps sounded as Bee walked hurriedly away, wiping her face, until she crested the hill and Delta could no longer see her.

Delta rested her head back against the headrest, squeezing her eyes shut. She wanted to get out of the truck and follow her sister and *force* them to talk it out, but she couldn't leave Starling alone. She also couldn't leave Tag's house, though—not yet. Bee had no way home, and Delta was still hoping her sister would return any moment, sad and sorry and ready for a hug.

She opened her eyes and glanced down at Starling. His eyes were open too and stayed open, and Delta met his gaze full on.

Starling's eyes had worlds inside them, but his voice was soft and raspy when he spoke. "You are shaking."

"I know," said Delta. The words came out strangled. Then: "Bee hates me, and I thought you were dying."

"Your sister does not hate you."

"Oh, because you're such an expert on humans now?"

Starling quirked an eyebrow up.

Delta sighed. "Sorry."

"I *was* dying, however," said Starling softly. Then, even quieter, "Thank you, Delta Wilding."

"It was nothing," Delta said quickly, even though it *had* been something; it had been agonizing minutes of racing through town and pumping adrenaline and a head aching with worries.

He stared up at her. Her heart stuttered, jumping into the race.

"I should have asked how often you needed your drink," Delta said in a rush. "I assumed you were like humans, who can go days without drinking and I just—I'm sorry."

"You saved my life," said Starling. "Twice, now. There is nothing to be sorry about."

He closed his eyes.

"Starling?"

"Yes?"

Delta kept her eyes trained on the glittering lights of the Rockford mansion, at the shadowy forms of partygoers raucously running toward the guesthouse. Somewhere down amongst the people and the lights and music, Tag was there. He'd never felt so far away.

Starling was quiet. He gazed up at her for a moment, and then his dark orb-eyes flicked away.

There was so much she wanted to say, but she kept her voice light and easy. "I can see why you would hate it here. . . . You haven't really had the proper Earth welcome, have you? I mean, you've been dragged through the woods, you've hidden behind trees and under the bed. And now here you are at a party, hiding in a truck, after you almost died. Welcome to Earth, right?"

"I do not hate it, Delta."

"But you said . . ."

"I know what I said," Starling cut her off, his voice a mere rasp. He turned his head, broke eye contact. His curls splayed out across her leg, and Delta had the sudden impulse to run her hands through the soft strands.

She studied him instead. He was handsome—despite his few alien features, most of the time he simply looked like a decidedly good-looking boy. It was only when he stared at her with galactic eyes or smiled wide enough that his vampiric canines were on show that she remembered the startling *otherness* of him. But she couldn't help that she was intrigued by him, fascinated.

But it's not just that, is it? The thought came unbidden. No, she wasn't just intrigued. There was some strange sort of attraction there, and she couldn't help it. Her stomach squirmed, but she couldn't put it at bay. What was attraction, anyways? Chemicals? Features? She didn't know. All she knew was that he'd come to Earth and changed her entire world, and there was something about the way he moved, the way he looked at her. It was the energy that ran through him, the energy that showed in the golden gleam of his skin. Yes. It attracted her. Again the impulse came to touch his palm, his hair. To have some of his glow rub off onto her. To remind herself it was all real.

"Starling?"

"Yes?"

"What were you looking for, in the woods?"

She couldn't read his expression. His lips tightened in the corners, and then he flicked his gaze away, shifting on her lap to reach down and get another bottle.

"I promise I won't tell," she said, chewing on her bottom lip. Her eyes drifted to the window; night had finally fallen, and there were only the occasional partygoers who made their way from the mass of cars down to the guesthouse. The music was far enough away to fade to a quiet pounding in the background, a soundtrack over her life.

"It is a chain," Starling murmured. "A chain imbued with all my remaining energy—everything I would require to leave this place."

"Oh," Delta said, digesting this new information. Her thoughts caught on what he'd said in the woods, and she said, "Or stay."

"Or stay," Starling said, drawing out each word, as if he was picking them carefully. "I must find it soon, either way. It gives me energy." He held his arm out, turning it so his glowing veins shone up at them. "They are not as bright as when I first arrived. They will continue to fade. This place is a drain on my energy."

"We'll find it, I promise," Delta said, her voice loud in the darkness of the truck. She had just saved his life; she wasn't going to let him fade away.

Starling didn't answer, but he tilted his head toward her, his black eyes reflecting the dim light from outside. She couldn't read his expression as he studied her.

A strange intimacy flooded the truck; Delta was suddenly very aware that there was no one around but them. The party might've been a million miles away. "So you don't hate it here anymore? Who knew I was such a good dancer?" she said with a laugh, her hopes two-edged: a part of her wanted to diffuse the thick air with some lighthearted, throwaway comment, and the other part hoped Starling would continue the conversation. That this morning had meant something to him, too.

"Hmm." Starling made a noise in his throat, and Delta's face flushed; somehow the small *hmm* as he'd looked up at her had been worth a thousand words. She saw him visibly swallow, his throat moving, and then he held up the bottle and said, "Would you like some?"

Delta hesitated. "No," she said finally. "I'll have to drive us home. Anyways—if I drank, then you'd have to put up with a silly human."

"Ah," Starling said. "You would reveal all your secrets to me?"

"Maybe," Delta laughed. *Her secrets.* What were her secrets? That the weight of her dad disappearing didn't seem quite as heavy with something new to focus her energy on? That she didn't feel so alone with Starling here? That she was glad Starling's distrust of humans—of her—was beginning to slowly drain away? She put her arms down, one against the door and the other on her lap, just brushing the cool skin at the alien's shoulder. Electricity tingled at her fingertips. "Maybe if you're lucky. And will you reveal yours?"

He cocked his head up to meet her gaze directly, his orb-eyes depthless, and then lifted his hand to brush back an escaped lock of her hair with his long fingers. She stilled. The movement had shifted the blanket, and the blue tint of his skin was visible in the faint illumination from the windows of the Rockford house. His smooth flesh was cool on her suddenly hot cheek.

"No," he whispered. But he smiled, and even his wolf-sharp teeth didn't scare her.

20

THE PARTY WAS IN full swing. Tag had spent all day hanging twinkly lights on the eaves of the guesthouse and lugging cases of beer and spirits out of the Rockford cellar and onto the grass down by the vineyards.

But now the decorating was finished, and the guests were arriving, and although Tag was technically ready, he just felt so restless. Unmoored. He'd thrown himself into the decorating; he'd raided the neatly labeled boxes of Christmas decorations, and it had given his mind a welcome break from his father yelling and mother crying before they'd both stormed out of the house and left him alone with ringing silence. He'd gone a little overboard, unwilling to stop moving for a single second, and now strings of gleaming Christmas lights were hung on every bush, looped around every tree trunk, and draped over every surface it was possible to attach them to. It looked magical with everything alight. It was perfect, except for the fact that Tag would rather be anywhere else.

"Hey, Tag!"

"Hey, where's the keg?"

"I think I'm blocking someone's car, so if you're the shitty Corolla, let me know—"

Tag let the raucous laughter carry him like a wave, off the porch of the guesthouse, into the fray. He could do this. This is what he *did*. Smile, smile, shake someone's hand, smile, give a little captain's salute to the baseball team, smile, smile, *smile*. This was his life.

And he was good at it—too good at it, really. He realized that now. He'd hidden his self-awareness so far down for so many years that now there was barely any separation between Tag Rockford, the Mayor's Son, and just . . . Tag. The person he was inside. The only person who could see that Tag was . . . himself.

Tag sighed as he grabbed a beer from the Christmas-light-wrapped icebox and cracked the metal tab open with an audible pop. He could enjoy this; he just had to do what he did every other party, and drink until he didn't remember that everyone only came for the free booze, and almost all the people here actively disliked his family, and by proxy, him.

The sip of hoppy IPA turned sour in his stomach. He suddenly, desperately wanted to be alone, or at least somewhere away from the stares and the curling lips. Most of Darling now disliked the Rockfords in their giant house on the edge of town so much that they didn't even bother trying to hide it anymore; even the two seniors who had hung out with him and Anders at the Wishing Well now shot daggers at him. He walked by a group of girls; half of them glared while the other half giggled flirtatiously. One of them whispered to her friend as he walked by, the words cutting through the music easily: "Stop smiling at him, Hannah, I know he's hot but—I swear to God, he's such a privileged brat. Allison told me last week that—"

Tag's jaw tightened, but he continued walking, sliding into the darkness at the side of the guesthouse. He didn't want to know what Allison had said about him. *Come for the free beer, stay for the insults.* That should be the tagline of a Rockford party, he thought bitterly, edging into a patch of shadow and slumping down in the grass. At least here he could look up at the open sky, awash with stars. Here he could hopefully hide from his peers.

Maybe he *did* come across as conceited. *Maybe that's why Delta doesn't like me anymore,* he thought morosely. From his spot in the shadows, he saw Anders loping casually down the slope toward him. The lights from the party lit him up as though he was in a spotlight; he was certainly dressed as if he was onstage in a full-on suit. He was all the best things in life: confident, witty, kind. He was unapologetically himself. Tag wished he could be more like his best friend, instead of being slowly crushed under crippling parental pressure and disappointment and the steely eyes of his father. Everyone Tag was surrounded by seemed to know exactly who they were—Anders, the Wildings, his parents. Meanwhile he sank deeper and deeper into the depths of Rockfordness, and the waters were getting murky.

"Anders!" Tag whisper-called from his hiding spot as Anders passed. Anders stopped, walked back a couple of steps, and then grinned. He furtively slipped around the side of the house and joined Tag.

"Hey, man. Why are you, uh, hiding?"

"Because I can't stand these people," Tag said, his voice low. He cringed as soon as the truth was out, but Anders's dark eyes just roved over his face in a knowing sort of way.

"You're the one who invited them."

Tag groaned. "What was I thinking? They're the worst."

"They don't like you much either," Anders replied, a small smile on his face.

Tag's jaw tightened. "Yeah, so I've been hearing."

Anders's expression turned sympathetic. "People suck sometimes."

"Yeah, they do," Tag sighed. *Privileged brat.* He tried to shake away the words. They weren't as bad as *worthless.* They weren't as bad as *You're a disgrace to the Rockford family.*

You're a Rockford—act like one. But Tag was so tired of trying.

"You don't, though," Tag added.

"I know," Anders replied, his smile returning full force. "That's why I'm escaping this place in, what is it, two months?"

"And leaving me here in Darling to rust with the rest of these people," Tag said, but he couldn't help but smile back.

"It's your own fault," Anders said airily. "I did *tell* you to apply to college."

Tag sighed. "I know, I know." He'd never really made the choice to not go to college—not yet, at least—and in not making the choice, he'd missed all deadlines and the choice had been made for him. Tag had had a huge blowup with his father when he finally admitted that he wasn't following through with the Rockford expectation of an Ivy League education. It had felt so good at the time to yell at his father in righteous anger, to do something a *different* way. But now everyone would soon leave Darling and he would remain, stuck and alone.

He shook away the thought. That time wasn't here yet; they

still had months of summer. And as long as he could hide away with Anders, maybe this night wouldn't be so horrible after all.

He cleared his throat. "Anyways. Did you see Delta around?"

Anders's dark eyebrow quirked up. "No, but I think I saw her little sister."

"Where?"

Anders shrugged and waved a hand toward the party. "Out there. She was just wandering around, looking weird and moody." He cracked a smile. "Typical Wilding behavior, right?"

"Not you, too."

Anders shook his head in reply and smiled. "No, I don't mind her—you know I don't. I've spent enough time with the both of you over the years. I *definitely* don't believe that the Wildings are, like, *witches,* or whatever weird superstitious shit this town believes about them. It's ridiculous."

"Yeah," Tag replied, taking a long swig of beer. The can's condensation dripped down onto his fingers. "My dad believes that, I think."

"*No* he does not."

"Yeah, for real. Something like that, at least. It's always a fun time when your dad hates your girlfriend."

Anders raised an eyebrow at him again. "*Is* she still your girlfriend, though?"

"Yeah," Tag said, but his following sigh undercut the sentiment.

"You never really told me what—"

"Things just got . . . complicated. I don't know."

"You need to forget about her, dude."

Tag dropped his head back, leaning it against the solid wood of the guesthouse wall. The Christmas lights blurred into pinpricks of red and gold and blue and green, drowning out the faint stars above. "I can't," he said. It sounded more like a groan than anything else.

They watched people drunkenly gyrate to some years-old dance song that reminded Tag of the seventh grade.

"I know," Anders said finally, slapping his hand on Tag's shoulder. "And that sucks." He shook his head, and then his voice turned bracing. "Come on, come hang out with me and Colson." He waved a hand toward the party. The dancing people all took shots from Solo cups, half the liquid spilling out of the red cups onto their chests as they bellowed into the night. Through the haze of smoke and Christmas lights, Tag caught a flash of blond hair.

Bee.

Where Bee was, Delta usually followed.

"I'll find you and Col later, okay?" Tag said.

Anders held up his cup in a little salute and then trooped off to mingle in the crowd. Tag circumvented the group, staying to the edges, dodging drunken couples who were stumbling away from the party. Bee was in the shadows, standing alone on the fringes of the crowd, her arms crossed tightly over her chest, a cup in her hand. She stared at the firepit nearby, the reflected flames dancing in her eyes.

Tag hesitated, uncertain. Bee didn't look like she wanted anyone to talk to her, and despite what everyone seemed to think about him, Tag did not actually *try* to be bothersome.

But still . . . he wanted to talk to Delta. Where better than to have a non-awkward talk, just like old times, than at a Rockford party? If he and Delta could just sit down together by the firepit with a beer each as the music drifted over them, he knew he could make her understand how much he wanted to make things work.

He knew Delta still harbored a grudge because of last year's Mayor's Ball, and he didn't blame her—that had been a low point for him.

But maybe he could get Delta to understand what it was like to grow up with Tag Senior. Tag's heart jumped into anxious overdrive at the mere thought of his father.

Worthless. You're a disgrace. In the moment, everything had gone strangely blank, his father's words echoing around in the chambers of his mind. He'd slid off the car and followed his father before he'd really realized what he was doing, as though his feet were walking of their own accord. And by then it had been too late. He'd ruined everything. Everything had fallen apart afterward, and each attempt at talking seemed to make it worse.

Now was his chance to find Delta and have that talk, the one that would fix it all.

He hurried over to Bee.

"Bee, hey!" He tried to keep his voice light and polite: the Rockford way.

"Oh—hey, Tag!" Bee's voice, too, was equally light, but there was a tightness there, as though each word was carefully said around a lump in her throat. Now that he was closer to her, it looked like she'd been crying.

"Is Delta around?"

"Um, no."

Well, that was a lie. Bee's eyes darted around as if she could somehow disappear.

"She doesn't want to see me, is that it?"

"No! Honestly . . ." He couldn't read Bee's expression anymore, but something in it hardened. "She's somewhere around. I don't—I don't know where she is now."

"Oh," he said, disappointed. "Is she down here?" He glanced around at the people dancing and laughing raucously around them.

"I don't know," Bee answered again, her voice almost a monotone now. For the tiniest moment, her eyes darted to the gravelly walkway up to the parking lot, and then she was staring at the ground so quickly, Tag thought he might've imagined the first look.

But he wasn't imagining her watery eyes.

"Hey . . ." Tag swallowed. "Are you . . . okay?"

"Yeah," Bee answered dully, her voice muffled as she kept her head down.

Tag had used that same *yeah* in that same tone often enough to know it was a lie. "Sure?"

"I got in a fight with my sister," she whispered back.

"Been there," Tag said wryly, and his dryness worked—just as he hoped, Bee gave a choked snort of laughter and wiped her eyes with the back of her hand, finally glancing up at him. Tag gave her a hesitant half smile. "You guys will make up. In the meantime—go get a drink, everyone is down by the guesthouse."

Bee shifted from foot to foot. She opened her mouth to say something, but then shook her head. "Thanks, Tag. I will. Are you coming too?"

"I . . ." He sighed. "I really don't even want to be here right now. At my own party. How sad is that." He waved a hand toward the lights and music. "It's just . . ." He couldn't think of a word to describe the tightness in his chest, or the way all the lights blurred together. The way the music twisted itself into something too loud. So he finished with a feeble, ". . . a lot."

To his surprise, Bee nodded, her eyes faraway for a moment. "Yeah, I get that."

She gave a little wave as she sidestepped him and returned to the party. He saw the change come over her as she moved into the crowd: her shoulders straightened, and she threw back her hair as if readying herself for battle. She smiled; Tag could see the light reflecting off her grin.

Tag sighed again. He wished he was still able to do that, to put up his shield and plaster on a throwaway smile and pretend it was all okay. Now he just wanted to go to sleep.

He turned and walked toward the parking lot. No one even glanced his way. The ornate porch light of his house past the rows of cars beckoned him with the promise of a soft bed and a dark, quiet room.

He trudged away from the Christmas lights of the party, winding his way between cars, and then—he stopped in his tracks. There was the Wildings' rusty, dilapidated Ford, clearly the oldest car here. It was parked sideways at the back of the lot, as though they'd driven up haphazardly, in a rush. There wasn't a lot of light to see by, but Tag saw the shadow of movement from inside; the sweep of Delta's long brown hair as she leaned forward.

Delta. She had come to the party; she was here. Finally, he could talk to her without anyone else nearby. This is what they needed. The two of them needed to sit and talk in the darkness, where the truth fell easier between them.

This was the night when things would change—he knew it. Everything up until now had been such an uphill battle, but he didn't want to quit. If he could only make Delta see that he'd made a mistake . . .

If only he could get her to understand he wasn't the person she seemed to believe he was. Delta lived in shades of gray, but when it came to how she felt about him, everything was black or white. They were going strong or they weren't going at all. He was an angel or a monster. She loved him or she didn't.

He gritted his teeth and wove around the carelessly parked cars of careless kids. He could do this. He was Tag Rockford, and he wanted to make that name mean something new, something better, something *good*. A name—a person—Delta wanted.

Delta grew clearer as he got closer to her truck—he was only fifteen feet away when she looked up and saw him coming closer.

Their eyes met, green and blue.

The look on her face made him physically recoil. It was pure, undiluted fear that, when it was obvious she recognized him there, turned to a high-grade anxiety.

What was going on?

And then he saw it: *something moved*. A body shifted, and Tag caught a glimpse of dark hair and pale fingers before he saw Delta hiss something, panicked, and the body—the boy—ducked back out of view.

A boy.

Of course. It was so obvious. He was so *stupid*. He felt an embarrassed, angry flush start in his toes and begin to rise. All this time he had been throwing himself at Delta: apologizing, calling, texting, doing anything he could to fix them.

And she'd pushed him away, time and time again. Even the times she'd called *him* in the middle of the night, whispering that she missed him, that she wanted to try . . . she'd sounded confused even then, as if she couldn't quite believe what she was saying. And now he knew why.

He was a fool.

He was so, so stupid.

He felt sick to his stomach; half of him wanted to run and pretend this never happened; the other half wanted to hear what Delta had to say for herself. All this time, and she'd never once mentioned another boy.

Worthless.

Tag crossed his arms, his heart hammering in his chest, and waited for Delta to get out of the truck.

21

DELTA HAD ALWAYS dreamed strange dreams: she'd imagined that the lights on the hillside were descending, calling to her, taking her away to the far-off reaches of the universe, and farther.

She never once imagined the lights on the hillside would descend and stay. There are some things dreams can never prepare you for, and this was one of them.

This was her burden, her delight. Sitting in the truck with Starling had seemed almost unreal, with his head on her lap, his soft, dark curls spreading out like a blanket over her jeans. Her single heartbeat jumped in sync with one of his, keeping up a frantic pace. And then she'd broken the eye contact and looked out.

Looked out to see Tag Rockford's light blue, searching eyes staring right back at her.

The panic had hit her immediately, almost before her eyes could make sense of what she was seeing. *Tag. Standing there. Staring at me.* Her adrenaline ratcheted up, and her first thought was to just throw the truck into drive and *go*. But knowing Tag, he would follow. He stumbled back from her, reacting to her expression, and it was this that made the frenzied alarm recede somewhat, leaving her brain slightly clearer.

She couldn't let Tag see Starling, but she also couldn't ignore the broken look on his face. She felt torn in two directions, both boys needing something from her, and she didn't know which way to turn.

But doing nothing would be worse. So she opened the truck door, just the tiniest crack, and slid her body out. She would try to calm him, try to placate him—*I do want to talk, now is just not a great time*—and they stood facing each other with arms crossed.

Tag's entire body was stiff and tense. He let out a sharp breath, then turned eyes accusingly toward her. "Who's in there?"

"No one," she said. *Damn it, Starling, why did you look out?!* Obviously Tag had seen Starling through the window, although he couldn't have gotten a great look or surely he'd be freaking out more. This was the reaction of a boy finding another boy in his on-off-again girlfriend's truck, not the reaction of the Rockford heir finding an alien. Delta supposed she didn't *really* know what that reaction would be, but she could imagine.

She couldn't let the Rockfords near Starling.

But it seemed Tag had other ideas. His gaze was set, focused. "There's someone in there," he continued. "What the hell, Delta? Why—just—why didn't you tell me?"

"There's no one," she repeated. "There isn't anyone."

Tag's eyes went flinty. *He is just like his father.* She knew it wasn't completely fair, but the minute his eyes went hard, Tag Senior was all she could see. However, when he spoke, his voice was far from angry. He just sounded drained, as though all the power and energy and soul of him had seeped onto the gravel at his feet. And *hurt* was all that remained. "Why are you lying to me?" he asked. He sounded so detached. She'd never heard him speak like this before—he seemed as exhausted as she felt.

He was supposed to be like a Rockford. That's the only Tag she knew—the only Tag she *let* herself know.

She was about to respond with another lie—*I'm not*—but Tag just shook his head and continued, "Why won't you just tell me the truth? What, I don't even deserve that?"

Delta looked down at her feet; it was easier than Tag's deep-set blue eyes. His very presence made her feel so conflicted: angry and sad and in love and awkward, all at once.

It doesn't matter what you feel. You have to protect Starling. She took a deep breath, pulling her mind back to what was important. Not Tag, not this party, not any sort of high school drama. *Starling.* That was all; that was everything.

She had to get out of here before she did something stupid, like tell a Rockford her secret.

"It's just a family friend," she said, trying very hard to stay casual. "He's lying down. He had too much to drink."

Tag gave a derisive snort. "Yeah, okay. I'm not stupid, Delta."

"I never said you were stupid." She felt tears come to her eyes in a head rush of emotions: she *hated* this, and the truth was on her tongue. No matter what she did, someone would get hurt. She couldn't tell Tag about Starling, but not telling Tag was somehow breaking her heart. She'd never have expected it.

"Well, you obviously think I am. There's a boy in your truck and you're pretending it's a family friend? Are you serious?"

"Just drop it, Tag!"

"Why wouldn't you *tell* me if you were seeing someone else? You just let me keep throwing myself at you like an idiot?"

"I don't think you're an idiot!" Tears had begun to spill over her cheeks; Delta brushed them away, staring beseechingly at Tag from beneath a veil of salt water. "I just didn't—" *Trust you.* The words were on the tip of her tongue, but she let them drop and instead said, "I didn't want to hurt you."

She could see Tag visibly shaking; his fingers were trembling, his face pinched. He looked like he was about to cry, something she'd never seen him do. A part of her didn't even think he *could* cry: that was Tag, always stoic, always detached, always polite.

"Too late."

"Tag . . ." She moved forward, hesitantly, reaching out to touch his arm. "Tag?"

"I don't care, Delta." She knew it was a lie; they both did. He jerked his arm out from under her fingertips and turned away. "You could've said something, though. What, were you just planning on having me show up for the Mayor's Ball and *then* tell me you're dating someone else now?"

"That's not—no!"

"I should've expected this, I guess." He let out a harsh laugh. "God, I'm stupid."

"Tag," she repeated helplessly, holding on to his name like a lifeline, as if he would hear it and realize that she was drowning in indecision.

"I'm over this, Del. You know how I feel. And I . . . I know how you feel." He gave a strange, tight smile, a smile that could give Bee's loaded smiles a run for their money.

"You know what, whenever my dad said to stay away from you, I never listened. Never." His smile twisted. "But maybe he was right."

Delta stumbled back as if he'd physically pushed her away. *"Tag."* It was a gasp. He didn't mean it. *He couldn't mean it.* She waited for him to take it back, to apologize. But he didn't.

Instead, he turned away, his hands shoved deep in his pockets. Gravel crunched loudly with each step as he walked away.

A whisper of cold wind curled around Delta and she shivered. The want to call him back, to run after him, was pulling at her fingers. The lights of the party backlit Tag, and he disappeared over the crest of the slope.

Delta waited a moment for him to reappear. He always did; that was Tag's *thing*. They fought, and they said things they half meant, and then Tag always came back.

The music from the party echoed up from the guesthouse. Delta shivered in the night air, her throat clogging up with tears. Then she turned and walked woodenly to the truck, sliding in beside Starling without another look back at the party's lights.

"Your friend Tag?" Starling asked.

"Well." Delta forced out a bitter laugh. "I doubt he'd agree to that anymore. Just add him to the list of people who hate me now."

"I do not hate you," Starling said quietly.

Delta's heart was in her throat, squeezing all the air out. She'd wanted Starling all to herself. No prying eyes, no leading questions. No hometown boys who made her teeth clench and her heart constrict.

She'd wanted Starling to trust her, and she'd done it. And if in doing so, she'd built walls up against the only other two people in her life—so what? She and Bee could make up later, and Tag? Her feelings were always all over the map with him. She bit down all other feelings except that flutter in her chest that informed her that Starling was looking at her with a measured expression, and there was no distrust or disgust there at all. But still they didn't speak; the air was so charged, Delta could have cut it with a knife.

She texted Bee, staring hard at her screen and trying to blink away the tears before Starling noticed. We're still here. You coming home?

The reply came within seconds: no.

Delta texted out half a long paragraph before taking a sharp breath in and deleting the whole thing. Instead, she typed a single response, something she knew would get under Bee's skin—k.—and then dropped her phone in one of the cupholders. She was shaking, energy and anger and Tag's bitter words coiling tightly beneath her skin.

She wasn't even sure how she made it home; but by the time she parked by the back of the Wild West, her hands were trembling and all she could feel was Starling's penetrating gaze from the passenger side. Was she imagining that she could hear each breath he took? Was she imagining the feel of his three hearts thudding against the seat?

She turned off the truck and took the key out of the ignition, dropping them into her lap with a harsh jangle. She slid her eyes toward Starling and the bottle in his hand. "Feel like sharing?"

She didn't know why she said it; she was feeling so on edge from speaking with Tag, what he said to her, and now she was alone with an alien who made every atom in her body light up like a live wire. She wanted . . . she *wanted*.

She wanted to be a little bit dangerous.

The corners of Starling's mouth ticked up, and he held out one of the half-finished bottles of gin. Delta wrinkled her nose—*not that dangerous*—and gestured to the small bottle of Fireball on the floor by his feet.

She didn't say a word as she cracked open the top and took a long swig. It burned her throat, sharp and sweet and honeyed with cinnamon, and although she knew the immediate effect was just in her mind, she met Starling's gaze and smiled, all teeth.

"Alcohol makes humans silly," Starling told her, although he sounded a little out of breath. "It makes them not think."

"Yes," Delta breathed. She couldn't seem to look away from his celestial eyes; they pulled her in, a black hole. "I don't want to think anymore." She raised the bottle to her lips and took another swig, making a face at the syrupy-cinnamon taste. It tasted like . . . like long nights with Tag, lying in the back of the pickup truck, looking at the stars.

Delta looked at the fallen star before her now and raised the bottle for another sip.

"Let's get inside," she said. She felt almost giddy now, as if she was rocketing toward something that would forever change her. She thought it had to do with the way Starling looked at her under his lashes. Starling gathered up the empty bottles and together they slid from the truck. "You can finally eat the fries

I brought you," Delta whispered to him. "Just wait until you try them . . ." She reached the back door and fumbled around the Fireball bottle for her keys, and then unlocked the door and flicked on the kitchen light.

"Hello," a mild voice said, just as a figure stepped out of the darkness beside them. Delta shrieked, jumping back in shock. She dropped the bottle; Starling's hand stretched out, lightning-quick, inhumanly quick, and caught it. He ducked his head, curls falling over his face, but as Delta stared into the face now illuminated by the light, she knew there was no hiding.

"Sorry," Ramona Schuyler said, but she didn't sound very sorry. She was wearing jeans and a Duke University crewneck. Her sheriff's badge was pinned to the sweatshirt like some sort of strange Halloween costume. She waved a twirly finger at the Fireball bottle. "I let the first two sips in the car go, but you're pushing it now." She smiled, and her eyes flicked to Starling's ducked head.

Delta saw the change in her face as she took in the figure before her. She watched as the sheriff's eyes widened, as the glow from his skin became more apparent, as the woman clocked the strange tattoos over his lean body. Starling raised his head and stared back at her with his fully black eyes, and the sheriff stumbled backward in fright.

"Delta, get behind me!" she said, her words rising almost hysterically. A quick fumble at her belt and she was holding her Taser, pointing it at Starling with miraculously steady hands. "Delta!"

"No, no!" shrieked Delta, then took a deep breath. She tried to keep her voice calm, although she couldn't help it from shaking. "Sheriff Schuyler, *please*—I'm not in trouble, and there's no danger here. I know this is unbelievable, but I promise he comes in peace."

She saw the sheriff mouth the words to herself: *he comes in peace.*

"Please," Delta said again. "Let's just talk." She grabbed at Starling's arm; he stood still as stone, blinking deliberately slowly. "He's my friend."

For a moment the sheriff stayed frozen.

Delta, you are so stupid. The words whirled through Delta's head. If only she had noticed the sheriff's dark car parked in the shadows, if only she had hurried Starling into the house immediately, if only Starling's nearness hadn't made her feel like she was a fire, slowly burning from the inside out . . . if only, if only.

And then Sheriff Schuyler wordlessly tucked away the Taser and turned wide eyes on Delta. "I think," she said, her voice low and hoarse, "we should go inside."

Delta unlocked the door. The sheriff filed inside first, hurrying over the threshold with a sharp glance at Starling. Delta followed more slowly. She locked the door behind the three of them and walked through to the living room.

Starling sat down next to Abby, lying in the corner of the couch. She woke up briefly; just long enough to sniff at his hand before snuggling down into the cushions. Sheriff Schuyler sat in the armchair across the room, and watched this interaction with a mixture of interest and lingering fear.

"Your dog likes him," she muttered.

"She does," Delta agreed. "And dogs are good judges of people, aren't they?"

The sheriff gave a short nod and sat back, her fingers laced tightly together. "So."

"So."

"So," repeated the sheriff.

"So I found an alien," Delta said in a rush.

The sheriff flinched, then let out a big sigh. "Jesus. Is this real?" She waved her hand in the direction of Starling but didn't look at him. "Is this some kind of prank?"

"No," said Delta. "That meteor that fell? That was Starling. Please don't tell anyone, *please*. I'm trying to keep him safe, that's all."

"Starling," whispered the sheriff.

"Starling Rust," Delta replied.

The sheriff's hand drifted back down to her Taser, as if she was reassuring herself it was still there. She took another deep breath, held it, and then let it out in a wavering gulp. "This is . . ."

"I know," Delta hurried to cut her off. "I know it seems impossible, but it really happened, and he needs our *help*."

"So . . . that light-covered clearing in the woods behind your house?"

"That was him. That's where he landed."

"Landed?"

"It's where he landed when he fell," Delta amended.

"From where? Where did he fall *from*?" The sheriff's words were raw, barely making their way out.

"The sky," Delta said. Then she shrugged, a little helplessly. "That's all I know. That's all he remembers."

"Delta saved me," Starling broke in, speaking directly to the sheriff for the first time. He met her eyes; Delta watched as the sheriff was drawn into their gravity. "She's saved me multiple times now."

"You—you can speak . . . ?"

"Yes," Starling said gravely, and Delta watched as the sheriff clenched her jaw and shut her eyes as if processing was taking up too much brainpower for anything else.

Finally, she gave a tiny half nod and murmured, "Okay. And the people who broke in . . . ?"

"They were looking for whatever fell—they were looking for *him*, although I'm not sure they know it," Delta said. "I'm just so glad they didn't find him. You're not from Darling originally; you don't get it. The people here . . . they don't like us. At all. We've *always* been the weird ones, the outcast family on the edge of town. And if they found out about Starling, especially *here*, with *us*, I think they might do something reckless." *Reckless* was one way of putting it: Delta's worst-case-scenario thoughts were filled with scenes too horrible to even mention out loud.

"Hmm." Ramona examined her intertwined fingers, but kept glancing up from under her lashes to sneak looks at Starling. "But you never considered telling the authorities? Anyone? I don't know, the FBI?"

"The FBI?" Delta gasped out. "No!"

Ramona held up her hands. "Okay, okay, not the FBI."

"*You* were frightened of him—think of what the reaction would be if the world knew about him!"

"I see your point," the sheriff murmured. "But Delta, you're a teenager."

"I'm eighteen," Delta snapped back.

"Right," the sheriff said. "A teenager."

"I . . . everything is fine." Maybe if she said it enough, she'd start to believe it. "Everything's *fine.*"

"You can't be expected to hide an alien away in your house forever."

"I can for as long as he wants to stay. You have to promise me you won't tell!" Delta suddenly felt desperate, frenzied. Had this woman *never* seen a single movie, watched a TV show? Calling in the government was a surefire way to get Starling locked up somewhere more secret than Area 51.

"I promise, Delta, I promise," the sheriff said soothingly. "I just meant . . ." She paused, her calm eyes surveying Delta as if wondering exactly what words to use to tactfully make her point. "I mean, the very *being* of Starling alters life as we know it on Earth. It not only calls into question everything we thought we knew about the universe, but the very laws of science itself. You didn't think maybe it would be better dealt with by someone other than an eighteen-year-old?"

Starling leaned forward, resting his elbows on his knees and looking seriously at the sheriff. He was still bare-chested, his celestial markings on full display, his light-imbued skin glowing. His depthless black eyes gleamed, and when he spoke, his sharp-edged teeth edged over the side of his lips. He looked like nothing less than an ethereal creature, a being from the stars. "Do I not get a choice in who is told?"

"I . . ." The sheriff looked flustered; she kept glancing around the room, her gaze falling on anything but the alien before her.

"I wish to stay with Delta," Starling said, and although his voice was low, there was no mistaking the stony resolution in his tone.

"Delta," Ramona said, "think rationally. You took your *secret* alien friend to a party with half your school there."

Delta paused. "How do you know that?"

"Oh, please," said Ramona, with a hint of a smirk. "I'm a sheriff. It's my job to know what goes on in small towns." She paused, and Delta knew they were both thinking of Starling. "When sixty percent of Darling's population drives to the Rockford place, I take note. And," she added casually, "you both reek of alcohol—"

"It isn't what you think," Delta interrupted.

"I need your human alcohol drink to survive on this planet," Starling added.

"Starling almost died today." Delta's hand trembled; a part of her suddenly wished she could reach over and grab Starling's, just to have something to hold. "We knew we could get alcohol at the party. He stayed ducked down in the truck the whole time."

Ramona was quiet for a moment, then said, "I can help with the alcohol situation until Starling leaves."

Relief rocketed through Delta's body. "Thank you, thank you," she whispered.

"And how long will that be?" Ramona asked.

Delta's head snapped toward her, eyes wide. "What do you mean?"

Ramona's gaze lingered on Starling. "How long until you leave?" It wasn't a question but a command. Ramona's voice left no room for anything else.

She felt Starling shift under Ramona's glare, until his black eyes met hers, his expression inscrutable, and she braced herself for what she knew he'd say: *soon*. Right? But in the truck, when she'd reminded him his chain had the power to keep him here as well, he hadn't contradicted her. *You know he doesn't want to stay*, she told herself sternly. After all, if *she*, born and raised within the confines of Darling, wasn't happy with the prospect of being stuck there forever, she couldn't expect a man from the stars to be content to waste away in Darling, among humans.

Delta leaned forward and answered for him. "There's something he needs before he's able to leave." Darling was a tiny town, and there were only a few places they'd have to search to find the chain for Starling to harness the energy to leave Darling. Earth. *Her*. "It shouldn't be too long," she said, barely able to whisper the words.

Silence hovered around them, except for the ticking of the living room clock. Delta could practically hear the whirring of Ramona's thoughts as she reviewed all her options. Her eyes kept flicking to the alien across from her as if he might disappear in a puff of smoke. "I don't like this," she said finally, standing up and crossing her arms.

"And you don't have to. Trust me. *Trust me*, Sheriff Schuyler. Please." Delta stood too, holding out a firm, beseeching hand toward the sheriff. *Please just leave. Please just go.* "There's nothing to worry about."

"There's everything to worry about." Ramona sighed. "This isn't a secret you can keep for long, not in a town this small. It's only a matter of time before all of Darling finds out about him. And if you're right about this town and its people"—the sheriff rubbed her temples—"which, I'll admit, I've only been here a few weeks and have heard more superstitious stories about your family than I'd care to admit, it would be in his best interest, and *yours*, Delta, if his time here is as short as possible."

Her words sank claws into Delta's mind, and she couldn't bear to look at Starling for fear of what she'd see on his face. When Ramona turned and walked into the hallway, she jerked her head toward Delta, beckoning her to follow.

The sheriff took a long look at the cabinet blocking the broken front door before heading to the back. Delta stepped out beside her. The night was so quiet; it was hard to believe that just a few miles away was laughter and dancing and music and *Tag*. Here in the darkness, she could pretend none of it was real.

She stared up at the canvas of stars. Which orb of light was missing from the sky—what star had fallen and was now in the Wilding house? Ramona turned her face to the sky as well.

"Delta," she said, her eyes still up, and for a heart-stopping moment Delta thought she was going to change her mind about helping them and march straight back inside and take Starling away from her forever. But instead, she tilted her head to the side and raised her eyebrows, and Delta saw a tiny glint of shared understanding there. "Are you sure this is a good idea? I can stay here with you tonight. He could be dangerous."

"Sheriff Schuyler, if Starling was dangerous, don't you think I would know by now?"

"Things can be dangerous without even trying," the sheriff murmured.

Delta shrugged helplessly. "But I trust him."

"I can see that," Ramona said, "and that's exactly what I'm worried about."

Delta couldn't explain why she wanted to be near him: maybe it was because she knew deep inside their time was limited, an hourglass slowly emptying of sand. Her nearness to the alien, to the universe, was coming to an end with each breath; they were dancing on borrowed time. She had always known it, but the sheriff had brought it to the forefront of her mind, unable to brush away.

"I'm fine," she said finally. "Thank you, though."

"Hmm," said Ramona, her piercing eyes locked on Delta's.

"Promise," said Delta. "I swear."

"You'll call me if you need me?" the sheriff asked. "Anytime."

"I will," Delta said fervently, wanting more than anything to get back inside.

Sheriff Schuyler made another skeptical *hmm* but then gave a wary nod. "Okay. Delta—be careful." She turned and headed for her car, the black paint melding with the darkness outside. With a smooth roar, the car started up, the headlights shining like lamps in the night.

Delta watched her go, then looked up at the twinkling stars once more before shutting and locking the door behind her.

22

THE WOMAN WAS RIGHT:
he had to leave.

Starling sat alone on the couch, his head in his hands, Abby sleeping soundly by his side. The whirlwind of the night tore through his mind: everything from the feeling of falling unconscious to rousing briefly in the Wildings' truck as they raced to help him, his head in Delta's lap, to the brief glimpse of the human boy through the front window. And now here, right back where he started.

Delta had warned him about the reactions from townspeople, and to see the look on the woman's—Sheriff Schuyler's—face when she took him in for the first time had made it all too clear. He now understood that other reactions would be much, much worse.

He stood, coiling his fingers into fists and then unrolling them, trying to calm some of the frissons of nervous energy that were snapping through his body. He paced around the living room, rounding the coffee table, passing a bemused Abby, roused from sleep by his footsteps. Turning into the hallway, he saw the sheriff and Delta standing side by side through the thin windows on each side of the front door. He couldn't read Delta's expression, and another twinge of nerves thrummed through him. The pull of the closet door was strong even here by the front door, and he eyed it warily.

Still afraid to open it? he thought bitterly to himself. *How human of you.*

The energy inside called to his, and Starling felt himself drawn to it, stepping closer as if someone was dragging him firmly by the hand. He edged up to the closed door. He could feel the *throb* from inside, like a heartbeat.

Just open it.

But what would happen? Would he remember the crash— would the energy counteract with his and drain him dry— would he be simply sucked away into the closet's gravity to somewhere new?

He stared at the carved wood, at the dull bronze handle.

"What's wrong?" he heard from behind him, and Delta sidled up next to him, close enough that her arm brushed against his. She glanced between him and the door, noticing his attention. He forced his eyes away from the gravitational pull and back to her.

"Nothing." He knew immediately that she saw right through his lie.

"You sure?"

"Yes," Starling said.

"Really?" she said, and then quickly sidestepped him. He reached for her, but his fingers just grabbed at her waist as she threw open the door.

The closet was a small space, dark and gloomy, with stacks of shoes and raincoats hung from pegs. Delta's reaction upon seeing the empty space was immediate; her shoulders sank and her mouth turned down.

But she couldn't feel the energy.

It hit him like an electric shock, coursing out over him in a wave. Starling's knees almost buckled, and he threw out a hand, bracing himself against the wall. Dust from the old floral wallpaper coated his fingertips as he breathed, his three hearts pounding in strange synchronization.

"Starling?!" Delta's voice sounded far away.

Starling breathed deeply as the particles roiled out of the closet. To Delta, it was empty. But Starling realized now what he hadn't before. As the energy hit him, Starling remembered.

He remembered falling.

Light, pouring out over him. The clap of pure power that pulled him here, and . . . pulled another out in his place. The energy in this closet was overwhelmingly strong. Strong enough to tip someone through that fragile veil in the universe.

"I remember," he said, his voice gravelly.

"Remember what?" Delta still sounded anxious, and he forced his eyes open to show her that he was fine.

"How I got here."

"You fell."

"Yes," he said, the word low in his throat, and then he held up one long-fingered hand. They both looked at it, and Starling tried to see his body from Delta's point of view: skin glowing with its dim glow, streaked with strange markings. So unearthly. "This is you, here." He held up another hand, placing it closer to—but not touching—the other. "This is everything else. And there is *so* much more. Sometimes, such as when the moon grows full and stirs up energy, this happens." He clapped his hands together suddenly, and Delta jumped nervously. She looked at his palms, pushed tightly together as if praying. "It makes it easier for certain things to slip through."

"What sort of things?" Delta whispered.

Starling's eyes rose to hers. Could she see the infinite worlds in them? His voice was nothing but a rasp when he replied, "Things like me."

The universe pushes and pulls; it balances.

Balance. He realized it now; when he had slipped through the thin space, something else took his place.

Balance. Two ends of the magnet, holding each other apart, keeping each other separate.

He remembered what she'd told him about her father. Gone missing, through the closet.

No no no no no no . . . His expression must have been horror-struck as the truth of the matter became clarion-clear in his mind, because Delta's worried voice, full to the brim with confusion, asked, "Is everything okay? What's wrong? Starling?"

Delta. Delta and the way she'd saved him, over and over again. The way she laughed when she danced and the way she rolled her eyes at him. The way her single heart beat so furiously within her small human chest.

"Yes," he said, his voice faint. *What was he supposed to do now?*

This was—the word came to him in an instant, and it seemed so banal, so *human*, but he couldn't think of anything better—*unfair.* Everything about it was unfair.

Why shouldn't he stay?

He was here, and that's all that mattered.

No—because he was here, someone else was not.

A soft touch on his arm made him look up, shaking away the thoughts. He felt sicker than when he'd first landed: that had been pain in his bones, in his body; he could deal with that. But this? This was worse.

How did humans *do* it? His three hearts were pounding in their disparate rhythms; his stomach was squeezing. Was this what dying felt like—this was worse than when his body had been going into shock from dehydration. His insides were being gnawed upon, swallowed by some maw inside him. *Push and pull. The universe demands balance.*

"Starling?" She spoke softly, like speaking too loudly might startle him.

"Yes," he repeated. He tore his gaze from the open closet. "Yes, everything is fine." He might've smiled; it felt to him like he was baring his teeth in agony, but Delta smiled back, so he must be a better liar than he ever thought.

"Good," she breathed, firmly shutting the closet door. "In that case, I have something I want to show you."

A shudder of excitement coursed through him, momentarily burning away the pool of guilt and confusion. Her nearness was electrifying.

"Will you come with me?"

She looked so earnest, and she gestured toward the back door through the darkened kitchen. She knew nothing of his inner turmoil and—*maybe*, thought Starling, *it's for the best.*

A saying he came across while reading one of Delta's books wormed its way into his mind: *what she doesn't know won't hurt her.* It wasn't true; he knew it wasn't true, because he could see the effect of the Wilding father's disappearance on both girls every day, but it was enough to push it briefly from his mind.

"I will," he said gravely. He wanted to see her smile.

She turned and led the way to the door, opening it with a shiver as a gust of cold, damp air snaked its way into the kitchen. Going outside—that was good. The fresh air and green earth of this planet would help to banish his guilty thoughts. He wished he could forget.

Let me forget.

Let me not care.

And when she stepped out the door, Starling followed, close enough that his fingers brushed the back of her hand with each step.

23

THEY SET OFF

together, the girl and the alien, walking side by side as they cut across the wet grass. It had started to drizzle with rain, and a thick mist hung over the trees before them. The trees beckoned, eager for more secrets. The air was still and moist, heavy with the sweet fresh smell of pine. The lichen was damp and slick underfoot, but Delta tried to keep up with Starling's quick—yet silent—pace through the forest. She followed the gleam of his skin lined with golden veins and inky black lines as he walked, not disturbing even a twig along the way: a mere evanescent apparition, a ghost flitting, transient, between moss-covered tree trunks draped in ivy.

The silence was heavy between them; Delta could almost see the charged particles racing back and forth from her body to his. She led the way farther into the forest, turning a hard right to skirt horizontal to her house.

The Wishing Well was almost directly between the Wild West and the houses of Darling; technically it was on the Wildings' property, but it was far enough from the ramshackle house that no one in Darling really considered it as belonging to the strange family on the edge of town. There were signs leading to it from the main road; during the day it could become as much of a tourist trap as something could in a town with a population just over three hundred. But all the Darling kids knew that when twilight descended, the well became *different*. They found it easy to pretend that the small stone well in the middle of the woods was truly magical. That it could truly grant wishes.

Only the Wildings knew it was probably true.

"Delta," Starling said suddenly, his voice breaking the silence. His fingers brushed against her again, and Delta considered just grabbing and holding his hand. Would he pull away? "When you were talking to that human boy—Tag. You know him well?"

"I . . . I guess so. Why?" Delta was guarded. She didn't want to talk about Tag, not here so deep in the woods.

"Watching you two together . . ." He trailed off.

"Well," Delta said, "there's a lot of history." She paused, remembering Tag's expression, how it moved from aching to angry. *My dad said to stay away from you—maybe he was right.* She added, "And a lot of hurt."

"And a lot of good, if I am not mistaken?"

He wasn't, but Delta frowned. "I don't want to talk about Tag."

"Did you love him?"

"I . . ." Delta opened her mouth, lost for words. "What do you even know about love?"

Starling was quiet for a moment, then said softly, "More than I thought I did."

Delta didn't answer: her thoughts whirled around her as Starling's words filtered through. What did he *mean*? A hot blush rose up her neck and cheeks, even though of course he didn't mean—couldn't mean—*her*. She could barely see Starling next to her in the pitch-dark woods, but somehow that made his disembodied words all the more intimate.

"And do stars . . . do stars *feel* things?" she whispered.

There was only silence, but she knew he was listening—she could tell by the way his breath caught and his head turned just slightly to the left.

"No," Starling replied, but she thought this reply sounded hollow.

"Are you sure?" She knew he did—she knew he felt *everything*, she could see it in his eyes. She just wanted him to admit it.

Starling's rough laugh gave another appearance, but it didn't sound remotely cheerful. "Delta. I am not a human."

Her blush deepened, although at first she couldn't quite understand why. "I know. What does that—"

Starling let out a word in his language, and although Delta didn't understand the distorted hiss, she understood perfectly the sharp tone it was verbalized in. "I will be leaving this planet, and I am not a *human*!"

"I said I *know*," said Delta again, her voice rising.

Starling slowed, then abruptly grasped her hand, pulling Delta to face him. His star-speckled eyes were soft, and Delta's breath hitched. "I cannot change what I am, or the fact that I cannot stay," he said finally. He looked around the woods, gestured to the dripping trees with his free hand. "I should not *be* here, Delta Wilding. You should not get involved. I should not let myself get . . . *invested*."

A sudden lump in her throat had her swallowing back an onslaught of tears. "So," she said, her voice thick, "you don't want to be friends with the *human*? Because you're so much better than us?"

Starling was already shaking his head. He looked utterly defeated. "I do not know what to say. I am not a human, I am not a person. I'm just . . ." He waved a gently glowing hand in the air. "Stardust."

"But so am I," Delta said, her voice almost a whisper. She felt like if she spoke too loudly, something would break: maybe the trees around her, maybe her heart, maybe the fragile, unlikely relationship. "We're from the same universe, aren't we? And we're both made of the dust of stars that collapsed billions of years ago. We may not be the same, but here we are, talking together. *Living*. You still deserve to live, to feel. I think you know it too, deep down. You can't lie to me, Starling—I know that you've felt things."

Starling closed his eyes as if he could block out the sound of her voice. "I'm not a human," he repeated.

"Right now, I can see that you're feeling tense and frustrated, like you want to lash out."

"I am not feeling *any* of that," Starling snapped. He sighed, then rubbed his long fingers across his face.

Delta smiled at him wearily. "Look at you. Feeling conflicted and edgy—you're more human than I am."

"That will never be true," snarled Starling, and then he removed his hand from his face and started walking again, his steps bordering on harried. She followed a half step behind him, close enough that she could still lead them in the general direction.

They finally emerged in the small clearing where the well sat unassuming in the center. Unlike the clearing they'd found the unconscious Starling in, this clearing was well-trodden, the strangeness contained in an almost clinical way by the passing by of the occasional tourist. The dewy grass had been crushed by hundreds of feet over many years. An obvious path led away from the clearing, curving its way back toward town. A small wooden sign on a picket wedged deep in the dirt had DARLING WISHING WELL carved inelegantly into the wood.

Delta had been here multiple times, especially after Tag decided it was a good place for hanging out and making out and his "kickbacks" as he liked to call them. Even though Delta had always felt a tiny frisson of *something* in the clearing, it had never seemed very magical, not with Anders drunkenly singing and Tag staring broodily at the canopy of leaves above them.

But as she and Starling stepped forward, pushing past rain-slicked branches, she *felt* it. Starling stood close to her side, close enough to feel his skin brush against her arm, and she chanced a glance toward him, trying to read his expression. He was soaked in starlight and rain, and the small stone well was reflected in his orb-eyes.

He said nothing, just stepped forward to run a long, black-marked finger across the mossy stones.

"Do you like it?" Delta whispered finally, giving up on trying to decipher the inscrutable mask of his face.

Starling met her gaze. "Yes," he breathed. "There is . . . energy here."

Delta looked down at her scuffed, damp Vans, as though she might be able to see this energy coursing through, shining like wires beneath her feet. She couldn't, obviously—there was nothing but crushed stalks of grass—but she could still feel what Starling meant. There was a pulse to the air, a vibrancy that made the light of the moon milky and the leaves shimmer in shades of jade and emerald.

"This is a special place," Starling murmured. "Darling is a special place. And you . . ." He trailed off.

Delta held her breath. *And you* what? *I'm what?*

But Starling fell silent again, even as his eyes bored into hers.

"I'm what?" she whispered, letting out her breath.

Still, silence.

Then suddenly there was Starling's voice, not making its way through the airwaves, but wrapping itself intimately around her thoughts. He spoke directly into the corners of her mind. *You're like nothing I've ever experienced, Delta Wilding. And nothing I ever expected.*

The feel of his voice in her head was like a caress, and the tone in which he spoke was even more so. His rock-on-rock rasp normally sounded so matter-of-fact, but now his words were soft, gentle.

Starling stepped away from her, forward toward the well. He waved a long-fingered hand gracefully toward the wooden sign and changed the subject. "The Darling Wishing Well?"

"Yeah," Delta said, giving a hesitant chuckle. "It's pretty silly, I know. But my dad believed in it." She winced as she spoke. She shouldn't have brought up her dad; tears rushed unbidden to her eyes, and she brushed them away impatiently. *Do. Not. Cry*, she told herself sternly. *There's no need to cry. He's not gone. He is* not *gone.* She couldn't let herself think that way, not when she had to be the strong one. "Every time I've ever come here, I've wished for my dad to come home. It hasn't happened yet—so maybe this Wishing Well doesn't work after all."

She glanced toward Starling to see if he'd respond, but he was staring down into the depths of the well, his mouth tight.

"Starling, you know a lot about the universe, don't you?"

"But not everything," Starling replied. "No, not everything."

"But a *lot*. You're from the universe; you're . . . *magic*. Do you know where he is? Can you bring him back?"

The expressionless mask crept over Starling's face once more, smoothing out the lines in his furrowed brow.

"Do you?" Delta asked again.

"Everything has a price," he whispered.

"What's that mean?" she asked. *A price?*

Starling paused. He ran a long finger on the cold stones of the Wishing Well, then slowly shook his head. He paused, then said stiffly, "I cannot bring him back."

Delta sighed, nodding, and dug her nails into her palms to keep herself from crying. She'd expected the answer, but a part of her still hoped that somehow Starling might know how to help. "I understand. It's okay." It wasn't, but she couldn't say how she really felt. Once she started putting words to the horrible pit of roiling anxiety and anger and stress inside her, would she ever be able to stop?

She brushed rain and tears off her face with a frustrated hand, then stuck her fingers into her jean pocket. There wasn't much in there, what with girls' pockets being made much too tiny to fit anything of real importance, but there was some lint, a folded receipt that had gone through the wash a few too many times, and at the bottom, some loose change from the morning. It seemed ages ago that she and Bee were at the store, fielding suspicious glares from the other Darling shoppers and talking to Tag as if nothing had changed, and then casually picking at fries at the Diner. Everything that had happened after—Starling almost dying, careening to the party, desperately dripping alcohol to his lips, his head on her lap, Tag's hurt eyes staring at her through the windshield, Ramona Schuyler apprehending them outside the house—seemed to frame this moment, standing quietly side by side by a wishing well.

She pulled out two of the smaller coins—two tarnished pennies lay on her palm.

"Here," she said softly, nudging him with her elbow.

Starling took a penny obligingly, holding up the copper coin and examining it closely. "What is this?"

"Coins," she replied. "Money. But here in the woods, here at the well, they have a different use." She gestured toward the Wishing Well, sitting innocently before them. The polished, dewy stones gleamed in the moonlight pushing through the canopy above.

One of Starling's eyebrows quirked up. "Does it, now?" His voice was slow, ponderous, and then he grinned. His sharp canines edged over his bottom lip, and Delta abruptly realized she had never seen someone so beautiful, so *fascinating*. All thoughts—all wishes—flew out of her head except for one: *Stay*.

"Now," she said, breathless, "we close our eyes and make a wish, then throw our pennies into the pool." How many coins and flowers and lighters and bottle caps met their watery end in the Darling Wishing Well? How many people over the years had stood exactly where they stood now, hoping upon hope that their wish would be the one that came true? And how many of those wishes did the universe deign to fulfill?

For so long, she had hurried through the woods a few times a week with a pocketful of pennies and stood by the edge of the Wishing Well, wishing on penny after penny that her dad would come home. She was starting to believe that maybe there were wishes too big for even the universe to handle through a well.

And so, side by side with the alien, she wished for something else. For the first time in over two months, she wished for something new.

Stay. Stay with me. Stay here. Stay in Darling.

Delta knew she couldn't bear for someone else to leave her. She couldn't bear to be the only one holding the boards of the Wild West together.

"Are your eyes closed?" Starling rasped.

Delta squeezed them shut tightly, until little sparks of light burst behind her eyes. "Yes. Are yours?"

"Yes."

"Then make your wish."

Silence. Then she heard a tiny splash as his coin hit the water and sank. She kept her eyes shut as she tossed her coin. She wanted this magical, celestial boy to stay.

She opened her eyes: and there he was, right in front of her, six inches away. He was so tall, he had to bend his head to look down at her, and his gaze was dark and steady.

When he spoke, it wasn't aloud, but twirled into her mind. *What did you wish for?*

He was so close, she could barely form a coherent sentence— they'd been this close before, closer even, but somehow this seemed so much *more*. He smelled like the woods around them, as if the rain and moss and fresh, damp air had been absorbed into his skin.

She didn't say anything, but she didn't have to. He knew what she wished for.

Stay.

Starling closed his eyes.

"Delta . . ." There was no mistaking the tone of his voice. Delta flushed, embarrassment rushing over her. She stepped away, pressing a damp hand to her flaming cheek.

"I'm sorry," she whispered. He still didn't look at her, and she took an awkward step backward. "Do . . . do you want me to go?"

"Go?" He gave a single shake of his head. "No."

The too-hot feel of skin eased slightly at his words. It was good enough for her. Good enough for now.

"A part of me can't help but think . . ." Starling continued, staring hard at the well. Delta wondered briefly what Starling had wished for, if anything. "That despite knowing I should not become involved here, perhaps . . ." He trailed off again, then made a low noise in the back of his throat as though trying to pick and choose the correct words. "Perhaps this was—meant to happen."

Delta let out a half laugh. It certainly was not what she had expected him to say. "Meant to happen? What, you coming here when my dad is gone? Falling into our backyard?"

"Meeting you? Yes."

Delta froze. He still wasn't looking at her, but that weighty feeling had returned to the clearing. *Look at me, look at me . . .* But the overwhelmed part of her wanted him to not reply, to not speak, to leave and not look back. "You believe in fate?"

"You do not?"

"I think the universe has a lot of coincidences."

Starling turned to look at her then, drawing her in as if his eyes held their own source of gravity. She couldn't help but stare back, to stumble closer to him. He opened his mouth once, twice, and then spoke directly into her mind.

I think that the universe is rarely so careless.

She couldn't look away from his starry gaze. Were the galaxies suspended there reflected in her own green eyes?

"Maybe you're right," she whispered. It felt necessary to whisper now, with the gentle drizzle and the deepening of night around them. "After all, you never bet against the universe."

Almost as if he could read her thoughts, Starling silently whispered into her mind: *I don't think the universe would do well betting against you, Delta.*

Her breath caught in her throat; his eyes were so bright,

watching her, tracking her expression. Delta wasn't quite sure why, but the tickle of his words in her mind made her want to cry. She sucked in her bottom lip, trying not to let the tears rise. It also made her want to trip closer to him, to listen to his pounding hearts. To raise her head to his, to stare into his eyes and . . .

Starling reached over and took Delta's hand.

He will leave eventually, and if he's really leaving, you have nothing to lose.

Delta didn't let herself fully think about what she was about to do; she moved only on want and desire and the tingly, heady feel of Starling's voice wrapped so intimately around her thoughts. As his warm and callused fingers wrapped around her own, she turned toward him, stood on her tiptoes, and pressed her lips against his.

24

SHE WAS KISSING

him. He knew exactly what was happening, but even with his infinite knowledge, it took his body a moment to process. It was only for a mere second—by the time he'd fully realized she was kissing him, she had already taken a step back, watching him with red-stained cheeks—and then he and Delta stared at each other in silence.

"I—I'm sorry."

He wanted to tell her not to be sorry. He wanted to tell her so many things. But how could she understand that his hesitancy wasn't about her, not really? It was about the situation. The uncompromising, lose-lose situation he'd somehow quite literally fallen into. He was not a human. While he was here, her father was not, and he knew deep down who she'd choose.

He could not stay.

He wanted to stay.

You're more human than I am. He heard Delta's voice saying those words in her language over and over again until they lost all meaning. *You're more human than I am.* It wasn't true, not in the least, but human minds were so small, so fragile.

He knew Delta couldn't truly wrap her mind around the sheer magnitude of what he was.

The universe in a boy's body.

She just saw the boy.

It cannot work. It will never work. You cannot stay. You are not human. He repeated this to himself, the words running together. *Can't work—can't stay—not human.*

Delta's mouth was set; she stood like stone and stared at the Wishing Well. There were tears in her eyes, tears that started to fall now in earnest.

Can't work—can't stay—not human.

But humans were selfish, and here he was, selfish as the worst of them.

He wanted to stay.

Starling felt his hearts begin to beat as one until his body was nothing but hearts. His own reminders faded into nothingness, until in his mind there was nothing but blissful darkness. Carefully, he unlaced his fingers from Delta's, and splayed them out across her cheek instead. He'd half hoped the movement would dissuade himself, but the celestial markings wrapped around his hands—the reminder, the reminder!—immediately became meaningless as she turned her face toward him.

She was so . . . *beautiful.* Beautiful and fragile. She had a quiet voice, a sad mouth, and a yearning heart. Just like him, she had stars in her eyes. He could see it in Delta's gaze, in the set line of her lips. No, whatever that girl was made of, it wasn't just flesh and blood and bones. She was made of stardust and a heavy soul, just like him. Maybe it was true what he'd said—that somehow the fibers of the universe had conspired to get him here, to the strange town and strange house, containing one very strange girl.

He felt her breath hitch as he leaned forward, his mouth hovering millimeters above hers. He tasted her warmth when he finally pressed his lips to hers. She responded immediately, as though she'd been waiting, *hoping*. He felt her warmth radiating from her skin, the flutter of her lashes against his, felt her one heart beating frantically against his trembling three. At first he tried to keep his mouth closed, hiding his sharp teeth safely behind cold lips, but she was so soft that he soon relaxed with an outward breath, drawing her closer against him. Every part of this body of his was lit up, on fire. Her human tongue ran along his teeth, and he shivered against her. Everything about her was so small, and fragile, and human.

Although . . . Delta was seeming less and less human with every passing moment. She seemed so much *more*.

He broke away, finally, but stayed close. Very gently, he rested his forehead down upon hers. The tears that had been clinging to Delta's lashes had been transferred to his, and he blinked them away.

His hearts continued to beat as one, finding rhythm together so that they pounded painfully inside his chest. It was something they only did when his body reacted to . . . well, feelings. Strange, passionate, wondrous human feelings. He closed his eyes; he could hear Delta breathing, he could feel the warmth of her breath as it hit his neck, but neither spoke.

What was there to say?

His warnings to himself flooded back in a giant rush of guilt: *You cannot stay. You must leave.* And now they pinpointed on Delta: *You cannot stay with her. You must leave her. You must not get attached . . .*

But he had. Somehow he had. The universe had seen the gleam of a human's eye, and he couldn't stop himself from staying close to her. He wasn't supposed to feel this way; it shouldn't happen that when he kissed Delta Wilding, his inhuman hearts beat as one with fear, with lust, with *wanting*.

He was not supposed to be experiencing human emotions. *None of this should be happening.*

Tell her.

Tell her it will never happen.

But he remembered tossing his burnished penny into the water with a *plink*. The wish he had made—to himself, to the air around him, to something more.

Let me find a way to stay.

25

THE SAME MOMENT

that Starling pulled Delta into his arms and kissed her was the exact same moment Bee, almost two miles away, started to cry.

These things weren't related, but they happened so simultaneously that they could've been.

Bee had been having a good time at the party, the type of good time when you manage to push away everything that hangs over you. Bee had been in full-on *push-away* mode: she wasn't thinking of Delta or Starling or their empty, dad-less house. She wasn't thinking of the conversation she'd had with Tag. She was just *being*.

But the feeling didn't last for long. Real life always manages to push its way in.

She stood on the outskirts of a small group of girls from her year, hovering as they giggled drunkenly and arranged tequila shots on the porch railing of the guesthouse. Everything around Bee was twinkling with lights; the guesthouse looked magical, like a movie set. Had Tag done this all himself? She took a sip of beer; it was cold from the icebox and fizzed at the back of her throat. She knew she should be trying harder to insert herself into the group's conversation, but she couldn't quite seem to keep up with the gossip. Unlike Delta, who always stood off to the side at parties, either lost in her own thoughts or speaking solely to Tag or Anders, Bee usually found *mingling* so easy— inserting herself with smiles and gossip and flashing, bold eyes. But it wasn't happening tonight.

Bee stuck her hand into the pocket of her jeans and felt the thin links of the chain she'd found—it was still warm, even in the drizzly rain that had begun to fall. As if the heat had flowed from the chain up her fingers and into her bones, she abruptly felt a hot rush of anger, followed by the sudden urge to burst into tears. She gripped the links tightly, wanting to throw it, wanting to break it, wanting anything that had to do with Starling Rust far, far away from her. She knew this was how he could leave—but she *saw* the way he looked at Delta. How they danced in the living room together, so close. How Delta's eyes lit up at the very mention of him.

He wasn't going to leave.

He wasn't going to leave. She clenched her fingers around the chain, trying to force back the sheen of tears that came to her eyes. If she gave it to him now, he would use it to stay forever. It would no longer be Delta and Bee. Never again. It would always be Delta and Bee and Starling, and Bee knew without a doubt that the third wheel would soon be shed and Delta and Starling would speed away into the sunset forever, never looking back.

Leaving her behind.

She looked around, eyes drifting from her laughing class- mates to a freshman throwing up in the bushes to Anders, dancing closely with his boyfriend, Colson Hawk, who'd graduated from Darling Academy the year before. She backed away, taking up position on one of the stairs leading up to the guesthouse, where she could oversee everyone. No surprises. It was only a moment before, out of the corner of her eye, she saw Tag coming again over the crest of the hill, in the direction she'd been coming from when he'd first stopped to talk to her. His head was down, his hands were stuffed deep in his pockets, and he was staring at his steps with a tense expression full of frustration.

What was Tag doing coming down from the parking lot? He'd said he was going up to the house . . . and yet . . .

And yet now he was coming back with such a strange look on his face. . . . Bee's stomach dropped as if she'd just missed a step.

Had he seen Starling?

Would that be a good thing or a bad thing? She didn't know. If he had, it would be a little bit her fault; after all, she'd been the one who told him Delta was still here. What if he'd gone to find her? The reckless, angry part of her didn't even care. So what if he saw the alien? It would serve Delta right for being so secretive. For being so *obsessed*. For forgetting about her own sister.

The angry part of her wanted to scream, just to let out some of the *feeling* that was bursting out of her skin. Every inch of her felt hot and itchy.

She stood up, needing to move, and headed over to intercept Tag.

"Hey," she said loudly. Her fingers trembled around the slick beer can.

Tag's head jerked up, and he slowed to a halt. "Hey," he replied, his voice low.

"What were you doing up there? I thought you were leaving the party." She tried to keep her tone light.

"I did leave," he said. "Now I'm back." Each word clipped.

"Oh. Okay. You okay . . . ?" She could tell something was wrong, she just didn't know what.

"I talked to Delta." His words were weighted, but she just couldn't suss out their true meaning.

Did he know?

"About what?"

"Us." His mouth twisted. "About how she doesn't trust me."

"She does." It was a lie.

"She hates me."

"She doesn't hate you, Tag," Bee said quietly. No one knew Delta like Bee—that's what she liked to think, at least—and she could see the hurt and confusion when Delta talked about Tag. The things that looked a lot like dislike, but weren't, not really.

"Okay," he replied, still with that twisted, bitter smile. "She does, but it's whatever."

It clearly wasn't whatever. Bee wanted to point this out, but swallowed it back. "Is that . . . all you guys talked about?"

At this, Tag's expression sharpened. His blue eyes snapped to hers, narrowed and shrewd. She could almost see the wheels working in his brain, turning and moving and putting things together. But when he spoke, his voice was measured and calm. Each word seemed deliberate, like he was a politician on a stand, delivering an address. "Is there something we *should* have talked about, Bee?"

The way he said her name had her wanting to reveal everything. He was such a mix of charm and calculation. Bee had the feeling that she could say anything and Tag would be able to twist his response to fit. Everything about him was deliberate, every response carefully chosen. Bee couldn't tell if it was a facade or not. Maybe this was why Delta felt so confused about her feelings for Tag—could she even tell which parts of him were real?

"Um—no?"

"Are you sure?" His eyes were *very* intense, like ice chips.

"I . . ."

"Because I saw the boy."

She felt winded at his words. *I saw the boy.* It had to be Starling—but he hadn't said *alien.* Did he still not know? Or had he seen Starling and simply couldn't wrap his mind around the truth of what he'd seen, never mind say the words out loud?

"What did you see?" Her voice was tiny, small, barely there. *I won't tell him if he's wrong, but if he's right* . . . Either way, Delta would be furious if she told.

Bee couldn't decide if she cared anymore. Because furious would be better than nothing. If Delta was yelling at her, at least they would be doing something *together*; they could argue and scream and do all the things that sisters did. It would be better than Delta holed away in Starling's room, sitting on his bed, each time shifting closer and closer. . . .

Anything would be better than her sister slowly forgetting she was there.

"I don't know what I saw," Tag said finally. "Someone—someone in the truck. Delta said it's a family friend of yours." It was a statement, but she could hear the question within it. *Is this someone really a family friend? Who is it? Who is he?*

A family friend. Delta had called Starling a family friend. Bee clenched her hands around the links of the chain once more. Starling was no friend of hers—he was taking her sister away from her, little by little. And he'd promised her that he wouldn't. She'd thought it was enough then; she'd thought the only danger was in this boy from the stars physically taking Delta from Darling. But somehow Starling had taken her sister without her ever leaving the house.

The anger reared its head again, and it mixed with the beer in Bee's stomach into something hardened and uncaring. She wanted Delta mad. She wanted Delta here.

She couldn't let Delta forget her.

"It's not a family friend," she said, her voice bitter. Her jaw was aching from being so tightly held. She pulled her hand from her pocket, the chain dangling between them, glinting in the glow from the strings of Christmas lights. "It's an *alien*. It's a *star* who fell into our backyard. Yeah, it's true, we're not *alone* in the world. We have an alien in our house and he's going to take Delta away."

She said this all very fast, and very loud, and her voice finally broke on the last word. She looked blazingly at Tag as if daring him to laugh in her face or disregard her sentence. But Tag's face had gone utterly white. Pinched. Bee could see the whites of his eyes.

"What?" he whispered.

She felt suddenly bad for the way she'd sprung it on him. She and Delta had always been around this sort of strangeness; she forgot that the rest of Darling wasn't as clued in to the mysteries of the universe.

"Um . . . yeah." Now she was uncomfortable. It hit her then, the truth she'd blurted out.

"Are you messing with me?"

"No! I was . . . kidding."

"Bee, what the hell?"

"Look, I was joking, okay?" She was babbling now, trying to backtrack. As soon as she'd said the truth, guilt had dragged her under. Not to mention what she'd be inviting by admitting everything—more whispers, more insults, more *Those strange Wilding sisters. They aren't normal.*

All she wanted was to be normal, and this would shatter any hope she had of staying that way in a town that already distrusted them. "It was a *joke.*"

"A joke?"

"Yes! Yes, okay?"

Tag squinted at her, his fingers clenched. "You don't look like it was."

Bee felt on the verge of tears, all the secrets she'd been holding inside fighting loudly to get out. "I . . . What do you want me to say?" she cried.

"I want you to tell me the *truth!*" Tag answered, his voice emphatic.

"It's a boy," Bee said, the word tumbling out.

Tag recoiled, his mouth tightening, frowning. His eyes flashed at the word *boy*. "I *knew* it. I knew it! Do I know him? Is he from school? Is—"

She'd started, and now she felt like she couldn't stop. The words were coming of their own accord. "No—I was telling the truth before. It's not just a normal boy, it's . . . something else. It's the thing that landed near our house the night of the earthquake. I'm sorry I told you like that—I just felt you needed to know." This was only a half-truth; she'd wanted to tell *some-one*, and Tag had happened upon her at the worst possible time. "Did you see it, that night? The light falling from the sky?" She spoke desperately, quickly; she *needed* Tag to believe her on this.

Tag took a sharp breath in. His calm facade was quickly sloughing off, and he looked bewildered and not the smallest bit okay. He no longer looked like a Rockford who had every-thing figured out; he looked like he was concentrating on not falling apart.

He rubbed his forehead. "Is this some kind of trick?"

"No."

"Did Delta put you up to this? To make me look stupid?"

"Tag—of course not."

"Are you drunk?"

"No. Not really." She held up her beer. "This is only my second."

He squinted at her, as though trying to determine she was absolutely not lying. "So you're telling me that that *meteor* was a person?"

"Yes. Person-ish. Starling looks—"

"Starling?"

"That's his name. Starling Rust."

Tag stared at her, lowering his voice as a couple left the party, sidestepping Bee and Tag in the middle of the path. "That's impossible, though."

Bee shrugged helplessly. "I know. But it happened."

Tag shook his head. "No. This isn't real."

"It *is*," Bee insisted. She felt guilt with each word, but also an overwhelming sense of relief. Secrets and lies had been bottled up inside her, and now they'd all tipped over and everything was spilling out.

"No."

"Yes."

Tag started pacing, his hands still shoved deep in his pockets. *"No."*

"You said you saw the light falling. Did that seem *normal* to you?"

"I—I don't know."

"And you said you saw a boy in the truck. Did it look like a normal boy?"

Tag gave a half-hearted shrug, which Bee took to mean he definitely had seen something strange. "I didn't get a good look," he muttered finally. "But I think his skin was . . . glowing." He rubbed his forehead, then ran a shaking hand through his hair. The gelled strands stood on end as if he'd been electrocuted. He looked utterly undone. "I thought it was the moonlight . . . or something."

"Yeah," Bee said. "Glowing. He does that."

"Jesus. I don't even know what to say." He was shaking all over now, pacing back on forth across the thin path. Pebbles flew out from under the soles of his shoes each time he turned.

Bee held out the chain; it lay coiled on her palm like a snake. Tag certainly was staring at the links as if they were dangerous. And maybe they were—she knew nothing about what this thing was, except that she'd found it in the clearing covered in Starling's light when they were looking for something lost. She knew it probably was the item he'd been searching for. She still didn't understand why she didn't reveal it. She still didn't understand what it was.

Maybe it was the fact that Starling was dangerous, and Delta didn't see it. Or maybe it was the fact that Starling was obviously trying to take her sister away. Or the fact that Delta obviously wanted it to happen.

Bee clenched her teeth, her fingers going stiff.

Yeah, maybe it was that.

"This thing belongs to *him*."

"Why do you have it?" Tag's voice was faraway, his face still drained of color. He wasn't even looking at her; he was staring at the lights of the party. She could see the Christmas lights reflected in his blue eyes. What was he thinking about?

"I found it," Bee said. "And I kept it. I just want him *gone*. I don't want to give him anything he wants." The chain was so warm in her hand, she could almost imagine it was alive. She shook herself—*that's stupid, Bee, don't be ridiculous, it's a chain*—and continued, "This chain will give him more power. Power he can use to leave or stay."

"Leave?" Tag said.

"He won't do it," Bee said with certainty. "He doesn't want to leave. We can't give it to him until we're *sure* he'll use it for the right reason."

The chain was hot with energy—she could feel it coursing through her fingertips. All at once the heavy feel of this otherworldly, magical *thing* in her hand repulsed her. "I don't even *want* it anymore," she whispered, and then, even louder, "I don't *want* this!" She clenched her fist around the chain and then threw it as hard as she could. They both stared at where it had fallen amongst the neat rows of grapevines that pushed up against the Rockford guesthouse: even from a distance, they could see it dully glowing in the dirt.

"Good riddance," she said. The anger drained from Bee, turning quickly into a sour sort of worry. It was the type of worry that burrows deep and keeps burrowing until it cannot hear any excuses or soothing statements.

"Is Delta safe from this . . . this . . . ?" Tag trailed off, unable to say the word. He was still staring at the lights as if he'd gotten lost in them.

And Bee made a choice. She wasn't *aware* it was such a turning point; no one realizes something is a catalyst until it's much, much too late. "No," she breathed. "I don't think she's safe with him." It was only when she said it out loud that Bee realized she truly believed it. Her sister wasn't safe. Delta was so starry-eyed in the face of anything otherworldly; only Bee could see through Starling's mystique to the *danger* he was. If Delta left with Starling, she would never return. Or worse—she wouldn't survive. And if he stayed, they would always be hunted. They'd have to go on the run—and would Bee be included in those plans?

Starling had danger written all over him, and even if Delta didn't realize it, Bee did.

She had to look after Delta now, as Delta had always looked after her.

"Then . . ." Tag finally tore his gaze away from whatever thoughts he'd been delving deep into. His expression was fire; it was conviction. "I'll do whatever it takes to help."

Bee felt her shoulders lighten. Together they would find a way. With Tag's help, they could make Starling leave. She would do what was best for Delta, even if Delta didn't know it yet.

That's what sisters are for, after all.

"Let's start now," Bee said immediately. She could see it now in her mind's eye: Starling leaving by tomorrow morning, Delta falling into her arms, happy and realizing it was the right thing to do, and that Bee had *saved* her.

She ignored the squirm of guilt. This was all for the best.

Tag's expression softened, taking on a wry look. "Now? We should probably talk more when it's not three a.m. and we're not surrounded by other people."

"I guess," Bee allowed.

"I think I better get you home."

"I don't want to get home."

"Yeah, yeah. Come on." Exhaustion flowed off him in waves.

"I'll catch a ride with Delta later." She remembered her response when Delta had asked if she was coming home; her short, sharp *no*. Still—she knew Delta would still be in the parking lot, waiting for her. Annoyingly diligent. The hovering big sister, like always.

Tag paused. "Delta left already, Bee. She left with . . ." He swallowed hard. "With *him.*"

For a moment, Bee didn't breathe, and she could feel her face growing hot, too hot, as if she was burning up. All the times Delta had waited for her in the car flickered through her mind, one after the next. Delta knew that Bee's *no* meant *not yet*, not *not ever.* And yet Delta had left without her. Left to go home with Starling to do who knows what, all alone. Unless they didn't go home . . . What if Bee arrived to an empty house, devoid of sisters or aliens or fathers or *anything?*

"Okay," she said woodenly. "Let's go."

Tag cocked his head toward the parking lot, and Bee followed him back up the slope. She knew she was doing the right thing, but worry was overriding everything. She swallowed the sick feeling back down, hoping that once she was in Tag's Porsche, away from the raucous laughter and strings of bright lights and the smell of spilled shots, she'd feel better.

As Tag drove gracefully out of the Rockford gates, easily guiding the ostentatious purple car onto Main Street, it became clear to Bee that the quiet and the dark wouldn't help her one bit.

Because worry, if anything, expands in the darkness.

Main Street was completely shut down, a street of dark buildings and puddle-speckled asphalt. Most places are dark at both the impossibly late and impossibly early hour of three thirty, but there was something ghostly about Darling's darkness, as if when the lights were out, the town might slide away into nothingness. It was the type of darkness that lets thoughts burst free, unbidden and flowing, into the air.

Bee's thoughts were a maelstrom.

Tag shifted into fifth gear as Main Street turned into the two-lane highway. He coasted along, focused on the endless straight road passing beneath the tires. Bee watched him from the corner of her eye.

Why can't she just be with Tag and be happy? Bee thought.

She wanted to cry again. She usually quite liked a cry, because she liked to be hugged and soothed with her family's loving hands. But there was no one here now to console her, and she certainly didn't want to burst into tears in front of Tag. So she just stared hard at the dark grass rushing by outside the window, her whirlpool of worry and grief and stress eddying in her stomach.

She wanted her sister to stay. She had to *make* her sister stay, and find a way that didn't result in Starling staying with them. He had to leave, and leave without Delta. Bee was terrified of change, and if that made her selfish, so be it. She told herself again and again: *This is for Delta's own good.* Because if Delta left, where would she go? Would Bee ever see her again?

I can't lose another part of my family.

If their father was still here, it wouldn't be like this. . . .

Bee gave a great, gulping sob. *If their father was still here.* That was her secret. That was her shame. That was what she had been keeping from Delta for almost three months now.

It was her fault that their father was gone.

Of course, it wasn't *really*, but Bee couldn't see past the events leading to his disappearance. To her, they were inextricably linked, and it was all because of her.

She had come home from the Diner all those months ago, where she'd been having a nice, normal gossipy lunch with girls from school, to find her father in his study waist-deep in papers and maps. His glasses had been perched on the bridge of his nose, and he'd been frantically scribbling coordinates. A radio on his desk was tuned to a station with a "witness" detailing the most recent UFO crash, and he'd turned to Bee with the *light* in his eyes and practically yelled, "It's happening, my girl!" before launching into what was supposed to be an explanation. To Bee it had just been a long string of garbled catchwords: "Now's the time!" and "Energy!" and "Thin space!" and "Portal!" He kept smashing his hands together, as if to illustrate *something*.

It probably had something to do with the fact that Bee had just returned from a lunch with completely normal, rational, average girls who also happened to be very popular; it probably also had something to do with the fact that they'd made snide comments about Bee's *odd* family: whatever the reason, Bee snapped. The words coming out of her mouth had surprised even her, but she hadn't seemed to be able to stop.

"What is *wrong* with you? Why can't you just be normal?" she'd screamed. "Why can't we just be a normal family who doesn't believe in fake, *stupid* things?" She'd kicked at a pile of papers on the floor; they'd launched themselves into the air and become satisfyingly ruined. Her anger propelled her: she continued to yell at her father, who stood looking shocked at this unexpected outburst.

"Bee, Bee!" he'd finally exclaimed, waving his hands around to catch her attention.

All she could remember was the tight feeling in her chest, the feeling of embarrassment. Truly, she believed all her father did. But she didn't want to believe it. She wanted to be normal. She wanted to fit in.

"Bee, my girl, everyone has doubts sometimes, but—"

"You've wasted your life, Dad!" she'd screamed. "You've wasted it looking for something that *just isn't there!*"

"It's all true!" he'd replied, excitement replacing the confusion that had settled during her tantrum. "Look, I'll *show* you!"

He'd sprinted from the study, his coat flapping around his heels, and run downstairs to the closet in the hall. She'd been standing at the top of the staircase when he'd poked his head out of the closet, hair standing on end, fire in his eyes.

"I'll prove it to you, my girl!" he'd said, a smile identical to Delta's lighting up his face. "There's so much more out there, and I've figured it all out, I've found a way through! You'll see!"

And he'd snapped the door shut. By the time she'd hurried down the stairs and thrown open the closet door, there was nothing there but rows of shoes lining the floor and rows of coats on hangers.

He'd gone into that closet to prove to Bee he was right. So she wouldn't be embarrassed by her father, by her family. And he had been right about whatever strange things he'd been talking about—the portal and the thin space and that now was the time—because he'd never come back out.

All her fault.

"Are you okay, Bee?" Tag asked softly.

She hadn't realized she was crying now; salty tears streamed down her face, running over her chin and making the collar of her shirt damp. *All her fault.*

What would Delta say if she knew her own sister was the catalyst of their father's disappearance?

"I'm fine, thanks," she gulped. Tag had parked near the front door, and the Wild West was dark; no lights shone from the windows. She tried to summon up one of her classic Bee smiles, but nothing would come.

"Is Delta inside?"

"Yeah," Bee sniffled.

"Can I come in and talk to her? I want to make sure she's okay, especially if—if *he's* there."

"I—I don't know."

"Bee," Tag said, his voice verging into a beg. "I just want to make sure Delta is safe. Please."

Bee finally nodded, and together they hurried to the back door. The ground had turned to mud under the rain's constant attention, and Bee and Tag splashed through it. She pulled off her shoes at the door and fumbled with the lock. Her head was pounding; a reminder of both the party and her driving thoughts. Each word was like a kick to the head: *All your fault. All your fault.*

Delta. She had to see Delta. Tag followed her closely; was he feeling the same?

She hurried up the steps in her wet socks, dripping water in a trail along the hardwood. Delta's bedroom door was propped open, and Bee wedged herself inside.

There was no one there. Delta's bed was empty. Bee's stomach was in her throat as she ran across the hallway to Starling's room. No one. She hurried to his window and looked out over the woods and the backyard. Nothing. There was no one at all.

No, no, no, no, no . . .

"Where is she?" Tag asked, his voice low. Bee heard a current of panic run through it. "Is she okay? Has he *kidnapped* her?"

Had he? Bee's thoughts roiled, jumping into overdrive. *This couldn't be happening.* Where was her sister? Had she *left?* Had she run away with the alien, with the star, without even telling Bee? Had Starling grabbed Delta and run, disappearing into the sky? Half of Bee wanted to scream and half of her wanted to stand stone-still as her mind flew through every worst possibility. Everything was wrong; the world was imploding around her.

Delta was gone.

Bee was cold and wet and shaking and crying, so much so that she almost missed seeing the movement down at the tree line.

"Oh!" she said, a tiny sliver of sheer relief running through her.

Tag strode to the window and stood next to her, peering out the foggy panes at the woods below.

Delta and Starling, walking together. Their fingertips brushed up against each other's as they walked. The were still in shadow and the rain obscured their expressions, but Bee watched as they stopped and the smaller figure looked up at the taller, then went up on her tiptoes and pressed her lips to his.

Bee's jaw was so tightly clenched that she almost choked on her heart as it rattled around erratically. She turned from the window and left Starling's room, taking the steps one at a time.

Slow, measured footsteps. Any split-second relief she'd had upon seeing Delta come out of the woods had disappeared in a flash, and now everything was so much worse. She had never felt so hollow, so alone.

Tag swore, his words harsh and loud and dripping with bitterness, then turned to her and ruffled her hair like she was five years old. "Well. See you later, Bee." He swallowed, and she saw his fingers clench, unclench, then clench again as if a beating heart ran through his fingertips, as if they just couldn't help themselves. "Tell Delta I said hi." Each word was like a shot.

He left then, as if he couldn't bear to stand there another second.

But Bee couldn't help but watch, entranced, horrified. Down below, she heard the back door open, and she hurried upstairs to her own room, locking the door behind her. She had just crawled into bed when her phone buzzed in quick succession, startling her.

we know

keep your eyes open, Wilding

we're coming

Bee stared at the text, her jaw clamping down tightly, fearing she might be sick. Someone knew. Someone was watching. For a moment Bee considered waiting for Delta and Starling downstairs, but although the idea of a confrontation had seemed righteous and necessary at the party, with her anger and Tag's anxious disbelief fueling her, now . . . now she was just tired. Bone-tired, and guilt-ridden, and scared.

She just wanted Delta, but Delta was too wrapped up in

Starling. Too wrapped up in anything besides living here with Bee.

She threw herself down onto her bed and pulled the blanket up over her head, creating a dark cave deep under the covers, where there was nothing but her own damp breaths and her own heartbeat and her own fingers holding tightly to themselves.

Bee cried quietly in the darkness, but no one came, because no one was listening.

26

TAG DROVE, HIS FOOT

pressed down on the gas, his hands gripping the wheel at ten and two. The night pressed in around him, the stars like glittering diamonds cast onto a dark cloth. The stars mocked him, hanging heavy in the sky and crushing down, the brightness blinding him. They rocked in their places, taunting him.

And one had fallen from its place in the sky to take *his* place. To take everything from him.

It was impossible. *Impossible.*

But he couldn't stop his brain from replaying what he'd seen with his own two eyes. Delta and a boy—a strange, tall, faintly glowing boy. *Starling.* He would almost think he'd imagined it, except that Bee had been right there beside him, and he had seen them—seen them . . .

She doesn't want you.

The words came loudly as he remembered how she'd stood on her tiptoes to stretch up and kiss the inhuman figure at the edge of the woods. *She doesn't want you*—he knew it all too well now, and no matter how much a part of his brain shouted the impossibility of it, he knew what he'd seen.

One of those bright pinpricks above was currently in Darling, with Delta. Making Delta smile, and laugh, and everything Tag couldn't seem to do no matter how hard he tried. Darling lay behind him now, a tiny collection of darkened houses, but Tag didn't look back. He didn't want to imagine Delta and the star inside the dark and gloomy Wild West.

Instead, he kept his eyes on the lane divider, the glowing white lines flashing by as he accelerated. What would happen if he just *drove*? Just drove and drove and never stopped? If he urged his Porsche down this straight dusty road and then through the winding mountain pass and beyond, out of reach of Darling's eccentricities and the impossibilities it held within its houses?

What if he left everything and everyone behind? A part of him wanted to do it, just to see if anyone would miss him. Tag's foot pressed down harder, and the Porsche responded under him, purring along so fast, the winking stars above blurred into a swash of gleaming white.

Or maybe that was because of his tears.

No one would miss you.

You're a Rockford.

They'd rejoice.

His stomach turned, his knuckles going white against the leather steering wheel as his fingers tightened. It was just all so unfair. No matter what he did, he could never be what this *Starling Rust* was—something more, something otherworldly. Rockford or not, Tag would always just be the boy from Darling.

The boy Delta would never want.

A strangled shout was building in his lungs and he gritted

his teeth against the release, lifting a hand to furiously brush his traitorous tears away. It would do no good to scream, or cry. This was something his father had taught him—one of the lessons that had truly sunk in. The only important thing was to take *action.* All he had to think of was the next step.

What was the next step now?

Leave Darling and never return.

He could already hear his father's voice in his head respond-ing to that: *Rockfords never run from their problems.* Rockfords never did quite a lot of things, it seemed, or maybe Tag was just epically bad at being a Rockford. He was sure that's how his dad would see it.

And what would Delta say? Well, nothing. She'd ignore him until she was lonely at four in the morning and couldn't sleep. Although now she had someone else to turn to . . . someone Tag could never compete with. Someone who Bee thought was *dangerous.*

The determination rose in Tag—he had to stay.

What's the next step?

Making sure Delta was safe.

How do I do it?

Ways rattled through his head, some difficult, some illegal, some that would surely backfire in his face. And then suddenly—it hit him. It was so simple, so obvious.

There was one person in Darling who hated the Wildings and anything associated with them. One person who was sus-picious of the meteor already, and who would do anything—literally anything—to keep Darling safe and secure.

The thought of it put a bad taste in his mouth, but maybe doing something for the greater good was like that. He was being a martyr, really, but he had to remember it wasn't about him. It was about Delta, and Delta's safety. Even if she didn't believe it. Even if she didn't know it yet.

Even if she would never, ever forgive him.

But then again, Delta would never forgive him for simply being a Rockford.

Do what needs to be done.

Be a man.

Be a Rockford.

Tag screeched to a halt by the side of the dark road, and under the canopy of watchful stars, pulled his phone out of his back pocket and texted his father.

27

DELTA WAS GETTING

used to the little moments with Starling: waking up to find him in the kitchen, opening a bottle that the sheriff had left in a bag outside their back door; the way he gave that now-familiar half smile when something amused him; the sound of music drifting out from under the door to the guest room. It was getting easier and easier to pretend that this could be her life.

It was a fresh, cooler-than-usual morning, and Delta was in the living room, Starling on the couch beside her. Bee sat perched in the armchair, suspiciously quiet and sitting silently and staring out the window at nothing, as she had been ever since the party.

Not that Delta noticed.

"Delta?" Bee muttered.

Delta was reading, but she kept getting distracted by Starling, who was also reading. Somehow the mere sight of him with a book propped up, one thin finger leafing through the pages, drew all her attention.

Bee's hair was up in a ponytail, and if Delta had looked at her, *really* looked at her, she'd have noticed that her sister's face was more drawn and more pinched and more like Delta every day.

But Delta was thinking about Starling, so she didn't notice a thing.

"What?"

"What?" Bee replied.

"You said my name."

"Oh, right." Bee was quiet, then mumbled, "Can I talk to you?"

This made Delta glance at her sister. Bee's tone was so . . . sullen. What was *wrong* with her? Bee was never sullen. Even when mad, she gave tight smiles and sharp looks. She didn't pout and stare morosely out the window—that was Delta's thing. Delta closed her book. "Yeah. What's up?"

"Out in the hallway?" Her sister unfolded herself from the armchair and jerked her head toward the door of the living room.

Delta followed, only to have Bee shut the door firmly behind her and stare at her with a decidedly angry expression, arms crossed.

"Uh, what's going on?" Delta asked.

"When is he leaving?"

"Who?"

"*Who*, are you joking?"

"What is wrong with you? Why are you being so weird?"

Bee gave a one-shouldered shrug, ignoring the comment. "Just wondering. I feel he's been here a long time."

"Not that long."

Bee's eyebrows shot sky-high. She muttered, "Our money is basically gone." The unspoken words were *because of him*. Both girls heard them loud and clear.

"He doesn't use that much of the money. He doesn't do

anything except drink his alcohol, and we don't have to get that, now that the sheriff is helping out."

"Still. *Still.*"

"I think," Delta said, trying to keep her voice down so Starling didn't hear, "you're not seeing the big picture here."

"*I'm* not seeing the big picture?" Bee said, and her voice rose to a yell. "Are you *serious*?"

"Yes, you. What is wrong with you?"

"*You* are the one not seeing the big picture," Bee screamed, strands of blond loosing themselves from her ponytail. She took out her phone and brandished it at her sister, waving a text message in front of her face. "*Look!* I got this text, and I don't want to be a part of this anymore!" Her face was blanched, her freckles standing out all the more prominently.

Delta took the phone and scanned the text, her jaw tightening as she read the threatening words. *Breathe*, she said. *Just breathe.* They had the sheriff on their side now, after all. "We'll keep our eyes open," she promised, handing Bee's phone back to her. "I'll let the sheriff know."

"You're ignoring *all* the danger! Just having him in our house is dangerous! People are mad, people already hate us, and now . . ."

"Bee, calm down," Delta said, trying to sound soothing. "Honestly, you don't need to be worried."

"But I *am* worried!" Bee cried. "And then if he ever leaves—what then? We have no money, Delta! No *anything*! And oh, the tiny little issue that if he was found, we would probably go to jail! What would happen to us? We would be in so much trouble! I don't care about Starling; we have the rest of our lives to worry about!"

Delta was thinking that she didn't feel the rest of her life would be very exciting once Starling left, but she felt it probably wasn't the time to point this out. All she knew was that their lives now contained Starling, and that was everything.

"We won't be in trouble."

"You don't know that. This is what I mean—you're not thinking straight *at all*!"

The hallway around them was completely still; Delta and Bee standing with their arms crossed might've been the only people left in the world. Then Bee pushed by her sister, striding over to the closet. She threw open the door and gestured inside at the coats and boots. "Have you checked in here recently? Do you even *care* anymore?"

"Care? Of course I *care*!"

"Doesn't seem like it when all you do is have heart-eyes for Starling!"

"Shut up, Bee," Delta hissed. "I check the closet all the time. And what the hell am I supposed to do, huh? I can't *make* him come back! I don't know where he is, I don't know what to do, so if you're so all-knowing, then *please*, let me know! I'm doing the best I can!" Her voice shook, but Bee didn't even seem to hear. She slammed the closet door and stormed down the hall to the kitchen, stomping out into the backyard.

"Bee!" Delta called out to her sister's retreating figure, but Bee didn't turn around. Delta waited a full minute on the off-chance that Bee might come back, but Bee just slid into the

driver's seat, started up the truck, and jerked the wheel violently, so the truck shot away down the unpaved road.

Delta's stomach squirmed with guilt and she chewed again
on her bottom lip. Maybe she'd been too harsh with her sister. She knew her focus had been on Starling since his miraculous arrival, and Bee had never had to compete with anyone for
Delta's attention. But didn't Delta deserve to be happy too? Bee
was right that there was danger, but there *always* had been—
that's what her sister didn't seem to understand. Starling was
harmless—it was their town where all the danger resided.

Every part of Delta's body was conflicted with itself.

But as soon as she saw Starling sitting on the living room
couch with Abby asleep next to him, all the guilt and confliction
disappeared, only to be replaced by veins of fire and a racing
heart. They hadn't discussed what had happened in the woods,
but the memory of it had replayed every day in Delta's mind,
over and over again. Starling drawing her close, Starling's lips
pressing to hers . . .

Starling gently stroked Abby's head with his long, graceful
fingers as he stared out the front window at the unseasonably
cool day. On the coffee table was a half-drunk bottle of cheap
gin, and next to it was a book. What was he thinking about?
Was he also replaying the memory of their kisses?

"Hi," she whispered, standing in the doorway, trying to calm
her heartbeat.

Starling glanced at her, and his lips edged into a small smile
that made Delta feel like sinking into the floor. "Hello, Delta,"
he replied, tongue flicking out over the syllables. He was now

wearing the clothes they'd got for him at the store during the weekend: a pair of jeans and an old grey crewneck that said DARLING ACADEMY on the front and CLASS OF 1994 on the back. and she couldn't help but grin; his clothes looked so *normal*, until you noticed each one of his unearthly features. "Is . . . everything okay?"

"Yeah. Bee is just . . . being Bee." She hesitated; he must've heard Bee shouting at her, heard *what* she was shouting. "It's not a problem."

"I am sorry."

"It's not your fault," Delta replied, walking toward the couch and, after hesitating only for a second, settling down next to Starling. She kicked off her shoes and tucked her legs up underneath her. "Don't worry about it at all—we're both really glad you're here."

Delta reached forward for the book on the coffee table, her arm brushing his knee. "What are you reading?" she asked. She *did* want to know, but mostly she'd wanted an excuse to lean closer to him. *Thank God Bee isn't here*, she couldn't help but think. She now had hours upon uninterrupted hours of time alone with Starling. Her body thrilled at the thought. When Bee was around, Delta was overly conscious of every look and move toward the alien.

Now, though . . . now she could do whatever she wanted.

She turned the thin volume over in her hands, stroking a finger down the worn spine. "*The Wind in the Willows*?" Ever since Starling had said his first word to them, everything had been moving at the speed of light: he now spoke English like he'd been speaking it all billion years of his existence, and he'd memorized the letters in a single millisecond. Since then, he'd been tearing through every book she owned. "My dad used to read me this. Do you like it?"

"Very much so," he rasped.

"I'm glad," she replied softly.

He blinked once, languid and slow, and shifted closer to her. Hesitantly, he reached out to touch her cheek with the tips of his fingers, and began: "Delta, I have to tell you—" when he was cut off by a loud, short knock on the back door.

Alien and human froze.

Delta, practical as ever, was first to break free of the paralyzing reverie. "Get upstairs," she hissed, and Starling was off like a shot, if shots were silent and graceful. His speed, so much faster than a human's, made it hard for Delta's eyes to focus on him; it was like her brain couldn't process the way he moved, the way he was there one second and halfway up the stairs the next.

Delta moved to the door, hand trembling on the doorknob. The knock came again, and Delta flinched back: somehow that second knock told her everything she needed to know. Whoever was on the other side of the door was not a friend.

This was not going to be a courtesy call.

This was not going to go well.

She opened the door, and the sight of the mayor confirmed this.

"Ah, Delta Wilding!" said Mayor Rockford. He was smiling. Delta didn't know what to say—she didn't feel this greeting really warranted a response—so she didn't reply, instead leveling a contemptuous stare that would have left a lesser man tipping his hat and running away. But the mayor was rich enough that he had no fears about his security, especially not at the hands of one teenage girl. Delta was used to being underestimated, and in most situations, she would love to prove him wrong, but this visit felt different. The last time the mayor had been on their porch, he'd been intimidating, threatening. Now he was . . . happy. Something had made him happy. Something had happened to make him stand like he owned the place.

A pit developed in her stomach, sinking lower and lower. Something had happened. Something very bad was happening or about to happen, that was clear. Only bad things could happen when the mayor was around.

"Delta, Delta, Delta," Mayor Rockford said again.

"What?" Delta snapped finally. Her head was ringing with her name falling from his lips in that horrible, jovial voice, and she remembered when he'd called her something else, the word spit to her: *Whore*.

She tried to push it all away and put together some course of action to steer herself through this treacherous conversation, but she couldn't plan when she didn't know what was about to happen.

And she *really* didn't like Mayor Rockford's serene smile. He was too calm. All the threat was gone. He looked like . . . Delta's stomach plummeted. He looked like a man who already knew he had won.

The mayor didn't waste any time. "Delta Wilding," he began,

his tone shifting into full-on mayor. "My son has come to me with the most *fantastical* story."

If Delta's stomach had dropped before, now she felt like it had disappeared completely, leaving nothing but an empty hole behind. A gaping black hole, sucking all her breath away. Her mind was spinning—did Tag say something to his dad about the family friend? He thought she was dating someone else, yes.

But what did that prove?

He didn't know anything else; he *couldn't* know anything else.

Play it cool, Delta. She swallowed and forced herself to tense up. *Don't fall apart. Starling's depending on you.*

"Oh really? About what?"

"About the meteor." Mayor Rockford paused, then said, "He was under the impression that it was not a meteor at all, but a person."

Delta's mouth was so dry, she could hardly force the words out. "That's impossible." It was the merest whisper.

"It is, isn't it?"

"Yes."

"So is it not true?"

"No, it's not true."

"So, my son is lying?"

Delta just stared up into his flinty blue eyes and didn't reply. She hated him, every inch of him. Every sanctimonious smile, every tilt of his head. He clasped his hands in front of him— hands that were so like Tag's, the hands of the wealthy, long and graceful and elegant. Hands that could sign bills and drive fast cars. Hands that could fit around a neck.

She was shaking, burning so hot with hatred that spontaneous combustion seemed very much on the table.

"In any case," the mayor continued, "any sort of claim like this has to be taken seriously. For the good of Darling—you understand. If there *was* any truth to this impossible occurrence, the proper authorities would have to be called."

"Authorities?" Delta whispered, but her mind was just screaming, *Tag? Tag? Tag did this?*

"Oh yes." The mayor was enjoying himself now; his fake, simpering smile had widened past the point of false sympathy. "Don't worry, you don't have to do a thing. I've taken care of it all. The FBI are on their way. Depending on what they find, they'll have the full force of the military at their disposal."

It was every worst-case scenario come to light. Tears sprang to her eyes before she'd even processed the full impact of what he was saying: her body had heard and responded; her head would figure it out eventually.

"You can't," she got out. Her voice sounded desperate to her own ears, and she hated that she couldn't make the desperate tone leave. "Please."

"I thought Tag was lying? If that's true, you have nothing to worry about."

Delta and the mayor stared at each other. There was absolutely nothing she could do, nothing to say. She just had to get him out of here and start figuring out how to get Starling safe. Hidden. And she had to do it quickly.

"That's true," she said, her voice shaking with each word. "I guess I have nothing at all to worry about, then."

Mayor Rockford smiled at her. "I'm sure you're very glad Tag informed me. If *any* part of this story is true, then it's high time some adults came to take over."

"I am glad," Delta whispered. She began to close the door—politeness didn't seem to matter much anymore. Being polite hadn't ever gotten her very far with Tag Senior, anyways. "I'm sure you are too."

"Oh?"

"Yeah," Delta said. "Glad to know that your son turned out to be a Rockford through and through."

She slammed the door, sliding every lock into place with loud, resounding clunks. She knew he heard; she didn't care. Where before she'd been on the verge of tears, now everything seemed cold. Her rage had hardened into ice.

She hadn't wanted to understand at first. She hadn't wanted to believe that Tag would really fall so far. That Tag would betray her. She had no idea how he'd found out about Starling— did Tag see Starling hiding in the truck? No, she was sure he'd been ducked down when they talked at the party. Was it—her stomach dropped farther—Bee? It couldn't be. Bee might be mad at her, but she'd never do that.

No matter how he'd found out, he'd taken that information and given it to the worst possible person.

Her whole body was shaking, trembling with suppressed rage, with suppressed—everything. She clenched her jaw so tightly, she thought it might break.

It was because of this hard rock of barely contained rage inside that she took the steps up to Starling's room slowly, one at a time, and when she entered his room, she couldn't seem to describe what had happened in anything other than a monotone.

Maybe Starling had the right idea after all, she thought, and the rock tightened and clenched. *Experiencing no emotions would be better than this. Anything would be better than this.*

"Tag . . . Tag told."

"Tag? The human boy?"

"Yup." Each word was short and sharp. She knew that she had hurt Tag when he'd seen the figure of Starling in her truck, but this . . . She felt hot and sick. She felt *betrayed*. After everything . . . he had gone to his father.

Starling went still on the bed, looking altogether bewildered.

"Who?" he said, his voice grating.

"Tag told his dad. The mayor of Darling. And . . ." Delta's voice caught in her throat. "He's called in the FBI. The government—people who will take you away to who knows where. We have to get you out of here." She brought a shaking hand to her temple. Her face felt flushed, and her head was pounding as she met Starling's black eyes. "Starling, I'm so sorry. I never should've told *anyone* about you, because somehow Tag found out. And now you'll have to hide."

"I can hide. Anyway, humans cannot kill me."

"But they can injure you, can't they? They can take you away. And do *horrible* things," Delta said, her voice breaking. "You were right the whole time about humans, okay? We can be stupid and thoughtless and mean. And I don't know where your chain is, I don't know how to hide you from the FBI . . . This is all just . . . *too much*."

Starling was still staring at her, eyebrows furrowed. He sucked in the sallow skin at his cheeks. Slowly, like he was still determining what had happened, he said, "And this is happening because . . . Tag told someone I am here?"

"Yes," Delta whispered.

Starling looked like many words were running through his head. Finally, he settled on, "Why?"

Delta shook her head and shrugged at the same time, a strange flinching movement that she felt summed up perfectly how she was feeling. She wanted to hug Starling, she wanted to cry, she wanted to scream. She didn't really know how to answer him—she didn't know *why*. Why does anyone do anything?

She didn't understand anything anymore. All she knew was that she didn't know Tag at all. Why had he done it?

Tag and the mayor were just people who did things.

That was all anyone was.

"Welcome to the human race," said Delta.

28

STARLING WATCHED AS
Delta called the sheriff, her words clipped and said without a trace
of fear or anger. She sat on the living room floor, legs drawn up
to her chest, her phone on speaker. It was so strange; he'd always
noticed the fluctuating emotions of these humans, but now Delta
seemed more like him—or how he wished he could be. As she
informed the sheriff of the news and asked if they could come stay
at her house, she sounded detached and cold.

As soon as she got the go-ahead from the sheriff and hung
up, Delta collapsed her head onto her knees and drew a circle of
arms around her, all her energy seemingly used up. Bee sat on
the couch, glowering. She'd come back to the house hours after
she'd stormed out, now armed with a to-go bag of fries from the
Diner, and had listened, silent and tense, as Delta explained what
had happened while she was gone. Starling watched as Bee's
mouth tightened when she heard what Tag had done; watched
as she threw herself down on the couch and crossed her arms.

Starling couldn't think of one single thing to comfort them.
He wasn't used to comforting, or even being able to comfort. He
wasn't used to the influx of human feelings that rushed through
him. But when Delta mumbled a muffled "This is such a mess"

from her cradle of arms, he couldn't help but place a long-fingered hand on her back.

From the horrified look Bee gave him, he might have just karate-chopped Delta in the spine. But he didn't remove his hand until Delta sighed and slithered upright again.

"Thanks," she murmured in his direction, not glancing at either of them. "I'm going to bed." She got up and left the room.

Bee leaned forward. Her freckles stood out in the lamplight, speckles on her skin so prominent, it looked as though they were trying to escape the flesh that bound them. Her eyes looked brighter than usual, although it might've just been the light. "I told you to stay away from my sister," she said in a low voice.

"Yes," Starling replied. What else was there to say?

"And have you been?"

"No," said Starling.

Even though it was obvious this was the answer Bee had expected, tears sprang unexpectedly to her eyes.

"I thought we had an understanding. You leave Delta *alone*," she hissed.

"I know," Starling sighed. "I know I have to, I just . . ." He couldn't tell the young human the truth—she hated him enough. If she knew that him being here was the reason their dad couldn't come back? Well. It would be chaos.

But it simply wasn't fair. He didn't want to go. He found it so hard to stay away from Delta; despite the fact that everything in his body screamed at him to stop, he didn't want to listen to himself. It was just him, alone in the farmhouse, surrounded by humans. The thought thrilled him.

He was here and their father was not.

Push and pull.

But he didn't want to go. He loved it here; he realized it now for what it was. *Love.* He loved the wet, earthy smell outside his window after it rained, and the crisp pages of Delta's books as he read. Walking next to Abby as she sniffed lazily around the edge of the woods. The bright swash of stars above, farther away than he'd ever known. The way the music shifted through the rooms of the old house, refracting off the walls like light, bouncing back to them. His hand on Delta's waist. His lips on hers.

"You're putting her in danger, you realize that, right? Now the FBI are coming to Darling and it's all because of you."

Starling sighed again. He wanted to stay on this planet. Delta had twice saved him; couldn't he be the savior now? Maybe their life would pass by always running, always moving . . . but they would be together, and he would be on this strange, wonderful planet.

"Stop sighing," Bee said, the words tumbling out her mouth. He glanced up to find tears glittering in her eyes. "You have to *do* something about all the problems you've made! Will you leave? Are you going to leave? Tell me the truth!"

He couldn't say a word.

She opened her mouth again as if to speak, but then with a sudden sob she hurried out of the room, wiping her eyes furiously, leaving Starling by himself.

It was so much easier when he had no feelings. No guilt.

He only waited until he heard Bee ascending the steps to the third floor, and then he went to find Delta. *I don't want to go. I shouldn't have to leave.*

"Delta?" Starling spoke softly as he opened the door to Delta's room, his eyes latching onto the small, curled form on the bed. Delta was sitting by the headboard, arms wrapped around her knees. Tears ran down her cheeks, disappearing into the collar of her gray-and-green Oakland A's sweatshirt.

"Oh. Starling." Delta wiped the back of her hand over her face, glancing at the alien. The sight of her there was making his stomach *feel* in a fluttering, uncomfortable way. "I was just . . ."

"You are crying."

"Yes," said Delta simply.

"Why?"

For a moment he thought Delta wouldn't answer, but then she bit her lip and managed, in a brittle voice thick with tears, "Everything . . . is a mess. Such a *mess.*"

And then she was crying again, and her hand came out, curled into a fist, and slammed down into the pillow of her bed. "A mess," she said, slamming her fist down again. The pillow sank obligingly beneath her fist. "I miss my dad. I'm so mad, so—so *hurt*—by Tag. And I don't know how to protect you. I'm so far in over my head that I feel like I'm *drowning.*" She hit her pillow again as a sob broke free.

He might not have understood all her emotions, but he understood the want to take all the energy and feelings and take it out on something else. As though from far away, he heard himself saying, "Do you want to try that on something more substantial?" He was so aware of himself, of her . . .

"I don't want to hit you."

"Why?"

"Because I don't want to hurt you," said Delta.

Starling laughed. The idea was preposterous. "You won't."

"I know I won't *physically*. It's not about that." She shook her head slowly, the makeup she'd lined her eyes with streaking down her cheeks in black rivers, then sank her shaking fist back into the pillow. It deflated with a sigh. "When you care about someone, you don't want to hurt them."

"But you would never—"

"You don't want to *try* to hurt them." She met his eyes, gave him a watery smile. "I don't need to take out my mess on you."

"It is because of me that you are in this mess."

"I don't care," Delta whispered.

"You lie."

"No. No, I'm not lying."

"How can that be true?" Starling rasped. "How can that possibly be true?" He took a step toward her, then another, reaching out to her. She placed her small hand in his, and he felt his joints click softly as he folded them around her fingers.

"Because," Delta said, eyes rimmed red. "Having you here— here in the house, here on Earth . . . well, it's worth it. It's a mess, but it's worth it."

Her eyes welled up again, and Starling didn't pause to think before he pulled her closer. She fell against him, burying her face in his borrowed shirt. Her body was so tiny compared to his, so soft, so warm; he could hear each harried beat of her heart, each sharp breath, and he could feel the wetness of each tear acutely against the space at his neck where the buttons of his shirt revealed his skin.

It was nothing. It was everything.

He was so caught up, so unbelievably caught up in this girl, in this world, in the feelings that were hitting him all at once, that he didn't even remember all the reasons why he should step away. All he knew was that Delta was crying, and then she was sniffling, and then she was turning her face up toward his.

"Starling." She reached up, curling her fingers around his neck. She looked at him with no fright, no disgust. "You can feel human emotions, can't you?"

"What?" he replied, and his stomach suddenly felt sick as he was once again reminded of the differences between them. *She is human. I am not.* He couldn't stop forgetting.

"I know that you're not emotionless. Maybe you were once, but now . . . you can feel. You *do* feel."

"How?" he said, and his voice sounded raspy even to his own ears. "How did you . . . ?" *How, indeed?*

"Well. It's obvious," Delta said.

"I am not a human. I do not feel."

Delta was so close to him. She stood on her tiptoes, and her breath was on his lips when she said, "You're lying."

And he was. For the briefest half second, it occurred to him that perhaps he should just swoop Delta up into his arms and kiss her and, perhaps, not stop. Because Delta was right; despite how adamantly he denied it, he *was* feeling everything; every strange human emotion was seeping into his celestial skin.

Despite what seemed possible, he did have a soul. And his entire soul was burning to be with Delta.

"I do not—"

"Okay, okay. You're not fooling anyone." And she laughed.

It was her laugh that did it. He let his fingers crawl their way into her hair, and bent slightly, curling his thin shoulders inward, bringing his face down to hers. Their lips had barely touched when Starling put his hands on her shoulders and, as gently as possible, stepped back and pushed Delta away from him.

The guilt was eating him alive. He couldn't do this, not with what he knew. He'd thought he'd be able to push the fact of her father's disappearance from his mind, but it was impossible.

"Delta. We should not."

"I . . ." Delta stumbled away, a variety of emotions flitting across her face, which flushed. Her mouth opened, closed, opened.

"We cannot be together."

It was a whisper, an echo of a whisper. "I understand."

"If I could, I would—but it just isn't possible. And this . . . this thing between us . . . it will just make everything harder when I go."

She set her mouth, and kept her eyes on the floorboards, and said: "Yes. I know."

Delta, ever the brave. Ever the rational.

There was a long silence: from Delta's point of view, the silence was horribly loud and filled with unshed tears.

"I'll see you tonight," he said finally. "When we leave for the sheriff's." But all he could think was, *It will be different then.* He sidestepped her and crossed to the door.

"Starling—wait," said Delta. Her voice was so small, the words forced out. He paused and turned back. She shifted from foot to foot, the very picture of agitation. "I have to . . . tell you something."

He waited, a strange feeling—was that *nervousness?*—beginning to stir inside him. He already wanted to walk back toward this human girl and sweep her up and do all the other things he'd read about in her books. It was hard enough walking away and not looking back.

Delta blushed, then said in a rush, "Starling, I *know* we shouldn't, but . . . I want to. I want to be with you. And not just because you're an alien. Not because you're a part of the universe. Because . . . because I've never felt happier than when we sit next to each other on the couch. And I think—I really think—we might be able to make this work. *Us* work. There *has* to be a way. You said it yourself, the universe brought you to me. It's not a coincidence." She stopped, realizing what she'd just said. It wasn't elegant. But it was true. "I want you," she said again, then looked right at him. "Do you want me?"

Starling paused. The room was too small; it pressed inward over his bones. It saturated itself with his hesitation. Because *yes*, he did, and there was no way he could tell her. There was no way he could act on it. Not here, not now.

Delta didn't wait to hear his response; she took his hesitation and formed her own conclusions. Her face drained of color, leaving only two bright spots of red high on her cheeks. "Never mind. It's okay. I mean—you're an—you're from the stars, and I never thought that maybe you don't . . . I mean . . ." She swallowed hard, audibly, then said in a rush, "You probably don't even—I shouldn't assume you'd even want a, um, *relationship* or whatever—you might not even *do* that sort of thing—"

"Delta . . ." He stepped toward her, reaching out to rest his long fingers on her shoulder.

She jerked away, not looking at him. "No. It's fine. It's okay. You don't have to justify anything. I don't . . . I don't need you, Starling. It was just a silly . . ." She stopped and took a deep breath. "It was a silly, stupid human thing. Let's just forget this ever happened." She straightened her spine and kept her eyes on the floorboards, then stiffly walked out.

Starling didn't follow her.

He wasn't human, and he didn't know he was supposed to.

29

THE THREE OF THEM

stood in the darkness outside the Wild West, duffel bags packed full of clothes at their feet and Abby at Delta's side, stoic and watchful. All the doors locked tightly behind them, all lights flicked off. Its wooden porch creaked behind them, as if it knew they were leaving, and was saying goodbye.

There were no stars out tonight, and a haze drifted low over the roofs of Darling; fitting, Delta thought. Fitting for a night like tonight. Her cheeks were still red from Starling's rejection, and she felt they might possibly stay that way for the rest of eternity. She stood apart from both of them, busying herself by checking the zippers on the duffel bags—Bee's kept springing open to reveal shoes and dresses and winter coats and all sorts of things she certainly didn't need for a short stay in June.

She knew Bee noticed the strange coldness between her and the alien, but she wouldn't meet Bee's gaze, and so they all stood in complete silence until a black shape turned off the main highway and made its way up the dirt road. Abby gave a worried sort of yip, and Delta rubbed her ear comfortingly.

"It's okay, girl," she whispered. "That's help coming."

The sheriff's Escalade, with all its lights off, was a ghost in the night. It was just what they needed to transport an alien through a town like Darling.

"Bags in the trunk, dog in the back seat," Sheriff Schuyler whispered without preamble. She stayed far away from Starling's dimly glowing form, but she did give him a jerky sort of nod. "The faster we can get out of here, the better. Who's driving your car over?"

"Me," Delta said immediately. Starling needed the protection of the sheriff, and Bee was still her younger sister, even if they weren't on speaking terms. Delta was the dispensable one. It made her feel grimly strong, to drive the noticeable car in this escape plan, and she slid into the driver's seat of the truck without another word.

"Remember not to park out front," the sheriff told her through the open window. "My house is at the other edge of these woods, so drive all the way through into the backyard. Get as far into the trees as you can. I'll find a tarp we can throw over the truck; hopefully that will be enough for the time being."

"We can just leave it here, I guess?" Delta whispered back, although her heart gave a pang at the thought of leaving their father's truck behind. Her fingers tightened on the wheel.

"I considered it, but at this point, I think it's best to have every method of escape possible." She nodded firmly to Delta. "We'll meet you at my house."

Delta waited for the Escalade to leave, a shadow cutting through the night, before she slid it into drive and started off. The Wild West got smaller and smaller behind her, and for a moment Delta was tempted to swing the truck around and run back inside her childhood home. Run upstairs and hide under the covers like she used to do when she was overwhelmed. And her dad would stroke her hair and Abby would lie on her feet and the house would settle around her and sometimes turn on comforting songs it thought she might like. And Bee would always be there to crawl into bed next to her.

And now her dad was gone, and Bee and Abby were looking out different car windows, and the house was in her rearview mirror.

There were no cars out on the main stretch of road, and she drove in silence, listening to the rumble of the truck and the turning of the tires as they carried her on. In the distance was the Diner, still awake even at midnight. There were only two cars in the lot, parked like statues in front of the large glass windows. One, the dilapidated Corolla; the waitress's car. The other . . . Delta stiffened in the driver's seat.

It was almost automatic, the way she slowed the truck and swung it into the parking lot. Where just moments before, her thoughts were a whirlpool, now there was just a dull sort of roar. She parked as far from the Diner as possible, half-hidden behind the spiky Joshua tree. Then she got out of the truck and crossed to the front door of the Diner, her eyes locked on the tousled blond hair and slumped body of the boy who sat inside.

30

THE LIGHTS IN THE

Diner flickered, bathing Tag with a fluorescent pinky-red glow. He was alone, apart from the wayward waitress who, like him, had her cheek slumped in a cradle of her hands. Alone. Alone in the red leather booth, sipping a thick vanilla milkshake through a bendy straw: the lone prince of a deserted, dusty kingdom.

The waitress narrowed her eyes at him over her fingertips, shooting him a look of unreserved disgust.

The prince of a kingdom that didn't want him.

Tag eyed her back for a moment, then sighed and buried his head again in his fingers, letting the bluesy song playing over the sound system lull him into a stupor. It wasn't worth asking what her problem with him was—he knew what it was. It was the same damn reason he hated himself, but there was nothing he could do.

He was a Rockford.

He'd proven it to himself the night of the party, proven it beyond a shadow of a doubt. As he'd been driving along, the single fast car on a deserted road with a star-laden tapestry above, telling his father had seemed like the best idea. The *only* idea. It had been a way to relieve some of the jealous anger rising up in him against Delta. It had been a way to maybe, just maybe, get his dad to smile at him.

And his dad had. He'd come home early from his trip and brought Tag into his office and forced the whole thing out; every strange and impossible detail. He'd even clapped Tag on the back as he left the room, already pulling out his sleek phone, already dialing numbers, and Tag had been left standing on the bloodred Persian rug, feeling sick and sluggish.

Like he'd just done something very, very wrong.

He was so *done*. He just wanted to forget what Bee had told him; he wished he'd never seen the face behind the dusty truck windshield. Everything about it was impossible. He wanted to call Anders and tell him to bring a bottle of *anything* so they could just sit and talk about nothing. But Anders would know something was wrong—and how could Tag tell him what it was? He couldn't even admit it to himself.

If someone told him he'd dreamed the past few weeks, he might've believed it.

The door jangled, and he jerked his head up. Delta stood there while she scanned the Diner; it only took a split second for her wild eyes to land on Tag, alone in his booth. She let the door swing shut behind her as she stalked toward him.

He let the chewed-up straw drop from between his lips back into the almost-drunk milkshake, sitting up straight in the booth. Trying to act as if he hadn't been slumped over, half-asleep and dour, just seconds before. He blinked, and Delta slid into the red-upholstered booth seat across from him.

"Hello, Tag," she said. Sitting so close to him, he saw she was trembling, as if she was not a girl but a storm with skin, the tempest just waiting to break free and unleash her fury. There was an urgency to her, an underlying wildness. She smiled, and the smile hardened into something violent red. "Of course you're here."

"I'm always here," he finally said, his voice barely more than a murmur. He knew the yelling was coming, and there was nothing to do about it. Better to get it over with. He cleared his throat and said, "I guess my dad talked to you."

"He did," Delta said. Her fingers were clasped together on the Formica table, her thumbs tapping each other wildly. She didn't meet his eyes; her gaze was burning a hole in the center of his chest.

"I was going to tell you—I wanted to talk—"

"I don't want to *talk*," Delta snapped.

"To anyone?"

"To *you*."

"Look, Delta . . . I'm sorry."

"Sometimes *sorry* doesn't cut it, Tag," Delta said, her voice sharpening. That was fine: he supposed he deserved it. He would welcome the anger. He wanted the fight. Delta being mad at him was better than Delta ignoring him.

"I get that. I just . . . ," Tag began helplessly. "I thought you were in danger. *Are* in danger. I mean, Del. An alien. In your house! Can't you understand how wild that sounds?"

He watched Delta absorb all of this. Watched the thoughts swirl in her eyes, his words start to sink into her mind. Maybe he could get her to understand. See things from his perspective.

But just as he thought there was a chance, he saw her eyes start to darken, black pools of resentment and confusion. And it was then that Tag realized he wasn't Tag to her anymore. He was a Rockford, a jealous, angry, bitter Rockford. He couldn't stand that look—not from anyone, but especially not from Delta.

"Yes, I can," Delta finally said. "But your *dad*? He hates me. *Hates* me."

Tag sat silently, then took a long sip of his milkshake. "I didn't know what else to do." He watched as Delta sat back in the booth as if he'd knocked all the air out of her, then followed up with a short, sharp: "That's something you understand, yeah? Feeling so far underwater that you're drowning and not knowing what to do?"

"Yeah," Delta murmured after a moment.

Tag sighed and leaned back into the booth. "So I made a choice. Okay?"

Delta put her elbows on the table, then slumped forward, her head in her hands.

"I'd do anything to take it back, though," he added, forcing himself not to reach out and touch her cheek, her hand. "When I realized what he was planning on doing, who he was planning on calling, I begged him not to."

"What the hell did you think would happen?" Delta mumbled, her voice muffled.

Tag shrugged helplessly. The past few days had seemed unreal, nightmarish. "As soon as I told him, I wished I hadn't. You have to believe that."

Delta glanced up, but then said, "I do."

"Oh—really?" He hadn't thought it would be so easy. The rest of his excuses pooled on his tongue, unsaid.

"I said I believe you, not that I *forgive* you."

"Maybe one day?" He smiled, but it felt weak. It was hard to remember a time when his smiles were brilliant and languid and could say more that his words ever could.

Delta finally met his eyes, and her expression was cold now, all the fire and anger drained away. "No," she said.

Tag sighed. He deserved it. He deserved it all. But still, his stomach twisted as he realized that for Delta, it was over. Really and truly over. Their relationship, their friendship, everything. He had ruined it all in one fell swoop. Just like him to do something so destructive.

Just like a Rockford.

"Maybe I don't care if you forgive me." It was a bald-faced lie. He was angry, but he still loved the wild, tempestuous girl before him.

"I think you do."

"I think," he said, "that it doesn't really matter anymore, does it? Not with *him* here." He mimicked her pose, slumping down onto the table.

He hadn't wanted to deal with it, with *anything*. He'd wanted someone else to take over. Look where his meddling, his desire to please his dad, his sheer arrogance, had gotten him. Had gotten them all.

He was always on the wrong side. God, he had enough self-pity to drown in.

Come on, Tag, sit up straight and be a Rockford. The voice in his head sounded a lot like his father's. He shivered, but sat up and tried to smile. It was a grimace, a farce of a smile, but he was proud of the effort.

"Tag," whispered Delta, her voice scratchy.

"I really am sorry."

Delta sighed. "How did you even find out?"

Tag opened his mouth, then shut it. So Bee hadn't said anything yet. Well, there was no point in throwing her under the bus. No need to wreck another relationship. He could take everything on his own shoulders. It could be his fault; he had to be okay with that.

"I saw him clearly in the truck," he said, the lie heavy on his tongue.

"No you didn't, you would've said something," Delta said, and her face scrunched up with anger. "Why are you still *lying*?"

Tag just shrugged again and set his cheek down on his palm. The gravity of this night was pulling at his bones.

Delta laughed then, and it was pure, undiluted bitterness. "I should've known, I guess. It's just like you to—"

"Is it like me?" Tag interrupted. "*Is* it though, Delta?"

"Yes," she said staunchly.

"*Why?* Because I'm a Rockford?"

"Yes!" Delta cried, throwing her hand in the air. "Yes! Exactly! And you prove over and over again that all you care about is getting a pat on the back from your dad!"

"You have no idea what I care about," Tag said, and he could hear his words growing sharper as his own anger grew and responded to hers. "And you have *no* idea what it's like to grow up with a dad like mine."

She fell silent at this, watching him. He couldn't read

her expression—maybe that had always been the problem between them. They each wholeheartedly believed they knew the depths of the other's soul, when in reality neither understood the other at all.

"All I wanted to do is help you. Everything that I've done, I've done for *you*."

"I didn't ask you to help," Delta said.

"I *know* you didn't!" Yes, he knew he'd messed up, but Delta hadn't been perfect either. Why couldn't she realize that he'd only been trying to help? "And why not? We've been friends for so many years, haven't we? Why would you not trust me? Why do you *never* trust me?" It was a hollow sort of feeling knowing the depths of Delta's distrust. She couldn't even *pretend* she wanted his help. She couldn't even pretend she still cared for him.

He watched Delta deflating before him. She sank her elbows down onto the table and was silent for a moment, staring at him with her glittering green eyes. "I . . . I do." It sounded like a question.

Tag snorted. "Yeah, okay. Now who's lying?"

Delta was just staring at him, her mouth open, eyes wide. Finally she rubbed her fingers over her face; all the fight had gone out of her. "Remember when all this was easy?"

"You and me?"

"Yeah."

"Yeah." Tag swallowed hard. Who knew when else he would be able to speak to her like this, uninterrupted by sisters or fathers or misunderstandings? He had to keep talking; he had to get it all out. "I know I'm not perfect," he whispered. "But sometimes I think you hate me because it's easier than admitting to yourself that you like me."

Delta's eyes widened even more, if that was even possible. "Tag," she breathed, then swallowed, seemingly lost for words. "That—I don't—I don't—I don't hate you."

Don't you? "You see me in such a bad light," Tag answered, and although he'd tried to say it with power, with anger, his voice broke. *Because you know it's true.*

"I see you how you actually are," Delta whispered. Her knuckles were white, straining against the skin.

Tag shook his head, and it took a few long breaths before he felt like he'd be able to reply without his voice breaking again. "Do you, though?"

"Yes." But she didn't sound very sure.

"I don't think you do. I think I see *you* clearly."

"You don't."

"See the problem?"

Delta dropped her head, so all he could see of her was the bridge of her freckly nose. "How do you do it?"

"Do what?"

"Make it so I'm not mad at you."

"Ah, well," Tag said dryly. He suddenly felt exhausted. "We all have our talents."

"What you said before? I don't always see you in a bad light." Again, she didn't sound sure. She kept biting her lip, and she couldn't meet his eyes.

"Delta," Tag replied, tilting his head back against the booth

and watching her out of half-open eyes. And he said the thing
he'd been slowly realizing over the course of many years and
ups and downs and read-between-the-lines fights. The truth
that had come to a point in the past few days. "I don't think
there's a thing in the universe that would make you think better of me."

"That's not true."

"It *is*," Tag shot back immediately.

"Everything would be different if you hadn't left me there
that night," she whispered. They both knew the night she meant;
almost exactly a year ago, it was the night that sent their relationship down a hole too deep to climb back out of. They each
saw it in the other's eyes—the lights of the party; their carefree,
tipsy laughter mixed with kisses; the twisted expression of his
father's face as he hissed his hateful words.

She was probably right. Everything would have been different if he'd been able to be braver that night. But there was more
to this imploding relationship than that.

When Tag spoke, he spoke each word clearly, so she couldn't
pretend she hadn't heard him. "Everything would be different if
I was the one from the stars."

He grabbed his mostly drunk vanilla milkshake and sipped
at the dregs, if only to give himself something to do with his
hands. What did people *do* with their hands? His couldn't stop
shaking. Delta was so *still*. She was completely silent, her chest
moving rapidly up and down in short shallow breaths. What,
Tag considered, had he actually been expecting her to say to
that? She had no defense for the truth, and she knew it. Tag

had neatly knocked down her excuses, one after the next.

"You okay?"

Silence.

"You want me to leave?"

"I want," Delta said, "for you to fix what you started."

Tag pushed himself up straighter, grabbed his keys, and then inelegantly fished some crumpled bills out of his pocket and laid them down on the table. Some things were deeply ingrained, and Tag's surface-level manners were one of them. So he swallowed all his mournfulness and stuck it into his echo chamber of a heart, then managed a brittle smile as he stood. He could feel the waitress's glowering gaze watching him as he began to walk away. Delta didn't try to make him stay—of course she didn't.

When he was about ten feet away, he turned back, fixing Delta with his blue, blue eyes. He knew they were just like his father's. He knew Delta held it against him—knew the entire town did. The waitress snapped her gum behind the counter and watched the exchange. Let her gawk. He couldn't bring himself to care.

"Look, I know I fucked up. Okay?"

She tilted her head up toward his; he couldn't read the expression exactly. It was just *watching*, void of emotion. Like she was carefully filing away everything he said or did so she could use it against him later. She wouldn't be the first. And he wouldn't let it stop him now.

"But so did you, even if you won't admit it. You can't say you've been *nice*. You can't say you've really *tried*. I'm fucking desperate, Delta, because I don't want to lose you, and I was just trying to protect you from yourself. Because despite it all—I still want you. So if you want to talk—if there's some way I can help make it right . . . well, I'm always around." He straightened up, giving a curt nod to the waitress—she ignored him, of course—and walked to the door of the Diner. The bells on the door jangled furiously as he opened it.

"I'm sorry. Sorry for—" *For betraying you. For snitching. For choosing the wrong side for too long. I'm sorry for what happened at the Mayor's Ball. I'm sorry I won't make leaving me behind easier for you.*

I'm sorry I'm a Rockford.

I'm sorry I will always be a Rockford.

He knew the same thoughts were going through both their minds. There was nothing really left to say. "Sorry for everything," he finished. Then he turned on his heel and let the door slam shut behind him, announcing the departure of the Once and Future Rockford, the boy who would never be king.

31

DELTA STARTED UP the truck and pulled back onto the main road, flicking off her headlights so she could drive the streets of sleeping Darling in darkness. The only person in Darling who could punish her for driving this way had done it herself, with a hidden extraterrestrial in the back seat; Delta felt she was pretty safe, all things considered.

Was it possible to make yourself sick from sadness? She didn't even know what she was sad about. Tag's voice, brimming with hurt that *she'd* caused. The things he said—every time she thought of it, her stomach heaved.

You have no idea what it's like to grow up with a dad like mine.

Why do you never trust me?

You hate me because it's easier than admitting to yourself that you like me.

Everything would be different if I *was the one from the stars.*

Delta felt unmoored, drifting alone on a choppy, angry sea. All this time her conflicted feelings toward Tag had seemed *right*. She'd thought her reactions were justified because *she knew Tag*.

But maybe she didn't. Which meant that all this time . . . she had been wrong. She had been *cruel*.

Her thoughts were paralyzing; she was freefalling. She could feel herself tuning out, as if her mind was very deliberately making a choice not to consider that particular line of thought. It was saving itself from the fall. It was, after all, a long way down once you jumped.

And then the second string of anxiety roiling within her was the ever-present knowledge of the truth that Starling couldn't stay with her. That soon she'd have to say goodbye.

Tag, Starling.

Darling in one boy, the universe in the other.

No good solutions. No answers, just hurt. How had it come to this?

She peered into the gloom as the outline of Sheriff Schuyler's house appeared. The new sheriff was in one of the first houses on Main Street, barely a mile and a half from the Wild West. Her backyard was large, the grass long and uncut, and edging onto the boundary of the woods. The sheriff's house had only one light on, and Delta steered the truck up the driveway, past the side of the house, and out into the backyard. The trees bordering the yard were spaced far apart, enough for Delta to carefully pull the truck so it was mostly hidden behind the tree line.

She threw the truck into park, then sat with her cheek pressed against the cold glass of the window. She felt numb, frozen in place.

Sniffling, she lifted her head for a moment to rub the salty tears from her eyelashes. She caught a flicker of movement from the house, and she peered out the window. A stiff wind blew the treetops into one another, making them wave about like dancers caught up in some wild, undone dance.

And then she saw him, moving toward her like a shadow, like a ghost. He disappeared behind a tree, then reappeared behind another; he moved sinuously, as if his feet didn't even need to touch the ground. She was the Wilding, but Starling was wild. She saw it now in the way he half turned to slide past a tree, neat and controlled but somehow natural, like the forest greeted him as not an intruder but a friend. Like the forest knew he was something not of the earth, that he was so much more.

Delta brushed the rest of her tears away, slid out of the truck, and followed him into the woods.

"Starling?" she whispered, edging around the trees. She wrapped her coat around her; it wasn't cold, but there was a brisk wind—strange for the summer, but that was just how Darling was—and she couldn't stop shivering. Where was he going? Was he leaving *now?* Her heart began to beat faster. No—he wouldn't. He wouldn't leave without saying goodbye, and he hadn't found his mysterious *chain* that would give him the power to go. Unless he'd found it and hadn't told her yet . . . "Where are you?"

The darkness wrapped around her, inky black.

A twig snapped to the right of her, and Delta jerked around, only to find herself face-to-face with Starling.

Hello, Starling said into her mind, a caress against her thoughts. The word was so simple, but it was said so intimately that she abruptly stumbled back a step as she remembered how she'd divulged *everything* to him, how she'd said she wanted him.

How she'd asked if he wanted her, and he hadn't said a single word.

How she'd left, and he hadn't come after her.

"Did I frighten you?" Starling said.

"No, you didn't." She flicked her eyes toward him; he was looking at her very seriously, but she noticed that his glowing skin had definitely faded. He looked . . . unwell.

"You are late. I was worried."

"I got distracted," Delta said. "There was something I had to do." She could see Tag's drowsy eyes in her mind, his mouth as he said: *Everything would be different if* I *was the one from the stars.*

Starling gave a slow shake of his head, then met her eyes. "I think we should talk about—earlier."

"It's—fine." Her voice was stiff. She didn't care. She couldn't have that heart-shattering conversation with Tag and then *this*, not even ten minutes later. She wrapped her armor tighter around herself. She shut herself inside.

"You are upset . . . This is my fault."

Delta shrugged. Tiredness washed over her in waves. She was drowning in it. She should be sleeping right now, and instead she was standing small and scared in the woods with an alien, her head ringing with Tag's admonishments and the FBI—and possibly the military—on their way to take away the most incredible person she'd ever met. Bee had told her over and over they were in danger and she'd continuously brushed off her sister's warnings, and now they were all holed up in the sheriff's house. Delta reached out a hand to a nearby tree trunk, steadying herself as her knees threatened to buckle under the weight of everything.

"I have caused so much trouble for you, Delta," Starling said. She didn't reply, and although her eyes were cast down at her feet, she felt the air shift as he took a hesitant step toward her.

"Don't," she muttered.

He paused. "You will not even look at me?"

She gave the tiniest shake of her head.

"I am sorry for this mess."

"Don't be," she said tightly, staring at her shoes. She'd pushed Tag away, and Starling had done the same to her. Everything between them was a tangled and convoluted wreckage, even as she wanted to fall against him, fall into him. He was so close to her—one more step and she'd be there. She was breathless with the nearness of him. But he'd made it clear. His silence spoke for him. She couldn't push it; she couldn't keep fooling herself that this man made of stars would ever want a small, fragile human being like her.

"Delta . . ." She saw him reach out. Felt his long, spindly fingers brush the back of her hand so lightly that if she hadn't seen it, she could've convinced herself she'd imagined it. "I believe I am more than you bargained for."

She met his eyes. Inky black stared at flecked green. Two set, emotionless mouths and two clenched jaws. So similar and yet so impossibly forbidden, two ends of the same magnet.

"Yes," she said. "You are."

She'd been desiring something more her whole life, and the proof of its existence was standing before her. This was all so much bigger than her, and yet all she could think of—all she *wanted* to think of—was the little things. Starling—not Starling the star, the alien, or the sheer, near impossibility of the fact that it had happened here, to her—but Starling, and the way he'd kissed her back by the Wishing Well. Starling curled on the couch, reading a book her dad had read her as a child; Starling watching bemusedly as she'd danced in the living room, and the sharp-toothed smile that he'd had when she'd grabbed his hands and pulled him into the dance. Starling, and what exactly he'd meant by *I am more than you bargained for,* and why the hell she still wanted to collapse into him, despite it all.

She wanted to collapse.

She'd wanted something more than Darling for so long. And now she just wanted simplicity, she wanted her dad, and she wanted daily walks with Abby, and Bee to be obnoxious, carefree Bee, and being around Tag to be easy, and Starling to stay.

She'd always wanted to be different.

And now everything was over her head, and she was drowning in bills and the weight of the majesty of the universe, and Bee looked to her to be the adult, but just because she was eighteen, she wasn't really an adult. She didn't *want* to be an adult, not anymore. . . .

The things she wanted and didn't want could fill multiple books.

She had to be unemotional—the way Starling used to be. "Well. You'll be safe here with the sheriff." She made herself keep her voice even and light, not filled with feeling. "I'm glad we could help."

"Yes," said Starling guardedly.

"And soon we can find your chain, and then you'll be able to go."

They stared at each other; the rest of the world might've dropped away or imploded in on itself and they wouldn't have noticed.

"Right," Starling finally agreed, his voice barely there.

Delta's throat clogged with tears. They built up, pressure in her head, pressing against the back of her eyes.

This planet would never truly be his. And she would never be his. He'd made that very clear. He couldn't stay.

I am more than you bargained for.

Yes, you are.

"Well," Delta began. "I should leave, then. I'll give you some time to be alone."

She turned, eyes stinging, but had barely taken two steps when fingers caught hers, whirling her back around. She felt him squeeze her fingers, pulling her closer, and had the briefest glimpse of a quick smile that turned softer by the second, and then his eyes fluttered closed and his lips met hers. Delta's mind went blank, empty; nothing was real anymore except for the feel of Starling kissing her, his tongue pushing against her lips, her teeth. His arms wrapped around her, and he backed her up until her spine hit a nearby birch and she wrapped her legs around his waist, lifting herself off the ground. One hand hooked around her thigh, holding her tightly against him, and his other hand slipped under the hem of her shirt. Every touch lit a fire, and his fingers dragged themselves down the skin of her back. She was caught between him and the tree, and she couldn't do anything but kiss him and savor the wonderfulness of it all.

This is how she'd wanted it to be. This is how she *knew* it could be.

Starling broke away with a gasp but stayed so close, she could feel the frantic beating of his three hearts pressed up against her chest. His gaze was heavy, his eyes pure black as he brushed his mouth against her cheek, leaving a trail of tiny kisses down her neck. She couldn't place his expression; desire, yes, but something else. Something desperate, something sorrowful.

Her mind caught up to her on what was happening, and despite the fact that his face was a centimeter from hers, despite the fact that he gripped her waist, she felt oddly . . . shy. She cleared her throat. Her face was made of flames.

Slowly, as if he didn't want to, he released his hand from her thigh, setting her feet back down onto the ground. "I . . . should not have done that."

Delta shook her head, breathless. "Yes, you should have."

His gaze was measured, but she knew her feelings were playing out in hers. She couldn't hide from the look in his eyes.

"I . . . I can't help . . ." He trailed off, waving his hand in an accidental sort of way, as though he couldn't find the words for what he wanted to say. "I can't help myself around you. I want to *stay*." Starling caught her hands in his own, his rasp almost pleading. "What do I do, Delta?"

"You stay, Starling. Stay with me." She said the words so quickly, so she could get the truth of what she wanted out in the open before reality closed in around them. Because how could he? The FBI were on their way—the best-case scenario was that somehow they could head off the feds and hide Starling until they were gone. And then—and then *what*? Forever hide in the Wild West?

And yet—*stay with me.* She wished so badly it could be true.

Starling shook his head in her direction, then studied her, unblinking, and under his heavy gaze Delta forgot where she was, she forgot the storm headed for them, she forgot everything and lost herself in his swirling eyes. He hesitated for just a moment, then placed a hand on Delta's shoulder, his long fingers grazing the back of her neck. He stepped forward, still pausing, as though everything inside was telling him to stop, and brushed his cold lips against her hairline, pressing the tiniest of kisses there. Then he stepped back, staring toward the house. His eyes flicked up toward the starry sky above, as if he was trying to divine some sort of sign from the heavens.

When he looked down at her, his expression was changed. There was no more indecision: there was nothing but craving. He closed the gap between them and caught her chin in his fingers, studying her expression, her green eyes. Then his hands dropped and in one movement he swooped her up, moving her legs around his waist once more and holding her with one strong arm as he turned and strode to the truck, opening the door and depositing her onto the long front seat.

He braced one hand on either side of the open door, his arms spread wide in the shape of wings. He stared in at her, his dark hair falling across his face, obscuring his eyes, and then slid in and shut the door.

Both were silent; Delta was holding her breath as though one false move would have him retreating out of the truck and back behind closed doors at the sheriff's house. His white shirt clung to his skin, and now he had come close enough for her to see the stark lines of his tattoos through the thin cotton. He looked tousled, his dark curls rumpled, and the tip of one of his pointed teeth protruded onto his lip. In the darkness, his swirling black eyes were like bottomless hollows in the recess of his face.

But he didn't scare her. Not one bit.

He smiled, his sharp teeth flashing, and she had never seen someone so beautiful; she'd never been so struck with desire.

Delta stared. Her stomach was in her throat. Her eyes were adjusted to the dark of the yard, but his body and face were still mere shadows.

"At the Wishing Well," he said, "I wished for you."

It was everything. He'd told her: now the wish wouldn't come true. But in the moment, with her heart dropping and her entire body on fire for him, she couldn't bring herself to think ahead. There was just now. Just this single split second, stretching away into infinity.

"I . . ." She leaned forward, wanting to touch him, but he held up a hand.

"But there are things I need to tell you," he finally rasped. "Things I should've told you before."

"Starling, it's okay," Delta whispered. She pushed his hand away and pulled him closer, her hand curling at the nape of his neck. "We can talk about things later."

He smiled a pained half smile. "Later?"

"Yes."

"What if there is no later?"

"Of course there will be." They locked eyes, each seeing the truth on the other's face. Delta felt the wave of tears rising, and she wrapped her arms around him, clutching him so tightly, she could feel his three hearts beating erratically to different rhythms, before beginning to pulse in sync as he reacted to her touch. His body was filled with coiled energy. It was bursting out at the seams, leaking from his skin.

His breath was hot against her cheek as he whispered, "Yes, of course there will be."

And then he kissed her again, fiercely, almost desperately, and it was different from the other kisses, because there were no thoughts of stopping. There were no thoughts of anything, except the feeling of Starling's arms wrapping around her, edging her so her back was flat against the seat, and her legs wrapping around him, and the sound of their hearts suddenly beating as one. His eyelids fluttered closed, his hands were in her hair; his hands were tugging her top up and over her head. She felt slightly self-conscious—the human before the eyes of the universe, small and bare and different. *Human.* But then Starling hissed, *"Delta,"* and his fingers gently traced circles on her waist, and it wasn't an alien before her but just—Starling. Here they were, together, and the rest didn't matter.

His sharp canine nipped her bottom lip; she tasted rust.

"I'm sorry," he rasped.

She smiled against his lips. "I'm not."

His forehead rested against hers, his marked hands splayed against the bare skin of her back. "Delta, this will make everything harder when it ends," he said, almost pleadingly.

"It doesn't have to end," she replied, breathless, the lie falling easily between them.

"It does," he said, but he tucked a lock of dark hair behind her ear and ran a tattooed finger down her arm anyways, tracing a path through the freckles. "And it won't end well."

"Starling," she said. "I don't care."

And then their lips met once more. It was breath on breath and exhausted limbs relaxing. It was a kiss that was more than a kiss; it was an avalanche, and Delta felt her soul sigh, smile, and settle in. And in that moment, he was not an alien, and he was not made of stars. He didn't look different or sound different. He didn't arrive in her life by crash landing like a shooting star. He was just Starling, and he was hers.

32

BEE SAT AT THE

sheriff's kitchen table in the dark like a mom waiting up for her wayward children. She kept replaying the party at Tag's, the way she'd thrown the chain as far from her and Tag as she could, off into the rows of grapevines bordering the Rockford mansion. She'd heard the rumble of their truck as Delta pulled into the woods behind the sheriff's house, and then moments later she'd heard the soft click as the back door opened and shut. She'd come into the kitchen to speak to her sister, but instead had watched as Starling slipped stealthily out into the night. Another secret she had to keep.

Bee remembered when she'd used to love secrets and gossip. It seemed like a different person, a wholly separate Bee. She barely recognized that person anymore.

When the kitchen door creaked open and the two figures crept in, she sat up straight, clasping her hands together. She felt cold, as though all her body heat had leached away into the floorboards, leaving her just a shell.

"Delta? Where were you?" Her voice shook as she flicked on the light switch.

Delta and Starling blinked in the sudden flare of light, the illumination displaying tousled hair and red cheeks. Bee looked away, a blush rising on her own cheeks from embarrassment, and a tiny part of Bee piped up inside her, *Look what Starling's done!* Made it so Delta would never be content in Darling again. Tag would never be enough. California would never be enough. Bee would never be enough.

But somehow the anger that had fueled her for so long just wouldn't rise to the surface. She just felt drained.

She just wanted her sister.

Starling, bright-eyed, his curls tangled at the nape of his neck, moved hurriedly across the kitchen, his eyes darting to Bee's and then quickly glancing away. He slipped out the doorway, and as Delta moved to follow him out, very deliberately avoiding Bee's gaze, Bee reached out a hand and caught her sister's fingers.

"Wait," she whispered. It might as well have been a shout from the way Delta stopped abruptly, then slowly turned toward her. She couldn't read Delta's expression; it was as if Delta had slammed up walls as soon as Bee spoke. Bee waited a moment to see if Delta would start—a *what*, a sigh, *anything*, but when she didn't speak, Bee cleared her throat. "Just wait." And then, her voice even softer: "Do you remember when Dad took us out of school for a week to drive down to Roswell?"

Delta's eyes widened; Bee could tell she'd caught her sister by complete surprise. It made sense, though, as all their conversations now ran sharply south as soon as they started, ending in patchy red cheeks and tearful eyes. But after a moment of silence, Delta tucked her tousled hair behind her ears, then replied "Yes . . . ?" almost warily. As if she wasn't sure why Bee wasn't shouting at her.

I don't want it to be like this.

It doesn't have to be like this.

Bee tugged on Delta's fingers, kicking at the leg of a chair with one foot. "Sit with me?"

Delta sat, and silence drifted over the two of them before she said, "And Dad made us listen to his crime podcasts the whole way down. For like twelve straight hours."

Bee nodded, then let out a half smile and continued, "And we stayed in that motel overnight, and you convinced me that you could magically turn me into, what was it—a giraffe? Yeah."

With a choking laugh, Delta grinned, her teeth reflecting the overhead lights. Bee hadn't seen her sister smile at her in so long that she just *stared* for a moment, as if she'd seen something unfathomable. It hit her then: Delta was happy. *Happy.* For once, the thought didn't terrify her, as if her sister's sadness was the thing holding her to this town. After their dad had disappeared, she'd watched as Delta had grown more and more inward, sinking down, caving in on herself. But now . . . she was smiling again. Why in the world had Bee wanted so much to destroy that? Her vehement assertions that Starling was dangerous seemed less accurate now, in the harsh kitchen lighting.

She didn't trust him—but Delta did.

And Bee trusted Delta.

Bee reached out and squeezed her sister's fingers again, tightly enough that Delta shook her off with an affable *"Ow, Bee."* She still had the remnants of her smile around her face, and her eyes were faraway. "Yeah, I really wanted you to believe I was magic. And then do you remember the next day—we all ate at that UFO-themed diner in New Mexico, remember?" Delta continued. "And then we spent days sitting in the back of the truck while Dad took like, readings of the air pressure."

Bee managed a smile. "Yeah. D'you . . . Delta, do you think *all* the things Dad believed in are real?"

She watched her sister's eyes track to the open doorway and then flick up the ceiling, as if she could see a glowing trail left behind by Starling as he'd trooped upstairs.

"I'm not sure," Delta said finally, her eyes drifting back to Bee's. They had the same eyes, green on green; Bee thought it was a little like looking in a mirror. "But I'm sort of inclined to believe *a lot*." Her eyes turned speculative as she continued watching Bee. "Why are you thinking about that trip?"

To remind you how much you mean to me, Bee thought desperately. *So you remember that we did have good times, that we did laugh, that there wasn't always this wedge between us.*

"Just thinking," Bee said, but she meant it like *I love you.*

"I haven't thought of that trip in a long time," Delta said. "And d'you remember when we came back, the whole school avoided us like we'd brought back some disease?"

"Well, they did that anyways," Bee said, her mouth turning down. She hated thinking of how much their own town feared them with a single-minded, cultish hatred. But her own efforts to make herself as normal as possible, as un-Wilding as possible, did next to nothing. Maybe it was time she stopped trying.

"True," Delta replied.

Her voice was light, and it made Bee reply, almost desperately, "Doesn't it *bother* you, Del?" For a moment she froze, hoping she hadn't accidentally turned the conversation into stormy waters. "I just mean—I just mean that it bothers me," she finished. "And you always seem so . . ." She searched for the perfect word to describe her inscrutable, unflappable big sister who sat before her and took everything in stride. "Calm. Unconcerned."

Delta's eyes grew wide, and Bee was just thinking how to backtrack when Delta started laughing. Bee stared at her. *What . . . ?*

"I'm sorry," Delta said, her laugh fading out with a little cough. She put her cheek in her palm and her eyebrows shot up high. "I'm sorry, but—what? *Calm?*"

"You're always calm—" Bee said uncertainly. And Delta *was*. Delta always knew what to do; Delta was always there with advice and certainty and guidance whether Bee wanted it or not.

"Unconcerned?" Delta continued with another giggle, although there was a wild look in her eyes. "Bee, I'm *drowning*."

"D-drowning?" Bee stared at her sister like she'd never seen her before. "No, you're—"

"Terrified," Delta finished. "All the time."

It was only when Delta reached forward, frowning, to wipe the tears off Bee's face that Bee realized she was crying. And then once she realized it, she couldn't stop, and the tears became a river.

In response to Delta, Bee cried, "I *miss* you," and the words were so anguished that Bee wouldn't have known it was her who spoke if she hadn't felt her mouth form the words.

"Bee," Delta said, and there were worlds contained in the

way Delta said her name. Somehow Delta's single *Bee*, filled with sadness and exasperation and tenderness and affection and layered over with a huge dose of eye roll, said everything.

Bee scooted her chair forward, pushing it so it knocked up next to Delta's, and the sisters wrapped their arms around each other.

"I'm right here," Delta whispered. "I'm not going anywhere."

"But one day you will," Bee said, her voice muffled, her face pressed against the soft sweatshirt covering Delta's collarbone.

"One day *you* will too," Delta said. "Isn't that what you want?"

Bee swallowed hard against the lump rising in her throat, and when she didn't answer, Delta pushed Bee gently away, meeting her eyes. "Beatrice Wilding, we are a *team*," Delta said, her voice fierce. "We will always, *always* be a team. You and me. The Wilding sisters. *Us*."

"Us," Bee whispered back, and for the first time in a long time, she smiled, and there was nothing sharp or bitter underlying her expression at all.

"And nothing, or no one, will ever come between you and me."

Bee's heart felt like it was slowly fracturing with relief, as though it had been made of rusted iron and had just been cracked open. She *hadn't* known, that was the problem, and hearing it from Delta made Bee want to burst into tears and crawl onto her sister's lap like she was five years old.

And then she remembered what she'd done. Her smile faltered. Would the Wilding *us* continue even when Bee revealed all her secrets one by one? They pulled at her with grasping claws, and she suddenly decided that she had to come clean.

This was her chance, with her cheek pressed against Delta's quickly beating heart, when the air was warm with forgiveness.

"I did something bad," she said, all in one breath. *There.* It was out. She felt Delta stiffen slightly beneath her, but her hand didn't stop stroking Bee's ponytail.

"Okay," Delta replied, her tone guarded. Bee could tell she was trying to keep her voice light, and thought that perhaps her sister didn't want to break the spell cast by their heart-to-heart and reminiscing either. "Whatever it is, we'll deal with it."

We. We'll deal with it.

Bee squeezed her eyes shut and sucked in a deep, wavering gasp of air. "I—Del, I know where Starling's chain is. It—it is a chain, right, the thing he's looking for? The thing he needs to give him more power?" The admission dropped heavily onto the kitchen tiles.

"Yes," Delta breathed. She pushed Bee off her slightly, but it was with gentle hands. "You know it's a chain?"

"Yes," Bee whispered.

"You *have* it?"

"I did."

"For how long?"

"Ever since—ever since that night in the woods," Bee said miserably. "Delta, I'm so sorry . . ."

"It's—" Delta took a deep breath. "It's okay." She managed a small smile, then shook Bee by her shoulders.

"I thought he would use it to stay on Earth," Bee mumbled. "In Darling. Or take you away somewhere. And I just—I just couldn't . . ." Bee's lip trembled, and she leaned against Delta once more.

To Bee's surprise, Delta's lip was trembling too. "I think," she whispered, "that it's past that now."

"H-he's not staying?" Bee said, the words shaking with confusion. "But you just came in together and I thought . . ."

Delta sighed and gave a half-hearted shrug. "The most important thing right now is figuring out a way to keep him safe, right, what with the FBI"—her voice grew softer with each word— "and the military, and the townspeople, and . . ." She swallowed, then smiled that brittle smile again. Bee saw right through it. "But it's okay, because I can find a way. I can do it. Now that we have the chain, it will be easier."

Bee bit her lip.

"I *can*," Delta repeated, then held out her hand expectantly.

Bee stared at Delta's outstretched palm, her heart sinking. Here was part two of the Very Bad Thing she'd done. "I don't have it anymore."

Delta's gaze turned sharp as a tack. "Oh?"

"I . . . I threw it away."

"Where? The trash?" Delta replied, alarmed, and Bee could already see her mind racing, trying to figure out how to sift through miles of landfill. "Oh, Bee . . ."

"No," Bee whispered, lowering her voice as much as she could, as if the truth of what she'd done could wink itself out of existence if Delta couldn't hear her say it aloud. "It's at Tag's."

There was a long pause as the air deadened around them, and then Delta groaned, long and low. *"Bee."*

"I know."

"Tag? *Tag?*"

"I know!"

Delta shut her eyes for a moment, and Bee stared blindly out across the table to the darkness outside. Pure, unrelenting blackness pressed up against the windows, and the wind had picked up. It seemed a storm was coming.

Bee turned back to see a storm in Delta's eyes.

"I know it was wrong," she said immediately, and she saw Delta visibly soften. Maybe they were both just overly tired and feeling emotional, but every sentence landed. Bee apologized; Delta listened. *Why haven't we been doing this the whole time?* Bee wondered, although she couldn't exactly place what between them had changed to make it so.

"I'm not mad. I'm just—" She sighed again. "I saw Tag tonight, at the Diner. He isn't exactly my biggest fan."

"Sure he is," Bee said encouragingly. This is how Tag and her sister *were*: back and forth, up and down.

"Not anymore," Delta replied darkly. "Do you know where it is?"

"I threw it away, somewhere in the dirt," Bee said, her voice small. "I don't know if it's still there. No one saw me throw it away except Tag."

"So . . . that's how Tag knows . . . because *you* told him."

Bee nodded, biting her lip, mouthing another *sorry* in Delta's direction. "He thought he was protecting you, he really did. I told him . . . I told him Starling might be dangerous."

"And so Tag told his dad." She was speaking slowly, as if the words were slotting together a picture. Then she hung her head, staring at her shoes. "He was trying to *help* . . . just like he said."

She paused, then turned to Bee despairingly. "God, Bee, I think I've messed up. I told Tag I see him clearly—I really thought he would choose the Rockford way. I thought he told his dad just to hurt me. But I think . . ." She gulped. "I was wrong."

"What are we gonna do, Del? Do you think he'll still help us?"

"I don't know, but we need to get the chain," Delta said immediately. "Being here without it isn't good for Starling—have you noticed how his skin barely glows anymore? This town is draining his energy away. He *needs* that chain. To leave or stay. Right now, he needs it to survive."

"Then we'll need Tag, won't we?" Bee whispered.

Another groan.

"You have to call him."

"It's two a.m.," Delta shot back, then bit her lip. "And how am I supposed to talk to him after what I said to him earlier?"

"Text him," Bee said firmly, nudging Delta's phone across the tabletop. "Right now. Tell him to come over tomorrow morning. Tell him it's important. That you need his help. He'll come."

"How are you so sure?"

They were whispering to each other now, the rest of the house silent and settled around them. It was late, but it suddenly seemed as if the two of them were suspended in time, as if the blinding white kitchen lights were the only real thing in the universe.

Bee smiled softly. "Because sisters know these things," she said, and her smile turned determined as she continued, "and you really don't have any other choice."

33

DELTA CLOSED HER

eyes, listening to Starling's even, unconscious breathing.

She hadn't been able to sleep a wink after leaving Bee, and had spent the last few dark hours staring at the ceiling, her mind whirling. She couldn't seem to stop checking her phone, in case Tag had replied, but every time she checked, there were no new notifications. She tried calling him over and over. No answer. *Of course*. And they were losing time.

The conversation with Bee the night before—all those whispered words in the dead of night—had carved out some of the sick, heavy feeling from inside. But in the absence, more insidious thoughts wormed their way in.

What if Tag ignored the text and never showed up? She could go sneaking around the Rockford estate to find Starling's chain, sure, but whereas until now the mayor hadn't truly had a reason to stick anything to her, finding her trespassing would surely push him over the edge.

Or what if Tag did come, and agreed to help retrieve the chain without any suspicion, but the FBI arrived early and whisked Starling away to who knows where? Every time she closed her eyes, she'd suddenly jolt awake again, sure she heard the sound of car tires pulling up outside the house.

She could see the horrible scenes playing out on the dark ceiling, crawling with shadows of the trees outside. The FBI, dragging out Starling in handcuffs. The military storming Darling with medical equipment created to subdue an alien. What would they *do* to him?

She felt sick to her stomach, and she rolled onto her side, her eyes springing open once again. Starling was fast asleep, his face slack and peaceful with the light of dawn creeping its way over his features as the sun rose. His skin glowed in the growing light—faintly. Always too faint now.

He could stay, Delta told herself firmly, gently stroking a finger across his forehead, brushing back the dark curls. She would find a way.

And if you can't?

She tried to imagine what it would be like if he left. The sudden jerk back to the everyday as reality swept in—as the most incredible thing she'd ever known drifted away, falling through her fingers like sand. The looks of the townspeople, sour and suspicious as ever.

Or would Darling simply whirl on without him, erasing the memory of their magical weeks together, its people moving like players on a chessboard, forcing their way ever onward? That, Delta thought, was how time was moving for her: too fast, rocketing forward, dragging her along with it. Because that was the first thing about chess: once you moved into a space, you couldn't go back. You couldn't retreat. And you knocked someone—something—out of the way to get there. Delta sighed. Was that what she had done? Burst her way onto the board, forcing her way through with sharp elbows and sarcastic remarks and moody looks, pushing aside Bee and Tag and everyone she met along the way in an attempt to get to Starling and keep him safe with her?

Her head ached, but Abby had begun to pace near the bed, and so Delta rubbed her temples and got up, tugging on a sweatshirt and a pair of sweatpants from her hastily packed duffel bag.

"Come on, girl," she said to Abby, who followed her downstairs. Bee's door—the door to Sheriff Schuyler's crowded, messy study—was still shut tight, and Delta hoped that her sister, at least, had managed to get some sleep. Her eyes itched with exhaustion, and she yawned, blearily rubbing her face and trying to feel more like a wide-awake, clear-headed person.

The sheriff was already up, sitting at the kitchen table with her forehead propped in her palm and a huge mug of black coffee before her. "Morning," she yawned. "Did you sleep okay?"

"Not really," murmured Delta. "My mind wouldn't shut off."

"Yeah, same," Sheriff Schuyler replied. She pointed at the pot of coffee on the counter. "Coffee?"

"With cream. Thank you," Delta said, backing out the door and letting Abby run free around the backyard. The chilly early-morning air swept around her, but the shivering felt good; it sharpened her hazy, tired thoughts into a mantra: *Get Tag. Get the chain.* It wasn't a plan, not in the least, but the words were something to hold on to.

She could figure this out. She could be what Bee thought of her:

Always calm. Unconcerned. Someone who could calmly assess

situations and not feel like she was drowning. Who could walk upright and meet the dour faces of the townspeople without feeling like she was balancing precariously, unsteadily, on a knife's edge.

A person who could take on the world. Who could hold herself up and not fall.

The FBI, the townspeople, the mayor, Tag . . . Could she ever be that person, brave and sure of herself?

She didn't have a choice. But Delta found she suddenly didn't *mind* not having a choice, not about this. She would do what she had to, to keep Starling and Bee safe. She would be the spine they could hide behind.

She checked her phone again. Under her message to Tag, tiny letters proclaimed *READ: 7:58 a.m.* Still no reply, but she couldn't wait for him long—the mayor's threat weighed heavily in her thoughts, continuously reminding her that weren't safe, *they weren't safe.*

Even when met with suspicion in the streets, Delta had never felt unsafe in Darling. But now she had something to lose, and every noise had her jumping in fear. Every crack of a tree branch had her whipping around to peer nervously into the woods behind the sheriff's house.

"Abby!" she called, and Abby came bounding back toward her. Delta hustled her dog back into the kitchen, trying to keep from peering over her shoulder. Too scared she would see someone watching.

Starling and Bee had joined the sheriff at the table, Bee shoveling spoonfuls of sugar into her frothy white coffee and

Starling sipping steadily at a vodka-filled coffee mug embla-zoned with WORLD'S BEST SHERIFF.

Delta's eyes widened at the sight of him: he looked more exhausted than either of them. Had he looked like that last night? No, she was sure he hadn't—the woods had been dark, but she would have remembered if he'd looked this sickly. He was wear-ing a pair of jeans and a sweatshirt, and the ethereal glow to his skin had almost completely faded away, leaving behind pale, pallid skin. Dark, bruiselike circles rimmed his eyes as he met her worried gaze. It made him look slightly more human—if you didn't meet his depthless eyes—but to Delta, he just looked ill.

"Are you feeling okay?" Delta said, her voice pitched low.

There was a pause, and then Starling replied, "I am," in a stilted way that made Delta think immediately he was lying.

"Starling?"

He sighed and held out both hands, twisting them back and forth so they could see how the shimmer, so brilliant and golden when he'd first arrived, had leached away. "I must find my chain."

Bee choked on a piece of toast, then exchanged an apprehen-sive look with Delta, who cleared her throat.

"R-right. Okay. I guess we should catch everyone up . . ." She glanced between Starling and the sheriff, who had gotten up to lean against a countertop, holding tightly to her coffee mug. Every so often her eyes would flick toward Starling and she'd edge a centimeter or two along the counter away from where he sat. "Starling, your chain is at Tag Rockford's house. I've texted Tag and asked him to come over so we can explain to him what we need, but . . . honestly, I'm not sure if he'll come. I talked with him last night and it didn't go . . . great." She swallowed. *"Didn't go great" is one way of putting it, I guess.* "Obviously it'll be easier to get it back if we have Tag to let us in and out of his property. Otherwise, we'll find another way." She reached across the table and took Starling's hand—it was very cold. "I promise we'll get it to you soon."

"And the FBI?" Bee piped up, looking at Sheriff Schuyler. "Do you have any information on when they'll be here? Are we completely in the dark?"

"Yes," the sheriff replied grimly, setting down her coffee with a loud *thunk* on the counter. "Unfortunately. I doubt the mayor would trust any new folks in this town, but I think he knows I'm helping you, or at least has his suspicions." She paused, then continued, "He's stopped by my house quite a few times armed with thinly veiled threats about ridding this town of outsiders." Her lip curled.

"Yeah," Delta said, a sour feeling filling her stomach. "That's kind of his thing." How would they be able to keep Starling—or themselves—safe if they didn't know exactly what was coming, or when?

"So, these FBI," Starling began, his accent thickening over the words, "might arrive at any time?"

Delta nodded slowly, his words sinking in. *At any time.* She remembered the feeling she'd had while standing in the sheriff's backyard: the prickle at the back of her neck that whispered, *Someone's watching.*

"And they will take me away?"

Starling didn't sound scared, Delta noticed; he was the only one of the four of them who spoke as if he was discussing the suddenly frigid weather outside. But did he truly know what was to come? He learned so quickly; in many ways he could already pass for a human. But he hadn't been here long—not long enough to know what fever-eyed, scared officials might do to an alien. She squeezed his hand hard as her own stomach contracted with fear, her imagination delving into all the worst possible outcomes: laboratory tests, locked cells, a media frenzy—or worse, a complete chokehold on all information, trying to force the Wildings to pretend that nothing had ever happened.

Starling squeezed her hand back, and for a moment she was right back in the woods, these same hands holding her up, his body pressing her against the tree. Back in the cold truck, their shared breath fogging the windows, his lips on hers.

"It will all be fine," she said aloud, *too* loud, and her voice shook. Because *it has to be fine*, because *I can't bear it if it's not.*

"Delta," Starling said, looking directly at her. The rest of the room dropped away. His teeth gleamed in the overhead lights as he shot her a smile, crooked and reassuring, meant only for her. She remembered him when they'd dragged him away from the crash site, back through the woods, her heart thundering as she beheld the unconscious, impossible being. And now—his glow had faded, the circles beneath his eyes had grown, and he was no longer this unknowable thing. He was still impossible in so many ways, but he was also so achingly familiar now. "I am not afraid."

"You should be," she whispered. He had no idea—he was still

so innocent of this world in so many ways; he'd been insistent that humans could not kill him, but he didn't realize all the other horrible things they *could* do. She'd tried so hard to make him believe humans were good. But now they were hiding out against the threat of government intervention—so maybe Starling had been right about humans all along.

"I trust you," he replied simply.

Delta's heart was raw, it was shattering. *You shouldn't.* These were the words she'd longed to hear him say. He'd been so suspicious, and that suspicion had gradually softened to acceptance, and then—and then, *at the Wishing Well, I wished for you.* She'd made him trust her, and where would that get him now?

The sound of crunching toast broke through the quiet, and then Bee cleared her throat and said, her words full of fear, "Why would the mayor even *tell* us that the FBI is on the way? Is he playing some kind of game?"

"Of course he is," Delta replied immediately, grateful for the chance to slip back into stoic, I'll-take-it-from-here Delta. "This is what he wants—us scared, hiding. It'll make it all the sweeter for him when he can drive us out and take Starling away."

"Will he go to the Wild West or . . . do you think he knows we're hiding Starling here?" Bee whispered.

It happened as soon as she spoke: a series of knocks sounded at the door, sharp and loud. The four of them froze; Delta's heart thundered into a frenzy. *No, no, no—*

"Starling," the sheriff hissed. "Stay back." She waved at him frantically, and he edged into the pantry, shutting the door behind him with a soft snap. Ramona then turned to Delta, and while her features were composed and impassive, Delta could tell she was thrown, and she reminded herself that this was all new for Ramona as well. Not many people took sheriff jobs in small towns thinking they'd have to deal with aliens and undermining mayors and incoming feds. No, this was a Darling special. "You and Bee stay back as well," she said seriously. The knocking sounded again, more insistent now. The sheriff took a deep breath, then moved into the hallway.

Delta and Bee stood close together, crushed between the doorway and the spice rack. Delta held her breath as she heard Ramona call out, "Hello? Who is it?"

There was a reply, mumbled behind the heavy wooden front door. It was definitely a man's voice, and Delta's stomach dropped, her fingers turning white as they clenched Bee's.

But then—she heard the door opening, and turned confused eyes on her sister. Ramona wouldn't have let just anyone inside so easily. Which meant—

"Through here?" came the voice again, and now that it wasn't low and muffled by the door, Delta heard it bell-clear and knew exactly who was at the door, and why.

"Tag?"

Delta moved into the hallway; there, at the other end, hovering uncertainly by the front door, stood Tag. He looked in complete disarray, his hair limp and un-gelled, his face drawn, his hands shoved deep into the pockets of his sweatpants. Perfectly put-together Tag was nowhere to be seen; this Tag was crumpled and tired, as though he'd had at least as bad a night as she'd had—worse, maybe.

"Tag," she said again, his name coming out in a squeak. "You're here?"

"You asked me to come," he replied tightly. She could see him putting on his armor against her: it was all too clear in how he angled himself away from her and refused to let his eyes stray anywhere in her direction.

"I know," she replied, "I just . . . I wasn't sure if you would. I didn't think you would, after last night . . ." She trailed off as Tag stiffened. A muscle ticked in his jaw.

"Well, I'm here," he said. "And I parked two blocks away, so no one would see my car outside."

She couldn't think of anything to say except a fervent "Oh my God, thank you." And she meant it. That was all there was to say: *thank you* for coming even when you hate me, thank you for trying to help me, thank you for being reliably Tag Rockford. It suddenly didn't seem like such a bad thing at all.

Ramona cleared her throat and sidestepped Tag in order to peer out the front windows and then lock—and then double-check—the door. "Seems all clear."

She then strode up the hallway, meeting Delta's eyes as she went. "Delta? You might want to do some, uh, *preparations* before Tag meets . . . ?"

Ramona raised her eyebrows as she edged back into the kitchen. Delta held her breath, standing frozen in the hallway, her mind reeling as she tried to figure out exactly how to prepare Tag Rockford to meet an alien. *Her* alien. In the kitchen she heard footsteps, then the creak of the pantry door opening. More footsteps. Soft voices. Tag flinched at the very sound of them.

"I know about him," he told Delta suddenly. "The—the—" He shook his head, the word seemingly stuck in his throat.

"Starling," Delta finished for him, then added hesitantly, "The alien."

Tag met her eyes then. His expression was perfectly neutral: it was his practiced politician look; Delta had seen it effortlessly roll out at years and years of Rockford events. Whatever he was feeling, he was managing—for the moment, at least—to keep it buried deep. "So it really is true?" he said, and Delta thought she detected the tiniest warble in his voice. The hallway light was harsh above him, bringing each twitch of his jaw and bob of his Adam's apple into full relief.

"It's true," Delta whispered.

"And he's not—" He swallowed again, as if a scream was trying to escape. "Dangerous?"

"Not at all," Delta replied. "Not to us."

"Are you sure?" Tag hadn't moved an inch; he still stood against the front door, even though his eyes kept darting toward the open arch at the end of the hallway that led to the kitchen— and to Starling.

Are you sure? Yes, she was. Completely. Delta flushed, feeling the echo of Starling's lips on her throat. Could Tag tell? Did he know?

All she said was, "I'm sure."

Still, Tag didn't move.

"Do you want to meet him?"

His neutral expression took on a hint of incredulity. "N-no." The word was out too quickly, and Tag winced. "I mean, I'm not *scared.*"

"You can be," Delta offered. "It's okay if you are."

"You're not."

Delta shrugged, if only to hide that she was suddenly uncomfortable, too awkward. "I'm a Wilding, Tag. This is basically what I was raised for."

"You're really something, Delta Wilding," Tag said after a moment, and Delta couldn't tell if he meant it nicely or not, although his voice was mild. She wouldn't blame him either way, really, because she *was* really something. She could be a lot of things. Hasty and sharp and judgmental and too starry-eyed for her own good. A bad sister, a bad friend, a bad girlfriend.

"About last night—" she began, but Tag finally took his hands out of his pockets and waved away her words. "I was so wrong—" Again, Tag shook his head, interrupting her.

"We were friends once," he said. "Weren't we?"

"Yeah," Delta said, almost desperately. "Yeah, we were."

"Do you think we still can be?"

"God, I hope so."

He regarded her silently, then said, "So do I." He paused for a second, thinking, then added: "This doesn't mean I'm not still mad at you."

"I know."

"Because I really am."

"Yes."

"But it means that if you need my help—"

"I do—"

"Then I'll help."

Delta felt herself go weak with relief. With Tag on their side, getting in and out of the Rockford estate would be easy.

Starling would have his chain back and would be fully suffused with every bit of his celestial power. Safe.

Tag was shifting now, peering past her down the hallway. Finally he muttered, "This cannot be real." He jerked his head toward the archway. "He's really in there? An . . . an . . ." Deep breath. Hands clench, unclench, clench. "An alien?"

"Come and meet him," Delta said.

Tag sighed, a long gust of air, and then rolled his shoulders back. "Honestly, Del," he murmured, "I'm pretty sure every single thing that's happened the past few days has been absolutely, categorically impossible."

"Yeah," Delta said with the hint of a smile. "I'm pretty sure you're right."

"This town . . ." He shook his head and looked down at her through his tousled hair. His true-blue eyes were bewildered but clear. "I just have no idea what is going on in Darling anymore."

"Join the club," she replied, and led him down the hallway toward Starling Rust.

34

STARLING LEANED against the counter and listened as the human boy's footsteps came closer. He could hear the boy's terrified heartbeat galloping away. What had Delta said about this boy? *There's a lot of history. And a lot of hurt.* And when he'd asked if Delta loved the boy Tag Rockford, she'd changed the subject.

He didn't like the idea of his chain at this human's house, such power being handled by ignorant hands.

Hands that had touched Delta.

He was *feeling* something, something he didn't really understand: a sharp little pinprick of an emotion close to anger, followed by guilt and a flicker of sadness, of longing. Was he . . . was he *envious*? He'd read all about it in the books on the Wildings' shelves, and now it was zinging through him. He allowed it to roar through him in a wave, this newfound human feeling.

Envy.

Which was, really, very human of him.

He shook his head. This was what it had come to, then. A celestial being, envious over the life of a teenage boy.

Delta came through the arch first, followed by *him*. Tag Rockford moved hesitantly, carefully. Starling saw the boy's hands shaking and watched as he stuffed them into his pockets in the hopes that no one would notice. This boy was so very . . . human. Hair blonder than Bee's, a face blanched by apparent nerves, eyes the palest blue. This was the boy that Delta had loved, at some point. He was completely the opposite of Starling in every way. The strange jealousy formed into something else: a horrible sense of loss. No matter what Starling did, he would never be human. He couldn't give her everything she needed. How could they be fated for each other if every second together brought another obstacle?

He is just a human, and I am celestial, he thought, but the words were hollow, and did not comfort him in the least.

Tag came to an abrupt halt as soon as he entered the kitchen. The only sound in the room was breathing, or lack of it: Tag's breaths came almost as a pant; Delta was holding her breath, her eyes wide and anxious. Bee's eyes were flicking from face to face apprehensively, and Sheriff Schuyler sipped her fourth coffee of the day, staring into the liquid inside as if it was her only lifeline in a vast and tempestuous sea.

"This is Starling Rust," Delta said finally, the words tumbling over each other. "Starling, this is my friend Tag Rockford."

"Hello, Tag Rockford," Starling said, trying to keep his voice low. Trying to keep his unearthly accent from taking hold of his syllables and twisting them into the hiss that so entranced Delta but was sure to shock any other human. His appearance would more than do the job: even with the otherworldly glow of his skin fading day by day, there was no mistaking him for a human.

Tag just stood there. Starling could see the whites of his eyes around the icy blue of his irises, until the irises almost disappeared into the growing dark of his dilated pupils.

"Tag, you okay?" he heard Delta mutter.

"It could be," Starling said casually, feeling suddenly very bold and like he'd enjoy acting on the human jealousy that twined its way around his three hearts, "that he's starstruck."

Delta met his eyes and gave him a look that said she knew exactly what he was doing and to *stop it immediately*, but he just smiled a slow, wicked smile at her and after a moment she looked away, her cheeks staining a deep pink.

She wanted Starling; he could see it in her eyes. Even though he wasn't human, she wanted him.

And Starling wanted her. *I deserve to stay*. He pushed out the other truth, the single word that kept crawling its way into his thoughts. Balance.

Because you are here, someone else isn't.

Push and pull.

Balance. It grew louder, louder, a scream inside the starry darkness of his mind.

No—he deserved to stay and be happy.

The human boy had opened his mouth, displaying a row of perfectly shining teeth, and took a few deep, quavering breaths before fixing Starling with a direct stare and saying, as if he couldn't quite believe the words that were coming out of his mouth, "N-nice to meet you."

"Thank you for helping us," Starling said in return. His voice verged on a rasp, and Tag took an involuntary step back.

"Yes, really, thank you," Delta added, rushing up beside him and pushing on his shoulders to get him to sit down. Whereas she'd been quiet before, words spilled from her now as if a constant stream of chatter would single-handedly keep Tag from going into shock. "Let's all sit and talk—no, Tag, don't worry, Starling will sit over by me. We need your help, Tag."

Starling crossed the room to take the seat next to Delta and pulled his coffee mug of vodka toward him. He could feel the weight of Tag's eyes tracking his every movement, as if the human thought that any moment he would disappear, proving it was nothing but a trick of the light.

"First things first," Delta said, twisting her hands in her lap. She took a deep breath. "There's something at your house we need, and we need it *soon*, before the FBI arrive." Her eyes narrowed and turned piercing as she looked at Tag. "Do *you* know when they're arriving?"

Tag was staring down into the cup of coffee that Ramona had placed in front of him. He took a tiny sip, then said, "Do you really think my dad lets me in on anything?" He kept his eyes cast down at the table; he seemed to speak easily as long as he didn't look directly at Starling or his swirling black eyes. "No, I don't know. But we have to move quickly—I get it. What's at my house, though?"

"It's a chain," Delta began hesitantly. "It . . . glows."

There was a pause, and then Tag said, "That necklace thing that Bee threw into the bushes?"

Bee winced.

Starling sighed inwardly, everything turning crystal-clear as the information filtered through. *Bee.* Of course it was Bee: strong-willed, scared Bee, who just wanted her sister. Who'd found his chain and kept it secret, safely hidden away from the alien who would use its power to stay. He found he didn't blame Bee—he couldn't. She had made a choice, just like he was making a choice.

Push and pull. Balance.

It's my *choice,* he told himself fiercely, his eyes roaming over the humans before him. *It's my choice to make. To stay.* He couldn't let himself think of the consequence: their father, unable to return home.

"That's the one," Delta said. "It's important." The edges of her mouth tightened as her eyes flickered to Starling's, tracing over what he knew were his suddenly sallow features. He was so far now from the body she'd dragged from the woods, and yet she still looked at him with stars in her eyes.

Tag sighed. "Don't get mad."

"Oh God," Delta said.

This time it was Tag's turn to wince. "My dad has it now."

"Oh, Tag," Delta sighed, squeezing the bridge of her nose. Starling wanted to reach over and touch her shoulder, her hand, *anything,* but the memory of brushing up next to her as they walked through the woods, her voice saying *There's a lot of history,* echoed in his head. He kept his long fingers clenched tightly in his lap.

"Yeah," said Tag, and he shrugged. "I gave it to him when I— when I told. I thought he might need *proof,* y'know? It turns out he didn't—he believed me right away. He was on the phone calling people within like, five minutes." He scrubbed a hand through his hair, making it stand on end. "He put it in his desk drawer."

"Locked?"

Tag shrugged again helplessly. "I'm rarely allowed in my dad's study. He keeps the door locked when he's not in there, but I don't know about the drawers."

Starling leaned forward. "So we will have to find a way in while he is gone?"

"*We* are not doing anything," Delta said immediately. She turned toward Starling, her face pale. "Starling, you're not coming. If I get caught, well, I'm just Delta Wilding, the town outcast—so who cares?" Her mouth twisted with the words. "But if someone saw you . . ."

A well of frustration rose in Starling. He tried to breathe away the flood of feelings but found his lungs were tight. Everything inside him was rigid, sticky with emotions. He could remember thinking humans were weak for having so many emotions, but his memory came back through a haze. Because how could he ever have thought that? These feelings were dragging him under. It was all he could do to stay ahead of them. His throat tightened, unable to form any words. He couldn't stop curling his fingers in stress: clenching them into fists before releasing them on the table, repeat, repeat, repeat.

"Starling, please," Delta whispered, and despite the overspill of strange human emotions threatening to drag him under, her voice still pulled him back into her gravity.

"You are always saving me, Delta," he replied, his voice raspy, stone on stone. "You must let me return the favor."

"Please," Delta whispered again. "I can't put you in danger, not after all we've done to keep you safe. This is the best option. Will you . . . will you trust me on this?"

Trust her? He could never have imagined it, but meeting the Wildings had changed it all. Changed everything. He *did* trust her, completely, with every molecule of stardust inside him. Finally: "Yes," hissed Starling, the *s* drawn out like a snake in the grass.

Delta smiled, although she couldn't possibly know the effect she had on him. Her smile was hard-edged, like the curve of a blade. It struck Starling that her smile was quite like his: wolfish and dangerous.

The very air was electric.

She turned back to Tag. "We can sneak in when your dad is gone." Her steely smile now turned strained, but her voice was as light as if she was laying plans for a relaxed summer day. "It'll be easy. In and out. We'll be back here with Starling's chain by tonight."

"Small problem," Tag interjected, but by the look on his face, Starling surmised whatever the human was about to say would be slightly bigger than a *small problem*.

And then Ramona groaned. "It's the Mayor's Ball tonight."

"Tonight?"

Tag nodded grimly. "Tonight. And my dad won't be going anywhere. My house will be overrun with—well, almost everyone. It already is—when I snuck out to come here, there were already people cooking quail and cleaning the chandeliers."

"High society," Bee said with a sigh and a perfectly executed eyeroll. "Could that be good, though? Even though he'll be there—risky—there will be so many people, he could easily be distracted."

"We'd just have to wait for the right moment," Delta added.

Tag's eyebrows shot up. "You're really suggesting I break

into my dad's office in front of the entire town?"

Delta lifted a thin shoulder and fixed him with a stare. "No. I'm suggesting *we* do."

Ramona coughed. "You do know I'm standing right here. The sheriff. Remember me?"

Delta crossed her arms, the corners of her mouth kicking up into a smile. "This is all hypothetical, of course."

"Hmm," said Ramona.

"Are you going to turn us in?" Delta continued.

"No, of course not," Ramona said after a short pause. "I'm going to help you in whatever way I can."

"If we get caught, we'll need it," Delta replied.

"You need to be careful," the sheriff said. "I'm serious, Delta. Be careful tonight. I'd very much like to keep my job, if possible. I just want everything to go back to normal after this." Her eyes slid to Starling; he smiled sharply in return. "Relative normal," she amended.

Delta nodded firmly and turned to Tag, who spread his hands, an acquiescence. Bee cracked her knuckles, her face blanched; Ramona made another little *hmm* noise and poured another cup of coffee, then went to stand near the front windows, peering out through the curtains as Darling surged onward outside their house. They were stuck in the eye of the storm, whirling in the gyre, unable to escape.

So there was a plan.

This is all because of you. Starling moved uncomfortably in his seat, far too aware that he was the reason these humans were reeling, throwing themselves headfirst into deep waters. For him. His stomach twisted again. *So he could stay.*

And yet how could he? He wanted so much to stay, but his mind had latched on to the action of *staying*, not on whatever came afterward. He was so obviously otherworldly—after the wind died down and they were left with the aftermath, would they all truly be able to fall into a normal human life? Relative normal—that's what the sheriff had said. But how could anything ever go back to normal, even a new normal, after their world had been so shaken by his arrival?

He hadn't been in their lives long and already they were here, bright lights shining on wan faces, plotting and planning. All for *him*. He'd brought targets onto the Wildings' backs, and everyone associated with them.

And it would never stop. They would always be in trouble, always be hiding, for as long as he was with them.

For a moment he opened his mouth—to say what, he didn't know. To finally tell the truth, to explain how every part of him contradicted itself. How the guilt was eating him alive.

You deserve to stay.

Delta wanted him—that was what made all the secrets he held worth it; Delta wanted him to stay, and *he* wanted to stay, and it didn't matter if by staying he caused more problems. He shut his mouth, his lips closing over the hint of his sharp teeth, and sat back in the spindly wooden chair in silence. Revealing nothing of his thoughts. Thinking of the plan to come.

And so the five of them all sat crowded around the scratched, secondhand table, knowing they were all mulling over the exact same thing, but none of them knowing what to say.

35

DELTA SWEPT DOWN
the hallway toward Tag, her dress silky as it brushed against her legs with each step. It was Bee's dress, the one her sister had been planning on wearing to the Mayor's Ball, back before Starling's world-shifting arrival. Back when the Mayor's Ball had just been an event, one single night of champagne and fake laughing and slow dancing in the glittering rooms of the Rockford mansion. The dress was ethereal and floaty, composed of layers of white and gold. It contoured to her every curve, the overlay of lace and sparkles moving with her, catching the light. It was a dress completely at odds with the mess she was stepping into.

It was a dress perfect for grabbing attention. Perfect for causing a scene.

She felt glowing, starlike. She felt like a human who had fallen in love with a star, and maybe even a human that the star could want to stay with in return.

It had felt ridiculous sitting in Ramona's study while Bee curled her hair into long, loose waves using Ramona's fifteen-year-old hair curler. Starling had watched silently from the doorway, his eyes very dark, and Tag had driven back first to his house to get his suit, and then over to the empty, lonely

Wild West to pick up Bee's dress for Delta to wear. Delta had protested this at first, sure that someone was watching their every move, until Ramona had reminded her that it was completely normal for her to be attending the Mayor's Ball; until Tag fixed her with a half smile twisted with bitterness and said, "Del, I can't tell you enough how *very* little anyone in my family notices what I do." And so she'd let him leave without another word. Because what could she say to that?

Tag at the Diner, his voice dripping with exhaustion, sounded in her head: *You have no idea what it's like to grow up with a dad like mine.*

Delta was beginning to realize how very right he was.

She'd grown up with a dad and sister who were *there*, and that in itself was more than Tag had. Bee following her around, bickering and gossiping and sticking as close as if she'd been glued to Delta's side, had always annoyed her, but even frustration—even anger—was better than being fully ignored. Forgotten. Drifting along in the world, unmoored.

She couldn't imagine. She didn't *want* to imagine.

When Tag returned, a suit-sized garment bag and Bee's dress on a wooden hanger tossed over his arm, all she could do was squeeze his hand, her smile faltering, tremulous. He smiled back like he knew exactly what was on her mind.

And now she was descending the stairs, walking carefully along the hallway carpet with her feet strapped into a pair of her old heels, unearthed by Tag from the depths of one of her closets. "Okay," Delta said, suddenly frozen in place by nerves. Tag was at the front window with Ramona, standing with his arms crossed over a pressed black suit. Delta swished the skirt of her dress around, if only to give herself something to do with her hands, and her voice grew higher. "Are we ready? Tag?"

"Ready," Tag said. He seemed nervous as well, but Delta couldn't tell if that was from what they were about to attempt, or the proximity of Starling, who stood silent and sentinel on the lowest step of the staircase. Or maybe he was nervous at the mere fact of doing something his father wouldn't like. That scared Delta, too, as much as she tried not to let the mayor and his smile with too many teeth get to her.

She didn't want to do this.

She had to do this.

"Remember," Tag murmured as she walked toward him. "As far as anyone knows, we're just attending the Mayor's Ball together. Just like we planned."

Just like we planned—his words rang in Delta's head like a bell clanging back and forth. Standing in the Diner with Tag as he'd asked her to the Mayor's Ball seemed like a dream. Something that happened in another life; something she might've simply imagined. Her life was divided now into pre-Starling and post-Starling. So much had happened in such a short time. So much had changed.

"Just like we planned," she echoed.

Then she turned to face Starling. He had crossed to the doorway, slouched there as if someone had propped him up and then stepped away. But there was a gracefulness to him that no amount of human clothes or human movements could hide. Even in the mundane setting of the sheriff's hallway, even with the gold in veins turning to a sallow gray, he was still utterly magical.

He pushed away from the doorway and caught one of Delta's hands in his own. He leaned close and tucked an escaped lock of her hair behind her ear, and Delta shivered. "If I don't get a chance to tell you again," he whispered, his head lowered so they were cheek to cheek, "you look—"

"What are you saying?" she interrupted, leaning back, trying to examine his expression. "If you don't get a chance to tell me again? What do you mean?"

"Just in case," he murmured. "You—"

"Stop," Delta said fiercely, her breath catching.

"You look—"

"Tell me later," she said, the words somersaulting over each other. "Tell me after."

She held his gaze, daring him to speak. Finally, he blinked, breaking the standoff. His thumb brushed her cheek.

"After," he said simply, his voice even, impersonal.

Her heart thundered—she knew he could hear it. "After." She stepped back, and Starling's hand drifted down. "Once we have your chain, we can do anything, go anywhere. You'll be in control then, and we won't have the mayor—or this town—hanging over us."

"Be careful," was all he said in reply.

Delta couldn't answer. She'd nodded so easily at this when Ramona had said it, but now, it was a thing she felt she couldn't promise.

"Good luck," Bee said, frowning. Her lower lip trembled; Delta quickly looked away. "And come home soon."

Delta nodded, then tucked her hand into the crook of Tag's

arm. *Just like we planned.* In so many ways she was going through the same motions of the year before: dressed up, made up, standing next to Tag Rockford.

Together, they left the sheriff's house, Delta's high heels clacking on the porch. The sidewalk was cracked, weeds pushing their way diligently through, reaching up through the concrete. The thick heat of the early morning had dropped into a cool breeze, and the verdant leaves trembled above them in the last stretching rays of the afternoon sun. They walked the two blocks to Tag's Porsche in silence, with nothing but the sound of their footsteps. A part of Delta kept expecting a sudden siren to go off, and for the calm world around them to fracture as armed men descended down. But there was simply stillness.

The streets were deserted, and although Delta knew it was because the townspeople were already up at the Rockford estate, Darling still seemed like a ghost town; she and Tag might've been the last two people left in the world. It was almost eerie, and for the first time Delta felt like she didn't belong in the town itself. She knew the *people* here didn't like her, but she'd always felt like the town was *hers.* And now? Now it felt like she shouldn't be walking these streets; like Darling had caught her in a snare and wouldn't let her go.

In her mind it had always been Darling and the Wildings as one team, poised against the rest of the town. As if Darling had chosen them—but for what? Noticing all of Darling's oddities caused them nothing but trouble.

She'd thought the town was on her side, but now, as Tag pulled away from the curb and drove down Main Street past the houses of everyone who thought she was a curse on this town, she felt like *she* was the interloper.

The dilapidated Victorians began to blur into one as Tag picked up some speed on the empty street, and Delta wondered again which of these people—these *neighbors*—had been in her house. Which of them regarded the Wilding family as so very abhorrent that sending threatening messages to them and breaking into the Wild West in the dead of night seemed like something necessary?

She knew it had been the mayor's plan—all of their troubles always had the mayor at the center of everything—but the townspeople had followed along. If the FBI arrived—*when* they arrived—would any of the townspeople side with the Wildings? Somehow she doubted it.

But, Delta thought as she glanced at Tag, at least she had him now. And the sheriff, and Starling. They could be outcasts together.

"Thank you again, Tag," she said. His face was illuminated for a moment as they passed one of Main Street's rare streetlights, then fell back into shadow.

"You don't have to thank me, Del."

"Yes, I do," she said softly. "After everything, you still came to help. I was such a bad friend. A bad—" She hesitated. "A bad girlfriend."

Tag's hands tightened on the wheel.

"Yeah, you were," he said. "But I wasn't perfect either. Maybe now . . . maybe now you'll see me more clearly." Ahead of them, another car finally pulled onto Main Street from one of the cul-de-sacs, heading toward the Rockford estate. Another late partygoer. The car's headlights swung past them in the growing darkness.

The gravel road to Tag's house loomed out at them, and Tag slowed and put on his blinker.

Click-click-click-click—

"Maybe," continued Tag, "you'll see now what I've been trying to tell you all along."

Click-click-click—

Delta eyed him as he turned the car up his driveway. She could already hear music faintly from somewhere up ahead.

"That you're not your father?" she said.

"That I'm not my father," Tag agreed.

They reached the top of the incline, the gravelly circular lot outside the Rockford mansion stretching out before them, already filled with cars. He edged the car onto the grass and turned off the ignition.

"I'm scared," Delta said in the sudden silence, her breath coming out in a big *whoosh*. It felt like a big admission somehow. "I dragged an *alien* through the woods. And now I'm going to a party and I'm terrified."

"It's going to be fine," Tag said bracingly. "In and out." He brushed his palms together. "Easy. Just like you said."

"Right," Delta said. "Easy." Nothing in her life ever seemed to go how she planned. She stared out the windshield a second longer. *But Starling needs his chain. He needs me.* "Let's go," she said, her voice shaking.

And Delta and Tag got out of the car and headed toward the lights of the Rockford mansion.

36

STARLING BECAME aware of two things as he paced the black-and-white Formica tiles of the sheriff's kitchen. One, he had a headache that was pressing against his temples and scratching its way through his head, as if his skull was much too small to encase all the thoughts and feelings battering his brain. The second was that he was utterly in love with Delta Wilding.

It didn't feel *good*. Wasn't love supposed to make you happy? He tucked his head down, blinking as black spots danced across his vision, reminding him of how very much he needed his chain. The realization that he was *in love* filled him with a sharp and sudden fear that he didn't quite understand, as if some great chasm had opened up inside him. He should have told her when she stood in the hallway in her ethereal dress.

Told her that it seemed like she was the magical one after all. That he loved her.

But she'd stopped him, and he hadn't pushed the words out. Worried that if he did, the rest of the truth would come spilling out with it.

I love you, and I am here when your father is gone.

Why couldn't he have simply stayed far away from these

humans, and not gotten involved? He could have ignored them completely and gone searching the woods each night until he'd found the chain for himself. He wouldn't have Delta, but maybe that would have been for the best.

He could've saved all of them a lot of trouble.

By staying here, you will always cause them trouble.

"Stop *pacing,*" a voice snapped, and he halted briefly to look at Bee, who was sitting at the kitchen table with her chin propped on her hands. She eyed him back.

"I must pace," he replied, stepping over Abby, who lay on the floor with her head on her paws, half-asleep and supremely unconcerned. *At least one of us isn't worried,* Starling thought.

"Must you?"

"If I do not, all I can think about is Delta in trouble."

Because of me.

Bee sighed, and he waited for her sharp retort, but none came. Finally, she whispered, "I'm worried too." She groaned. "I hate just *waiting* here for them to come back."

"I know," Starling said, his voice low. He glanced up as Sheriff Schuyler came into the kitchen, a police walkie-talkie clipped to her jeans. White noise occasionally erupted from the walkie-talkie, a babble of unintelligible voices and sounds, before falling silent once more.

"I haven't heard anything yet," she announced. "At first thought, I wouldn't think Mayor Rockford would have all this happen tonight, when he has his big party—but maybe that's exactly what he wants. Everyone preoccupied, gathered at his house. Allowing others to do whatever they want in secret."

"But no one knows Starling's here," Bee said.

"Not yet," the sheriff replied grimly. "In a town this small, it's only a matter of time."

It could've been a coincidence that the sheriff's phone started ringing then, a loud and jaunty tune bursting through its speakers that was completely at odds with the drawn, nervous atmosphere. But Darling, Starling thought, rarely did anything by coincidence. Darling played its own games.

Darling did what it wanted.

And so when the sheriff picked up the phone with a quick "Sheriff Schuyler," Starling watched her carefully, his stomach squirming. He didn't know much about humans, but he was certain that nothing good would come from this call.

He watched the sheriff's face as she spoke, even though she gave nothing away with her words: "Yeah. No. Hmm. Got it. Okay." But he could see the way the corners of her lips turned down with worry—Delta's did that too.

"Right," she said, hanging up. She was definitely frowning now.

"The FBI?" Starling said, surprised that his mouth had gone dry; he was celestial, he shouldn't be frightened of some human officials. But the Wildings' constant worry, filled with whispers of tests and examinations, had rubbed off on him.

"No," Sheriff Schuyler said. A line had appeared between her eyebrows. "No, it seems many of the townspeople are gathering."

"Aren't they at the ball?" Bee asked.

Starling could tell the sheriff was holding something back; he just didn't know what. "No," she said slowly. "It seems some Darling residents haven't quite made it yet. I'll have to go check it out, see what's what."

"Where are they gathering?" Starling asked, and although his voice was pitched low, he knew the sheriff had heard him by the way her eyes flashed.

She put on her coat and grabbed her keys and belt from the hook by the door. "Stay inside, don't come out. Not for anything. Got it?" She hurried down the hallway, keys jangling loudly as they smacked together, and the door slammed behind her.

Bee took a deep, wavering breath. "She didn't answer your question."

"No, she didn't."

"And she forgot her walkie-talkie." It sat on the table, abandoned in the sheriff's sudden rush out the door. What could be happening that the sheriff hadn't paused for an instant? "I don't like this," Bee continued. "Do you think something's wrong?"

Yes, he thought something was very, very wrong. He didn't know what, but that *feeling* was there. That something had happened, that the world was tilting just a little too far off its axis. He felt off-kilter.

"Everything will be fine," he said instead, because he suddenly couldn't bear to see Bee Wilding—so like her sister, even in ways she didn't realize—scared. "You do not have to be frightened," he continued, then echoed what he'd said to Delta when the townspeople broke in. "I am here."

He met Bee's eyes. They were exactly like Delta's, down to the flick of the eyebrow, the soft darkness of the lashes. For a moment he thought Bee might scoff at him; he could tell it was her first instinct, could see the skepticism on her face. But then she took a deep breath and nodded.

"Thank you."

The walkie-talkie on the table let out a sudden squawk of white noise, and Bee jumped with surprise, but no voices came out, and after a few moments the sounds faded away. Still, Bee's face had gone as white and pinched as if she'd seen a ghost, and she chewed anxiously on her bottom lip.

A thought flitted through his mind—something ridiculous, something Bee would never agree to. But before he could talk himself out of it with reasons why he shouldn't, he stood up and held out a hand in her direction. "Let's dance," he said.

Bee looked at him, fear leaving as confusion took its place. For a moment she just stared at his outstretched hand as if she thought she might be hallucinating it. Then: "Dance?" she repeated uncertainly.

"Don't worry, Bee Wilding," he said, managing a smile. "I come in peace."

He saw the moment when Bee made up her mind; he watched as her lips quirked up and she pulled out her phone, scrolled through the lit screen, and then set it on the table as tinny music sounded from its speakers. Her eyes turned shy, and very slowly, she placed her small hand in his. He wrapped his tattooed fingers around hers and pulled her forward.

They moved haltingly, awkwardly, stepping back and forth. With a push of his hand, he raised his arm and twirled her through. Bee gave a surprised laugh, and for a single moment her face broke into a smile that was so sparkling, she seemed lit from within. As if she, too, had gold running through her veins.

And he knew, without her saying a word, that she hadn't smiled like that in a while.

Maybe since their father had disappeared.

I deserve to stay.

Doesn't what I want matter?

"I love your sister," he said abruptly as they rotated in place on the tiled floor.

"I know," Bee said simply.

She twirled out, flourishing her fingers, then spun back toward him, a breathy laugh barely leaving her lips.

"I think that I was . . ." She trailed off, then said in a tiny voice, "Selfish."

"We can all be selfish sometimes," Starling said, pulling her back into movement. *I am selfish,* he thought, although his repeated mantra of *I deserve to stay* was growing smaller and smaller each time he thought of it.

"You don't need to make me feel better," Bee said. "I know what you're thinking—humans are so dumb and selfish. Maybe you're right. But . . ."

Starling spun her around, his three hearts beating. Should he admit to Bee the truth?

"But Delta's happy," Bee finished. "And so I'm glad you're here too."

I deserve to stay.

He loved Delta—that was the truth of it. And now here was Bee, making peace. So why did he feel like he was doing something very, very wrong?

He spun her around, and around, and around, until he couldn't remember what the Wrong Thing was; until they were both half-sick with the movement and Bee's carefree, brilliant, all-teeth smile edged back out. He was still twirling her with abandon when the walkie-talkie on the table crackled once more with white noise and then, quite suddenly, a loud, tense voice, barking commands.

"This is Blackburn, requesting backup and firefighters at the Wilding place, I repeat, backup and fire."

Starling and Bee came to a stumbling halt, Starling grabbing at Bee's waist as she almost went careening into the sheriff's granite countertop. They stared at each other, breathless, chests heaving.

"Did that just say—" Bee began, and the fear that suddenly entered her eyes was a living thing. It was not the low-lying fear that could be tamped down by twirling around a kitchen to music piped through a phone. He could see it roaring inside her. Her pupils were huge, black holes that almost matched his.

She turned toward the back door and he grabbed at her hand. "Bee—wait. The sheriff told us not to leave—"

"'And fire,'" Bee cried, her voice breaking. Her hands lifted to make shaking air quotes for the words. *"And fire*, Starling. Why—w-why do they need firefighters at my house?" She tried to tear her hand from his grip, but he held firm, his spindly fingers wrapping around her jerking wrist.

Backup and fire.

What was happening at the Wild West? There was an expanding rock in his stomach; his whole body was filling with lead.

"Starling!" she yelled. Abby was whining from the corner, wound up by the palpable air of pure anxiety that was roiling through the room. Bee pulled again, trying to get free. "Let me go!" It was a scream. "That's my *home*! Everything I have of my dad is there. Everything of my mom! Let *go*!"

The pain in her voice struck all three of his hearts. He let go of Bee's hand, his thoughts so loud he wasn't able to think, to move. Abby was barking, the music was still blasting from the phone, and Bee was choking out horrible sobs that sounded like she was suffocating.

This was because of him. Somehow he knew it—because what else would be the reason? The Wildings had lived in Darling for years and years, and his arrival had stirred up everyone at their worst.

"Can you drive?"

Bee hiccupped, her breath ragged, but she nodded and grabbed the Ford's keys off the countertop.

"Then let's go," Starling said, his stomach sinking. *Stay inside, don't go out. Not for anything.* But Bee would leave with or without him, and surely she was safer with him there to help?

It was a desperate thought.

They're safer without you, another voice whispered in his mind, its hiss cutting through all the other whirling thoughts. *You're the reason they're in this mess.*

But when Bee opened the door and ran out into the backyard, throwing the tarp violently off the semi-hidden truck, he followed anyway, giving Abby a pat on the head as he left.

Bee's fingers shook on the wheel as she reversed through the trees, then did a jerky, squealing U-turn on the grass and turned onto Main Street. Starling's hands were shaking too, trembling uncontrollably. He stared hard at them, willing them to stop as his lungs squeezed painfully.

Bee's foot slammed against the gas pedal, and the speedometer jumped upward as she accelerated, the truck groaning in protest as the wheels skidded on the asphalt.

His three hearts ricocheted off his ribs in horrible synchronicity, their pulsing twined together with heavy fear. He was shaking, panting, taking on Bee's terror; what was happening to his body? He was feeling *everything*, all at once.

"It's okay," he said, then repeated it, again and again, the strange words blurring together as they slipped past his sharp teeth. "It's okay, Bee, it's okay, it's okay, it's—"

Even the words sounded fake, like they held no meaning anymore as the dark houses lining Main Street shot by. Were their windows dark because their inhabitants were at the ball, or because they were at the Wild West?

"It's okay, it's okay, it's okay—" His mouth kept moving, kept saying those words, because Delta had taught him more than she ever would've thought about being human, and Starling knew that sometimes you flat-out lied in order to hold somebody together.

"It's okay, it's okay—"

But Bee was crying, and it wasn't okay.

Starling knew that all too well.

Bee left the houses of Darling proper behind, the flat expanse of scrubby brown fields stretching out in all directions. She moaned at the sight ahead of them, the only thing on the horizon that was out of the ordinary. The thing that was horribly wrong.

Fire filled the sky, crimson red and leaping gold lighting up the night. The Wild West stood alone against the sky, framed by the dark mass of woods and the hazy outline of mountains in the distance. Smoke billowed from the windows, and around the base of the house were cars and a couple dozen people, screaming and shouting and throwing things at the Wild West's walls. A rock hit a window; the glass panes shattered with a splitting crack.

What would they do if Bee pulled up in the midst of them?

"Pull off!" Starling yelled.

Bee kept driving, tears streaming down her face, and she cried, *"No, no!"*

"Pull off the road!" he shouted again, grabbing the wheel and tugging it to the side. The truck jerked to the side of the road, veering erratically, its tires screeching, before Bee slammed her foot on the brake and threw it into park. It shuddered to a halt with a violent lurch and was still.

Bee stared out the dirty windshield and the scene before her, the maroon-streaked sky. Starling saw leaping flames reflected in her eyes for a moment, before she put her head in her hands and began to scream. It was an awful howl; Starling had never heard something like it before, and hoped he never did again. From behind them, somewhere in town, sirens began to wail in the night.

"My dad!" she screamed. She turned wild eyes on Starling, grasping frantically at his arm. Her nails raked down the skin, leaving angry red scratches in their wake. "Starling—the closet! The closet! How will he get home?"

Her breath was ripping itself from her body, and Starling pulled her across the bench seat toward him, tucking her small body under his arm. Holding her tightly against him.

"That's not how it works," he said. "The portal will be there no matter what—do not worry—it's okay—"

Bee was shaking in his arms. Everything seemed so unreal. It couldn't be happening. The stalwart house; the Wildings' home . . . gone.

His eyes roamed over the horrible scene before him as Bee continued to shake and cry against him. There was the sheriff's Escalade, parked haphazardly at the edge of the property. He remembered the reason she'd left: *It seems many of the towns-people are gathering.* They didn't know that the Wildings were currently at the sheriff's—that made it all the worse. They'd come here, with their flames and rocks, ready to smoke out the Wildings and the secret inhabitant they were hiding in their house.

Him.

The people of Darling had done this, but it was his fault. They were trying to burn the Wild West to the ground, the Wildings' one and only safe haven. All because of him.

He stared at the mob before him as Bee's wail echoed in his ears, mingling with the growing sirens. The fire trucks raced by them with lights revolving.

He'd been fooling himself when he thought he could stay.

Delta might tell him the mess he'd caused was worth it, but it wasn't. Nothing was worth this. He was . . . he was *selfish*. He had come down to this planet without warning, and these girls had shattered his defenses one by one. Delta had knocked down his walls, one smirk and human eccentricity at a time.

He loved her. Which was why he had to leave.

He held Bee tightly to him, staring out the front windshield without really seeing. The flames and smoke turned into a swash of brilliant color behind the tears that began to drip down his cheeks. All the back and forth, all the guilt and the questioning and the secrets and lies . . . It all fell away as he watched what he had caused. It didn't matter what he deserved, because the Wildings deserved better. They deserved their father, not a man from the stars who would give them nothing but a life on the run, a life of worry and pain and other people's suspicion and hate.

Without a word, he shut off the headlights and took Bee by the shoulders, facing her solemnly. He felt calm, now that he knew what he had to do.

"Breathe," he said, staring right into her eyes, brushing back her hair. "Breathe." She returned his stare, green eyes frenzied. There was no way he could explain to Bee that the words were also for him: he felt like all the air had been sucked out of the world, like gravity had increased its pressure a hundredfold, like his three hearts might just cave in and shrivel up. He was slowly breaking, fracturing, under the weight of what he had to do.

Oh, humans, he thought. He would miss them: the dependable, curious sheriff; even Tag, with his wholly human ways. And Bee—yes, he would miss Bee, with her protectiveness and fiery smile; and he thought maybe, just maybe, she might even end up missing him. All of them, with their emotions and feelings and curious ways. And Delta.

Delta.

Her strength, and her half smile, and the way her eyes brightened when she glanced his way. The way she kissed him, the feeling of her soft hair against his cheek. The feeling of her body against his as they danced together on the living room rug. How there was something inside her that was more like him than she ever could've believed.

Bee took a gasping breath, her eyes streaming, her nose running. She tore her gaze away from him and stared out the window at her house. Smoke had started to spiral into the sky.

The sky—*that* was where he belonged; he'd forgotten. Delta made it easy to forget. But the truth was there, cold and unflinching in the light of the fire. He wasn't made for this world. He would always cause trouble for the Wildings whether he wanted to or not.

Bee was crying silently now, her face streaked with tears and dripping mascara. "I don't understand," she whispered, choking out the words. "Why—*why*?" And then, with a sudden gasping scream, "Delta! We have to get to Delta!"

"What do you mean? Why?" His thoughts were whirling; he couldn't put the pieces together.

"Starling, *think*! These people"—she waved a trembling hand toward her house and the people surrounding it—"came here for us. For *you*. But everyone else who hates us—who have *always* hated us—are with Delta right now at the Mayor's Ball. We have to get her out of there!"

He stared at her—how could he have not considered that? Here he thought he was so strong, so smart. But Bee knew humans more than he ever could. They should have never let Delta go to the party—she was walking unknowingly into the lion's den.

Bee was still speaking, the words tripping out over each other in her panic. "What if the mayor was behind this? Starling! What do we *do*?"

Adrenaline coursed through him, a fiery rush of fear following close behind, and he squeezed Bee's hand tightly.

"We need to get to Delta *now*."

"But if they see you—"

"Bee, I do not care," he ground out. "We have to make sure Delta is able to get out of the Rockfords' house."

Bee didn't protest again; she swung the truck back onto the road and sped up, roaring along in the direction of the dark houses of Darling and, beyond, the twinkling of the Rockford estate while the charred wreckage of the Wild West smoldered behind them.

Starling glanced back once, but the smoky haze filling the sky soon obscured the house, and then all Starling could see in the rearview mirror was loss, and an ending.

37

THE ROCKFORD ESTATE

was in a glittering, gorgeous uproar.

Delta and Tag walked up the long, curving driveway, past old, rumbling cars parked every which way, and most of Darling's citizens were unloading themselves and trooping toward the sparkling windows of the mansion. The two of them joined the throng, her heels skidding slightly on the gravel, and Delta clutched Tag's arm for support.

The scene around them on the walk up to the mansion was, Delta thought, the most Darling thing possible: everyone sliding out of ancient Volvos and decrepit trucks, dressed to the nines in ball gowns and suits, laughing daintily like they were the highest of society.

"Are you ready?" Delta whispered. She could feel eyes on her, and she slipped her fingers into Tag's, clenched his hand tightly as all the hairs on her arms stood up. She knew she was being watched, and she made herself take a deep breath.

Just like we planned.

She was a Darling citizen; she was allowed to be here. She was doing nothing wrong—at least, nothing anyone here would hopefully find out about. As she and Tag filed into the grand entrance hallway of the Rockford mansion, past its double front doors, both flung open wide, her stomach squirmed as she remembered their plan. It wasn't a great plan; it wasn't even a very good plan. It was a careless plan, thrown together by a teenager who'd been forced to act like an adult, who had nothing else to lose. It was a wild plan, outlined by a scared, starry-eyed kid with everything at stake.

But she didn't need the plan to be perfect, or foolproof, or smart.

She just needed it to work.

Wait until the mayor is distracted. Break into the office. Find Starling's chain.

Run like hell.

"I'm ready," Tag replied, looking a little sick as he moved fully into the entrance hall. The Mayor's Ball was already underway; the hall was a huge room with sweeping double staircases curving up either side of the room. Identical chandeliers hung high above, their thousands of crystals twinkling in the warm golden light. Waiters were edging through the crowd with rotating plates of hors d'oeuvres; the air was thick with the smell of stuffed mushroom caps, crab bites, and canapés. Delta snagged a mini bruschetta off the nearest waiter's plate. Champagne was flowing and the live band played from a raised dais set up in the corner of the hall, filling the gilded, marble room with slow guitars and haunting violins. The room was packed; Delta couldn't decide if that was a good thing or not. It certainly made it less likely that the mayor would see them breaking in; however, it heightened the chance that anyone else might.

Delta and Tag shuffled through the crowd until they were pressed up against the carved paneled walls.

"We really can't get caught," Tag muttered, his eyes glancing from person to person.

"I'm not planning on it," Delta murmured back.

"My dad will *kill me.*"

They both looked toward the other side of the room, where the mayor was standing on the bottom step of the huge, sweeping staircase, shaking hands and kissing cheeks. His blue eyes were ice chips in a colder, harder face.

Delta shivered despite herself and squeezed Tag's arm. "Noted."

A weary-looking waiter with a teetering tray of champagne flutes sidled by, and Tag grabbed two, passing one to Delta with a Chiclets smile. The bright flash of teeth was completely at odds with his wide, frazzled gaze.

"Liquid courage."

"I'll drink to that."

They touched their glasses with a clink. The champagne was cold and fizzy as it went down her throat, and when she glanced at Tag, she saw his too-blue eyes and the lazy way the corners of his mouth quirked up, all perfect, all Rockford. But there was nothing of his father in his face at all.

I don't think, Delta thought, *there ever really was.*

They were half hidden behind a large, leafy potted plant, peeking out at the dancing horde. The white-and-black floor tiles had been polished so much, Delta could see her reflection; she looked worried and unsure.

"His office is down there," Tag said, nodding his head

meaningfully toward a long, elegant hallway stretching out behind the nearest staircase. An accordion partition screen-printed with ornate flowers half covered the entrance. "Let's get as close as we can."

They began to move, trying to make it look natural. They were gripping each other's hands so hard, both their knuckles turned strained and white, and with each step Delta was sure their footsteps were echoing through the packed hall. She kept her eyes on the ground, watching where she walked, but she could feel the guests staring at her. She couldn't see Anders anywhere, so there was no break from the raised eyebrows, the scowls, the looks of distrust. They pulled at her attention like every watcher had its own circle of gravity.

"Are people looking?" she whispered to Tag, afraid to look up and see for herself.

"Yup," he muttered back, his face set and grim. "They're looking at you, I think."

"We have to get out of here," she said, a sharp, sudden fear settling deep in her bones. She wanted to grab at Tag's hand and pull him in the opposite direction, away from the party, away from the mayor. But she couldn't—she had to get Starling's chain.

She thought of Starling's sallow skin, his exhausted expression, the bruises under his eyes. For him she could be brave.

As she brushed by a man in suit pants and a white shirt with his sleeves rolled up, he leaned close and hissed, "What're you doing here, Wilding?" His breath reeked of beer. "Nobody wants you here."

"Ignore him, just ignore him," Tag intoned, pushing Delta in front of him.

The entrance to the hallway was close now; it beckoned to her. There was the endgame; they were almost there. Behind one of those doors was the key to Starling's freedom. They could go anywhere they wanted, and he would always have his celestial energy, and be strong, and . . . she would be happy.

"Laugh," said Tag abruptly, right in her ear.

"What?" she said, startled.

"Laugh," he said again forcefully, and as soon as Delta let out a confused, fake, high-pitched giggle, Tag grabbed her around the waist, hugging her against him and gently pressing his lips to her neck as he simultaneously swung her around the corner of the open archway: out of the entrance hall and into the hallway.

"Tag!" she hissed, a deep strawberry flush starting up her cheeks, stumbling away from him. "What was that?"

"That," said Tag, "was the diversion." He lowered his voice and dragged the partition back across the entrance to the hallway. "All those people watching you? They saw us go here together, not creeping around like *spies*, but—" He broke off and coughed. "For other reasons."

Delta pressed her lips tightly together.

"It worked, didn't it? Now come on, follow me. The quicker we get in, the sooner we can be done with all this."

The hallway stretched back into the rear of the house. The floor was covered with plush maroon carpeting, and the dark wood walls seemed to suck in the light from the brass lamps.

They were shaped like the heads of hares, and Delta shivered under their blank, bronze-colored gazes.

Tag led her along the hallway. Their feet sank low into the carpeting; Delta felt like she was walking on sand. And in a house like the Rockfords', it was bound to be quicksand. Any minute she might be sucked under and swept away. All the doors were identical, and all were shut.

Tag stopped before a carved door midway down the hallway and took a deep breath. The handle was shining gold, so reflective she could see both of them looking out, tiny people trapped there, faces distorted in the metal. Delta took a deep, wavering breath. She couldn't stop looking over her shoulder; even in this empty hallway, the feeling of someone watching her closely was almost overwhelming.

Tag reached out and pressed down on the handle.

The door swung silently open.

Delta stared, first in at the darkened study and then at Tag. "I thought you said he keeps this door locked?" She checked over her shoulder again, back down the hallway to where the crowd whirled and twirled to the sweeping music. No one was there; none of the party guests near the partition screen even glanced their way. Delta clenched her fists. *No one is looking. No one is watching.*

"He—he does," Tag whispered, staring bemusedly at the handle that had opened so very easily.

"Tag . . ." Delta swallowed hard. The inside of the office was fully dark, a heavy curtain pulled across the window behind a large black shape she assumed was the desk. But she couldn't make out anything, and she was again hit with the need to run, to get out. She didn't want to step into this shadowy room and have the door close behind her. "Don't you think that's too easy? That the door just happens to be open?"

"I . . . I do," Tag said, but then he shrugged, his movements jerky and helpless. "But what can we do?"

"D'you think he knows?"

Tag flicked his eyes from the room to her. "I . . . God, I hope not. Come on—let's just get out before he notices."

I don't want to, I don't want to . . .

Delta stepped across the threshold. Tag followed quickly, closing the door almost all the way and snapping on the light switch. Immediately, they were bathed in dazzling light, so bright that Delta had to screw up her eyes against the sudden glare.

The mayor's office was before her; Delta felt like she'd been dropped into the belly of the beast. Tag's father, of course, was nowhere to be seen, and although the small rational part inside Delta *knew* that this would be the case, because they had both seen him mingling with guests, she couldn't help the hot swell of relief that washed through her at the sight of the empty room.

The same dark red carpeting was on the floor, the same gleaming dark walls. But where the hallway had felt muffled, this room felt truly oppressive. The room was quiet and still, but had a strange anticipatory feeling, as if the walls were holding their breath. The behemoth of a desk sat squarely in the center of the room, its presence filling the space. Delta could barely stand to look at it; it was as if the mayor himself was seated before her. Atop it was a beautifully carved chess set. The players were arranged mid-round, frozen in motion. Frozen in time.

Tag nodded toward the desk; his lips were pressed tightly closed, and Delta wondered if he, too, could taste the threat in the air. Maybe it was just the fear curdling in her stomach, but she tried to breathe shallowly all the same as she crossed to the back of the desk and crouched down.

From her place facing the desk, the bookshelves by her side looming over her, her stomach twinged with the slightest sense of something *wrong*. It was a moment before she realized what exactly had caused the suspicion: a bottom drawer was ajar. Just one drawer, just slightly cracked open, showing the tiniest sliver of darkness. But it was open.

It was almost a dream, the way Delta knelt before the open drawer. She only noticed her hands were trembling when she saw them outstretched, fingers curling around the wooden handle. *This was it.*

Delta pulled the drawer open; it slid toward her silently. Inside were piles of papers, some paper-clipped together, some loose and crumpled. A decorative dagger with an elegant bone handle sat atop the papers, and next to it . . .

A chain lay there, small and frail and more *normal*-looking than she ever would have expected. Except for the glow. She reached forward and picked it up; yes, a definite golden glow permeated the thin links.

Tag came and crouched beside her. "So that has all of St—" He stopped, swallowed, and tried again: "All of S-Starling's energy inside it?"

"Yes," Delta whispered, running a finger down the links. Relief was trickling down her body—she had done it. She couldn't help but shoot Tag a grin as she said, "Let's get back to the sheriff's."

She carefully closed the bottom drawer, leaving it open just a crack, and then they crept back across the room together, feet sinking into the carpet. Delta paused by the chess set and then, lightning-quick, moved the queen.

Checkmate.

She wondered who the mayor was playing against, and if he'd ever notice the change. She hoped he'd stand there, confusion blooming on his hard face, and then he'd look for the chain and realize what had happened. Beaten by the town outcast. Bested by a Wilding.

"Come on, come on," Tag whispered, but he was smiling. She met him at the door, and he pointed to the thick carpet behind them, where the indentations of their feet were slowly fading as the thick fibers rebounded. "See?" he said with a smile so buoyant and wicked, she couldn't help but smile back. "Like we were never even here."

He opened the door.

"Unfortunately," said a soft, dangerous voice. "It's much too late for that."

The mayor stood there in the hallway, dressed in a perfectly pressed suit, his white-blond hair shining eerily in the light of the bronze hare lamps from above.

"M-Mayor Rockford," stammered Delta. She felt as if she'd plunged headfirst into a lake of frigid water. *Run like hell—the last part of the plan.* But she felt frozen in place, too stunned to even try.

"Delta Wilding," the mayor echoed back to her. He was smiling, all teeth, like a dog about to bite. It was such a brittle smile, Delta could've snapped it in half.

"May I ask what you are doing with my son in my office?"

"Nothing," said Delta as she clenched the chain as tightly as she could in her fist.

Mayor Rockford's horrible smile grew wider, and an eyebrow kicked up as he noticed her hand. "Nothing? Really?"

"Dad, stop," Tag interjected.

"Do *not* tell me what to do, Taggart," his father said. He reached over and grabbed Tag's arm, his fingers tightening, viselike. "I thought I told you to stay away from this *Wilding*. You would've done well to listen to me."

"Get your hand off me," Tag muttered, trying to jerk his arm out of his father's grip.

"I am surprised to see you here," Mayor Rockford continued, staring at Delta. She took a step back under his gaze. "Especially considering the state of your house."

Delta stared back at him. She felt cold all over; cold and sick. "My . . . my house?"

"Don't worry," the mayor replied. He grinned again, a rictus grin that had Delta stumbling back another step. She hit the paneled wall with a painful thump, the edge of the panel digging into her spine. "We've done nothing but improve it."

"What did you do?" Delta said. She took a deep breath as the mayor's words settled in, seeping down into her bones. She spoke again, each word tearing itself from her tongue in a sudden shout. "What did you *do*?"

"Tonight is a good night for Darling," the mayor said, and where his voice had been gloating before, it was now soft again, each word underscored. "Tonight marks the end of the Wilding gang and any of the freaks they hide in their guest room."

And Delta remembered the feet she'd seen as she lay huddled with Starling under her bed. What would have happened if the sheriff hadn't arrived when she had?

"Delta." Tag hissed her name, breaking though the buzzing in Delta's head.

"Shut up," the mayor sneered at Tag. "What kind of Rockford are you?"

Tag was staring at his father, his face pale except for two spots of bright red high on his cheeks. "Well," he said, and Delta was surprised to hear his voice was controlled, although she heard it shaking. "I don't want to be your son. And I sure as hell don't want to be a Rockford—not if being a Rockford means being anything like you." Then he glanced at her and said, "Run like hell."

And Delta turned and ran, her breath coming in sharp gasps. *Starling.* She had to get to Starling. Her fingers clenched down on the chain as she knocked the partition to the side. Her heels sounded noisily on the shining tiles, loudly announcing her flight. Delta felt half-crazed; her hair floated in tangled curls around her shoulders as she pushed through the crowd. "Get out of my way!" she yelled, but even louder was the shout of the mayor from behind her: it was a bellow, the type of low roar that makes people sit up and listen.

"Get back here, Wilding!" he yelled suddenly, and the music

came to a crashing halt as half the room turned to see the commotion. "Stop her!"

A few guests, confused and tipsy, made to grab at Delta's arm; she dodged them, just barely ducking out of their way, and continued onward, her eyes fixed desperately on the open doorway. A cool breeze floated in from outside, scented with a hint of smoke.

"Stop her!" the mayor roared again, and this time it wasn't simply drunk guests who moved to grab her, but multiple Darling citizens, all dressed in elegant gowns and suits, all with hard, suspicious eyes. She was only halfway across the room, struggling to push her way through a bemused crowd, when two men hurried to the front door and pushed the opulent front doors closed. They shut with a solid *thunk*, the sort of noise that sounded very final.

Delta had wondered how many people would turn on her if the mayor ordered it. Looking wildly around at the throng of people advancing, it seemed she was about to find out.

"I haven't done anything!" she screamed at them. "Get away from me!"

Tag struggled through the crowd toward her, and across the room she saw Anders, champagne flute still gripped tightly in hand, elbowing people out of the way in an attempt to help.

It was then that the lights in the chandeliers began to flicker, their crystal-adorned frames swinging, quavering in a nonexistent breeze, causing Delta's glimmering dress to reflect with a disco ball effect. A few of the townspeople stopped their advance and looked up at the chandeliers above. They flickered again, then went out. The room was plunged into complete darkness. It was a darkness that Delta was familiar with; this wasn't the musty, oppressive dark of the mayor's study—it was the gleaming perfect black of Starling's eyes. The darkness of a starless night, when the only star had fallen from its place and asked to come in.

Screams rose around her, echoing off the tiled floor and multiplying in the high ceilings. Delta pushed her way past stumbling bodies, not caring who she forced out of the way. *Get to the door—just get to the door, and you can run.* She was almost there, as far as she could tell; the crowd wasn't as tightly packed here, and when she hit a wall, she scrabbled her way along it, searching desperately for a handle.

"Where d'you think you're going, miss thing?" rasped a sharp voice right in her ear, and an arm wound around her waist. Delta screamed, pure fear dropping like a stone into her stomach. She kicked out as hard as she could, flailing wildly in the darkness, until finally her elbow connected with something soft and fleshy, and with a grunt the man released her.

There was a bang—more people began to scream—and then the lights flickered dimly, once, twice. Suddenly, without warning, the chandeliers burst into full brightness.

The front doors had been thrown wide open.

And Starling Rust was standing in the doorway.

38

DELTA THOUGHT A
couple of things in that moment. The first was that she was
dreaming. The second, hallucinating.

Because it couldn't be true. It couldn't be real.

She felt suspended in a bubble, watching his face, watching
the way he let out a breath when he saw her. Watched his fingers curl in on themselves, then straighten out again.

She had been so careful to hide the truth from everyone,
but here he was, striding toward her silently, purposefully.
He certainly didn't seem to care if they saw his true self now.
He turned his tumultuous eyes on the crowd, and the screams
and exclamations were rising now. Some people sprinted for
the door, keeping to the edges of the room to stay as far from
Starling as possible. A few people stayed where they were, and
although they were first frozen on the spot with champagne
flutes in their hands, with a rising roar they once again began
to advance toward her. Anders and Colson broke into the fray,
their voices joining the din as they yelled at the crowd to stop. A
furious-looking man with a bloody nose was being hauled away
from her by Tag, but when Delta looked around, she couldn't
see the mayor anywhere.

For a moment, confusion and shock and fright descended onto Delta like a sledgehammer, rooting her in place. But then Starling was there—finally, miraculously, he was there, real as anything—and he touched her elbow gently, his long fingers caressing the skin there. And Delta found her voice.

"Everyone stay back!" she screamed, thrusting both hands out toward the crowd. "Stay away from me! Stay away, you don't know what I can do!" The room echoed the sentiment back to her, amplifying her voice, and the crowd, so intent on pressing forward before with their frenzied eyes, *stopped*. It was as if she had cast some spell on them, as if they were captivated, locked in place. As if they really believed her. She couldn't do anything—she knew that; the rational part of her knew that. But there was a hot, rising feeling within her that felt like maybe she *could*. Like every time a neighbor had hissed *witch* at her, it had taken root somewhere deep inside, and had grown until their words became true.

"Stay back," she cried again. "And don't you dare come any closer, any of you." The fear on their faces was evident, and she knew it wasn't just because of her but because of the strange man before them. Trusting that their fear would keep them back, she turned to Starling and raised her hands to cradle each of his cheeks, checking for injuries. *Why* was he here? Had something happened?

"You are safe," Starling murmured.

"What's going on, Starling?" she asked. "Where's Bee? Where's the sheriff? What are you doing here? You need to be *hiding*."

"No," he said, his voice totally calm, as if they were discussing the weather, but his eyes were scanning the room, pushing the people back farther. "Were you able to find the chain?"

"Yes, I found it," Delta said, pressing the warm, glowing links into his palm and clinging to his arm with her other hand. "Starling, what's happening? Are you okay?"

He met her gaze for the first time, and although his words had sounded serene, his eyes held a hurricane within the whirling black orbs. "No," he said again. "But soon I will be."

"What does that mean?"

"It is time that I leave," said Starling. "Right now. And I'm not coming back." He touched a finger to her face, and for the first time she noticed the dried tear tracks that carved down her skin. "I'm sorry, Delta." The thin chain was clenched tightly in his hand, his skin glowing in earnest now. He was lit from within.

"N-no," she whispered. "That doesn't make sense. Why are you saying this? You have your chain now; you have the energy you need to stay here . . ." It was all she could manage. It wasn't supposed to happen like this—she'd retrieved his chain, she'd *done* it. She was supposed to wake up with buttery light streaming in and find him glowing golden next to her, every day, forever.

This was a fairy tale.

That's how her fairy tale was supposed to end.

"Starling," she said, not even bothering to keep her voice low. "Listen. Listen to me. I don't know what's happened tonight, but there are ways—we can leave Darling *together*, with Bee, and we can be together—"

Starling shook his head. "No."

"But . . ." She couldn't stop the desperate edge from entering her voice. *"Why?"*

His hand stroked up and down her cheek as if he was reminding himself of something. Of what, she didn't know, but she leaned into his touch regardless. "With me here you will *always* be in danger." He turned his gaze on the remaining townspeople, who trembled under his stare. One fainted dead away, sagging into the arms of her peers. Glasses smashed to the floor; champagne crept its way over the tiles.

"I don't care," Delta said fiercely, turning back to him, wishing more than anything she could speak directly into his head like he could to her. "I don't *care*, Starling."

"You should," Starling said, eyeing the crowd behind them. He took her hand and pulled her out the open front doors. Delta heard the crowd murmuring, as if they were all coming to after being collectively stunned, some strange, shared daze.

She followed Starling down onto the gravel, just out of sight of the grand hall's interior. The air wrapped its cold fingers around Delta, and the smoky scent she'd smelled before was much stronger now. Starling was still pulling her, but she stopped firm, making him whip around and face her. By the way he stared just over her shoulder, refusing to meet her gaze, she could tell something was right on the tip of his tongue, something he didn't want to say.

"What's going on?" she asked softly, and as she spoke, she saw his face grow a pained, resigned look. He reached up and ran the back of his knuckles down her cheek. The touch crackled with energy; his skin glowed brighter every second.

She leaned into his gravity, but his expression turned blank and hard.

"I'm going."

The words rang in her head as the ground beneath her toppled, the world tilting off course. She was crying now, without ever realizing when she'd begun. She tasted salt with each word. "I don't—"

"You don't what? You don't *understand*? I will never be human. I do not belong here."

"Yes, you do!"

"It is not worth it," Starling said, and his voice turned bitter. "The cost is too high."

"The cost?"

But Starling was still speaking, one hand wrapped tightly around the chain, the other stroking Delta's hair. He leaned in close, fixing her with his dark, soulless gaze. "They set fire to your house, Delta. Your *house*."

Delta's heart dropped, her breath stolen from her in one fell swoop.

"The people in this town took it upon themselves to do something about—about *me*," Starling said. "About the Wildings and whatever they had hidden in their home."

"Fire," she repeated, her voice nothing more than an echo.

"It was still standing when Bee and I left," Starling said softly.

Delta reached out, grabbing at his arms. "Bee's not hurt?"

"Not hurt," Starling confirmed. "She's in the truck. She'll take you—" He stopped, *home* hovering almost tangibly in the air before them. Starling sighed, then continued, "She'll take you back to the sheriff's."

"And you."

"Delta," Starling said, and the way he said her name was a caress; it was a kiss in the dark. His orb-eyes turned gentle, so gentle she felt like her heart was already breaking, because she could hear the goodbye. "As long as I'm here, I will make it worse. Me being here is just happenstance, and now it has to end."

"But—" Delta sucked in a breath. "You don't believe that."

"Yes, I do."

"After everything? We did this all for *you*—so you could stay!"

Starling closed his eyes for a second, squeezing them shut as if riding out a wave of physical pain. When they opened, they were emotionless. His voice was monotone, raspy, close to how it was the first time he ever spoke to her. "You have to just let me leave, Delta. Don't make me say any more. I promise you that it's the right decision. It will be worth it. You will understand."

"I can't just *let you leave*! This isn't a goodbye! This isn't right!" She tripped toward him, speaking the words that coalesced out of years of wanting more, years of wishing to be whisked away by something magical. "But what about us? What about everything we've been through?"

"It was a dream. Nothing more. Our time together is but a tiny performance on a stage billions of years old." Starling's voice simmered with something like frustration, his fingers clenching.

"Not to me," Delta whispered. Why couldn't he understand

that to *her* this was so much more? This was her life. It was a part of her life that she'd never forget, never get over. "I thought you wanted to stay."

"I realize now that it doesn't matter what I want."

Delta's voice was nothing more than a sigh. "It matters to me." There was a tightness in her throat, one she couldn't swallow away. "You said . . . you said it was fate. That *we* were fate!" Delta's heart was beating painfully fast now; she knew that Starling could hear it. "I hoped we would be together."

"Oh, Delta," he said, his voice tender, each word lisping out over his celestial tongue. "Look at us. What kind of world would it be where we could be together?"

The sob broke loose, and Delta's voice came out quiet and shaky when she whispered, "A good one."

For a moment Starling moved as if to take her into his arms, his fingers stroking down her skin, and then he stepped away and shook his head. "It was a mistake, Delta. We were a mistake—"

"Don't say that!"

"—I should never have let it go as far as it did." He caught both her wrists in his fingers. His touch was gentle, but his mouth was set. His breath whistled out as he sighed, and then he simply said, "And then my biggest mistake. Your father."

"My father?" She repeated the words slowly, shaking her head. "What are you taking about?"

He was quiet for a moment, his eyes almost beseeching, and Delta all of a sudden knew he'd try to project the words into her head, and she also knew she wouldn't be able to bear what he whispered.

"Tell me," she demanded. "Out loud. Tell me!"

She saw his throat bob as he swallowed. A stream of light from the glittering windows of the Rockford mansion illuminated the side of his face, his lips tight.

"Tell me!"

He gripped her fingers. "Delta, as long as I am here, your father cannot return. It is a cosmic balancing act, and when your father slipped out, I was pulled in." He put her palms flat against each other, his larger, marked hands surrounding them. "The universe is so very thin."

Delta heard his words in the way that a person underwater might hear voices on the surface: faraway, unreal.

This isn't true.

It's not.

This isn't happening.

There was a roaring in her ears that was becoming louder and louder, but when she spoke, her voice was nothing but the merest trace of a whisper. Her lips barely moved.

"What?"

"You heard me."

"How long have you known this?"

"Too long," Starling whispered. "I was selfish. It did not seem fair to me, at first, that I would have to leave simply so another could return here. And you made me want to stay, Delta. But it's also because of you that I have to leave." He pulled her in close. She let herself be pulled.

It couldn't be true. *It couldn't be true.* Starling could bring back her dad. It was one or the other. There was no question, of course, but her body still felt frozen, her mind rejecting his explanation, the truth in his words. Tears crystallized in her eyes, blurring her vision, blinding her. She closed her eyes, let them fall. His hand rested near her collarbone, and she tried to memorize the feel of it, the weight of stardust on her skin.

Her chest felt like it had caved in. She was suffocating.

Then a sneering voice cut through the night behind them, each word clipped and cold. "Well, well. It seems the people of Darling were not able to get the job done."

Delta whirled around, still clinging to Starling. The front door was cracked open and Delta could see movement inside, the crowd restless, rising out of their confused stupor. And sauntering out from the shadows and down the front stone steps was the mayor, an ornate silver pistol gripped in his hand; he examined it as if it was a surprise to find it there.

"So I suppose," the mayor continued, "that I'll have to take matters into my own hands."

"Starling, *run!*" Delta cried, shaking off the cold shock that rooted her in place. *Run like hell:* it's what they all should've done from the start.

Starling didn't. He put a reassuring hand on the small of her back and stood right next to her, calmly facing the mayor. This show of strength didn't comfort Delta in the slightest. A vein was throbbing in the mayor's neck, and his teeth were bared in a horrible grimace of a smile.

"All I have ever tried to do is *protect* this town. Protect my family. And I intend to see it through."

With a rustle and click, he leveled his pistol at Starling.

"No!" screamed Delta, her heart flying into her throat. "No!"

There was a wooden thud as the double doors were thrown wide, and then she heard voices pooling around her, melding together into one loud cacophony, and she couldn't tell if she was imagining it or if people were really shouting. Lights glimmered around them, reflecting brightly off the sides of the cars as the crowd streamed out from the ornate doors like a wave, flowing down over the stone steps, pressing closer, closer, only to hurry away once more.

It seemed like ages ago that she'd been scared as the townspeople pressed around her; now they hardly seemed real. All that was real was the mayor before her and Starling by her side.

Starling removed Delta's hands from his waist and began to edge her behind his body.

The mayor waved his gun toward Delta and Starling. Blackness pooled in his eyes—not the darkness of magic and galaxies like those in Starling's, but the flatness of hate and contempt.

Worthless.

Whore.

"Do you see the people who fester on the edges of my beloved town? Do you see what you have to pass by every day?"

"And who do *I* have to pass by every day?" Delta yelled at him, pushing Starling's tugging hands away. "People who break into my house, who threaten me, who have treated my family like trash for years? And all because of *you.*"

Starling was still trying to pull Delta behind him, but she resisted. She was so tired of hiding in the shadows, under her bed, inside her house.

"Ha!" The mayor let out a wild laugh. It was a loud laugh, unhinged. "I *protect* my town. Especially from threats like *that*."

As if in response, Starling's gaze drifted away from the mayor, as if he wasn't worried in the least by the shouting or the gun or the sudden rush of people circling around them. Instead, he tilted his head down to Delta's. His voice was searching. "I suppose, Delta Wilding, since there won't be a better time to say it, you have to know that I—"

The mayor fired his shot.

39

THE SCREAM NEVER

left Delta's mouth; it got tangled in her vocal cords, strangling her, choking her. But others screamed, voices melding together in a terrible discord. The crowd whirled closer, pressing in, and Bee's scream was the loudest of them all, gravel flying out from under her feet as she ran toward them, the truck door left wide open like a mouth gaping in horror at the scene before it. And suddenly Tag was there too, lunging forward toward his father, swinging his fist with a wild cry and grappling for the gun.

Starling crumpled to the ground, sprawled there like he was making a snow angel in the gravel. Something like blood began pooling from under his body; it was bright, shining gold, and as it spread, his skin's glow began to fade. He twitched slightly and then fell completely, deathly still. Delta fell to her knees beside him, the gravel slicing through her soft skin. All she could hear was her heart in her head, as though it was reminding her that she was here, she was still alive, *she could help him, she had to help him—*

She was vaguely aware of the chaos that had broken out around her: the crowd dispersing, running for their cars; the sheriff's siren screeching through the air, getting louder by the moment; high heels clattering and heavy footsteps thumping on every side of her in a mad rush.

Delta's hands were shaking as she placed them frantically on Starling's chest, feeling for a heartbeat, a pulse . . .

"Starling, no, no, no," she choked out. "You said they couldn't kill you! You can't leave like *this*! Starling!" His name was a scream, a plea.

She felt the first throb of a heartbeat right as Starling inhaled a gasping breath and sat up, his long fingers going up under his sweatshirt, scrabbling for something. A second later his hand reemerged, covered in his strange golden blood and holding the bullet. He dropped it onto the gravel beside him and slumped back to the ground. When he saw Delta, a weak half smile lit his face. Her hands were coated in the viscous golden liquid flowing from his body; beneath her fingers, just one single heartbeat continued to thud. It was faint, slow.

"Your father," he said, his voice faltering, "will be able to return when I am gone. No matter how I go."

"You're not dying, Starling, so shut up," Delta said tightly, her hands under his shirt. Her fear was a lance in her heart, and it made her words harsh. She could hear Ramona's voice shouting, commanding the mayor down onto the ground, and over it all Bee was crying so loudly, it crowded out everything else.

"I am, in a way," Starling said, the words trailing off into a cough. Gold flowed from his lips. "You can't destroy energy, Delta, but this body—this *body* is dying."

"*No*, you are *not*," she snapped. What did she do with a gunshot wound when the person shot was formed of stardust? Did she perform CPR? Mouth-to-mouth? Why didn't she know how to save a life? Tears dripped down over her nose, thick and fast, and she laid her head on his chest, listening to his single beating heart, the weight of her own shortcomings crushing her. She couldn't save him. She didn't know how to save him.

"Smile, Delta," Starling whispered. His breath stirred the hair on the top of her head. "He will be back soon. Very soon—I can feel him, Delta, trying to slip back through."

"But he's been gone for months," Delta said, her voice breaking. "Why hasn't he tried before, when you weren't here?"

"That's not how time works," he replied, each word faint. "He hasn't been gone for months. Not for him. Just—moments. Time passes in mere moments, Delta."

Shock welled within her as she imagined her dad disappearing and then whirling around to return home, just moments later, only to find the way back blocked by an arrival of someone—something—else. And on the other side of the door, her father's mere moment had stretched out, strung its way into days, weeks, months.

But now he could return, slip back through that thin space. And even as a part of her heart swelled, imagining her dad returning so soon, another part broke.

"It wasn't supposed to happen like this," she whispered, and it was so inadequate for what she wanted to say to him that her throat closed up. She couldn't save him, and she couldn't even *tell* him how she truly felt.

"I know," he replied. His voice grew fainter each time he

spoke. "But I was leaving anyways. Whether I go in this form or not, you will not know the difference."

"*Yes*, I will—God, of course I will." Tears dripped from her eyes down onto his neck.

"But either way, I will be gone from this world, and your father will return."

"Even before you got hurt, you decided to leave here—leave me—so my dad could come back," Delta whispered.

"Yes."

"Because you *care* about us."

Starling's eyes sucked in the light from the mansion; the chandeliers, the fairy lights twinkling on the hedges by the doors, all dimmed in the shining infinity of his gaze: she was the supernova, he the black hole. His eyes had entire worlds cradled within them. "Yes."

"Because you want me to be happy, and—"

"Because I love you," interrupted Starling. They hung there, suspended, the center of the universe. "Yes."

She didn't seem to be able to catch her breath.

Because I love you. Yes.

Delta squeezed Starling close to her as if she could keep him on Earth by sheer force of will alone. Her entire body was trembling, and he gasped in pain, shifting slightly as the puddle of golden light trickled farther, puddling out around him. The chain clattered to the gravel, the glow gone.

Delta picked it up, her fingers shaking as she touched the cold metal links. And that's when she knew. The energy was gone, and the chain was just a chain: worthless now. The glow that had vanished was the same glow leaving Starling's body. A star dying, its energy and light dispersing back into the universe. *No.* She couldn't believe that.

"You need to leave," she whispered, fitting the chain back into his limp hand. "You can still leave, I know it. *Try.*"

"Delta—" Each letter a gasp.

"Try, Starling!"

"Delta—"

"Tell me how to save you!" Her voice rose, dipping into the edges of hysteria. The dark, cold chain in his limp hand kept pulling her attention toward it, mocking her. She heard someone in the crowd utter a soft, sad little *oh*, and for a second someone's hand touched her shoulder, but she brushed it impatiently away. She could feel the weight of eyes on the two of them, but she only had eyes for Starling. "How? How do I save you?"

"Delta."

When she next spoke, it bordered on a scream that ripped from her tight throat. "You need to slip back through! Starling, please, this can't—this can't—this can't—" She took a deep, ragged breath in; her breath out was just a choke masquerading as a sob. Her nails dug into his upper arms, marked with their celestial tattoos, now faded to gray. "You have to—I can't—this can't—" Was she even making sense anymore? Her own words sounded like nonsense, like any meaning they might once have had had been torn away and scattered to the wind.

He was so still beneath her.

"You're an alien, you're *stardust*, you—" she cried, trying to expand her senses so she could remember every second, every press of the pads of his fingertips on hers, every sharp-edged smile. His galactic eyes. *Him.*

They were face-to-face, Delta hovering over him, her hands trembling on each of his cheeks. From somewhere beyond, she heard Bee's hard sobs. She felt the presence of others nearby, gathering around, but she didn't look up; she didn't want to take her eyes from Starling's for a single second.

"You are—just a human."

She met his eyes, then said, "Oh, Starling." Her voice broke, and she swallowed thickly, rubbing the heel of her palm into her eye until sparks exploded there, golden bright fireworks behind her eyelids. *"Starling."* She tried to say everything in the syllables of his name.

"I know," he breathed.

Delta tried to calm her breath, stop her tears. She pressed her hands into her eyes once more. Whether the stardust inside of Starling remained in the universe or not seemed to matter little, because he would no longer be *here.* He wouldn't have those long fingers or that sharp smile. He'd be gone. How could this be the end?

She finally glanced up, taking in the circle of wide-eyed townspeople, trembling in their evening finery. Bee stood amongst them, mascara streaked down her face, her arms wrapped around herself as if she, too, was holding herself together at the seams. Tag and Anders stood next to her, the blue and red lights from Ramona's Escalade flashing, strobe-like, upon their faces. The mayor was in the back seat, his face in shadow. Everything seemed far away, blurry and unrecognizable . . . everything except for Starling, gasping for breath before her.

She didn't care who was watching; she leaned over his body and hugged him close, clutching him. His arms enfolded her, keeping her snugly against his body.

"We were really something, weren't we?"

"We sure were," Starling murmured.

"Thank you," she whispered.

His smile was the edge of a knife, teeth agleam. A little strange, a little dangerous.

Delta kissed him anyways, and she was crying, because how could she go on in the mundane, normal reality when she had held a star in her arms? Their kiss was salt and ash. It tasted a lot like coming home.

It was this: the ground shaking that fateful night as light arced overhead, and knowing in her heart of hearts that something had irrevocably changed for better or worse. Seeing him there in the gold-strewn clearing; carrying home this boy flung straight from the stars. She could still remember her harried breath and sharp inhalations as she and Bee stumbled through the woods with the wrists of an absolute impossibility gripped in her hands: it was this she thought about as her hands cradled each side of Starling's face there at the Rockford house, as her tears transferred from her eyelashes to his.

It was this: the way the sunlight reflected off the glow in his veins as they turned in place on the threadbare living room carpet. His honeyed voice whispering her name. It was every sharp-edged smile, every silence where his starry-black eyes said more than words could. Tossing pennies in the Wishing Well instead of wishing on a star, because the star she would've wished on stood beside her in the darkness. It was his long fingers tracing down her back, tucking a lock of hair behind her ear, turning page after page of her books.

The memories of every touch. It was the strange tingling electricity that she sometimes felt flutter between them—that's what she felt now as their arms were entangled. It was something gold that matched the glow of his skin, something dormant that now rose up as she tasted the memories on his lips.

With a brief and cursory glance at the two of them, anyone might've thought it was just a boy and a girl kissing, and that the tiny shiver of honey-thick gold that left Delta when she breathed and entered Starling when he inhaled was just a trick of the light.

But they weren't, and it wasn't.

She kissed him once more, until his eyes fluttered close. She placed her head on his chest, as if the single heart still resisting the quiet dark was her own, and when it stopped, so would hers, and the shattering could begin in earnest.

Thump. Thump. Thump.

A single heart—it was so altogether human that she suddenly had the strangest desire to laugh. Starling had gone from distrusting humans to loving them, and soon his body would die like one. A short, harsh laugh loosed itself from her lips. How appropriate—she hoped Starling would've thought the same.

Thump. Thump. Thump.

Thump-thump. Thump-thump.

Delta rocketed up off his chest, staring at Starling, at the chest now rising and falling with two heartbeats. Carefully she placed a hand over his heart, just as a third rhythm stuttered into being.

"Starling?" she said, her voice rising. *"Starling?"*

He brought a hand up to her cheek and rested it there; she whispered his name once more, reminding herself that this was real, that somehow, *somehow*, his three hearts were beating in staccato songs once more. She trembled, eyes wide in disbelief, as his fingers drifted over her skin, gently dropping to her neck, her shoulder. She knew they had an audience; half the town was standing, watching; if she listened, she could hear the shock whispering its way through the crowd.

She didn't know what the townspeople of Darling were making of the scene before them.

She didn't care.

"Delta," he said, and although his brows were dark and furrowed, his eyes were filled with so many pinpricks of light, she could see herself reflected there; it was almost too bright to look straight at him. It was dizzying: Delta was seeing stars. "I should've known—" He chuckled, and raised a still-cold hand to brush the hair behind her ear. "Yes, I should've known."

"W-what?"

His hand drifted down and rested at the base of her neck. Her pulse jumped erratically beneath his thumb, and he continued, "I did say you were very strange."

"Yes," Delta whispered, trying to make sense of the murmured words. "I remember."

"Just a human." He shook his head. "Delta Wilding, you are so much *more."*

Her stomach dropped. *You are so much more.* She couldn't think of what to say—every question seemed to have drifted away, leaving behind nothing but fear-tinged wonder.

The chain was glowing now, and so was Starling: it began as a faint streak of light, and then it grew, spiderwebbing up his hands and neck. He shifted under her, pushing himself off the gravel with a grunt to stand, then taking her hand and pulling her up with him. He interlocked their fingers once more. Delta's breath was coming in as a gasp; she felt dizzy, completely out of sorts. She didn't know what had happened— she didn't know what *she'd* done, or what Starling meant when he said she was *more*, or why he was looking at her like she was a little bit magic.

All she knew was that her mouth had been on his, and every touch and every look had coalesced into one. She knew that she'd been wishing, the wish building in her brain like a fever; she felt hot, too hot, as if she was burning up from the inside out. But there had been something in the way he kissed her back, in the way he moved his hand to grasp the back of her neck. Something that cooled the heat in her cheeks.

"Are you . . . ?" She trailed off, unsure. He was glowing now, his skin brightening, no longer fading away into the cold, gray pallor from moments before. "Did . . . did Darling . . . ?"

"Darling? No, Darling did nothing," Starling said. A wind had picked up around them, and he stepped forward to clasp both her hands in his. Suddenly in her head his voice was there, the soft rasped words twining themselves up her neck, stroking at the inside of her feverish forehead with cool, invisible fingers. "This was all you, Delta."

"But what did I do?" It was a cry, and the wind whipped it away almost as soon as she'd spoken. She meant it more like *How did I do it?* because she knew what she'd done, somehow: Starling was alive, standing before her, suffused with golden energy. Her nails pressed half-moon crescents into his skin as if she could keep him in place by pure strength.

His eyes drew her attention; they were no longer the pure black of a void; they were bright, shining, the white flame of stars. He was glowing from inside, his veins filled with light until he was almost translucent. Just light in the outline of a boy.

His skin became hot to the touch, so hot she had to release his wrists; it was then that she knew it was time. The heavy weight of time coming closer and closer; she had run from it, she had tried to stop time, but time had found them.

Delta looked at him silently; and although there was glittering wetness in her eyes, she felt calmer now. She didn't want to let him go, but she had told him everything she needed to. She didn't have to scream, or wail for him to come back.

He pressed his palms together, his expression unreadable. But then she thought she saw him smile.

Do not forget me, Starling said. The words were a whisper in her head.

She met his eyes and reached down deep inside her, where that tendril of gold still curled around the base of her ribs. And without ever saying a word, she whispered back, *Never.*

Starling smiled. He'd heard her.

His eyes shined brighter and brighter, and a wind whipped up, a hurricane breeze that held them in its knowing eye, its diamond-bladed chill whirling their hair around them. They were caught in their own personal circle of gravity; Darling had given up its hold on the building blocks. The light inside him was seeping out, wrapping glowing, reaching vines around every inch of his body, and then he was shattering, fracturing.

The universe is so very thin, almost close enough to touch.

And with a brilliant explosion of ten billion particles of light and stardust, Starling Rust slipped away through the gap in the universe and disappeared.

The wind died away. Ash mixed with molten embers of light, and together they whirled through the air like confetti. Delta's eyes didn't leave the place Starling Rust had been; the spell surrounding them had been broken and the townspeople, once curious and captivated, were either frozen in time or rushing away in a frenzy. Delta's knees buckled, and Bee rushed toward her, her sister's thin arms wrapping around her before she hit the ground. Together they sank down, huddling in each other's embrace. Delta saw Tag hurry toward her as well, before being pulled back by Anders, who gave a brief shake of his head.

"Where did he go?" Bee cried, hiccupping, tears drying on her cheeks. "Did he—did he—"

Inhale. Exhale. Delta stared down at the spreading pool of gold: it was the only thing that showed it had been real, he had been here, *there, right there*, and now . . .

"He slipped away," she said to her sister, and Bee's arms

tightened around Delta. "Back through." She held up her palms, an inch apart.

The universe is so very thin.

She pressed her palms flat together, the memory of the feel of another's skin still on her fingertips.

Delta Wilding clung to her sister, and turned to look at the night sky, where a canopy of lights hung, twinkling stars strung across the expanse of black above.

Almost close enough to touch.

Every single light in the Rockford house behind them flickered and trembled in exhilaration. There was only the haze of the moon shining gently down on the rows of gabled houses and quaking aspen–lined Main Street, where streetlights flickered on and off in delight.

The Wild West sat alone against the sky, water-doused and charred and smoke-heavy but still standing. Somewhere inside its blackened walls a closet door opened, and a bespectacled man stumbled out and found he had come home, finally, after many moments and, in another timeline, many months away. The house sighed and settled, content, as the man fell to his knees.

And Darling smiled.

epilogue

THERE WERE TOWNS,
and then there were small towns, and then there was Darling.

It was hard to say exactly what the magic that ran through Darling's veins was, because it was magic of a strange sort, unable to be calculated or weighed. It was quiet; it didn't sparkle or crackle or bang.

Sometimes it glowed.

Sometimes it crash-landed.

Sometimes it slipped softly through a gap that no one knew was there.

It was hard to say if the Wildings had brought the magic to Darling, or if the town itself, in its impossible way, had torn off a small piece of its own power and dragged it up through the roots, slipping its own magic inside the walls of the Wild West.

Inhale, exhale. The magic seeped out of the walls, coating the skin of the inhabitants. And so the human hearts inside the Wildings took on a glow as a curl of gold nestled inside them, waiting for the right moment to emerge.

And they became just a little bit more.

The streets of Darling turned quiet, time marching onward, and the population carved itself almost in half as an exodus of townspeople picked up and left. Among those who remained, the suspicious glares turned into despair and apology, as if the town had been under a terrible spell for far too long and had just awoken.

The Wild West was a shell. But charred boards were replaced, and rooms rebuilt, and the Wildings and their father watched as the Wild West's peaked roof once more stretched up toward the sky, daring the stars to come and try to touch it. And the magic, untainted, unable to be destroyed by anything the humans could try to do to it, soaked back into the copper pipes and settled itself into the drywall and rose like dust from the new floorboards. Taking up residence once more in the home of the people it trusted.

Sometimes Delta thought she could see it: motes of magic, illuminated by a shaft of light, swirling in the air. Golden-bright energy, a glimmer from the corner of her eye. And sometimes while Delta was sitting in the Wild West's new kitchen, fat drops of rain pounding against the windows, the lights would flicker.

There was no way to tell if it was the electricity, or the storm, or something else.

All the Wildings were accounted for, and they all knew that the universe required balance, and so there was no way their man of stars could return.

Because it was impossible. *Impossible.*

But Darling dealt in impossibilities.

The porch light of the Wild West flickered in the darkness. There was nothing but the rain and the howling wind. Nothing but a creak of hesitant footsteps, a held breath, trembling fingers, wide green eyes staring down the hallway. *Impossible.*

There was nothing but silence.

And then there was a knock.

Because after all, Darling was a town unlike any other, and Darling did what it wanted.

✧

Acknowledgments

BECOMING A PUBLISHED author has been my dream since I was young, and now that I'm writing my acknowledgments of my debut book, words don't seem to cut it. My heart is full of thanks for the village of people who had a hand in this book at all stages.

The hugest thanks in the world to Taylor Martindale Kean, my superstar of an agent who took a chance on a writer with a big dream. I couldn't ask for a more talented champion of my writing, and I'm so grateful to have you and the Full Circle Literary team in my corner!

To Nicole Ellul, editor extraordinaire, who took this book and helped shape it into the best story it could be. Thank you for truly understanding the heart of *Starling* and working with so much brilliance and magic to make Delta and Starling's lives, world, and romance shine.

Thank you to the entire team at Simon & Schuster who worked so diligently on every aspect of this book! I am so appreciative of your effort and hard work. Thank you to Jen Strada for your copyediting skills, to Laura Eckes for your wonderful cover design, and to Sivan Karim for creating the cover artwork that took my breath away.

Allison, thank you for being my #1 hype woman, who read this book when it was just a rough short story for our creative writing class but made me feel like I'd penned a bestseller! Your unwavering support in anything I do has been a lifeline when the writing was difficult. Thanks for our Zoom dates and our wine nights and our magnificent plot-brainstorms. Sorry I put you and Marzi the dog (Marnie) in the book as drunk seniors, but you're in my book, as you deserve to be!

To Laura Urbano and Iza Korsak—thanks for reading early drafts, and for our ranting sessions, true crime discussions, and the *Starling* merch! Iza, thank you for using your photography skills to make me look so good in my author photo, and Laura, for our Dirty Martini and Airport Lounge dates that kept me sane. I wouldn't have made it through without you guys. #BookClubForever!

Thanks to Ross Allan (aka Best Friend Ross) for being the first to read this book—when I emailed you my manuscript I never thought you'd actually read it, but I'm glad you did! Probably because we're both Virgos, yeah? And thanks to my friends who have always supported my writing dream, especially Kate Dickinson, Sarah and Rachel Cefalu, Madison Murray, and Joe and Claire Harley. I'm lucky to have friends like you.

I have had some extraordinary teachers and professors over the years who have fostered my love of reading and writing: thank you to Andy Leiser, Teresa Finn, and Kim Magowan! And to Susan Ito, for assigning the writing prompt in your creative writing class that gave this book its start.

I have been a part of the YA and Bookstagram community since 2016, and have met SO many incredible people. Thank you to Tara, for being my beta reader and for all your fabulous feedback! Thank you to both Rachel Palmiter and Marcella W. for the stellar *Starling* artwork. Thank you to Liz Smith and Amber Dunlap for the hype and encouragement, and of course to my writing group, the #LitHappens ladies: Heather, Hannah, Tyffany, Shiza, Virginia, Becky, Sarah, Danielle, and Marissa. You all ROCK.

To Denise and Steve Chatfield, Alan Coniff, the Coniff-McBreen family—Amy, Mark, Lily, and Fred—and the Coniff-Kent family—Sarah, Alex, and Arron: thank you all for the excitement and love and support, and for making me feel like part of the family from the very first moment.

Thanks to my brother Nicholas, for being the first person to pick up my call when I got the book deal (yaaasss!), and to my brother Daniel, for always being up for some transatlantic World of Warcraft when I needed a writing break. A big thank-you to all my siblings: Angie, Dede, Raymond, and Alex, my sisters-in-law Borislava and Jen, and my nieces Lydia and Isla, for all your love and support.

Thank you to both my parents, who raised me in a house chock-full of books. To my mom—you made me realize I could be an author too, just like you. Thank you for all the advice and encouragement throughout my own journey to publication. I don't know what I would do without our long FaceTime calls! Thank you to my dad, for imbuing in me a love of fantasy and sci-fi, as well as for the Lake District retreats full of cheeky pints and hikes atop Darling Fell! And for reading the first page of *Starling* and then sending a text that said, "Finish that novel soon, seems like a game changer!" Look at it now . . . !

acknowledgments

Thanks to Jacky and Ginger Bunny and Junior, for their emotional support (and because I said I would).

And finally, I have to thank Henry, who was my boyfriend when I began writing *Starling*, my fiancé when I got my book deal, and who will be my husband by the time he reads this. Thank you for cheering me on when I was on deadline, ordering my favorite Triscuits from America when I needed a treat, and for always believing wholeheartedly in my writing and the fact that one day my book would be in bookstores. (Maybe now you'll read the book!) You're the reason that writing stories about romance is so easy.